VICIOUS WALTZ
FANG AND DAGGER
BOOK 2

JS HARKER

Developmental editing: Sue Brown-Moore (suebrownmoore.com)

Editing: One Love Editing (oneloveediting.com)

Cover Art: Reese Dante (reesedante.com)

For the readers and dreamers

PROLOGUE

Rural Indiana, 1947

The hunter swung his dagger with a wild impulse, but the despair in his eyes said he already knew his struggle was futile.

Blood dripped off his chin and coated Roger's shirt. Other splatters made his shirt stick to his arms, his abdomen, some trailing to his pants. He'd gotten sloppy while eating. The middle of combat was no time for a careful feast.

This hunter would be his third meal of the night.

Roger couldn't wait.

Easily, he dodged the hunter's swing. The hunter attempted another, but Roger caught his wrist and snapped it. With a sharp, pained cry, the hunter yanked free, and Roger released him. The fight in the living room where they were had moved into the kitchen and beyond. The other vampires had routed the hunters. He had the time and space to have some fun; the complete defeat of this hunter base was imminent.

The sooner it was wiped from the Earth, the better. The hunters had taken a farmhouse and converted it. Secretive locations were common in supernatural circles. Operating in plain sight was often the easiest way to disguise oneself. However, the base had been chosen for its isolation and deep basement. These hunters weren't merely coordinating their attacks and research; they were experimenting on supernaturals.

On living shifters.

On living vampires.

They'd even had a fey locked in an iron cage. The poor Unseelie had been left out for days in the summer sun. They'd been near dead when Roger broke open the cage at the beginning of the raid.

And hunters have the audacity to think they're righteous. Roger snarled at the man in front of him, enjoying how he cowered farther into the corner. A noxious odor of fear permeated the air.

Desire was Roger's usual playground, but his vampiric powers worked equally well on fear. He raised his hand, palm up, fingers forming a claw, and uncorked the hunter's fear from what little self-control he had left.

He dropped to his knees with a cry and pissed himself.

Roger snatched the hunter by his hair and dragged him upward. He ripped into the hunter's throat with his fangs. Hot blood hit his mouth again, but there was no sweetness to it. The taste wasn't worth the effort of drinking it; the fear had spoiled him. Roger dropped the man to the floor. Blood continued to spurt from the wound, and the man put his hands on it, attempting to stop the loss. He was pitifully sprawled on the floor and not even delaying the inevitable that well.

Fear was different than suffering. In the heat of the moment, Roger had wanted the man to feel every ounce of terror, but as his victim lay there dying, he couldn't help the tender strings plucked in his heart.

But he couldn't afford to show sympathy for the enemy. Seamus was somewhere in the house, and his orders had been clear. *No mercy*.

There were subtle ways of circumventing that. Roger had to act as if he wasn't doing the man any favors. So he grinned and glared down at the man. "Let me help you with that."

Then he put his heel on the hunter's throat and pressed down, down, down until *snap*.

A rustle and shot of movement caught Roger's eye, and he pivoted toward the source. Unlike the other dangers he'd encountered in the house, this one wasn't coming at him. Instead, someone was escaping through the front door.

Seamus had had one other order.

Kill every human.

Roger caught the hunter a dozen feet from the door. She screamed as he grabbed her by the arm and spun to face him. Wind blew her hair out of her face, and the grass under their feet cracked from dryness.

The hunter's stomach bumped into Roger. The sensation was disorienting enough that Roger looked down. His sense of hearing caught up to his consciousness, pushing past the obvious external sounds and zoning into the heartbeat in front of him.

The *two* heartbeats, actually.

With a primal scream, she clocked Roger across the jaw with her fist.

She was fighting for two lives with the conviction of survival. Despite the hellish retribution striking down the hunter base, she managed to keep her fear far beneath the surface of her thoughts. The desire to protect was wrapped around her like a suit of armor.

What is that kind of love like? To feel it? To be the object of it?

Roger released her.

She bolted for a car. As she hurried into the driver's seat, he slowly retreated toward the front door. The car tires spewed rocks from the country road, and the taillights glowed a ruddy color.

Watching her flee brought up memories of another time he'd spared a life. That mistake had resulted in the Gladwells becoming a lineage of hunters.

What would come of allowing this one to escape?

I hope I never know. Roger turned to step into the house.

Seamus stood in the open doorway. He was shorter than Roger by half a head, but his aura was colder than a gathering of a dozen vampires. His chin was covered in blood, and trails of it decorated his shirt. Grinning, he grabbed Roger's shirt and tugged him closer. His voice was slick as a metal roof in rain as he asked, "Had your fill, darling?"

Darling was a tricky word in Seamus's lexicon and almost as dangerous as his tone. He used both when he was well pleased, but also when he was about mete out a punishment. Had he seen the hunter leave? Was he tracking the sounds of the automobile hurtling across the road for safety?

The best course of action was to assume everything was fine. Roger had narrowly dodged more than a few punishments with the right word and a smile. He'd used the tactic relentlessly and had survived for two and a half centuries under Seamus's rule while older sirelings met their end.

Roger leaned in and dropped his voice to a husky whisper. "Not yet, master."

Then, he kissed Seamus, first plunging his tongue deep into his sire's mouth and then opening for Seamus when he pushed back. Kisses were a tug of dominance that Roger always let Seamus win. They were inconsistent lovers, but he remembered every trick.

Eventually, Seamus relaxed his hold on Roger and gently pushed him away. He groaned with a note of satisfaction. "You have a dazzling tongue."

Slyly, Roger smiled at him.

With the speed of a vampire master more than a millennium old, Seamus backhanded Roger. The blow came at a speed that Roger barely saw, but he didn't move out of the way. That would have only angered Seamus more.

The strike broke Roger's jaw. The blood he'd drunk had infused him with vampiric magic, so his jaw instantly began to heal. He kept his head turned and braced for Seamus's next slap.

But Seamus walked away from him. He stood in the middle of the living room and assessed the bodies on the floor. "Whenever I think you finally understand your responsibilities as one of my captains, you disappoint me. These hunters flourished in our territory for years, and you knew *nothing* about their activities."

Seamus hadn't known about them either. A shifter looking for his mate had brought evidence of the hunters' existence to Seamus, and hunting them down had become Roger, Dmitri, and Candide's task. Anton, Seamus's eldest sireling and a warlock, hadn't lifted a finger. And Seamus knew that hunters in their territory were nothing new. Hunters tended to be humans, and they lived their human lives until they struck. They were never bold enough to strike at the heart of Seamus's empire in Chicago, but they continued living in the territory. Though this twig of the Wright family tree was clipped, there were dozens more branches. It was likely another branch lived in the Great Lakes Coven's domain.

But demonstrating logic would only incur more wrath. Roger held his jaw, feeling it knit together. The pain was lessening. He'd endured far, far worse than a slap and a scolding.

Seamus glared at him. Disgust twisted his features, and frost began to congeal the blood on the floor. "And you let one of them go."

"She surprised me."

"I saw you back away from her," Seamus replied.

Pointing out that if Seamus had seen that, then he could have acted and stopped her was futile. Whatever Seamus's reason for letting the hunter go, the fault of the action would still rest on Roger. Arguing anything would only incense him further.

"She had a cross," Roger lied. A believer with faith strong enough to repel a vampire with a holy symbol was rare, but they did happen. He shrugged. "I didn't feel like burning myself to get to her."

Seamus smacked him. "You released her when you realized she was pregnant. This world doesn't need another generation of *vermin*. You have lived hundreds of years, and you still fail to learn the basic lessons. This weakness of yours to let prey slip between your fingers will be the death of you one day."

Compassion is not weakness. Roger held his tongue and buried that truth deep in his soul. Another vampire, an older one, had refused to kill at all once he'd gained control over his feeding, and Seamus had eventually murdered him in a rage. And as horrible as the night was, he enjoyed his life as a vampire. Blood, power, money, sex—those were amazing reasons to keep living. He didn't want to die.

His jaw was healing again, but he leaned in to playing up the injury and faked remorse for his action. "I'm sorry I'm such an idiot, master."

"At least you're smart enough to apologize," Seamus grumbled. "Though it's a good thing you're gorgeous."

Roger played with the gold ring on his left hand. It was a symbol of Seamus's coven and cursed to remain on him until he was strong enough to become his own master. "I do live to serve, master."

Seamus stepped forward, grabbed him by the jaw, and dug his fingers into the break. Pain flared, but at a level Roger sometimes enjoyed in the bedroom. He tried to pretend he liked it as Seamus said, "You're far from off the hook. These hunters had to have financial support from someone wealthy and connected to keep them from our notice."

"I may have the answer," Dmitri said as he came down the stairs. His Russian accent was less notable around Seamus. With Russia and America on the brink of annihilating each other, Seamus had ordered Dmitri to lessen his natural speech. However, Dmitri only bothered when Seamus was in the room.

Dmitri had sharp cheekbones and short dark hair, and his sleek black clothing made him extra scrumptious. His expression was too serious, but he'd been like that even as a human. He'd been Roger's lover. They'd risen from graves mere feet from each other, though Anton was his sire.

He had a pile of papers and what looked like a leather-bound journal in his hands. In his typical cold fashion, he handed the lot of it to Seamus. "From what I've found so far, the Fey Weather Court and the Enduring Circle of Chicago were supporting these monsters."

"Damned Seelie and mages," Seamus complained as he took the papers. He rifled through them. "Every time I think we've made peace with the bastards, they do something like this. I will burn them out of our city."

Seamus had been threatening to rid Chicago of every other supernatural group since they'd moved into the city after the Great Fire. Nothing would likely come of that threat said in anger.

"If you aren't too preoccupied," Candide called from a deeper room, "perhaps someone can find the keys so we can release the poor unfortunates in the basement! Some of our kin are down here."

Seamus made a motion for them to follow Candide's request for help but continued to read through the papers. Roger wanted to kick himself for not thinking about the keys sooner, and he prayed that the hunter he'd let go didn't have all the keys on her. The cages had silver components, and he'd rather not have to pull and break his way through them.

Dmitri found a keyring first, though Roger found an additional set on another dead hunter. The prisoners in the basement had silver burns, and some of them sported new scars. Nathaniel, a vampire descended from Roger through Ezra, had a milky-white right eye when he'd had a pair of deep blue eyes before. His left eye was unmarked, but a scar ran through the right. Somehow, the hunters had figured out how to permanently damage a vampire. That shouldn't have been possible.

Seamus, Candide, and a few of the other better-off captives helped divide the group into the vehicles. Luckily, the dead hunters had more than enough transportation for everyone.

Roger and Dmitri stayed behind to burn the horrible place to the ground. As the flames rose and the engines roared in their departure, Dmitri slipped his hands into his pockets. His accent was thick again. "We hurt them. They hurt us. We use that as an excuse to hurt them again. When does it end?"

Roger watched the flames seeking the upper floors of the house. He thought he saw movement in one of the windows, but it had to be a trick of the light. They'd made certain everything was dead before dousing the first floor in gasoline.

This wasn't the first house he'd burned. And he had lived long enough to see the loop that plagued Dmitri. At the center was Seamus, a volatile cyclone they had to endure night after night, decade after decade. Even if they killed every hunter, one would learn of him through some tragedy caused by Seamus, and then they would want to take out the evil vampire that had ruined their life. A tiny seed of Roger wanted to, but he didn't dare let that desire grow. Seamus was ancient, and Roger was nothing in the face of that.

Roger twisted the gold ring on his finger. *One night, I'll be strong enough to change my fate.* "We're immortal. In some ways, it never ends, Dmitri."

Dmitri shook his head and strode toward one of the cars.

Roger decided he'd stay as long as he needed in order to make certain the house became a pile of rubble.

CHAPTER 1

Taliville, Tennessee, October 2021

Roger ran his fingers over the inked words on the notebook page. The paper had the unique stiffness that came from so much ink sprawled across it. The rigidity made it feel fragile, on the edge of breaking. Or perhaps that was Roger projecting his own tender state of mind onto the inanimate object. While he'd asked Zack to dig into what the Great Lakes Coven had been doing for the last thirty years, he hadn't expected him to go further back. He hadn't counted on reliving his past sins.

Zack had filled two pages with details about the demise of the hunter base in Indiana, though he'd labeled it as "The Farmhouse Slaughter, 1947." The notes included information on how the hunters had tortured supernaturals, but the language was clinical and detached. He had all of the data and none of the emotion.

Roger flipped to the end of the entry. Zack had listed out those that died, but there, at the end, were ten words that would haunt Roger for weeks. *Sole Survivor: Ilene Wright. Grandpa was born three months later.*

Grandpa.

Though Zack's family had disowned him, he had still been born a Wright. He'd been raised as a hunter. Roger had wondered how Zack's family was connected to other Wrights he'd heard of. Before him lay one answer. Which man among the ones who died that night had been Zack's great-grandfather? How many others of Zack's ancestry had Roger killed?

If he followed that train of thought, he'd drive himself mad with guilt. At least when it came to hunters, killing them was self-defense. And even the momentary glimmer of that thought made Roger want to hang his head. But killing was part of who a vampire was. In his more than three hundred years, he'd rarely had a bout of guilt over his victims.

The guilt was easier to feel than facing the old fears clawing their way into his consciousness night by night. Thirty-two years ago, someone had cursed Roger into an enchanted sleep. To him, he'd fallen asleep in 1989 and woken in 2021 without knowing that time had passed.

Seamus wasn't the likely originator of the curse. While he could have had someone perform the spell for him, he was never so merciful in a punishment. The last time Roger had tried to leave the coven, Seamus had tied him to a post and left him to burn in the sun for a morning. He'd nearly died, and he'd never strayed far from him since.

While he'd been taken from the coven against his will, he and his blood brother Dmitri were spreading the story that he'd chosen his departure. Vampires sometimes grew bored of existence and disappeared for years or even decades from both human and supernatural societies.

In truth, he'd woken two months ago when Zack had broken the curse on his coffin. Instead of rushing back to Seamus's side, Roger begged the vampire master of Taliville, Nell, for the opportunity to regain his strength. Roger's gold ring had fallen off in 1989. He was finally strong enough to be his own master, but he'd never be free so long as Seamus lived. Nell's idyllic town was the heart of her domain and the perfect place to recover and train for the inevitable battles he would face.

Zack would be at his side when he left for Chicago.

But where was he now?

A month and a half ago, Callum Wright, Zack's older brother, had invaded Taliville in order to find Zack. Though he'd set his sights on killing Roger, Zack had interfered and taken a stake to the shoulder that had been meant for Roger's heart. The blow had nearly been a lethal one.

To provide more safety for her honored guests, Nell had invited Roger and Zack to stay in her mansion for the remainder of their time in Taliville. Once Zack had recovered enough, he and Roger shared a room. The pillow beside Roger's smelled deeply of sandalwood and a distinct mortal musk that belonged to Zack. As a vampire, Roger was almost entirely nocturnal unless circumstances demanded his attention during the day. Zack had to bridge the day and the night, often researching during the light and training during the dark.

He was also supposed to behave as Roger's pet, and protocol demanded that he should be with Roger at sunset. Even when he couldn't see it, twilight eased an itch in Roger's psyche. The sun had to be going down. Zack ought to be close.

Roger closed his eyes. Lately, he had experimented with the strength of his senses and powers. He stretched his awareness past his bedroom and sought what noises he could discern in the rest of Nell's mansion. Her home had a wide range of people, from visiting vampires to her mortal pets to her staff. As he came across a voice or a heartbeat or a footstep, he tossed it aside and searched for another. After so long with Zack, he knew the quiet tread of his steps, the gentle, steady thrum of his heart, and the melody of his voice.

"Yes?" Zack said, some distance away. Floors? Roger wasn't entirely sure when he fell this deep into what he could hear.

"A package," another voice said. One of the servants, Roger believed. "I didn't want to disturb your master with it."

"Good call. I've got it from here," Zack replied.

Simply hearing Zack's voice eased the fear raking deeper grooves into Roger's mind. As much as Dmitri wanted Seamus and Anton dead, as much as Nell was providing support, and as friendly as Josefina had been, Zack was the one who truly *chose* to be at Roger's side. There was no wondering if he might've betrayed him decades ago.

Roger trusted him, and that was a rare beauty he hadn't felt ... *if I'm being honest, in my entire life. Not like this.* Knowing Zack was on his way back to their room, Roger opened his eyes and picked up the notebooks strewn across the bed. He organized them on the desk where Zack had left them.

Everything else in the room was in its place. Their queen-sized bed was made, the connecting bathroom clean. There was no window, so there were no curtains to push aside to reveal the night. As they were leaving for Chicago the night after next, the bulk of their possessions were in the newly obtained luggage Roger had purchased.

Nearly all their possessions were new. Roger had woken with only a single outfit and little in his wallet. Through a generous loan from Nell, Roger would make his reentry into vampire society in a style appropriate to his position in the GLC. Zack had brought a week's worth of clothes and a few things he considered essential from his mortal home, but none of what he had was what someone of his status could show in public.

Roger doubted there was anything in Zack's wardrobe at

his parents' house that would have suited his station, but he would never know for certain. Zack's parents had disowned him after he stood with Roger and against Callum. Even sneaking in was out of the question—Zack believed that his family had "followed protocol" and changed the locks on their home.

Sensing Zack was nearing the room, Roger lounged on the bed, putting on an air of casual waiting. He didn't want Zack to glimpse the panic clinging to the edges of his thoughts.

A moment later, Zack came through the door with a package under his arm.

Zackery Wright was a young man a week shy of twenty. An element of his youthfulness had melted away into an adult's firmness. His gray eyes always had a quality of steel to them, and he was prone to frowning when he thought no one was looking his way. He had a lithe frame, shoulders only a touch broader than his waist. Though he wasn't sculpted, he was muscular.

Over the last few weeks, his skin had paled since he was living more nocturnally. His light brown hair was cut to a popular fashion and had a few blond highlights. He had on a thin layer of makeup that was common among pets. A little foundation evened out his skin tone, a little blush made his mortality apparent, and a trace of eyeliner brought attention to his steely gaze. He wore jeans and a polo that were tailored to his body.

As soon as he shut the door behind him, he was reaching behind to unclasp the black collar on his neck. A small round metal disk hung from it. Etched into it was a kraken in the style of Roger's vampire crest, and it marked Zack as belonging to him. Even if other vampires didn't know Roger's kraken, they would know that Zack was claimed. In Taliville, he might have been safe enough without it while interacting with the vampires and other supernaturals, but in Chicago, the collar would protect him.

Provided anyone still respects me enough to keep their hands off my "property." Roger smothered his newest fear and smiled at Zack. "You look dashing tonight."

"I look like an expensive-ass doll," Zack complained.

His attitude was more sour than usual, but this wasn't the first time he'd come back to their room with a grumble in his voice. Roger had never demanded the twenty-four-hour submission some masters wanted from their pets, and Zack would have never gone for it. However, his pets usually showed a *little* more deference than Zack did.

Then again, Roger was realizing he didn't miss the way some of his pets would treat him like an immortal masterpiece. Zack was clever and compassionate, and more than Roger had dared hoped to discover when he'd first entreated him to stop fighting him, but he never ignored Roger's flaws.

Because when they first met, Zack had been trying to kill him. He'd come to Taliville after reading an email detailing where a vampire could be found. Zack had followed through on the clues, discovered Roger's coffin, and broken into it. He'd hesitated before driving a stake through Roger's heart, and that momentary gap in judgment had given Roger the chance to bite him. Roger had been moving on instinct. He would have killed Zack if Zack hadn't thought on his feet and used the tools at his disposal.

And Roger had seen an opportunity in Zack that he hadn't had on his own. Zack had an enchanted silver dagger. Since Seamus was a vampire over a thousand years old, killing him could be tricky. Simply driving a wooden stake through his heart might not be enough. Though the stories were few, Roger had heard of vampires of great power surviving the apparent destruction of their bodies only to resurface again. Silver burned vampires, and Zack's family had spent generations working out the runes they carved into each blade. Zack's dagger would be key in taking down Seamus for good, Roger was sure of it.

At the very least, having a trained, brilliant hunter at his back had to up his chances of survival.

Before the end of their first night, Roger realized that he liked Zack, and as the weeks wore on, that like was only growing into something more each time he laid eyes on him.

But Zack's appearance as his pet was only a costume, one that he was quick to toss to the side anytime they were alone. He practically threw the black leather collar onto the desk. When he glanced Roger's way, he narrowed his eyes. Tension built in him, the kind that meant he was running through the data of what he saw and coming to conclusions.

That kind of scrutiny was a bit intense. Roger asked, "What's wrong?"

At the same time, Zack said, "You okay?"

How does he always see through me? Roger dropped his gaze and examined his fingernails for a fleck of dirt. Finding none, he sighed and looked up again. Zack remained pensive. Avoiding him would only be exhausting, so Roger sighed and said, "I took a few bad twists down memory lane. I only need to clear my head. What's causing your mood?"

"I spent the afternoon with Reed making content for the Fang app." Zack ran his hand through his short hair, messing with the styling of it. "No one told me I'd have to be a social media influencer when I signed up."

"To be fair, I didn't know social media existed when I asked you to join me," Roger replied.

Zack gave a noncommittal snort. "Yeah, well, if my family didn't hate me before, they will once they see what I'm up to."

"I thought the point of the Fang app was that only super-naturals used it."

Zack shrugged, his disbelief clear in his gesture. "If I'd been a little less obsessed with the Hunters' Information Network and physical books, I might have bothered to find a way in. And if I could have that thought, then someone else probably has."

"That doesn't mean your parents will see it," Roger said. Part of him longed to ask what the problem would be if they did, but he knew. Zack's family considered pets to be traitors to humanity. If the videos showed Zack enjoying his new life —which they would have to in order to maintain Roger's image as a great master—then his parents wouldn't approve.

"Whatever," Zack grumbled. He brought the package over to the bed and sat down. The box sat between them. "I also saw where this is from."

Roger glanced at the sender. His favorite leather shop in Chicago had remained open through the decades, and he'd been able to order a custom set of collars for Zack and another set for his dedicated donor, a shifter named Kit.

"Excellent," Roger said.

Zack bristled.

Gracefully, Roger slid off the end of the bed and went over to the desk. He took his time finding the letter opener, drawing out his movements in the slow, smooth way he'd practiced when he was a fledgling. Slick, enticing movements weren't an automatic part of the vampire package. Roger had put incredible effort into training his body to be like this.

And as he turned back to the bed and crossed the room, he noticed that Zack's breathing had evened out, the wall in his eyes was crumbling. Roger grinned at him as he opened the package. Inside were seven thinner boxes, shaped like necklace boxes, though a little thicker than a jewelry box would be.

"I seem to remember you becoming flustered when I mentioned having sex dungeons," Roger said. He drew out one of the necklace boxes labeled "Z, onyx" and opened it. "I'm surprised you hate the idea of the collars so much."

"If we were messing around with them in the bedroom, I might be okay with it," Zack said.

"Might be?" Roger raised an eyebrow.

Zack squirmed, and he suddenly wasn't meeting Roger's gaze. That wasn't unusual when they started discussing anything sexual. Zack had a hesitance in him. As close as they'd gotten, he still shied away from talking about what he wanted.

Roger reached under Zack's chin and tilted his head back up so their gazes met. "We have to be convincing in public."

Zack's gaze hardened. "I *know*."

"Do you know how I usually claim my pets?"

"You put a collar on them and fuck them senseless?"

Roger glared a fraction, and Zack had the decency to look embarrassed about what he'd said. After this long together, Roger would have figured Zack knew him better. He had spent two weeks waiting on Zack hand and foot, something even Zack had said was excessive. "I take them to dinner. We spend the night talking about limits. Only then do I take them home and have them prove themselves worthy of wearing my collar."

"I am not your *pet*," Zack said fiercely.

"But you are *mine*," Roger replied.

A warmth spread up through Zack, but a dull buzz countered the brush of lust that Roger felt. Zack had a hunter's tattoo on his hip, which helped negate mind-controlling magic like a vampire's ability to affect fear or desire. However, it wasn't one hundred percent, and Roger had spent enough time with Zack to know where the gaps in the defenses were. If he and Zack had the relationship Roger had had with other pets, he would use his powers to coax Zack's lust upward to make him more amenable. Arguments were taxing, and Roger hated when he fumbled. And he seemed to inevitably misstep with Zack.

Yet that would betray Zack's trust, and Roger wouldn't do that to him. Roger would have to try the old-fashioned way to seduce him.

"Perhaps I should actually claim you." Roger grinned and dipped his voice to a husky whisper. "We could make a game of it. I'm the big bad evil vampire, and you're the innocent youth I've invited to my castle in the mountains."

Zack pushed away Roger's hand and stood. "You want to play *Dracula*? Seriously?"

"I thought it might help you blow off some steam," Roger said.

"By being a victim?"

"Then we forget the claiming and reverse the roles." Roger sat on the edge of the bed and leaned back, propping himself up with one arm. Once the words were in the air, an electrical buzzing started in the back of Roger's mind. Though he didn't mind occasionally bottoming, the only one he'd ever been truly submissive with was Seamus. The roleplay he'd suggested to Zack didn't have to include such dramatic lines of dominance, but it was possible.

He hadn't meant to casually offer Zack the opportunity to dominate him. While they'd had sex more than a few times over the last few weeks, Roger was the top between them. What would Zack do if he took charge? Did Roger really want him to? He wasn't about to back out from engaging in some fun, but the nagging buzz in his psyche waited to pounce on every mistake.

For his part, Zack only stood at the end of the bed. He crossed his arms over his chest. "You're off again."

"I'm fine," Roger insisted. If he was ever going to lead the GLC, he would need to learn how to operate while under such clear scrutiny. Seamus only saw what he wanted to see, and Roger had grown accustomed to displaying the personas that pleased him.

But Zack saw through every one of those masks in a heartbeat. Roger couldn't help wondering if everyone else did as well and they were only too polite to say anything. *You know that isn't true. Seamus wouldn't tolerate you if you hadn't perfected lying to his face.*

Roger would simply need to prove to Zack that he had nothing to worry about.

Languidly, Roger rolled up from the bed and onto his feet. He was chest to chest with Zack, and he stroked his cheek. Zack was always so warm. A flicker of the hunger deep in Roger sought that heat like a moth, but he could keep it at bay for the time being. He tilted Zack's chin up and gazed deep into his steel-gray eyes. Zack was searching for something in him, so Roger held steady. The best way to avoid detection was to simply wait.

And in that moment, Roger saw the hints he'd been seeing for weeks. The tiny glimmers that Zack didn't hate everything about vampires despite being raised by hunters who did. Doubts were in his core, but he was young, and he would have been strange for having none. He was only on the cusp of discovering who he truly was.

Are you so sure you know who you are? Roger couldn't deny the question lying in wait in the corners of his mind. This time away from Seamus had been a relief in ways he hadn't predicted.

He could ignore the question by remaining centered in the moment. If he never stopped to think, he never had to worry about what revelations might come for him.

"Would it be so terrible to be mine?" Roger whispered. He ran his thumb down Zack's lips and over his chin and caressed his neck to his shoulder before gently sliding his hand up to cup his cheek again.

Zack stepped away sharply. The clever sting in his eyes faded as the doubts clouded. Roger started to reach for him, but Zack dodged backward, slipping away from his grasp. "I have practice with Josefina. I shouldn't be late."

Roger let Zack make it all the way to the door before he said, "You're forgetting something."

"What?" Zack said as he spun back to look at Roger.

With a flick of his wrist, Roger tossed the collar in his hand to Zack. Zack caught it without breaking eye contact with him. Gently, he said, "I'll see you later."

"Later," Zack replied. After putting on the collar, he ducked out of the room quickly.

A thousand ifs ran through Roger's mind, but he had no time to entertain any of them. He had his own training to attend to, and he would need to feed before that. Once he'd waited long enough that Zack was far away in the mansion, he slipped out of his room and headed out into the night.

CHAPTER 2

The ache in Zack's shoulder worked its way down his body until his left side cramped. Sweat stung his eyes and rolled down his back. Keeping up with Josefina drove the air from his lungs. Matching a century-and-a-half-old vampire step for step wasn't easy. Zack fought to maintain a neutral expression, but a wince was coming on. He ground his teeth together and kept moving.

Suddenly, Josefina stopped, raising her hands and stepping away from Zack. She was beautiful—Zack had yet to meet a vampire that was truly ugly and had a theory that vampiric magic might emit a low-level psychic energy that made everyone seem attractive—and had long dark brown hair that she kept in a braid. Despite two hours of practice, her dress shirt and slacks were immaculate. Not a drop of sweat dotted her brown skin. Since vampires didn't need to breathe, she wasn't panting either.

Zack was a smidge jealous.

Maybe more than a smidge.

"That's enough for the moment," she said.

Zack had left a towel on a chair in the middle of the ballroom. He went over to it and used it to wipe the sweat off his brow. A bit of makeup came off as well. If he was the type to admit his pains—which he was ignoring the best he could— he'd have confessed his ankle felt off and his shoulder hurt. He rotated his sore shoulder a few times, then dropped the towel onto the chair and turned toward Josefina. "Okay. Let's go again."

"Excuse me?" Josefina put her hands on her hips and arched an eyebrow. Any hint of warmth evaporated from her expression. Her sternness could match a black screen of death in seriousness.

Vampires wore many masks, and her serious demeanor was one of her most frequent. Underneath, she had a gooey center, and Zack had seen glimpses of it. After all, she'd given him a rainbow teddy bear as a get-well present and checked up on him while he was recovering. She claimed she was doing her duty to keep her lover's mansion safe. He was "hunter spawn" and needed watching. The excuse would have been believable if she hadn't brought him coffees and brownies.

So while Zack didn't buy her aloofness, he didn't call her out on being his friend. Vampires considered themselves masters of deception. Besides, they were supposed to be practicing vampiric protocols.

Knowing he'd broken it with his tone of voice and lack of proper etiquette, he widened his eyes and faked innocence. "What?"

Josefina picked up her phone from a nearby chair and turned off the foxtrot music. "Why do you always slip up when we're practicing ballroom dancing?"

"Because I know the rules," Zack said, a sliver of anger in his voice. He took a deep breath and plastered a smile on his face. He wasn't supposed to show annoyance or anger. In the GLC, that could be dangerous. Nell and her coven would only think he was rude, but everyone kept reminding Zack that Seamus's underlings were terrible.

"I'm already letting you slide. You're dressed inappropriately for an evening out with your master."

"That gossamer shit isn't clothing," Zack complained.

"Zackery, the clothing, the manners—all of it is important," Josefina said. "This has to be second nature if you're going to blend in with the upper echelons of vampire society in Chicago. You can't afford to break character around them."

The lecture was a common one he'd heard over and over the last two months. Josefina had repeated it at least twice a night in the last week alone. He could follow the rules, but they were like being bound in duct tape and tossed into the back of a moving vehicle. Though he had a far better view of his surroundings, he had the same amount of control over his destination.

But pointing that out wouldn't change a damn thing, so Zack made a sweeping bow. In a soft whisper, he said, "Please forgive me, master. How can I ever compare to the immortal night that truly occupies your soul?"

Josefina shook her head at him. "I can hear the sarcasm in your voice. False flattery like that—"

"Will be the death of me. I *know*." Zack ran his hand through his hair and let out a long sigh. Acting like vampires were a superior species meant to be worshipped was degrading, especially since Zack had been raised to hunt supernaturals and consider them all monsters. Vampires weren't glorious; they were predators who tormented the weak for sport. They were vile, evil creatures.

Zack tensed as his thoughts strayed into that familiar, now-unwelcome territory. When he was a kid, he hadn't firmly believed everything his family had said about supernaturals, but after he'd made a mistake in Detroit, he'd tried to keep their philosophies. Nothing he did earned his mother's trust, and the rest of his family remained unimpressed. He'd dropped out of college and dedicated himself to research and training, but he wasn't allowed on another hunt.

The family, his mother in particular, was never going to accept him as a hunter unless he proved himself. An email came in while his family was out on a hunt, and he figured it was his best shot to reclaim his dignity and become part of the hunter legacy. After all, he was the son of a Gladwell and a Wright. Fighting evil was in his blood.

The email had led to a hunt, which resulted in discovering Roger sleeping in a coffin. Zack had hesitated because, well, Roger was extremely hot. He wasn't proud that he'd slipped, but he held no guilt over not "finishing the job." At first, he'd been all right with his decision because Roger offered a bigger prize. Seamus was an infamous bastard that both Zack's familial heritages wanted to destroy. The closest anyone had come was in the early 1800's, and a whole branch of the family had died in the attempt.

Pretending to be a pet would get Zack closer than anyone else had ever been. He'd wanted to explain that to his brother, Cal. Once Cal had seen the bite marks on Zack, he'd decided that Roger needed to be put down.

Zack *liked* Roger. Like, *really* liked him, even then. Roger wanted him to open his eyes instead of viewing the world in the demanding black-and-white way his family had taught him. And Roger saw worth in him that his family never had. With that little bit of support, Zack had done what he always did: take in data and make conclusions. Vampires weren't a monolith any more than humans were. Roger *wasn't* evil.

So when Cal demanded Zack kill Roger and come back to the family, Zack had told him no. In the fight, Zack had seen Cal attempting to stake Roger in the back. Zack had pushed Roger out of the way and taken the blow.

For a second, Cal seemed like he was sorry to drive a stake deep into Zack's left shoulder.

Clearly, that regret hadn't lasted. By the time Zack woke from his surgery, his family had disconnected his phone and changed the passwords on the emails and the financials he'd been managing when his parents were on the road. Since he'd left his laptop at home, they'd accessed his social media accounts, and what they didn't change, they closed down. He'd been helping the family with every waking breath, and suddenly, he was just ... out. Discarded. Abandoned. *Deleted*.

Zack rolled his sore shoulder and tossed his towel back onto the chair. "Please, master. I would like to try again."

"My love and I have put a great investment into your health." Josefina slid her phone into a jacket pocket. "If I break you just before you leave, we'll have wasted a fortune."

Nell's mansion had three floors, a dozen guest rooms, two kitchens, a room for video games, and another for old-school games like billiards. There was a workout room, more bathrooms than Zack had had a chance to count, a huge library he was barely allowed to be in, and other areas he hadn't been permitted to investigate.

Her property included massive gardens and the additional building Zack and Josefina were in. A portion of the greenery was between the main house and the event hall, while the rest of it butted up against the lake that was in the middle of Taliville. Pixies lived in the gardens, and their tiny lights gave the area an enchanted feeling.

The event hall was for entertaining guests and separate from the main house so that vampires wouldn't have to be invited into her home. The largest room of it was the ballroom, where they practiced formal dances. Chandelier light gleamed off the polished wooden floor, highlighting the amber lurking in the natural material. Grand pillars around the center supported the thirty-foot ceiling.

Besides the physical signs of wealth, Nell employed a massive staff to upkeep the property. She essentially ran the town of Taliville, making investments and keeping employment steady. The other vampires of her coven contributed, and other supernaturals had businesses in the small town. She ruled over the fifth-largest territory among the American covens. What she and Josefina had spent on him, both in finances and effort, would only be a blip for the immortal.

But I make a useful pawn. Zack had had a conversation with Nell on his second night in Taliville. She had tested his resolve in the face of danger and then hinted at why she wanted Roger to succeed.

Seamus was consolidating power. In the last three decades, his coven had gone from over a hundred vampires to over four hundred. His territory extended from the Canadian border in the north to the tip of Kentucky, from Cincinnati, Ohio, to the Mississippi River in the west. A smattering of small, inconsequential territories separated Seamus's domain from Nell's. If he continued, he'd threaten Nell's domain.

Nell wanted them to take out the threat before open war happened. Her investment in them would return a huge bounty, and part of that bothered Zack. Being *used* slid under his skin and festered, but the best he could do for now was learn etiquette and train for the inevitable fight.

Adopting a serious tone, Zack nodded in deference to Josefina. Softly, he said, "I only want to make the most of that investment, master."

Josefina snapped her fingers.

Quickly, Zack slipped into the most common pet pose he'd have to adopt in public. He stood with his feet slightly apart, his head bowed and to the side, one wrist behind his back and his right hand loose at his side. His gaze remained on the floor, watching a spot not more than a few inches in front of his feet.

Every ounce of hunter training in him activated mental alerts as Josefina walked a slow circle around him. Her heels echoed in the otherwise silent room. An itch started between Zack's shoulder blades.

Instead of listening to the part of him that sounded far too much like Cal and did nothing but tell him he was an embarrassment, Zack focused outward with his other senses. Vampires had a subtle but distinct odor. Hunter lore called it devil's rot, but Roger called it the scent of the grave. Using his hearing, he could trace her movements.

However, he'd been practicing another tactic. The magic that sustained vampires made them cool to the touch. The older a vampire was, the greater the chill affected their aura as well as their body. One benefit of wearing so little around vampires was that Zack could stay aware of where a vampire was without overtly watching them.

Josefina was over a century old, and the air around her had a chill, like putting a hand on cool metal. Between the cold and the click of her heels, Zack followed her movements.

"There's a good boy," Josefina said.

Zack clenched his jaw. He couldn't react to her patronizing tone. Shouldn't say anything. *She's trying to do me a favor. They're going to say worse shit in Chicago.*

She's making you an easy meal, idiot, his internal voice that sounded like Cal said.

"Thank you, master," Zack replied quietly. "May we please continue the lesson?"

"No."

A flash of anger rushed through Zack. The only answer anyone seemed to give him lately was "no."

"We're about to have company," Josefina said.

"But, master—"

Josefina held up her hand, which was her signal for silence. Zack shut his mouth tightly.

A moment later, Reed walked through the entryway. He had a tray with a pitcher of ice water and two glasses. Nell had plenty of servants for that kind of task, but Reed always found an excuse to check on Zack during a ballroom lesson. Zack was pretty sure Roger had put him up to it. However, Reed was also the kind of person who naturally looked after others. Since they'd met, that care had included Zack.

Reed was around thirty years old. He was a white guy with sandy-blond hair and brown eyes. He taught a beginner's yoga class at the Taliville Gym, but his physique wasn't an athlete's. Along with his sweater and dark jeans, he wore a black leather collar with a crest tag that marked him as Nell's. Between his wardrobe and his glasses, he looked like a comfy professor. Usually Reed wore contacts, but every once in a while, he wore glasses. Both looks suited him.

Since he was bringing water, Zack could forgive him for intruding. He shifted his weight off his sore ankle absently, then caught the slight frown Josefina shot his way. Zack had let his mask slip and shown his pain. In an attempt to divert her attention, he complained to Reed, "She's refusing to teach me."

"We've done an hour of combat training and two hours of ballroom dancing. Even my endurance has limits," Josefina said.

"Besides, you're leaving in two nights." Reed set down the tray on one of the empty chairs and poured a glass of water. As he handed it to Zack, he said, "Is another half an hour going to teach you something you don't already know?"

"There's no replacement for muscle memory." Zack took the glass of water.

"And yet you stop behaving at every opportunity," Josefina said sternly. "Your gaze is up, and you're engaging in conversation without permission."

Her glare was ice-cold. A snarl was in his throat in response, but he quashed it.

"Aren't you being a little hard on him?" Reed asked.

"My sweet boy, I am teaching him how to survive. Don't undermine me." Josefina caressed Reed's cheek.

"Of course, master," Reed said reverently.

Pets usually belonged to one vampire, but Reed was in a poly relationship with Nell and Josefina. His relationship with them wasn't sexual—Reed was ace, and Nell and Josefina were lesbians—but there was love between them. Reed had told Zack that he got all the cuddles he wanted; Nell and Josefina had a human they trusted to help run their city. What they had worked for them.

Addressing Josefina, Reed motioned to the water. "Do you want some, master?"

Josefina stared at his wrist rather than the water. Her eyes turned the faintest red, a sign she was hungry. "Has Nell drank from you?"

"She had a nip the other night. Barely anything." Reed turned his wrist over, baring it for her.

Gently, she took his wrist and pulled him closer. She put a finger under his chin and tilted his head to the side. "May I, love?"

"Yes," Reed breathed with a sigh of want.

She was going to feed on him like it was no big deal. Being in the presence of a feeding seemed to be the one area of vampire society that lacked rules. Zack had no idea where his gaze belonged. Should he look away for their modesty? Or was not watching a vampire overwhelm a mortal and drink from them a sign of disrespect? Was ignoring them dangerous? Josefina was experienced, but what if she lost control? Did Zack need to be ready to step in? Interrupting a feed had to be against the rules and just so ingrained as something no one did that it went without saying.

Josefina wrapped her arm around Reed and bit into his neck. Reed gasped, and his eyes fluttered shut.

Watching a vampire feed was nothing like watching porn. Zack's gaze fell to his own wrist. He had a few sets of fading bite marks there. Roger needed blood, Zack was supposed to have the scars if he was a pet, and ... and feeding Roger was ... *hot*. Admitting it to himself was hard, but he liked the feel of Roger's fangs piercing his flesh. He liked knowing that Roger needed him in that deep, visceral way that felt more powerful than sex. It usually led to sex between them, or at least intensely making out for a while, and that was a confusing nest of thoughts Zack didn't want to examine.

Vampires constantly fed from others. Roger said the ones in the GLC did it as casually as drinking from a soda can. Zack had to get used to it. *Hopefully it stops turning me on.*

But Reed moaning as Josefina continued drinking from him only made Zack think of his own moans and needs.

"Thank you," Josefina murmured in Reed's ear as she finished. She hugged him.

"Always," Reed whispered.

They held each other for a long embrace before drifting apart. Reed took a clean handkerchief from his pocket and lightly held it to the wound. Josefina had been careful; the wound she'd made didn't bleed much after she stopped drinking.

"Looks like we're having fun in here," Roger said, his voice carrying across the ballroom.

Zack's belly flip-flopped and filled with butterflies. He turned to watch him enter the room.

Roger strode as if life were one long drama and the gleaming boards beneath him were the latest stage. He had broad shoulders, a narrow waist, an ass sculpted by a higher power, and long legs that added to his swagger prowess. At just over six feet tall, he was nearly five inches taller than Zack. His smile was cocky and sinful, while merriment lit his brown eyes. The small gold hoop earring in his left ear drew attention to his square jaw. Long black hair framed his chiseled face and draped over his shoulders. His raven locks made his white skin seem even starker and paler than he actually was.

Lately, he'd adopted a "coven captain appropriate" wardrobe. Everything he wore cost more than Zack wanted to know, but he always looked amazing. His shirt was dark red silk and had a billowing sort of look. The front was parted for the first few inches, showing off the curve of his pecs and his smooth skin. His pants were black and barely whispered as he walked. And it had to be magic the way his black leather belt and boots perfectly matched the shade of his pants.

Somehow, this amazing, hot immortal found Zack attractive. Digging into the coven's history had revealed a few details about Roger, even though Zack had shied away from directly researching him. He didn't want to think about the countless men Roger had been with over the centuries, and he didn't want to discover how many victims he'd left in his wake. Sometimes ignorance was better.

Still, Zack had learned through pieces of conversation and bits of gossip no one thought he was overhearing that Roger tended to have multiple partners. Pets, other vampires, demons, Seelie, Unseelie—the only thing Roger seemed to be picky about was that his partner identified as a man. No one in Taliville was boasting about sleeping with him recently, but that didn't mean Roger wasn't seeing other people. After all, Kit was his actual pet. Kit identified as nonbinary, so Zack wasn't sure the two of them were hooking up, but Roger usually slept with his pets.

I shouldn't be jealous about that. We've never talked about it. And maybe they aren't sleeping together. Just because they spent so much time together, Zack couldn't assume they were boyfriends. They'd never had that talk. Was he a casual lay for Roger? Something more?

Roger approached Zack and kissed his temple. Physical touch was common between pets and their masters, but Zack's stomach squeezed tight as he realized Reed and Josefina were witnessing Roger doting on him. Heat flared in his cheeks as he also noticed that Roger's mere proximity was turning him on and that was probably tenting his pants, and even if it wasn't, Josefina would be able to psychically feel his desire if she paid close enough attention, and ... The spiral continued roaring out of control, egged on by that nagging internal voice that insulted him.

"I thought I'd catch you practicing." Roger stroked the top of Zack's shoulder and then down his back.

"Josefina said we're done, master." Zack pouted. Putting out his bottom lip in just the right way had been how he'd bent Roger to his will during his recovery. He'd learned it when asking for another bowl of ice cream. "I've barely tried the foxtrot."

"He's been acting up," Josefina replied. "He's also hiding the fact that his shoulder's killing him."

Roger slid his hand up and around to put his finger under Zack's chin and tilt his head up. The smile on his lips could melt an iceberg. This was Roger at full charm, and Zack had no trouble picturing him as a pirate on the high seas or a gentleman thief in Georgian England or a bootlegger with a heart of gold. "Now, now, is that how a good boy behaves?"

The ground was slipping out from underneath Zack's feet. His hunter's tattoo remained dormant, meaning Roger wasn't laying on any supernatural charms to woo him. The pet role he played had few perks, but the way Roger spoke to him often caused a rush.

He murmured, "It's not hurting that much, master."

Firmly, Roger pinched Zack's chin between his finger and thumb and tilted Zack's head up farther so that Zack had to straighten instead of relax. *Masters manhandle their pets frequently*, Roger had said during one of their lessons. *Expect to see them in physical discomfort. Especially when they misbehave.*

Zack held out, biting back the building pain. Roger's grip smarted, but he'd been training for fights his whole life. The little bit of pain he felt was nothing.

"Be honest, boy," Roger said, his voice cooler and dripping with authority. "Does your shoulder hurt?"

The command in Roger's voice made something inside Zack bristle. He was sick to death of listening to other people. First, his parents and the rest of his family, now the vampires. Everyone thought they knew better than he did. But here he was, alive, on his own, and having to keep step with dangerous creatures.

"I really want to practice," Zack said, his voice tighter than he wanted it to be. He hated how young he sounded. "I need to be able to nail this."

Roger rumbled with an inaudible note of pleased annoyance as he released Zack. "I suppose I can't be upset about that. I have a little time before Nell's ready for me. We should dance."

Josefina put her palm to her face and then wiped downward. "You two are impossible."

"I think they're sweet," Reed said.

"Because you are a hopeless romantic." She sat down on a chair.

"And you like to hide your gooey center." Reed settled onto her lap, resting his arms around her shoulders. In turn, she wrapped an arm around him.

"Josefina, can we have a waltz, please," Roger said.

"We were working on the foxtrot," Zack said.

Roger raised an eyebrow.

"The waltz is boring," Zack complained.

Completely disregarding Zack, Roger looked away from him to speak to Josefina. "You're right. He is misbehaving."

Because, of course, Roger wanted him to use the rules. Zack was outside of their bedroom, so he was a *pet*. And he was supposed to like it. But this night was one of the last ones where he could get away with breaking the rules. "Can we drop the master shit?"

Roger glowered at him. The disappointment in his expression made Zack take a step back. "You understand that you can't just 'drop' it when we're in Chicago?"

When they were alone in their room, Roger had a warmth to him that could comfort Zack as well as tease him. Here, pretending they were in high vampire society, Roger was a marble statue. Beautiful and nearly unreadable and utterly a work of art hiding his own gooey center. This was the Roger he would have to deal with nightly once they left their safe haven.

"I'm sorry, master," Zack said sharply. "Josefina is right. I've had enough for tonight."

Without waiting for permission, Zack spun and stormed out of the ballroom. He made it to the path between the event hall and the mansion before he heard Roger calling after him. Muscles clenching, he turned to face Roger. "*What*?"

"You can't behave like this," Roger said in a quiet, scolding voice. He closed the distance so there was less than a foot between them.

"I know," Zack snapped. "It's all anyone's been saying for months."

"Do you think I like this?" Roger replied.

"You've been doing this for hundreds of years." The words were out, but Zack wished he could take them back as Roger stepped away from him with a distant glaze in his eyes. Zack twisted around so he didn't see the hurt in Roger. Because it didn't make sense. Roger had boasted about having sex dungeons when they met. He'd prided himself on being a "good master" in the past.

Before he met Roger, Zack assumed all the vampires lived as if humans were lesser than them. The family lore taught that vampires' pets were always half-dead, mindless sex junkies.

But that wasn't Zack's relationship with Roger at all. When Zack had cried himself to sleep, Roger had held him the whole time. He'd watched trashy movies and what had to be boring documentaries. He'd looked absolutely wrecked when Zack first woke from the surgery. He *cared*.

He's not turning me into some feeding bag. He's not. Zack wiped at his eyes and tried not to feel the weight of the collar around his throat. "I'm sorry. It's just … this is a lot."

Carefully, Roger stepped forward and put his hands on

Zack's shoulders. He kissed the back of his head and slowly wrapped his arms around him in an embrace. His tone shifted to one that Zack wanted to think of as his boyfriend voice. "If this is too much, we can find another place for you."

Because Zack couldn't go home.

The only place he might belong was Taliville, but he didn't want to stay without Roger. And the thought of Roger facing Seamus without him froze his inside. He wouldn't be able to sleep knowing Roger was putting himself in danger every night.

His only choice was to shovel down the shit and not choke on it.

So Zack pulled himself together and sealed his mask into place. He smiled the brightest he could and turned around in Roger's embrace to face him. "I'll be fine, master."

"Zack," Roger said tenderly.

The eggshell mask that Zack had constructed threatened to crack. He slipped away from Roger's side. "Don't, master. We're outside of our room. This is how it's supposed to be, isn't it?"

A shift came over Roger, like the closing of a hardcover book. "You have a point, sweetheart."

Zack nodded, not trusting his voice.

Roger nodded once in a silent agreement. "I'll see you later."

"Yes, master," Zack whispered. Then he turned and walked into Nell's mansion.

Zack would sink his dagger into Seamus's heart and complete a hunt that even Cal couldn't compete with. Roger would take over the coven and end Seamus's reign of terror. Everything would fall into place, and all that he'd sacrificed was temporary. He'd get a better life in return for the one he'd given up.

He just had to hang on.

It will be worth it. It has to be.

CHAPTER 3

Roger clenched his teeth to smother a groan as Nell's blade sliced through his leg. He swiped at her with his own knife, but she backstepped with an enviable grace. While her domain was currently at peace, Nell had defended herself and her people for ages. She was an ancient vampire a few decades older than Seamus, and she outclassed Roger in every skill.

Training with her was a lesson in humility, but Roger had made some progress. While he and Zack had trained together, he would fare better if he was the one to land the final blow in Seamus's heart. Vampires were immortals, never planning for the night they'd die. Among their own kind, one vampire could claim the possessions of any vampire they killed. That included leadership. Holding the title of coven master might be difficult, but Roger wasn't worrying about who might attempt to kill him for the role.

He feinted his next strike and kicked at Nell's knee, but she effortlessly dodged his attempt. With a growl, he relied on his supernatural abilities, and his speed increased. He hoped to catch her off guard.

But his use of powers broke the unspoken agreement

between them. Nell's eyes flared ruby red as she relied on her own vampiric nature, and she attacked with a speed and ferocity that Roger could only counter. They continued at breakneck speed, but each moment drained him. Though he was at full strength, he didn't have Nell's endurance.

He was going to lose. Just like he always imagined he'd lose to Seamus.

Desperately, he swung toward Nell's heart. She countered, taking hold of his wrist, and she used his momentum to flip him onto the training mat. She stabbed her blade through his back, a half inch below his heart.

Facedown on the mat, Roger couldn't reach the knife's hilt to pull it out. He was pinned. Metaphorically dead, like he was every time they did this.

"You're sloppy tonight," Nell said.

"I'm trying. That should count." Roger pushed against the floor. He managed to pry himself free of the mat, but the knife went deeper into his back.

"Let me." Nell yanked the blade out.

Roger winced at the pain but swallowed any noise he might've made. The knife was steel, and the wound quickly healed. He'd endured far worse.

Accepting his third round of defeat in ten minutes, he sat on the mat. The training room had a variety of weapons hanging on the concrete walls, but none of them would give him the edge he needed against an older vampire. Besides, Roger was focusing on using a particular knife because that was the weapon he intended to use against Seamus.

Nell had a twin to that knife. Both were replicas of Callum Wright's magical silver knife. While the enchantment would only work for Callum, the silver blade was a huge asset in a fight against many supernaturals, particularly vampires. Nell and Roger hadn't settled on who would own the original blade in the long run, but Roger was taking it with him to Chicago.

Callum had been forced to abandon his enchanted bowie knife and other weapons when he had to make a quick exit from Taliville. Seeing it as the only attainable vengeance at the moment, Roger took Callum's belongings and added them to his own. Thanks to him, he had a shotgun, a handgun, four one-liter bottles of holy water, regular and silver ammo for both firearms, ten stakes, six sets of plastic zip ties, and a length of heavy silver chain. Either it was an alloy, or somewhere along the line, the Wright family had invested a fortune to make the chain. Roger only knew that it had enough silver in it to burn like the sun.

In addition to those weapons, he could count on Zack and his equipment as well. Some of Zack's weapons had been stolen by Quinn, a sireling of Roger's who had had a grudge against Callum. Zack had unwittingly interfered with Quinn's revenge scheme and become the target instead. Out of necessity, Zack had killed Quinn.

Since Zack was publicly seen as Roger's pet, that gave Roger the right to claim Quinn's possessions, which included the contents of his hotel room in Taliville. Zack's short sword and crossbow had been in Quinn's room, along with Quinn's handgun and a particularly cruel set of floggers and whips. If Quinn had used them for pleasure, then he was playing rough with someone.

Roger examined the steel blade in his hand. Seers could read the future from bones or the stars or cards; could he determine his future from the look of a blade?

"How long do you think it will take you?" Nell said.

"To reclaim my dignity for another round? Eh, another few minutes at least," Roger replied.

Nell gave him a flat look that told him she did not find his answer amusing.

They both knew what she actually meant. She'd been asking the same questions for the last two weeks. When would he strike at Seamus? How? How long did he need to be part of the GLC in order to reassert his position? Would he be able to hold the territory from intruders seeking advantage in the turmoil of a leadership shift? She always asked these questions when the two of them trained alone, and he'd been doing his best to avoid answering.

Because the truth was, he didn't know. He didn't have a plan. There were too many variables. Seamus had ensured that the coven revolved around him. Roger needed to know more. To see everything, and maybe, *maybe*, then he'd have a chance at creating a foolproof scheme.

And there was, perhaps, deep, deep down, in the bottom of Roger's cold dead heart, the untethered hope that Seamus had changed and there was no need to supplant him. That somehow, after centuries, Anton was no longer the threat to others that he had always been.

He couldn't indulge that hope, couldn't let it grow. It definitely couldn't see the surface of his thoughts and plans. Anton and Seamus had been the same for over three hundred years. What could have changed in the last thirty-two?

Nothing, but still that tiny hope persisted and nagged him.

"The fewer people who know the plan, the better," Roger replied.

"I am not a random stranger in the middle of an orgy. I am a master vampire, and we are in the privacy of my home. A home I've allowed you to stay in," Nell said sharply.

"And I appreciate that." Roger stood. "But Anton has always had a way of learning things he shouldn't know. Divination magic is rare, but I wouldn't put it past his capabilities."

"That's a bullshit excuse for not divulging your plans."

Roger was floundering to find another excuse, although he kept his cool demeanor. Allowing Nell to know she'd gotten under his skin would be unwise. Before his pause carried on too long, his phone buzzed in his pocket. Smothering his smile of relief, he pulled it from his pocket.

His desire to smile fell when he saw who it was.

Dmitri. Not necessarily a reprieve, considering how their phone calls had been the last few times, but better than facing Nell's questions. Roger made a motion to Nell that he needed to take the call and turned away from her as he answered it. He squared his shoulders and forced a smile that he attempted to carry into his voice. "Dmitri! Hopefully you've called with good news for a change."

"Don't start with me. I'm having a shit night," Dmitri said, his Russian accent thick.

Roger rubbed his brow. Dmitri had been made the same night as him—Seamus was Roger's sire, and Anton was Dmitri's—and had known him as a mortal before that. They'd been lovers off and on as humans and then as vampires, though their relationship tended to crash and burn within weeks of reigniting every time. The last time had been in the 1920s, and Roger had sworn off romance with him for eternity.

But he knew Dmitri, inside and out. And with that knowing, he could picture Dmitri sitting behind an office desk, the windows displaying a powerful sight of Chicago at night, a pile of papers on his desk and a laptop open in front of him. Dmitri would be in an immaculate suit, tie perfectly in place, scowling at his screen.

"Good evening, Roger! How are you doing?" Roger said in a mock Russian accent. Then he dropped his imitation. "Oh, I'm *fine*. Thank you for asking, Dmitri. How are you?"

A thump happened on Dmitri's side of the call, and Dmitri lowered his voice. An office door shutting? "When I say 'don't start,' it means 'don't be a jackass.'"

"You are in a mood," Roger said. "What's happened?"

"I'm an idiot, that's what."

"It's taken you three centuries to realize that?"

"*Roger.*"

"All right, I'm behaving," Roger replied. "Are you going to explain?"

Another thump. Not a door. What was Dmitri shifting around? "Candide made a comment, and of course, she's right. I should have thought of it, but I've been running from meeting to meeting and preoccupied with sorting Quinn's disastrous finances."

"What sort of comment?" Roger asked.

"She remarked that your back dues would make a nice investment in a new club."

The implication of those words was a wind in the wrong direction. Roger stalked over to the far side of the room, though Nell would still hear both sides of the conversation. He needed the illusion of privacy before he lost his temper. "I was in a coma!"

"I know that, but that's not the story we're telling everyone else," Dmitri replied. "We're going with the lie that you chose to walk away."

That lie was the best story Roger had come up with. He wasn't sure who had betrayed him, and he didn't know how Seamus would react if he learned Roger had been thrown into an enchanted coffin by an unknown Unseelie for a mysterious reason. "Yes. And because I was gone without any indication of who or what might have killed me, the coven confiscated my wealth of nearly a billion dollars. How on earth could I owe *more*?"

"I'm preparing the argument that since your accounts reverted to us, you don't." Dmitri hesitated. "However, there's a consequence to that course of action."

"What?"

"If we consider your accounts forfeit, then even if I could track down your former fortune, I couldn't hand over a single cent."

"That's ridiculous. I can't possibly owe more than a few hundred thousand," Roger grumbled.

"Your outstanding coven dues come to around four million dollars."

"*Excuse me*?"

"You haven't been paying them," Dmitri said dryly. "We've done a price increase three times since you disappeared, and there are penalties for late payments."

That was ridiculous! Absolutely criminal! The amount would have been drops in the bucket over time, and if Roger had access to his accounts, he wouldn't have balked. Currently, he only had the money Nell had loaned him, a little less than five million after he outfitted Kit, Zack, and himself. There had also been a sizable deposit on their upcoming hotel suite and a few travel arrangements. The five million was supposed to keep him on his feet until he regained his fortune, inherited Quinn's money that was owed to him, or took control of the GLC and inherited Seamus's accounts. In the end, it would be nothing.

If eighty percent of the money had to go to paying his coven dues, then he would have to start watching every penny. But if he forfeited his claim to his old accounts, he'd lose far, far more.

Money was supposed to be the least of his problems.

And does the money matter now? If we win, I'll be filthy rich, and if we don't, we'll be dead. Roger hated gambling, but he didn't have a lot of choice. "Argue that I've more than paid my debt, and work on giving me Quinn's accounts."

"How will we explain your arrival in style?" Dmitri asked.

"Started investing in the dot-com buzz to begin my slow acclimation to the modern age," Roger replied.

"I like it, but we'll say clean energy. I have a company we can work with, though I'll need a few funds from you to make it work."

"You have how much money? Why do you need it from me?" Roger demanded.

"Because I am doing this *for* you, and nothing comes for free," Dmitri snapped.

"Fine. When I get to the city, we can set it up." Roger ended the call.

"Dmitri provides more bad news," Nell said.

With the best grin he could manage, Roger turned around to face her. "It's a tiny bump in the road."

Nell had a sharp look in her eye, clearly sizing him up and determining fact from fiction. Though he did his best to keep his expression relaxed, she only hardened and scowled at him. "What if Seamus doesn't accept this bargain?"

Then I'm in the middle of the sea with a leaky boat, no wind for my sails, and an albatross around my neck. Roger slid his phone into his pocket. "Then I'll convince him to."

"How?" Nell said.

Roger shrugged with one shoulder. "I have been surviving him for centuries. I'll figure it out."

"That has come to mind before." Nell's eyes flared ruby red once more. The color of her irises overtook her whole eye. The shadows around her grew thicker and darker. "You are a survivor, Roger. A lie here, a pretty tale there, anything to slide free. Anything for a smile, a caress, and the ability to waltz away without a scratch."

"Nell," Roger said, dropping his carefree act, "I don't know what you're thinking—"

"That the last three months have been nothing but a con," Nell snarled.

The temperature plummeted, and a thin layer of ice blossomed across the practice mat in a radius around Nell. Her scent of the grave was earthy and salty, a mix of the land she'd been buried in and the salt of the sea she'd called home for five hundred years of her immortal life. She was invoking power that Roger had rarely seen, and she was doing it without faltering like Seamus did. The shadows darkened the room, stretching out from the corners and toward the center.

A hard fear twisted in Roger's gut. She could crush him into paste. He had to find some way to convince her that he was honest. "Do you think I put myself in a box?"

"Perhaps you did," Nell snapped. "Perhaps it hasn't been thirty-some-odd years. Perhaps this has been Seamus's way of toying with my defenses. Of spying."

"Oh yes, and I conveniently staged everything with Zack?" Roger scoffed. "What would be the point of that?"

"If he's in on it, I will find out after I am done wringing answers from you." Nell raised her hands, her fingers poised like a marionette puppeteer.

Shadows lifted from the floor and formed four inky-black tendrils. When Nell motioned with her hands, the tendrils shot forward.

Roger relied on his speed to dodge out of the way of the tendrils' first attempt to grasp him. The ice spreading out from Nell was growing thicker, the mat becoming slicker under his feet. He nimbly darted out of the way a second time.

"Nell! You're being ridiculous!" Roger used the steel knife in his hand to cut through one of the shadows reaching for him while he spun away from another. The knife passed through the tendril without issue—and without causing any damage to it.

His throat hurt, and his stomach started to burn. He was reaching the end of his strength. *Or am I? Nell hasn't fed tonight, and she's doing this kind of magic.* What did she know that he didn't? At what age had she started to manipulate shadows? Was it truly something only an older vampire could do, or could he master them?

His racing thoughts distracted him, and he failed to pull his left wrist out of the way of one shadowy tendril. It looped around him and pulled, throwing him off-balance. As he tried to pull his arm free, another latched onto his right knee. Then the other two caught his other wrist and other knee.

With a jerk from Nell, the tendrils tightened and yanked him down to his hands and knees. Roger dropped the knife on his way down out of reflex.

"Poor, pitiful, *weak* Roger." Nell lifted her chin, her regal demeanor only elevated by the glow of her eyes. "Whose pawn are you? Seamus's? The boy's? Dmitri's?"

"No one's," Roger growled.

A tendril came out of the shadow beneath him and latched around his throat. It tugged on him, attempting to pull him against the mat.

What could he do against her?

I'm a vampire. A goddamn immortal bloodsucker of the night. I have survived for centuries. I will not be schooled like some disobedient dog.

With a snarl, Roger embraced his own power. A century had passed since he'd last fully indulged the magic within him. The power had a solid weight to it, like a sword in his hand, only his whole body was the sword.

The shadows had an unnatural movement to them from Nell's infusion of will and power. But he could feel the slither of them, and that was new. Beneath them, in some unseeable place, was a pit of cold power that he could brush his fingers against. He had never studied magic. He had no clue what he touched, but he recognized the strength of it. The danger.

She had control of the darkness in the room, but there was one shadow that should belong to him more than her: his own. He sought it, discovered it hidden among the others. The vagueness of it had his shape and a hint of the grave that smelled like him. Shadows having a smell was also new, but he didn't stop to admire that.

Mentally, he grabbed his shadow and pulled on it. Wrestling it from Nell's influence was like trying to take the lead with a forceful dance partner. He slid and slipped and burned with want.

And it broke free from her control. Relief rushed through him, and he almost lost his grip. But if she could make the shadows do more, then he could. He imagined a blade, sharp and dark, and sliced through the tendril holding his throat.

Nell's control faltered, and Roger pulled himself up from the floor. The tendrils were still looped around him, so he used the shadow blade to cut through the one on his right wrist. He gripped the blade's handle. It was ice-cold but real, and he used it to free himself of the other tendrils.

The ache in his stomach became fatigue in his bones. He had to drop the blade and let it become nothing more than a patch of gray on the mat once more.

The light in the room was brightening. The shadows were receding. A perpetual snarl was on Roger's lip, and he drew a ragged breath when he forced his gaze to Nell.

When she rushed him, he rolled onto the mat and grabbed the steel knife. Lightning speed was exhilarating, and he found a pace faster than before. He swung, and Nell moved out of range with less than an inch to spare. She was toying with him.

He gave in to the rage. He was a fighter. Had been since he'd had mortal breath in his lungs over three hundred years ago. He fucked and he fought, and he was damn good at both. His body knew the movements, knew to counter, knew to strike. The magic dulled any pain he would've felt from the injuries she inflicted in return.

The cold burn and deep ache grew. He couldn't keep it up.

Snarling and growling, he kept going. She *doubted* him. He had played by her rules, and now she believed the worst of him and attacked. He would show her he wasn't a pawn. He was strong. He was *Roger*, the vampire pirate, the gentleman thief, the goddamn terror of the night.

Nell flipped him onto the mat and then pounced on him.

Before he could sit up, she slammed her blade through his shoulder and pinned him to the mat. When he dropped his knife to grab its hilt, she took that one, shoved down his free shoulder, and nailed him to the mat with it.

"Enough!" Nell declared.

"You started it!" Roger spat.

"You can hardly blame me! We've been training for two months, and you've never shown me a quarter of what you've just done." Nell leaned back, though she continued straddling his hips. "I didn't know you had it in you."

Roger swallowed. Saliva was an odd sensation, something that happened when his hunger was rising. The swift change in tempo between them was disorienting. Nell's anger seemed to have evaporated, but he didn't believe it was entirely gone. Seamus hid his for weeks at a time when it suited him.

"Neither did I," he said, and his voice was rougher and colder. Hollow.

"Good that you finally discovered your power," Nell said. She pulled the knives from his shoulders and let his clatter to the floor beside him. She kept hers in her hand as she stood. The fight had taken a toll on her. Her dark skin had a pallor he'd never seen in her, and her eyes remained brighter red. Spots of blood, hers and his, dotted her suit, and there were rips and tears from Roger's blade and the need to move.

He'd driven her to the defense, and though he was starving, he'd nearly *won*. Slowly, he grabbed his knife and stood.

"Where does this leave us?" Roger asked.

"I have yet to decide," Nell replied as she made her way toward the door. The frost in the room was melting, causing little pools of water everywhere. "At least you are more than a pretty face, Roger. I was beginning to worry you weren't."

Somehow, being honest had made Nell lose her trust in him. *There is no winning against an elder vampire*. Roger started to run his hand through his hair but realized he had tied it back. He undid the ponytail and let his black hair flow down around his shoulders.

The dull ache of hunger persisted. He'd need more blood to recover the strength he used. Which would cost more money, which could be something he'd need to be more careful with. *How many more ways can I be fucked?*

CHAPTER 4

Having coffee at Sugar Moon wasn't the same since Blake went back to Chicago. Her replacement always had his friends at the counter that Zack used to take over with his research. Though coffee was life and the Wi-Fi was reliable, the black-and-white-tiled coffee shop just didn't hold the same cozy feeling it'd once had.

Plus, as the locals became more familiar with him, the greater his presence was. When he first came to Taliville, he could set up in the coffee shop and write down every scrap of rumor he heard floating past him, and no one noticed what he was doing. Anymore, people avoided him. Some people scowled at him, though that was rare.

Others stared and whispered. Despite their efforts, Zack still caught a word here and there. Visitor. Hunter. One of *those* pets. They talked about him like he was something between a trophy and a plaything. Taliville was a place where the supernaturals were an open secret, and people with collars or some symbol of belonging to a vampire were common.

In Chicago, there would be people who wouldn't know what Zack's collar meant. They'd assume he was being edgy or it was a sex thing. Whenever he was on a bus or train, people would stare.

Like you're going to take the bus. Everything you do has to be "in style." Zack closed the lid of his laptop. He'd only had it for a month, and it was far more expensive than what his parents could have bought him. Between it, the leather messenger bag, the collar on his throat, and the phone in his pocket, he was clearly kept. And that was before his clothes, hair, and general appearance.

He'd always been the kid in the back of the classroom with all the answers, the cousin left out of the games, the brother laughed at, and the son left behind. Now he had to be the center of attention—physically *and* digitally.

He opened his social media apps on his phone. Supernaturals had two for themselves that required invites: the Fang app and Night Deets. Posting on other platforms worked, but Zack had decided to focus on gaining views in these two places.

Making videos for the Fang app was annoying, but Zack was seeing some views on his newest ones. He wasn't sure he could call it a success, though. Zack was sitting at ... he double-checked for the second time that morning. Six hundred and twenty-six followers. *Not nothing, I guess. But is it great for the "head pet" of a GLC captain?*

Vincent Talmadge, Seamus's head pet, had a 100k following, which was huge on the app. He'd posted a new video, and Zack couldn't *not* click on it. The pursuit of knowledge demanded he know what Vincent was doing. *And maybe if I watch enough of them, I can figure out how he's made this a success.*

Vincent was a young pasty white guy. He couldn't have been any older than Zack, but his videos went back three years, all of them as Seamus's pet. Eyeliner brought out his blue eyes and makeup or a filter made his features flawlessly smooth. In this particular vid, he was primping for the camera and prattling on about his ideas for his Halloween costume to dress as Cupid. The background of his shots was hard to follow, but he looked like he was in Seamus's mansion.

Too bad his videos are too short to start making a map of the place. Zack sipped his coffee. He took out a pen and pad of paper and restarted the video. Any of what Vincent said might have a detail he could pick apart later. He made a quick transcription on his next watch.

At the very end of the clip, Vincent flopped onto a couch and put his head into someone's lap. He tilted his head back. His shirt was a gossamer, barely there layer, and the someone slid their nail down the cloth. The fabric parted, and a thin red line of blood beaded on Vincent's chest. Vincent craned upward, whimpering into the touch. When his gaze refocused on the camera, his eyes had dilated and had a glaze.

Seamus had put him under his charm, increasing Vincent's lust with his vampiric power.

"Gotta go," Vincent murmured, a moan in his voice. He winked. "Master's calling."

The video had been posted the night before, closer to midnight. Something about it bothered Zack, but a third and a fourth viewing didn't enlighten him. Was it the whimper? His trained biases creeping in and demanding that no one should look that happy as a sadistic vampire's property?

Zack sipped his coffee and flipped over to Night Deets. It was a microblogging site closer in spirit to places like Reddit and Tumblr, where longer posts were possible but not preferred. People spilled valuable details all over the place. Profiles had an actual slot for "sire/curse-giver," and people filled them out. *If I'd had access to this while on the HIN, I could've answered so many questions.* Zack had made an extensive "family" tree for Seamus's coven primarily using details he'd found from Night Deets. Of course, he was assuming that the information provided on the site was genuine. He hadn't been able to verify every name he'd stumbled upon, but he had a pretty good picture of the coven's bloodlines.

Including Quinn Turner's bloodline. So far, Zack had traced a dozen vampires back to Quinn, which technically led back to Roger since he had sired Quinn. But would those vampires obey Roger as the hierarchy demanded? Or would they be like Quinn, angry that Zack had been raised a hunter? Would he have to face another ambush?

Zack pushed away the memory of the night he'd finally killed a vampire and focused on the present. He skimmed Vincent's profile, but he wasn't as forthcoming on Night Deets as he seemed to be on the Fang app. Zack was still betting a bulk of that was performance. What was genuine about the guy?

"Can I sit here?" someone asked.

Zack looked up from his phone. A dark-haired man with a chiseled jaw was standing beside the chair across his table. Blake had nicknamed this particular guy as EWE—Extremely Well-Endowed. Over the last few weeks, Zack had learned his name was Carver. Even in the cooler weather, he was wearing a tank top, light sweatshirt, and tight biker shorts, which were formfitting over his impressively sized dick. He had a few fading vampire bite marks, including an older one on his thigh.

"I guess," Zack said.

Carver grinned at him while putting one hand on the chair back. He cocked his head to the side. "Only guess?"

Something about the way Carver was looking at him made Zack feel way too warm. Having a conversation with someone normal would be nice, so he took his laptop off the table and motioned to the chair. "Sorry, I'm in my own head. Go ahead."

"Freaking out about the big move?" Carver asked.

Zack froze as he was putting his laptop into his bag, but he pushed past the mental barrier. Of course Carver knew that Roger was leaving town. Taliville only had seven thousand people; news spread fast. *I've been posting about it, too.* Zack managed a smile by the time he brought his attention back to the table. "Only a little."

"Has to be exciting though. Chicago sounds amazing," Carver said. "The parties are legendary."

Dancing around the point was a fine art that Roger had told Zack he should appreciate, but he didn't have the patience for it. Instead, he did his best impression of Josefina, a bored affect with a tone bordering on nonchalance. "Is there something I can do for you, Carver?"

"You know my name," Carver said, his grin broadening. He put his coffee on the table and relaxed in his seat. His foot brushed against Zack's and rested there with their ankles touching.

This was an open *flirt*. Carver had done something like this before, verbal instead of physical, and Zack had had a minor brain freeze over it.

But this was something he needed to get used to. Everything in vampire society was charged with sexual energy. However, his ingrained panic threatened to overwhelm him. He was supposed to be the watcher, not the watched. Anyone observing him could tell his cheeks were flushing. They'd be able to *judge* and he would be found ugly or repulsive.

The fear was ridiculous, but it was there and Zack couldn't wish it away.

Luckily, Carver continued talking. "I've been wondering if I've been making an impression."

"Impression?" Zack asked.

Carver's smile dimmed, but remained. "With Roger."

Quickly, Zack scanned the visible bite marks on Carver. His examination must have been overt because Carver laid his arm across the table and rolled his hand over to reveal a bite mark on his wrist around five nights old.

Zack didn't have to look at his own, but he reflexively

touched it. The marks would match. *Don't get jealous. Don't.*
"He fed from you?"

"Four times, so far," Carver said. "How'd you earn it?"

"Earn what?"

Carver gestured to Zack's neck.

On instinct, Zack touched his neck and his hand smacked
into the collar and crest tag. He wanted to wrench it off his
skin once he remembered its existence, but he smothered that
desire. The first time they'd spoken, Carver had suggested he
could help Zack earn his pet collar by fucking him in front of
Roger.

Zack put his hands around his coffee cup. *Have they slept
together?* Did he want to ask the question? Did he need the
answer? Zack had thought he'd kept a pretty good track of
who Roger was feeding from, but there were times Roger
didn't drag him along to the donor house. Had he been
hiding sexual partners from him? *Don't get jealous. Don't get
jealous.*

Zack said, "Roger doesn't hand out collars like party
favors. He takes his role as master seriously."

"He's been a repeat customer," Carver said. "I thought he
might add me to his harem."

"The correct term for a group of vampire pets is
'collection.'"

"Collection sounds stuffy. You don't have sex with a
collection."

I have to know. Zack took a sip of coffee to give him time to
steady his nerves. Slowly, he returned the cup to the table and
raised his gaze to meet Carver. "Has he slept with you?"

"I keep offering but he never takes me up on it," Carver
said.

Why? Why hasn't he slept with Carver? Zack slowly turned
his coffee cup, rotating it against the table. The slightest
scrape noise eked out. *Don't overthink it.*

"Come on, share the secret. How'd you earn it?" Carver asked.

I freed him from a decades' long curse and happen to have a magical dagger that can kill his ancient evil sire and we're only pretending. But that couldn't be the story he shared. So far, when others asked, he'd been able to say they'd met on the internet and that was it. Carver clearly wanted specifics. Zack hadn't invented a clever story.

Carver gently touched Zack's wrist and pressed more of his leg against his. Zack's pulse thundered in his ears and his skin was blazing, but all of that was turning to ice in his veins. Because he didn't know how to do this. All of his research and studying and he had no freaking clue what to do with someone openly hitting on him.

Only ... he did have an out. Data slid into place and he carefully detached himself from Carver's touch. "I pleased him. And you shouldn't touch what's his without his permission."

"He's the strict leash type?" Carver raised his eyebrows in surprise. "I didn't figure him for that kind of vampire."

"My master has been more relaxed due to the nature of Nell's sanctuary," Zack replied stiffly.

Carver shrugged. "If sex with him is anything like his bite, then I can handle the leash."

Zack leaned forward and under his breath, demanded, "Why are you so intent on becoming his property?"

Carver raked his gaze over Zack before matching him, leaning in so their faces were only inches apart. "When you got to town, you were wearing worn out shorts and hand-me-downs. Now you've got a monogramed bag and expensive clothes. You're sleeping in the most impressive mansion in the state. He's hot and rich, who wouldn't want him?"

In his mind, Zack screamed at Carver. He pictured going off on a long rant of the bullshit he'd had to endure in the training alone and continued into a lecture about the dangers of the GLC. The reality of his life was on the tip of his tongue.

But he swallowed it. He drew in a steady breath. "My master is returning to his coven. The GLC is nothing like Nell's coven."

"Public feeding and fucking doesn't bother me," Carver said.

"I've been training for two months," Zack replied.

"I'm born and raised in Taliville. I know the etiquette."

Zack strangled the urge to shout and stood. Pulling on the coldest affect he could muster, he stood, slung his bag over his shoulder ,and swept up his coffee cup. "If you want to be his that bad, just ask him."

"Maybe I will," Carver said.

"Fine." Zack stormed out of the coffee shop.

Reed had warned him that there would be people who were nice to him because they thought he'd be an easy route to Roger. But the concept that people would *want* his new lifestyle caused the hunter part of his mind to short-circuit. The anger in him was irrational. He knew that. He longed to find a place to shove it because every dawn only seemed to bring out more in him. The constant deference and compliance he was expected to show to vampires, especially Roger, only drove that anger deeper.

Objectively, he knew submission was what some craved. He'd thought he might understand it and even want it himself. But only for Roger, maybe. Being in proximity to vampires had opened his eyes.

Zack unclenched his hand and double-checked the street as he crossed. He had a busy day ahead of him and only so many hours of daylight before he had to be back at the mansion. *I won't live like this forever. Once Roger is the coven master, everything will change. I just have to hold on.*

CHAPTER 5

Night had settled into the charming streets of Taliville roughly thirty minutes before Roger left Nell's mansion on a long walk. He had one of the thin necklace boxes. The last rays of light were gone, but the true darkness of night hadn't yet come. The town's streetlights were dim enough that the stars above were visible, though a few clouds flirted with the moon and the heavenly bodies.

Along his way, Roger nodded to a few familiar faces when they smiled or nodded in his direction. While there was a certain cookie-cutter aspect to the homes in the less affluent neighborhood, the houses had hints of individuality through choices of gardens or siding colors. Few had fenced-in yards, and those that had "Beware of Dog" signs had the distinct scent of shifter magic nearby.

Night had always settled Roger. Contentment was rare, but he found it in his steady pace. He made his way to a rather ordinary house and rapped on the door.

Nearly instantly, Kit opened the door. They were young, only a year older than Zack, and they wore a red collar with Roger's crest tag hanging from it. They'd dyed their hair a deep cherry red, which Roger found to be a shame because he liked their beautiful brown hair. That evening, they wore a plain black V-neck T-shirt with jeans. Their eyes were a brown-green hazel.

They brightened with a smile when they laid eyes on Roger. Though they were two inches shorter than him, they had a youthful lankiness to them that their style accentuated.

"Good evening," Roger said with a warm smile.

"Please come in, master." Kit opened the door and slightly bowed their head.

Roger stepped inside and gently shut the door. Kit's invitation hadn't been necessary since Roger had been in the house before, but their politeness was nice. "Are we alone?"

"Yes, master," Kit said.

"I appreciate the diligence, but we are in private. No need to keep up the pretenses."

A flicker crossed Kit's features, and they tucked a stray strand of hair behind their ear. The two of them left the small foyer and headed into the living room. A stack of luggage was beside the television stand. Various pieces didn't match the others and showed signs of wear. Roger had offered to buy them a new set, but Kit had turned him down.

Because they had their own things, not like Zack and I.

"Am I bringing too much?" Kit asked.

"Of course not," Roger said smoothly, burying the conflicting grief thinking about Zack occasionally brought up. If Zack hadn't chosen to stay with Roger, then he might not have lost his family. *Though what "family" tosses aside their child for knowing the difference between right and wrong.*

Roger sat on the couch and then held up the box he had brought with him. "I brought a present for you."

"They came in?" Kit joined Roger on the couch and eagerly took the box. "I thought Zack was wearing a new one during our lesson."

Roger relaxed against the couch, one arm resting on the

back, one leg over the other, and angled so he was in the corner facing Kit. "How are your studies going?"

"I've seen the manners in practice for ages, master," Kit replied. They furrowed their brow and set the box on the end table beside them. "Zack's making me memorize every supernatural species' weaknesses. I know that Chicago is a dangerous place, but I don't think knowing that demon-possessed people will vomit when presented with a holy symbol while invoking a deity matters, does it?"

"Zack believes knowledge is the best form of self-protection, and he is the head pet," Roger said.

"Am I going to have to fight?" Kit asked.

Fear trickled into the air with their words. Roger sifted through what he could sense of Kit's feelings. Overall, Kit thirsted for something *more*, a sensation that reminded Roger of when he would stand at the edge of a ship and stare out into the distance. But that lust for the place beyond the horizon was tempered with the fears of the unknown.

The fewer who knew Roger was after Seamus's position in the coven and planning to kill him and Anton, the safer the plan and those he cared about would be. One couldn't share what they didn't know. Kit had to remain in the dark for their own good.

"You have to remember, Zack was raised a hunter. His family trained him to watch for threats from every corner." Roger let the words sit for a moment, then added, "His cautious nature will help us stay safe. That's one reason I gave him the black collar."

"That and he's your boyfriend," Kit said. "And I'm just a donor."

Roger leaned forward and took their hands in one of his and touched their cheek with his other. Kit raised their gaze from their lap. He smiled at them, imbuing the gesture with as much warmth as he could manage. Joining Roger's collection and the coven should be a positive experience for Kit. He wished Zack could relax for a moment and find the adventure, but that wasn't Zack's way.

"I care for you," Roger said. "Don't doubt that."

"I don't," Kit said with a soft sigh. The trickle of fear faded. "You came to feed, right?"

"Yes, little fox," Roger replied. His hunger ached deeper, etching its way into his bones. He brushed Kit's hair back from their face and then trailed his fingers around to the clasp of their collar. "May I?"

"Yes, master." Kit's voice was quiet but filled to the brim with want.

The heavy desire in their tone only fueled the fire carving through Roger. His fangs were always present, but moments like this reminded him of their length and sharpness. Every nerve in him was sizzling from his thirst. And he used his own want for Kit's blood as a magnet to draw the lust upward in their consciousness. As he undid and slid Kit's collar off, they moaned and their eyes fluttered shut.

Roger drew them onto his lap, and Kit straddled him, one knee on either side digging into the couch. Kit was pliant to his touch—a side-effect of the magic Roger used on him. Still tugging on their lust, Roger gently threaded his fingers in their hair and pulled their head to the side.

Kit panted, their breath hot against Roger's cheek. They were a were-fox and naturally ran warmer than the average mortal. Their scent was laden with the smell of freshly washed fur and a mortal metallic zing.

Carefully, Roger tightened his grip on Kit's hair and used his other arm to hold Kit in place.

Then he sank his fangs into them.

Kit's gasp was a faint sound under the thunderous taste of fresh, hot, wonderful blood filling Roger's mouth. He sealed his mouth around the bite and swallowed his first mouthful. More poured in after the first, and he eagerly drank it down. Kit melted against him and mewed with desire. They latched an arm around Roger's shoulders while they rolled their hips downward.

Feeding from a shifter required more work than drinking from a human. Kit's healing ability began to close the wound, and Roger needed *more*. He bit harder, sinking his fangs in deeper, and held Kit tightly as they squirmed. Their lust sweetened their blood, and warmth filled Roger's core and oozed through him. Each crunch and suck and swallow coaxed Roger's predatory urges from the pit he locked them away in. Hunting was part of a vampire's nature and a part he didn't indulge often enough. He moaned.

"Are you fucking kidding me?" a voice demanded.

Someone yanked on Kit, trying to take them from Roger's grip. They cried, a mix of pain and surprise. Roger growled and continued to feed. Kit was *his*, and he wasn't about to give up his prize. He hadn't taken too much yet. He could have more.

"Let go," someone shouted. And there was the stronger smell of fur, like an animal's dander kicking up. An electric buzz tainted the high Roger was coasting toward.

With a primal hiss, Roger looked up at whoever dared to interfere with his meal. A man and a woman who bore striking resemblances to the person in his arms were standing in the living room. The man looked pissed while the woman paled and her eyes widened.

Their parents. Forcefully, Roger blinked and dragged his thoughts away from the wonderful scent of the blood mere centimeters from his lips. The taste of Kit lingered on his tongue.

"In our house!" Kit's father shouted. Both he and Kit's mother emanated a sharp fear that left a tang on Roger's lips.

The fear mixed with the blood in his system and became a heady undertow, one that threatened to intoxicate Roger. His hunger piqued instead of becoming sated. He longed to grab

Kit's father, rip open a vein, and drink him dry. *No. I'm not like that. I won't.*

In the distant past, he had indulged like that. Killed whole families with his sire, drained a brothel with Quinn and a few others another time. But the shell he had encased his emotions in had begun to crack, and Kit had slid through one of them. He couldn't bring Kit suffering. That wasn't right.

Roger released his hold on Kit and leaned back against the couch.

Kit took the opportunity to spring off the couch and face their father. "Dad!"

Kit's father—Mr. Mahoney, Roger assumed since that was Kit's last name—pointed his finger at Kit. "It's one thing selling your blood off at the donor house, but inviting one into our home?"

"It's not the first time," Kit snapped. "I've had him over like a dozen times."

"What?" Mr. Mahoney flushed a bright red. His anger was rooted in a deep fear, a familiar acidic burr bristling against Roger's awareness. It was the fear for another.

And utterly ridiculous in the present situation. As subtly as Roger could, he wiped any lingering blood from his lips. There was more than he anticipated, but licking it off his fingers in present company would be unseemly. "Continuing at the donor house didn't make sense, and I saw no reason to make Kit move into Nell's mansion when they could enjoy the comforts of their own room for a little while longer."

Mr. Mahoney frowned and looked between Kit and Roger with increasing confusion.

"Kit," Mrs. Mahoney said slowly, uncertainty in her voice. She pointed at the collar resting on the couch. "What is that?"

In a swift, entirely obvious move, Kit snatched the collar from the couch and hid it behind their back. "Nothing."

Their father reached for it. Both relied on supernatural speed—Kit to keep it away from Mr. Mahoney and Mr.

Mahoney in an attempt to take it from them. A human might have had trouble seeing the quick movements, but Roger could track them.

When Mr. Mahoney grabbed Kit's arm and roughly yanked on them, Roger zipped around to seize Mr. Mahoney's hand. As fast as shifters were, he was faster. He pulled Mr. Mahoney's hand free of Kit's arm and twisted sharply. Force and momentum demanded too much of Mr. Mahoney's wrist, and it popped. Roger thought he might have heard a crack as well.

With a howl, Mr. Mahoney backed away and held his injured wrist to his chest.

"Roger!" Kit exclaimed.

Roger snapped his head to the side to look at Kit over his shoulder. Cold enveloped him, and he said sternly, "Quiet."

Kit sucked in a deep breath and swallowed whatever they intended to say. Their eyes were wide. A desire emanated from them like a light caress, and it tangled with a buzzing fear, a mixture Roger had long ago learned meant a need to understand.

Mrs. Mahoney had put a hand to her mouth during the scuffle, but she dropped it as she went to her husband's side. She put her arm on his shoulders and leaned into him. "Why did you do that!"

"I had a point to make." Roger turned his full attention back to Mr. and Mrs. Mahoney. "Kit has chosen to become *mine*, which means they are under my protection."

"No fucking way are they going with you," Mr. Mahoney snarled.

"Dad," Kit complained. "Roger's right. I signed up for it."

"Why?" Mrs. Mahoney asked.

"Because he's offering a hundred grand a year, plus room and board *plus* clothing allowance and healthcare. All I have to do is dress up and let Roger drink blood every now and then," Kit replied.

"But you aren't staying *here*." Mr. Mahoney glared at Roger. "You're going to Chicago."

Before Roger could speak, Kit puffed up their chest, squared their shoulders, and stepped around Roger so they stood between their father and him. "People pretend that Nell's coven is perfect, but it's got problems, too. Vampires and shifters are always playing politics, and they don't care who gets caught up in their bullshit. At least in the GLC, I'll know who the bad guys are, and I can start over."

"Sweetie, people are moving past it," Mrs. Mahoney said.

Roger schooled his features to remain neutral. He had no idea what people would need to "move past" in regards to Kit. *Zack probably knows. He's a master of information.*

"They are not," Kit said. "The only job I can get is as a part-time waiter at the inn because you and Dad are friends with Teddy. When I tried working the donor house, Roger was the only one interested in me multiple times. I've got three friends, one of which is already in Chicago and one who's leaving tomorrow, no substantial income, and the only sex I've been getting is from a friend with benefits who's no longer answering me. What life is that?"

"You need to give it time," their father said.

"It's been four years! For a stupid mistake!" Kit clenched their fists. "You don't know what it's like having the town pretend you aren't here! Meanwhile, Nia holds court every time she's at a bar or the donor house. I'm suffocating. Going with Roger gives me a chance to find some happiness."

"Happiness?" Mr. Mahoney shouted. "Your great-uncle went to Chicago and died within a year! How happy is that?"

"Oh my God, that was sixty years ago!"

Mrs. Mahoney turned to Roger with a pleading look in her eyes. "Please release them from whatever agreement you made. They're still a child, especially compared to you, and the GLC is no place for someone as sweet as them. It's just too dangerous."

The three of them had sharp fears that were pinpricks against Roger's mind. Each had its own heat and thickness. Mr. Mahoney's was the fiercest of all, but the throb of Kit's fear of rejection pressed in equally.

Roger could reach into their psyches and untangle these fears or increase them. He could twist their parents into liking him, but *no*. He kept a smooth, emotionless expression. If he weren't a selfish creature, he might agree with Kit's parents and tell them to stay in Taliville. But he needed blood every night, and he couldn't drink frequently from Zack. And he needed the strength having a collection of pets would project. Other vampires wouldn't accept him as leader if they thought they could take him down.

"Kit has made their choice," Roger said quietly, intentionally lowering his voice so the others would have to focus on his words. "I won't revoke an opportunity on the begging of parents when their 'child' is, in fact, an adult. Kit is aware of the risks as well as the many benefits."

Only you haven't told them everything, have you? You haven't said you're going to war. Roger kept his chin high, his demeanor aloof. *Because it's not supposed to be a war but an assassination. Kit will be fine.*

"I have said everything I need to." Gently, Roger touched Kit's shoulder, and they turned to face him. "As I have promised, you can leave me at any time. I won't fault you for making the decision you feel is best for you. The car will pick you up before dinner tomorrow unless I hear differently. For the record, I hope to see you."

"Yes, master," Kit replied.

Roger glared over at Mr. Mahoney. "And if I need to collect you before that, I can."

"I don't think you will, but thank you, master," Kit said softly.

Roger kissed their forehead and squeezed their shoulder. He left the house before another argument began, but he could hear the heated voices as he made his way to the sidewalk.

Family. After three centuries, he sometimes struggled to remember his own mortal parents and siblings. His long stride carried him down the street, but his mind teleported him farther. Back to England, to the hovel he'd grown up in. Well, as grown as someone could be at twelve.

For some, memory could paint the past in overly warm tones, but he only found ice. The village Roger had lived in as a child had been small, barely more than an old churchyard filled with forgotten dead and farmers who passed from the exhaustion of their lives. His father had cursed at anyone in the house and lashed out with that anger. His mother had matched him in that temper. They had been tyrants. His siblings had been many. Roger wondered if his parents had even realized the night he ran away. *I doubt they noticed for well over a week.*

They certainly would never have worried like Kit's parents were currently doing. And that was all Kit's parents were expressing. Worry. Roger almost regretted injuring Mr. Mahoney's wrist, but the man had laid a hand on Kit.

Only it wasn't Mr. Mahoney's wrist that Roger truly wanted to break. In that flash of a moment, Roger had seen Callum Wright's face. Had heard Zack's *oof* as the stake slid into his shoulder with a wet sound. Had felt the ghostly strike of his own father's fist.

And like he had done for the last three hundred and fifty-two years, he smothered the pain of those moments. He had to carry on, and he couldn't afford to lose his temper like that. His rage and anger went into a chest that he dropped to the bottom of his mental sea. The waters would remain untroubled.

He continued into the night, and his thirst itched his throat.

CHAPTER 6

"Honestly, if I have to pick one more color, I'm going to scream," Zack said.

"*Honestly*," Reed said, mocking Zack's tone, "you should have had this done last week."

Groaning, Zack put his head on the table. He and Reed were tucked into the corner of the kitchen. While Nell's staff provided a buffet for the people who worked the house, her pets and Josefina's had dinner served to them an hour before dusk. Reed and Zack often skipped that in order to have a semi-private conversation in the kitchen while they ate. Since shifters worked in the mansion, they still had to be careful of what they said, but most of their conversations had been about social bullshit that Zack still struggled with.

Maybe, if I was picking suits for me instead of how naked Kit and I have to be, I wouldn't have a problem. He grumbled, "Give me some credit. Roger's gotten a dozen e-vites for Halloween parties, and he's given me no hint whose he's going to accept. And the themes range from Elizabethan to 'sexy dinosaurs.' And I've never been to a Halloween party before."

"Seriously?" Reed waved a hand before Zack could answer. "Ah, right. Every once in a while, I forget about the hunter upbringing. Halloween was probably about raiding some poor witch's closet every year, huh?"

Zack clenched his jaw. Obviously, his family hadn't been the picture-perfect version he'd convinced himself for years. The whole reason he had taken the hunt to kill Roger was because he'd been left behind. His mother had never forgiven him for letting a teenage, less-than-two-week-old vampire out into the world instead of killing her. But the girl had been a victim, turned against her will, Zack was sure of it. He'd done the research.

Though he'd seen only the best in them, his family had only pointed at his flaws. And there was a relief in not dealing with them in his day-to-day. The new people in Zack's life tended to accept him completely.

Except when it came to his fucking family and life before Taliville.

"My parents might have been focused on relevant threats to the goddamn world," Zack said icily, "but I was usually celebrating my birthday."

"I think that makes it sadder that you've never had a good Halloween party, then," Reed replied.

"That's because you grew up where it's Halloween every fucking day."

Reed closed the notebook Zack was filling with current clothing plans. "All right. I've poked the bear when you already didn't want to dance. This shit can wait. I could actually use your advice."

"Mine?" Zack asked.

"As you so eloquently pointed out, I grew up here," Reed replied. "I could use an outsider's perspective. Josefina asked me the question last night."

"Marriage?" Zack tapped his pen against the table. He was thinking through how being legally married would work for vampires. Technically, Roger's modern identity was fake, but it was real enough for the important paperwork. Vampires had figured out that system as it'd developed.

Reed laughed under his breath and shook his head. "God, no. Josefina asked if I wanted to become her sireling. She'd said she'd support me if I wanted Nell to do it instead, but she's hoping I'll say yes to her."

"Why the hell would you say yes?" Zack said, the question blurting out of him.

"For starters? Being able to be with Nell and Josefina for hundreds of years instead of a few short decades."

"But sunlight would hurt you, you'd be beholden to Josefina *forever*, and you'd have to drink blood. You'd have an eternity of bills and … and—" Zack held up his notebook. "You would never escape the bullshit of fashion."

"Some of us don't hate parties, Zack," Reed replied.

"You know immortality isn't guaranteed, right? You can still die."

"But it's far more possible as a vampire than a human." Reed sipped his tea. "Haven't you thought about being with Roger? Long term?"

Zack had been giving some thought to what would need to happen after Roger became the coven master. At some point, he'd have to decide if he'd remain his "head pet." Would sticking around and helping him mean that Zack wasn't pretending anymore? *Become his sireling?* The idea churned Zack's stomach. Humans could be vicious. He knew that. But vampires were still … *vampires.* Sires and sirelings shared a connection that Zack hadn't fully figured out. Some seemed like lovers, some like parents to children, and some completely discarded their sirelings out to the world.

"I'm guessing your advice is a 'hell no,'" Reed said.

Zack picked up a lone mozzarella stick left on his dinner plate and took a bite. His food was long cold, the mozzarella hardened instead of being in its melty state, but the flavor was there. He held up the half-eaten mozzarella stick. "Everything about this mozzarella stick changed when it got cold. Sure, it kind of looks the same. But it's not hot. Not satisfying the way it was."

"You're still eating it," Reed replied.

Zack shrugged one shoulder. "Maybe I'm desperate. Maybe I'm eating it remembering that it used to be warm. Maybe I'm thinking about how I wish I'd eaten it sooner. Maybe I regret taking the bite I just did and wish I'd spat it out instead."

"I get it. Life is a mozzarella stick."

"It's not a perfect analogy." Zack put the mozzarella stick down on his plate and wiped the trace of grease off on a napkin. "I don't know if you should become a bloodsucker. But you're not wrong for wanting to think it through, and if Josefina says you are, then you should dump her ass."

"She said I could have as much time as I needed," Reed said.

"Good." *I guess. But who would want to become a vamp? Seriously?* Zack sighed heavily and opened his notebook. "Do you think he'd really wind up going to a sexy dinosaur party?"

"You're the one in his bed every night. You should know."

"Right," Zack muttered. Which one would Roger pick? While Zack recognized the names of all the people throwing the parties, he honestly couldn't tell if Roger liked any of them. He hadn't interrogated Roger about his emotional connections. *Because then we might have to talk about us, and I don't want to.*

His phone vibrated. For a split second, he had an irrational hope that his family had contacted him, but they'd never responded to any of his texts or calls from his new number. Instead, when he checked his phone, he saw that he had a new message from his friend Blake. She'd sent a pic of her hand holding a cup of coffee while saying, "Can't wait to show you my new fave place! Get here already!"

"Was that Roger?" Reed asked.

"Blake." Zack slid his phone into his pocket. "Roger was going to see Kit and then stop by the donor house."

"I hate that you're leaving tomorrow night," Reed said with a sigh. "It's been nice having another mortal to talk to like this."

"You're literally surrounded by mortals," Zack replied.

"Not everyone sees things the way you do."

"Like a hunter?"

"With a natural intelligence. You're clever, Zack, and you're not afraid to be clever. You'll find a majority of pets like the coasting they can do. And why not? They're fed, clothed, have plenty of downtime. I don't blame them for wanting to vibe their way through life. Most of them are picked because they're pretty people who won't overthink their situation." Reed ran his hand through his hair. "Even Nell chooses people like that. Probably what leads your people to believe that we're all bite junkies, though that's not a thing."

"And if you become a vampire, what kind of person would you pick to be your pet?" Zack asked.

Reed's eyes widened, and then he relaxed, though his smile became rueful. "See, *that* is exactly what I meant. I hadn't connected those pieces, but you did."

"You were talking about it. It was an easy leap to make."

"Zack, I know the vampires have been harping on all the protocol, but I hope that you don't forget how amazing you are. Nell wouldn't have welcomed you into the house for a visit like this if you weren't special."

"I'll try to remember that when I'm freezing my ass off because no one will let me wear more than a vest and shorts," Zack replied. "I'm going to snag some alone time before Roger comes back."

"Don't forget, tomorrow night, goodbye dinner with the rest of the pets here," Reed said.

"Already got a reminder set." Zack picked up his note-book, waved goodbye, and headed for the bedroom he shared with Roger.

The trek felt fairly long. He had to go up two flights of stairs and walk more than halfway across the massive mansion to reach the door. His parents' house was a fifth the size of Nell's home. And it was weird that he was getting used oil paintings on the walls and uniformed servants completing tasks he would've had to do—like changing the sheets or doing the laundry. *Maybe I shouldn't be letting them do that.*

Zack cracked open the bedroom door and was greeted with a blast of cold air. The heat was on in the mansion, not the air-conditioning, and Roger's aura didn't chill a room that far. And the lights were out.

Zack popped the bedroom door open as hard and wide as he could. The source of cold shifted, moving fast. On instinct, he ducked, and he felt a woosh as a fist sailed over his head. His dagger was in the bedside table because he'd foolishly believed Taliville was safe and he didn't have to arm himself. He could sense the presence of the blade's magic since it was tied to his soul, but he couldn't drag it to him. He'd have to make it to the drawer.

First, he'd have to survive. After feeling the fist sail over him, he pivoted and swiped the light switch up. Soft illumi-nation filled the room, and he used his momentum to kick toward the cold source. He didn't connect, but the presence had to move away from him in order to dodge. He bolted for the bedside table.

A blur of motion stepped into his path. He threw himself to the left and knocked into the desk. He needed a weapon *now*, so he grabbed the letter opener Roger insisted he needed. It wasn't his dagger and wasn't silver, but it was at least something pointy to wield. He attacked and caught the edge of his assailant as the individual blurred out of the way.

Vampires always zipped to a space behind their target, so Zack pushed off the desk and spun.

But this vampire was *fast*. Before he finished moving, the cold presence was closing in, adapting to his tactic. When a hand grabbed for his throat, he reacted on muscle memory. He grasped the vampire's wrist with his free hand and applied pressure to the hand so it had to let go. Despite all their magic, physics and biology could still bring a vampire low. Zack moved to stab the vampire, but she grabbed his hand and yanked him to throw him off-balance.

And she had finally slowed down enough that he caught a glimpse of her face.

Nell.

She was testing him.

Again.

He tumbled to the floor, gaining control as he went, and rolled to end up back on his feet.

Nell was already on top of him, and though he struggled, she eventually pinned him to the floor. He was panting, face-down, and she was twisting his arm behind his back. If he didn't tap out, she was going to break his arm. He could feel it nearing that point.

Blinking back a pained tear, he snarled, "Mercy."

Nell eased her grip and backed away from him. She smoothed and straightened her clothing on her way, ensuring the door was fully shut. "Excellent reflexes. How did you know I was in the room?"

"Trade secret, master," Zack muttered as he sat up.

"Drop the formalities. They don't suit you," Nell said with a dismissive wave. She strode over to the desk.

Zack was about to thank her when he realized his notebooks were spread out over the desk, and Nell was approaching them with familiarity to their setup.

There were pages and pages and whole-ass notebooks about lore and rumors. He had theories on vampires and magic, and none of it was meant for Nell to read. He dashed forward and slammed his hands on top of the closest notebook. "Those are private!"

Nell smiled, the corner of her lips lifting, but there was a predator's gleam in her eyes. "I've known for a long time what you've been doing, Zackery."

How was he supposed to explain that this was beneficial for himself and Roger and not something to pass on to hunters? Would she believe that his parents had effectively cut off his contact with the hunter community? She could have killed him, and she'd stopped. *But what if she strikes again?* "Nell, I …"

She held up a hand. "You continue to impress me."

"I … do? Uh, thanks?"

"I particularly like this line, 'Nell is a professional badass with no patience for insubordination from guests and underlings alike.'"

"I wrote that after our first meeting." Zack cleared his throat. Though his hunter tattoo protected him, if he felt too much fear, she'd be able to sense it. *She may be strong enough to slip past my ward anyway.* "You, uh, can keep that notebook, if you want."

Nell slid the notebook off the desk and walked over to the bed with it. She sat on the end and crossed one leg over the other while she continued to skim through the notes. "You have a list of weaknesses in my coven. I'm not surprised to see notes on the security of my home or my donor house or even the town itself, but you have strategies here for social infiltration. How did you develop these?"

"I paid attention to who's talking to who and who's talking about who," Zack replied. "I don't think any of them would really work. Those are thought experiments."

"I don't believe you're far off. I've had my eye on a few of these people already. The tricky thing about vampires is that you can never be truly certain of their loyalty." Nell closed the notebook and set it beside her. "You can keep it. You may need bargaining chips in order to grow close to Seamus."

"And now that you're aware of what information I could give him, you can guard against it even if I don't warn you," Zack said.

"Precisely." Nell folded her hands and looped them around her knee. "Now, there is something lacking in your notes. What, specifically, is Roger's plan for defeating Seamus?"

"Regain his former position and then strike," Zack said.

"Regain *how*? Strike *when*? What is his timetable?"

"You know Roger. He can be aloof."

Nell narrowed her eyes. "Which is how he hides his cowardice."

"That's not fair." Zack had a journal under the bed where he'd listed out the details that he'd picked up over the last three months.

Roger had told him that everyone was a sad monster made of trauma when they first met. He probably had scores of them. The least of those traumas was that Seamus had paid Quinn to seduce Roger and turn him into a vampire—something that Seamus had revealed while Roger waited for Quinn to rise from the grave.

But Roger didn't talk about his past freely, and he always had a sad, wistful look in his eye when Zack tried to ask. The details Zack knew weren't for sharing. *I should burn those pages.*

Zack took in a steadying breath and forced himself to release his clenched fists. "Roger hasn't been exempted from Seamus's cruelty. In fact, he's survived it longer than anyone else."

"I thought that would motivate him to form a cohesive plan," Nell replied.

"He'll get there."

"Will he?"

Over the last two months, Roger's conviction hadn't faltered, but he had grown ... *lax* wasn't the right word. Complacent? But he was still catching up to the world's changes. Zack hadn't found any clues as to who could have put Roger in a coma. Not knowing who they could trust was making the trip back to the GLC tricky. Seamus might even kill them the first night. He had a reputation for being a capricious asshole.

"You want him to take charge of the GLC," Zack said slowly. "That means we can't just blow up Seamus with a rocket launcher on the street. Roger needs allies to have a better transition of power. And there's Anton to take care of."

Nell's expression became colder and unreadable. "If Roger should falter, or worse, do you intend to carry on ending them?"

"Yes," Zack said without missing a beat. "I'm a Gladwell on my mother's side. We've wanted him dead for centuries. And besides, the more I learn about him, the more I want to burn his heart out."

"That will do." Nell stood. "I hope that you'll warn me of any schemes against my people, Zack. I would hate for the trust I've placed in you to be misplaced."

She's the enemy, the voice in his head that sounded like Cal claimed.

She's an ancient vampire leading the best version of coexisting I've ever heard of. Zack nodded his head once. "Of course, master."

Nell chuckled softly. "I believe that's the first time you've said that and meant it. When Roger comes home, and nudge him if that isn't soon, bring him to my office. I need to speak with both of you."

Zack nodded again and was grateful she decided to leave after that. He shut the door behind her and sagged against it. What had happened that made her go through his stuff? Why hadn't Roger mentioned something to him? Had she read through his notebooks before? Why couldn't human minds remember everything so he never had to write anything down in the first place?

None of that mattered. He just had to put one foot in front of the other and keep moving. Pushing away from the door, he headed toward the desk and took out his phone. After sending a text to Roger, he packed away everything else he wouldn't need before they left the next night.

Nell was trusting him.

But everyone had their own angle. *I just have to work mine.*

CHAPTER 7

"You'll have to visit after I finish building my new house," Collin said. He was one of Nell's vampires that Roger didn't mind spending time with. He was currently lounging against his pet, a buff human with an almost intimidating amount of muscle.

Roger smiled through the impromptu invitation. Collin was a waifish vampire who had hardly been an adult when he was turned while their other companion, Evander, must have been closer to Roger's age. Without a good handle on calendars during the 1600s, Roger had lost track of his exact birth year as a mortal, but he figured he must have been at least twenty-four when he was turned.

The three of them, along with Collin's and Evander's head pets, had found a corner of a sitting room to call their own. Hunting in Nell's territory wasn't allowed, so Roger had settled into the donor house with a dry throat he wasn't sure he'd be able to quench.

Luckily, Collin and Evander had decided to spoil him since he was leaving. While he was listening to the conversation, his gaze was on the trickle of unclaimed mortals moving about. He played with two round, plastic, orange chits. With them, he'd be allowed small drinks, nothing too taxing for the donor. As he'd already had Kit's blood and another's, two more orange chits would satisfy him and even let him soak an extra bit of power. After the previous night's power expenditure during training, he was looking forward to the blood.

"Assuming you get around to building it," Evander said. He rolled his eyes and looked to Roger. "He's been promising this mansion for a decade."

"I will. I break ground within the year."

"Which is what you said last year." Evander stretched his legs out and put them on the back of his pet, who was filling the role of footstool. "Roger, any chance I could talk you into an exchange?"

"Perhaps," Roger murmured. The smell of shifter permeated the atmosphere. He was hoping for something human.

"I have a fantastic wine collection. Would you take the whole thing and give me your boy? The human one."

A twinge tightened Roger's awareness and brought his focus back to the vampires beside him, though he didn't turn his head to watch them. Vampires in Taliville didn't usually talk about trading their pets as if the pets would accept whatever their master said. In fact, Roger was certain Nell would be furious to discover Evander had made the offer.

However, a conversation like this in the GLC wasn't uncommon. Roger had never traded away any of his pets, but that didn't stop others from asking on occasion.

It shouldn't have bothered him this deeply that Evander asked. And Evander had boasted about the worth of the wine collection for weeks. Still, the twinge in Roger's mind became a clench, and he had to fight the urge to snarl and find the nearest piece of sharp wood to drive into Evander's chest.

"He's been obsessed with your boy," Collin said, sounding bored.

"He's remarkable," Evander replied.

"And not for trade," Roger said coolly. "I haven't gone to the trouble of training him for a black collar to give him away."

"Can't blame me for trying," Evander said.

The fuck I can't. Roger rolled the chit between his fingers. He should have suspected his parting present had a few strings attached. Evander had likely schemed for a week to figure out how to approach the topic with him.

Collin playfully slapped Evander's arm. "I told you not to try. You've fouled his mood."

"Nonsense," Roger said, faking a smile. His mood was sinking, but the inclination to write it off was a knee-jerk reaction. Happiness beget happiness. "You can't blame me for being a bit territorial. He is magnificent."

"He is," Evander said with a sigh.

Roger couldn't allow his anger to surface. At least Evander had a note of admiration in his voice rather than the basic hunger and demanding tone Seamus might have used. He didn't have a reason to be upset, not really. Why, then, did he want to rip Evander's throat out? Because he'd admired *Zack*? Zack, who was *his*, not in the way of pet and master, but his partner.

Oh God, I need to have the "what are we" conversation with him.

"And he's brooding," Collin complained.

"Not brooding," Roger replied. He flashed a wicked smile at Collin. "Thinking. You two should give it a shot."

Collin put a hand to his chest and dramatically gasped. "I am wounded."

There was a chance he was insulted and a chance he wasn't. Roger wasn't willing to put the mental energy into figuring him out.

Especially when he saw Carver Vega enter the room.

Carver was broad-shouldered. And since he was shirtless,

he was showing off his impressive physique. Typically, he wore jeans when he ventured into the donor house, but he had on a pair of black biker shorts that were hardly longer than boxers.

And he was exactly the sort of man who belonged in Roger's collection. Handsome, gorgeous, easygoing, a ready smile on his lips. Roger didn't salivate, but his throat dried upon laying eyes on Carver.

The matter wasn't helped by the fact that Carver had on a metal choke collar and a long chain hung from it, swinging with every step. The collar, the near nudity, the way he kept his gaze as close to the floor as he could manage—everything about his presentation had a meaning, but Roger hadn't seen anyone do such a thing while he'd been in Nell's territory.

But he knew what it meant. Did Carver? *He has to.*

Evander straightened, dropping his feet from the back of his pet and sitting up. "Oh my lord, is he making an *offering?* I thought Nell banned the practice."

"She did," Collin whispered.

Carver didn't hesitate in his steps. He approached the corner where Roger, Collin, and Evander sat. Without a word, he knelt on both knees and offered the end of the chain to Roger.

Carver was putting his life in Roger's hands. If Roger wanted, he could use the chain to pull the collar taut and choke Carver to death. In theory, no one would even have the right to interfere. Anton had killed a few would-be pets who had offered themselves in this manner.

Nell would put a stake in Roger's heart if he dared. He had no desire to cut Carver's life short.

A fresh, exciting buzz covered Roger. *I shouldn't entertain this. I am going into enemy territory, and he will be in danger if he comes with me.* But he couldn't embarrass the boy either. Roger took the chain from Carver and lightly held on to it as he stood. "Collin, Evander, thank you. It seems I have some busi-ness to discuss."

"Skip the discussing and claim him," Evander said. "The boy clearly longs for your embrace."

Roger forced a chuckle. "Wouldn't want Nell to revoke my visitation privileges on my last night." To Carver, he said, "Come along, boy."

Carver followed along obediently as Roger led him outside. His pulse had elevated, and the thunder of it echoed in Roger's ears. Waves of want were pouring off him, but then they always were whenever he was near Roger. That was one reason Roger had chosen to feed from him multiple times.

I did it too often. I led him on. Roger maintained his calm demeanor until he was certain they were alone. The night was cool, and no one else was taking advantage of the brick patio. Scattered around were various iron-wrought tables and chairs.

When they reached the middle of the space, Roger dropped the chain and turned around to face Carver. "What the hell did you think you were doing? Do you have any idea what that means?"

"That I'm willing to be yours, master," Carver said, speaking softly.

As a pet should. Like Kit could do. As Roger had been trying to get Zack to do for months. Unlike Kit, Carver's tone was an act. A rebellious desire was lying in wait, tangling with his lust.

Roger paced away from him. The need to sink his fangs into Carver's neck and seek his touch while he did so was growing.

"Carver, we need to have an open negotiation, drop the deference for the time being," Roger replied.

Carver lifted his gaze from the ground to watch Roger,

and he folded his arms over his chest. The action wasn't defensive but protective. A second later, he shivered.

"I'm an idiot. It must be freezing out here for you." Roger slid out of his suit jacket and put it around Carver's shoulders. Doing so brought them closer, and Carver's breath caressed Roger's wrist as he smoothed the jacket over his shoulder.

"Thanks," Carver said.

"Let's return to why you decided to make an offering to me," Roger said. Reluctantly, he withdrew from their near embrace.

"I thought I was dropping obvious hints the last couple of months that I was interested."

He had. Roger had ignored them. Indulging in his blood had almost felt like a betrayal, except he needed the blood, and Zack had said he didn't mind who Roger drank from. But taking on another pet was a different matter. Roger shifted his stance, preparing to let Carver down.

"Zack said if I wanted to be yours, I should ask. Since this is your last night in town and etiquette's important to you, I figured this would be the way to do it," Carver said.

"Wait, Zack *told* you to ask me?" Roger said.

"Yeah."

Roger leaned against one of the tables and folded his arms over his chest. So Zack and Carver had talked about this. Zack knew all the dangers and had told Carver to go ahead anyway. Why had he done such a thing? *I've been emphasizing that I needed to reenter the GLC in style. He's been doing the research. Two pets are rather few, and I have no guarantee that I'll have drinking privileges right away. Kit and Zack won't be enough for me to keep my strength up.* But did Roger want to put Carver in that kind of danger?

"Seamus seems to be accepting of my return, but I may be dead by the weekend," Roger said seriously.

Carver grinned and padded over to him. "Have a little faith. You're too hot for him to kill right away."

"You have no idea the amount of beautiful people he's murdered."

"I don't have a death wish, but you never know what day's going to be your last."

"I'd expect you to travel with me tomorrow night."

"Person I'm renting a room from would love to have it for her granddaughter."

Roger was struggling to find other complications Carver might turn away from. "Zack is my head pet. You will have to obey him as you would me."

"You're both my type," Carver said with a grin. "He has that kind of intense sexiness that you have to be born with, you know?"

I do. Roger watched Carver carefully as he said the next words. "I won't promise you a sexual relationship, but I also won't stop you from sharing your body with whomever you like. I only ask for your blood to remain mine."

Carver double-blinked. "Wait, really? Why?"

"Because Zack and I are close."

"Don't tell me you're one of those vampires who hate the word 'boyfriend.'" An iciness morphed Carver's grin from a sly one to a wary one.

So Carver did have a few morals with which he was willing to judge others. Roger leaned toward him. "I don't mind the word, but nothing is formal between he and I. I'm not going to declare his feelings for him."

Carver wrapped Roger's jacket tighter around him and shivered as the breeze kicked up. "But you don't want to mess things up between you."

"And given how the upper echelons of the GLC are expected to behave—"

"He's got to be your pet for appearances. Got it." Carver

stepped closer to Roger. "What I'm really hearing is seduce both of you, not just one."

Roger put his hand on Carver's chest and pushed him back a step. Another time, he would have taken everything Carver had to offer without consulting anyone. His relationships were always on the verge of breaking for one reason or another.

Or that's what I've told myself. He had never nursed anyone to health the way he'd cared for Zack. While he'd had lovers who were disowned from their families, he'd never been their primary comfort. But Zack was changing every night, and he had a pain in him that Roger wanted to ease. He longed to see Zack's shy smile more than he wished for another sunrise on an Atlantic wave.

"You are welcome to try," Roger said, his hand still on Carver's chest, "but Zack ... He has some mental blocks when it comes to passion."

"You his first boyfriend?"

Roger pulled his hand away and folded his arms over his chest again. "I don't believe so. He's comfortable with his sexuality, but the expression of it."

"Is that why he freezes up whenever I hit on him?" Carver asked.

"He panics when he believes others could be judging his more carnal reactions."

"Well, now I feel like an ass. I just thought it was 'oh no, I'm gay and just realizing it's panic." Carver moved so that he was at Roger's side, facing the same direction.

"If you push him or hurt him in any way, the deal we strike will be void." Roger let his eyes flare red as he added, "And depending on the depths of your crime, you may find your last day sooner than you'd like."

"You have to know that was intimidating *and* hot," Carver said.

"As long as you understand my seriousness, I don't care if you find it exhilarating," Roger replied.

"I got the message loud and clear. You and Zack are an item, and don't push my luck, or I'll dig a hole deep enough to be my grave." Carver smiled at him. "This mean you're considering me?"

Roger *ought* to say no. Returning with too many pets was as bad as returning with none. He shouldn't display too much wealth, especially since he had lost his massive fortune to the coven. Was three too many? Was it not enough? Josefina had three pets, and she was Nell's right hand, but they were a different coven. Candide, a captain in the GLC and one of his oldest friends, had a half dozen or more when it suited her.

But Roger would need blood. And Zack had told the boy to ask him.

"You have the right to say no at any point," Roger said. "I provide housing, healthcare, food, clothing—and you are expected to make public appearances in the clothing I buy. I don't demand for my pets to live in the dom/submissive life-style that we display in public, but you will be expected to follow rules and not embarrass me. After my authority, Zack is in charge. You'll be compensated a hundred thousand a year, which you'll receive in increments over that time. Quit early and I don't owe you the rest."

"Good beginning," Carver said. "Let's hash out a few more details."

They went back and forth on the agreement, amending only a few places while figuring out what they would need from each other.

As they were close to finishing, Roger received a text from Zack. "When are you coming back?"

"Soon," Roger texted back.

"Nell wants to see us. Her office. ASAP."

Roger frowned and promised he'd return shortly. He wrapped up his conversation with Carver by exchanging phone numbers and emails. The fact that contracts could be done without paper and still be binding boggled Roger, but he liked to embrace modern practices. At least he could make the adjustments in a matter of moments rather than taking multiple nights.

"If we're both satisfied and sign, then I'll have the car pick you up before dinner tomorrow," Roger said. "It'll bring you to Nell's mansion, and from there, we'll leave for the airport."

"I look forward to serving, master," Carver said.

Roger guided Carver back into the donor house. Thankfully, Carver had clothing waiting for him. Roger spent his remaining orange chits between two wonderful donors, and then he headed toward Nell's mansion. As he went, he texted Zack that they should meet outside Nell's office for expediency.

When he turned the last corner to the hallway, he spotted Zack leaning against a wall, arms folded tightly over his chest. His scowl was deep, without a hint of anger. He wasn't so much lost in thought but clearly navigating a labyrinth.

Roger paused to watch him. Something familiar about his features nagged at Roger's memory, but he'd lived hundreds of years. Some faces were bound to repeat themselves, and yet every time, they found a way to be unique. A minor expression, a gesture, a freckle or dimple.

Zack looked up from the floor, and the night could no longer remain a frozen moment. As Roger drew closer, he murmured, "She was in our room."

"What?" Roger whispered. Nell might overhear him even at this volume, but they could at least pretend they had an ounce of privacy. "Why?"

"She was searching for your plan," Zack replied. "She's pissed you don't have one."

Roger grimaced. His supposed lack of forethought would come to bite him in the ass.

Zack straightened and squared his shoulders before turning toward Roger. "How long has she been asking?"

"A few weeks. Last night, we had a disagreement about it," Roger said quickly.

"Fuck." Zack's gray eyes became hard as steel. "You should have told me."

"And what would you do about her annoyance?" Roger asked.

"Tell her that we have a plan. Because I *do*."

Of course he did. Zack had been raised to think of nothing but how to plot murders of supernatural entities and had probably devised six plans the night they'd met. Roger shook his head minutely. When Zack's scowl deepened with an element of anger, Roger closed the distance between them to only a few inches. "Your research has been essential, but it's not enough. We only have hypotheses about how people will accept me. Until I return, we don't know for certain what the reaction will be."

"You think I don't know how to account for that?" Zack snapped. "You haven't heard any of my ideas."

"Seamus—"

"Is a devious, sadistic bastard who's lived this long because he's a controlling dickwad who stamps out the first sign of a revolution," Zack replied. "You've said that a few times. But we're going to hit his blind spot."

"We have to be *careful*," Roger said.

"I know that." Zack tensed, his arms squeezing tighter together. Then he pursed his lips and said, "If you can't stop being terrified of him, we're fucked."

With that, he spun on his heels and headed for Nell's door. Only long years of practice kept Roger from gaping. What Zack had said wasn't entirely wrong, but that fear had kept Roger alive. He couldn't simply abandon it when they'd need his awareness to keep them alive.

Instead of arguing, Roger put on his best calm demeanor and followed Zack into the office.

Some vampires' homes felt like tombs, but Nell's style was elegant without being unnaturally pristine. Her desk was at the side of the room, far enough away from the door that it didn't crowd someone's entrance, but she could easily spot an intruder and defend herself if need be. She stood beside the gleaming mahogany, an expressionless mask much like Roger's gracing her features.

She wasn't alone.

The man sitting across from her, and therefore in the center of the room, appeared to be in his early twenties. He had short black hair, cool, fawny skin, and pale blue eyes. His suit was rumpled, with his jacket over his knees, his white shirtsleeves rolled up, and his tie loose. His hair had been styled spikier, but much like the rest of him, it was travel-worn. He had the slump of someone who had been awake far too long, yet he had plenty of energy in the calculating gaze he leveled on Zack and Roger.

Takashi Sato was one of Nell's trusted captains and one of Roger's ... could someone be considered an ex-boyfriend if they'd never gone on a date? They'd been lovers and had been close when Takashi came with Nell to Chicago in the 1920s. They'd reconnected at a meeting of regional vampires in Nashville in 1985.

"Roger," Nell said, "shut the door."

Ashamed that his own shocked reaction had caused a delay, Roger swiftly shut the door behind him. By the time he turned around to face the room again, he had forced his embarrassment below the surface and presented himself as the ageless vampire he was.

Takashi lightly sniffed the air. "Did you feed? Nell, why did he have a chance to do that while I haven't?"

"Takashi," Nell said, her tone firm.

Takashi sat up in his seat. "You summoned me from Cairo.

Halfway across the world, and I didn't bother to pack. I had to sleep in a coffin on a plane, and you know I hate doing that. Excuse me if I'm hangry."

Zack went to the far corner of the room and kept his hands loose at his sides. Was he armed? Should Roger have checked him for weapons? Surely he wouldn't try to murder Nell before they left Taliville.

I'm growing paranoid. Zack likes her and this place. He wouldn't hurt her. Roger slid his hands into his pockets and strode further into the room to stand near Nell and Takashi. "I wouldn't be surprised if your whining is an act and that your appearance is to put me at ease. Considering your penchant for disguise, I'm not convinced you're tired or hungry."

A small smile curled the left side of Takashi's mouth. His focus became razor-sharp, and he leaned back against his chair. "The years haven't dulled your memory."

"Nor my curiosity," Roger said. "Nell, what's the point of this meeting?"

"He's going with you to Chicago," Nell stated.

If Roger needed to breathe, he would've stopped. "Excuse me?"

"I need assurance that your friendliness hasn't been a ploy against my domain and you need the help," Nell said.

"Zack and I have things well in hand."

Nell glared at him with a coldness only a true immortal could master. "I will not see your mission fail, Roger. Seamus must be eliminated."

She had sent a warning flare last night, but Roger had ignored her. She didn't trust him, and he shouldn't have trusted her so completely. Staying in Taliville had lulled him into a false sense of security. He wasn't an ally; he was another pawn for her to manipulate across the board.

If he was ever going to lead, he needed to promote himself beyond the board and move his own pieces.

Too bad wishing doesn't make it true. Roger flattened his

expression into an equally hard glare. "You mean that you want a spy in my household."

"Takashi will be an asset to both of us," Nell replied.

"How do I know this isn't a scheme to take the coven?" Roger demanded. "What will stop him from staking me in the back, claiming the GLC, and acting as your vassal?"

"I do not want to annex that territory. It would be too much land to govern, too many disparate groups of supernaturals to keep happy, not to mention the Wrights. I am quite content with my domain."

"For now," Zack drawled. His voice was low with a note of seriousness. Desire flickered in him. Nothing sexual, not in the least, but Roger couldn't figure out the flavor of it without diving past Zack's mental shields. "Takashi came from Cairo, so clearly, you planned on adding him to our group before you checked our room."

"He caught my name!" Takashi said with a cheery grin. "What a smart little doggy."

Zack took a step forward with his right fist clenched. He stopped from taking another step when Roger motioned for him to halt. Already, Roger could feel a shift in the energy between Nell, Takashi, and Zack. There was an urgency and a readiness to pounce. Zack was good, and Roger could take Takashi without much effort. But Nell. They'd have a chance, but not without Zack's dagger and not with Takashi dividing their attention.

And I don't want anyone in this room to die. Roger shot Zack a pleading look.

Zack narrowed his eyes, then rested his attention on Takashi. "You're Takashi Sato. Nell sired you in 1895. You were a trapeze artist with a traveling circus that was wintering here. One night, you fell, and she decided to turn you. You spent the first fifty years by her side, but after World War II, you became her ambassador to other covens. Before Cairo, you were in Tokyo for three years, before that London for five, before that Dubai for seven—*should the doggy continue?*"

Takashi dropped his mask of pompous pleasure and smiled genuinely at Nell and then to Zack. His tone was respectful as he said, "You have done your homework, though you're bold to address me like this."

"Fuck you," Zack said. "You're clearly in on our scheme. How much of my research did you get to read?"

"I'm quite moved that you thought you might assassinate me by planting a potential pet in Los Angeles. Before this came up, that was going to be my next assignment," Takashi said. "How did you figure that out?"

"The LA and Las Vegas covens are considering merging. Since Nell seems to hate any territory bigger than hers on the same continent, I figured you'd be sent in to muddy the waters and sabotage any deals."

Takashi pointed at Zack but looked to Nell. "He is *clever*." Grinning broadly, he swung his gaze back to Zack. "You are absolutely wonderful. Did you know that?"

Zack double-blinked and then frowned at Takashi.

"Nice to see you getting along," Nell said.

"Not that it matters. He's not coming," Roger replied. When everyone looked his way, he did his best to keep his chin up. The world was tilting, and he was tumbling. He had to catch his footing before things spiraled further out of his control. "I have enough to handle without explaining his presence."

"You're not leaving without him," Nell said.

"You think Seamus is going to be all right with me returning with one of your *captains*? We'll be staked the first night."

"We have a night to sort out the approach."

"I have an idea, if I'm allowed to speak, masters," Takashi said.

Elevating Roger to Nell's status had to be Takashi's way of

worming into Roger's good graces. His respect might not be genuine. After all, he was her sireling. His loyalty would always be to her first. And with his connections, he could secure a rule in the GLC and present the territory to Nell if he wanted.

He was a potential traitor.

But Rover could also remember when Takashi was young and knew nothing of subterfuge. He had been sincere. They had been close, once.

"No promises," Roger said.

"I'm willing to listen," Nell said.

Takashi shifted his gaze from Nell to Roger and back as if judging their readiness to match his dance steps. "I could formally leave Nell's coven and petition to join the GLC."

"No," Nell replied sharply. "If anything happened to you, I wouldn't be able to retaliate."

"Openly," Takashi said. "You'd be able to exercise other paths."

Zack looked to Roger. "Could he still claim the GLC and work closely with Nell?"

"In theory, he could, but he would have more trouble from them and Nell's own people. Defending one of their own is one thing, but I doubt every vampire in Nell's domain would seek to defend the leader of a territory that technically wasn't one of them."

"Not to mention how the European vampires would riot," Takashi said. "They aren't in favor of how Nell runs the humans in her territory."

Takashi's plan made sense. Joining a coven and taking it over within a decade wasn't done without outside help. Roger's own claim would be strengthened by his age and that he was technically a founding member. If Takashi did betray him and claim the GLC, the other covens wouldn't have to physically attack Nell or Takashi. They could impose financial sanctions on the GLC if Takashi was seen to be leading it for her. Money and influence were as vital to a coven as blood.

"Could work," Roger sighed.

"Seamus could reject your application. Then you'd be in hostile territory on your own," Nell said. "I won't allow it."

"You have to think of the wider game, master," Takashi replied.

A game that Roger was hopelessly outclassed in. He searched Zack's expression for any hint of a reaction, but he stepped back to the wall and folded himself up.

"Zack?" Roger asked.

"I'm not opposed to help, but the string has to be cut," Zack replied.

"I am not releasing him from my command," Nell snapped.

"If you don't, he won't live any longer than Seamus," Zack said in a voice so soft Roger almost missed it. When he met Roger's gaze, there was an intensity in his steel-gray eyes that rocked Roger to his core. The world remained tilted, but there was support from Zack. Roger wouldn't fall flat on his face if he could hold onto him. Subtly, Zack nodded to him and then said, "I will eliminate any threat to Roger's rule."

Nell shifted her weight, and Zack mirrored her. The long hours Roger had trained with both of them warned him that they were heading to a fight. Takashi had his gaze on Roger.

"Think of it this way: you have nothing to lose," Roger said as he stepped around Takashi and between Nell and Zack. He faced Nell. "I'm not about to limit Takashi's communications, so he'll be able to report anything he learns. You'll have your spy, and I won't even mind. By giving up your claim over him, he may even be able to maintain a position among Seamus's elites even if something happens to me."

"And if Seamus decides to murder you the first night?" Nell growled.

"Then you'll have a cause to plot with others against him," Roger said.

Nell clenched her fist and pressed it onto her desk. "I don't like this."

Swiftly, Takashi stood and put his hands around her fist. "Please, master. This is the perfect option to satisfy everyone."

"I hate this idea," Nell said as she pulled her hand from his. She took out a sheet of parchment from her desk. Her lips were a thin line, and her grimace remained firmly in place. She took a fountain pen and wrote across the page. "Zack, if he dies, I will burn the Wright family to the fucking ground and use your ashes in a compost for my roses."

Roger started to open his mouth but quickly closed it. Why had she made *Zack* responsible for Takashi's well-being?

She must have seen his frown because she added, "I'm assuming, Roger, that if he's dead, you're dead. Because if you're not, you'll wish you were, but you'll never find that mercy."

"Ah," Roger said.

Nell pricked her finger and used her blood as ink for another pen. She signed the page. Then, she handed the pen over to Takashi. He repeated the ritual and signed the document as well. When they were done, she handed it to Roger. "There. I have officially released Takashi, my sireling and captain, from my coven. He is no longer mine. Once you show that parchment to Seamus and have it recorded, your fear that I might use him against you should be alleviated."

Roger gingerly held the page since the ink and blood needed a chance to dry. In less than ten minutes, she'd been convinced to drop her hold over an underling. Takashi would likely remain loyal to her out of love, faithful in a way that none of Roger's own sirelings had ever been. All the vampires he'd made had fought or resented him.

What is it like to have that kind of bond? To be so sure of someone else? Roger glanced up from the parchment to Zack. In the middle of the argument, he'd come to Roger's defense and treated Roger's rule like it was an inevitability. Doing so had answered questions Roger hadn't wanted to ask. Such as, would Zack want to stay by his side after Seamus was gone? *Apparently yes.*

"If I could, I'd like a moment alone with Takashi," Nell said.

"Of course." Roger motioned for Zack to leave the room with him.

Once they were in the hallway and on their way to their room, Zack murmured, "And then we became four."

"Five," Roger said.

Zack bunched his eyebrows, then relaxed. "Oh, right. Dmitri. Though if we're counting like that, we're still at four in Chicago since Kit doesn't know."

"There will be five of us traveling tomorrow." Roger lightly took hold of Zack's hand and pulled him to a stop. "I spoke with Carver earlier."

"What?" Zack asked, color draining from his face.

"He approached me while I was at the donor house and offered to become my pet." Roger frowned.

"And you said yes." Zack pulled his hand from Roger's. After checking that no one was in the hallway with them, he snapped under his breath, "You have been on Kit and me for the last two months to learn all these fucking manners. Why the fuck would you say yes to Carver the night before we leave town?"

The acidic glare in Zack's eyes burned through the protective layer of Roger's emotions. Numbness infected his lips and tongue, stilling whatever slick response he would have made. A part of him was flinching, waiting for the inevitable. But Zack wasn't Seamus. As angry as he could be, he never reacted the way Seamus did.

And yet. Roger flinched—not outwardly but *inwardly*. "He said you told him to ask me."

"Because I'm not allowed to speak for my 'master,' and he was pushing to know whether or not you were into him," Zack replied.

"Would you please calm down and tell me what's wrong?" Roger asked.

Zack narrowed his eyes and scanned Roger from head to toe and back to his face. The fire in his eyes shifted to a laser focus without any heat. Then he dipped his head and ran his hand through his hair. "I've been sucker punched a few times tonight. I guess since we have to worry about feeding Takashi, too, that it's not a bad thing Carver's coming along. And if he fucks up, it'll take the focus off of me. You realize you have to have a reason Takashi is coming with us. 'Just because' will be suspicious. People might think you're working for Nell."

"The formal release will ease most of those worries." Roger gently folded the paper and put it into his suit jacket pocket. "Takashi and I have been known to connect. We could say he's my boyfriend."

"'Connect,'" Zack repeated. "You've hooked up before."

"A few times."

"Right." Zack hugged his arms to his chest. "Yeah. That'll work."

"Zack—"

"I'm tired, okay? And tomorrow's a big night, and I'm freaking out about it." Zack turned and headed down the hall. "Don't worry about me."

Roger was out of words himself.

As soon as they were in their bedroom, Zack said, "I think I'm going to bed."

Tension underscored Zack's words and made his shoulders taut, but when he didn't want to talk, he remained silent.

Roger started to reach for him but went for his sleep pants instead. "I'll join you."

"You sure? It's a few hours until dawn."

"Like you said, tomorrow is a big night. I wouldn't mind a little quiet." Roger glanced to Zack. "Especially quiet spent with you."

A glimmer of a soft smile graced Zack's lips, and he relaxed his shoulders. "Okay."

They changed, Roger sending a quick text to Dmitri about the additions to the flight, and settled into bed. Zack curled up against Roger. His warmth and the weight of him brought an intangible peace to Roger's mind. He pressed a kiss to the top of Zack's head when he was certain he was asleep and held him through the night.

CHAPTER 8

Zack said nothing as he cuddled into Roger. Sleep took forever, but he gradually dropped into it. His dreams twisted memories into nightmares and ended with Cal coming for him with a stake. In the morning, he gently unentangled himself from Roger so as not to wake him—Roger was hard to wake, but caution was wise. He'd tried to choke him to death once when he was between sleep and wakefulness. But Zack had discovered that short of shoving Roger out of bed, he didn't wake during the day.

He said nothing bothered him to Reed before heading out for his last day in Taliville. He made posts in the Fang app and updated his status on Night Deets. One of them even welcomed Carver to Roger's collection with a pirate booty joke. He had coffee and lunch like he'd been doing for weeks. His final goodbye to the librarian was tearful on their part. They were going to miss him.

At his last dinner with Reed and the other pets he'd gotten to know, he smiled and made polite conversation and joked about how wonderful getting out of the small town for a big city would be. Kit was full of energy, and Carver soaked up attention, but at least no one was staring at Zack. He drank three glasses of wine when he'd meant to have one.

The wine made the nothing in his heart hurt less.

But in the shade of Carver's shadow, Zack was left to think. Roger had *crumbled* when faced with conflict. He'd caved to Nell's demand and Takashi's compromise and in a room of vampires looked to Zack for guidance. And he wouldn't be able to do that in Chicago because Zack would have to act like a lesser. Like something Roger owned.

And there was the way Roger wilted when Zack got angry in the hallway.

That wasn't the real Roger. The real Roger was charismatic and confident. He could charm the pants off anyone he wanted to, and he could make anyone feel desired. Wanted. *Worthy*. That was how he made Zack feel. He saw into him and turned him about until the shitty stuff fell away.

A good leader should be capable of that.

A good vampire leader couldn't cower, though. Not once.

What's bothering you more? the Cal voice taunted throughout the day. *The fact that your boyfriend sucks at scheming or that you've tied your fate to a loser?* Which wasn't a true thought. Or a fair one. Roger had baggage. Centuries of it. He'd be able to deal with it. They just had to get rid of Seamus and Anton so he could. *Sure. Because that guy really faces his problems.*

Zack caught himself clenching his fists so hard that he had half-moon marks on his palms more than once during dinner.

He had a fourth glass of wine with dessert.

The middle of fall meant the nights came on quicker, so by the time dinner was done, darkness had come. Zack finished up his goodbyes, left Kit and Carver waiting in the foyer, and made his way to the bedroom to check on Roger.

Takashi was in the hall, overseeing some of Nell's servants as they took the packed bags out of Zack and Roger's bedroom. When he spotted Zack, he smiled smugly.

The arrogance in his grin made Zack long to shove his silver dagger into his gut and twist it around. Takashi clearly thought he was the smartest guy in the room. The problem was that, as far as Zack could tell, he was *that* good. In every city he visited, he rubbed elbows with powerful vampires. Paris, Berlin, Atlanta, Dubai, Tokyo, Shanghai, Mumbai, New York City, Mexico City, London, Johannesburg, Toronto, Cairo —he'd traveled just about everywhere. To do that and survive, he had to be charming, talented, and intelligent.

Doesn't hurt that he's handsome. Zack dropped his gaze to the floor and made a small bow customary to greeting a vampire casually. "Master."

"I don't know why everyone complained about your manners. You seem better behaved than a bulk of the ones I've met recently," Takashi said, not directly looking at Zack anymore. "Are you ready, boy?"

"Yes, master."

"And the other two?"

"Downstairs waiting, master."

"Excellent." Takashi strode into the bedroom. "Lover, we are all waiting on you."

Zack stayed where he was and said nothing. Because there were others around. Because this was how it was going to be in public and there was going to be a lot of public time.

He'd need to trim his fingernails before the night was over, or he was going to wind up accidentally drawing blood.

"Almost ready," Roger purred.

"Are we eating on the flight?" Takashi asked lightly.

"Dmitri promised to send two donors along."

"Fantastic."

"Zack," Roger called.

For a heartbeat, Zack had hope that Roger was going to call everything off and say they were going to sneak in, murder Seamus, and then live fabulous lives somewhere else. Or maybe they'd just run away. And he hated that he wanted that future for even a second. He swallowed, but his throat stayed dry. "Yes, master?"

"You can wait downstairs with the others. We'll be along in a minute."

"Thank you, master." Zack gave a quick bow and then went down to the foyer.

Two SUVs came around, one for baggage and one meant for passengers. Kit and Zack climbed into the far back while Carver and Takashi took the center, and Roger rode up front while Josefina drove. The ride down the mountain was quiet, and Zack didn't feel the urge to change anything about that.

They went to a private airport where a small jet was waiting for them. The marvel of rising into the air didn't thrill him. He sat in his seat, tucked one leg up so he could wrap his arms around it, and put the fact that Carver was already shirtless out of his mind. The black collar around his own throat was a weight.

"Why do people always complain about airplane seats?" Kit asked as they shimmied against theirs. "This thing is roomy."

"I don't think regular planes have seats this big," Zack said.

"You've never been on one?"

"Naw."

"The last time I was off the mountain was my second cousin's funeral," Kit replied. "And then we only went to Gatlinburg. We were gone and back in a day."

"Hm."

Kit grabbed the arm of Zack's chair and spun him so they faced one another. In a low voice that Zack struggled to hear over the plane's engines, they whispered, "What's up with you?"

"Nothing," Zack replied. He glanced across the small cabin. Roger and Takashi had the two seats closest to the front of the plane, and Carver sat behind them, though his seat was rotated so he faced away from the window. There was a row in between Zack and Carver, but the five feet felt like two inches and six hundred miles at the same time. Carver had a drink in his hand and a smile on his lips.

And he was everything Zack was supposed to be. Uncaring what was going on. Fang scars on his wrists and throat and here and there across his body. Sexy and ready for a good time. *What everyone wants to see. Not moody, scrawny me.*

"Yeah, he's a surprise addition for me, too," Kit said. "And Takashi?"

"You know vampires. Relationships that just pick up from whenever they last saw each other, even decades apart," Zack whispered.

Kit leaned in. "Does that mean the three of you are a thing?"

Zack frowned at them.

"I thought you and Roger were an item."

Me too. Zack shrugged.

An interior door at the back of the cabin opened, and two people walked out. They showed no expression on their faces and wore gray bands on their arms just above the elbow. One presented a wrist to Roger, and the other offered one to Takashi. Without any preamble, Roger and Takashi drank from them. Afterward, they returned to the rear room of the cabin.

A flight attendant stepped out from the galley, bowed toward Roger, and said, "If you or your companion require more of them, master, they are available. I can bring either back here, or you or your companion can join them in the pen."

Zack jumped to his feet. "Do they *live* back there?"

The flight attendant's courteous smile faltered as her gaze fell on Zack. "Tonight's selection was provided by Steward's Garden."

Zack's stomach went cold, and he locked into place. He'd

come across the name more than once in his research. The place was owned by the vampire Marcus, one of Quinn's sirelings, which made him a descendant of Roger. Supernaturals didn't have to market, and vampires didn't blast every detail of their businesses on social media, not even Night Deets.

Steward's Garden was a "donor house." But unlike Nell's or even some of the other GLC houses, there were no protective policies. What little Zack had dug up about the business pointed to serious allegations of abuse and kidnapping—and inevitably murder. Vampires had to expend a constant effort to maintain their lust effect and dull a victim's senses. Zack had theories on how that could aid them in brainwashing and assist in long-term conditioning, but the two people he had just seen barely had a scratch on them. He swung his gaze from the back door to Roger and Takashi. "Were they shifters?"

Roger frowned with confusion in his eyes.

"No," Takashi said. There was a precision in his manners, something Zack had seen from Josefina and other mentors. He had the look of someone evaluating a promising equal.

The bands. I bet they're enchanted. Zack clenched his fists. "Someone in the GLC has perfected *mind control?*"

In a blur, Roger moved from his seat to stand in front of Zack. He said lowly, "You do *not* speak that way to me."

Zack opened his mouth, but Roger made a subtle gesture to indicate the flight attendant behind him. And Carver believed they were pet and master and would be living with them. There would be no true privacy to unleash his temper. Zack clenched his jaw and glared up at Roger.

Pretending to be a loyal pet was one thing.

Acting like he didn't care about the suffering of others was utterly different.

He snarled, "*Mind control.*"

With an elegant motion, Takashi drew the attention of the

flight attendant. "We are in need of some refreshments, dear. I'll have a manhattan. Boy?"

"Do you have fey spirits?" Carver asked.

"We do," the flight attendant replied.

"A shot of Winter's Brink and a double of the best mortal gin you have on the rocks," Carver said.

They were ordering drinks while two helpless humans waited like drones for the flight to end. Zack clenched his fists and glared up into Roger's eyes.

A coldness swept over Roger's features, and a mask Zack had never seen before snapped into place. He was cold and elegant and every bit the vampire Zack had imagined when he read the *From the Grave* series. Powerful. Drop-dead gorgeous. Unfathomable.

Zack sucked in a breath.

Roger put his finger on Zack's lips. "Don't disappoint me, boy."

Disappoint *him*?

This was what they've been warning you about, the rational part of his mind began. *You've been told over and over that you wouldn't like what you see.*

He imagined a thousand ways that he could help the people trapped in the back. His dagger was in his backpack at his feet. The glory of going through a private airport and private plane meant he hadn't needed to stow his weapon completely out of reach. He could use the magic of his dagger and a quick spell to undo the bindings of the armbands.

Of course, then he'd be stuck with two people who would be massively freaked-out on a runway outside Chicago that was operated by vampires. He could try calling his family, but what if they were out on a job? Halloween was only a week away, and they tended to stick closer to home to prevent any nearby threats, but they could be anywhere in North America. *If I crawl home, Cal will never let me hear the end of it.*

A worse possibility came to mind. And what if his family wouldn't answer? What if they wouldn't come?

And what would he solve? These two victims weren't the only ones.

He had to get to the heart of this and destroy the monster that was rotting a coven and ruining helpless people. But remaining perfectly complacent would burn his soul if he didn't think of a way to release the pressure. *Lucky me, the others are providing an easy answer*.

Breaking the staring contest without dipping his head in deference, Zack tilted away from Roger's touch and said, "Master Takashi, I've never had a cocktail before. What would you suggest?"

"An old-fashioned," Takashi said.

"Thank you, master. I'll try that." Zack sat down stiffly.

Roger stared down at him, but Zack refused to meet his gaze a second time. There was wrong and there was *wrong*, and he had to know that.

After an eternal moment, Roger went back to his seat. The coldness never left his eyes, even as he smiled at the attendant and ordered a sidecar. Kit asked for a lemon drop.

"I take it that alcohol has never been a source of interest for you, Zackery," Takashi said.

Zack frowned at him. "It hasn't, master. How did you know?"

"You seem knowledgeable on a great manner of subjects," Takashi said evenly. "However, no one can be expected to know everything, can they?"

There was a weight in those words. Zack tried to judge it, but the righteous fury burning in his belly wasn't quenched by the drink in his hand.

"Screw cocktails, then. We need to get shots going," Carver said. He nodded to Roger. "If you'll allow, master."

"Of course," Roger said, the distance still in his voice. "Do as you please."

And for the first time in forever, Zack drank.

A limo met them at the airport in the Chicago suburbs, and Kit discovered it had a private stash of booze. It wasn't nearly as good as the drinks on the plane had been, and there wasn't anything to mix with the hard stuff.

By the time Zack climbed out of the vehicle, the world had a definite sway to it. Despite the late hour, the hotel staff was moving with a ruthless precision to unload the luggage from the trunk and back of the limo.

The building in front of them was the local version of the high-end ultrarich locations that catered to supernaturals, especially vampires. L'Hotel de Monde de Nuit had bas reliefs in the stonework on the lower floors. The windows above the sixth floor were arched, and balconies dotted many of the highest floors.

Until recently, it was the tallest of the vampire hotels at forty-five stories, beating out New York's, Tokyo's, and Dubai's. The new Hotel Vampire in Atlanta had stolen the title with sixty-five floors. Filling such a hotel with only supernaturals could be a challenge, and Zack had seen a plethora of posts on Night Deets arguing that it shouldn't count since it allowed regular, completely-unaware-of-the-supernatural humans to stay within its walls.

"Ooo, we need a pic," Kit said, their speech slurred. They grabbed Zack's arm and tugged him toward the large fountain.

At the center of the fountain was a statue of a winged man stretching toward the heavens. Beneath him, several smaller stone figures clawed and grasped his lower ankle. One even hung from his otherwise free left ankle. Water splashed up from the jets, seeming to help the hands grasping for the winged man. The finer details were harder to make out, either because someone thought red lighting was decent enough in the dark or the alcohol in Zack's system was blurring his vision.

Kit pulled Zack around to the far side, and Carver saun-tered along behind them. The three of them took selfies, alter-nating who was using what phone. Zack was pretty sure his was trash and opted not to post it, but Kit and Carver were happy and posted theirs.

Roger snapped, and the glow of the moment dropped away to the misery that wouldn't be dulled. The crest tag lightly tapped against Zack's neck as he hurried over to him. The others followed behind him.

"All right there?" Roger murmured.

"Fine, master," Zack said. Because he couldn't scream. His dagger was in his backpack and on a cart that the bellhops were taking in, but he wasn't allowed to hold on to it. Denied the comfort of being armed among enemies, he sank into the remaining alcoholic buzz as they stepped inside.

The lobby's marble floors were shined to perfection. Massive chairs and deep couches made up a small lounging area near the front desk, while another seating area filled a space near what Zack thought was a gift shop. Then his research kicked in and reminded him that the store wasn't filled with knickknacks or souvenir T-shirts or even boutique clothing. It had "pet necessities." A little food, some water and snacks like any hotel might have. A few bits that could charitably be considered clothing.

And a whole lot of collars, leashes, harnesses, floggers, and other devices.

Instead of looking out, Zack focused upward. The ceiling was thirty feet up, and a huge chandelier hung in the middle of the lobby. Long crystals formed a sweeping spiral, and each one had a unique glow, no two showing the exact same shade of soft white light.

While Roger engaged a hotel staffer about some detail, Zack walked underneath the chandelier. There weren't any bulbs to illuminate it, and he couldn't spot any sign of arcane magic. Whoever had constructed it had either hidden their runes or it wasn't done with enchantments.

A rumor on the Hunters' Information Network was that a wizard had discovered how to grind pixies into a concentrated magical dust that could be used in glass to make it glow. He'd read it months ago and never considered the ramifications of it.

Nell's gardens had a whole community of pixies living in it. While they were troublesome when they wanted to be, they were intelligent, beautiful creatures. Destroying them for some pretty lights was about the cruelest thing Zack could think of.

Even ground into dust, they're worth something. Me? Mom and Dad tossed me away. Zack sank to the floor. If he kept looking up, maybe his tears would stop before they started.

"Zack," Roger called.

The others were heading toward the elevators. Zack scrambled to his feet and hurried after them. He wobbled as the elevator started to rise.

Roger had his arm looped over Takashi's shoulders, and they were whispering to each other. Zack didn't have a hard time picturing them in other eras. Smiling, laughing. Kissing. *Together.* And Takashi would have a chance to do that when Zack died. Takashi could be with Roger forever, and Zack was just a moment. Something to forget.

His descent into sadness was soaked in whiskey and rum and a hundred other things. When the elevator came to a stop at the forty-second floor, Zack flailed, just a little. Just enough to grab onto Carver on accident.

Carver grinned at him.

But he doesn't really want me. He wants Roger. Zack swallowed, another rock of potential tears joining the others forming in his gut. He followed Roger and Takashi out of the elevator and into the hotel suite.

The opening room was double the size of Zack's parents'

living room, and the ceiling went up to a second floor. Windows took up the far side except for a sliding glass door that led out onto the balcony. A sleek staircase on the right seemed to hover, but the support beams and structure were discreet. A full-service bar was nestled in under the stairs and landing to the second floor and near the exit to the balcony.

Excitedly, Kit took Zack's hand, and they explored. On the second floor, they discovered a sitting area that overlooked the floor below and two bedrooms, one of which Kit claimed. The style was minimalist and sterile, the linens incredibly smooth and the colors cool. The two bedrooms upstairs shared a bathroom, but each had its own unreasonably sized closet.

Directly underneath the partial second floor on the first was an office and an exercise room complete with a treadmill, weight machine, weight bag, elliptical, and solid floor mat. Across the way, they found the master suite that had the same high ceiling as the living room and gorgeous windows. The bathroom had a tub big enough for three people and a shower with five different heads that could probably fit all five of them intimately—and maybe squeeze in one or two more before it became too congested.

The whole place was ridiculous.

And this was where he was going to live for the foresee-able future. Roger would only buy a house once *Seamus* approved. That could take weeks. Months.

Months of playing nice. Of watching other people get hurt. Of gaining the bastard's approval so we can stab him in the back instead of the front. Zack stumbled over to the bar.

"You better be after a bottle of water," Roger said lightly, a smile on his lips.

Because everything was a show. Or was this the true Roger? Had he played Zack? Was this just a long con? No. No, he needed Seamus dead. He'd been sincere.

Hadn't he?

Zack didn't recognize any of the brands, but he spotted a bottle of vodka. He snatched it from the shelf and placed it on the counter. Then he hunted for a glass.

Just as he reached for one, Roger grabbed his wrist.

The anger came back. The alcohol couldn't keep it at bay. Zack stepped in closer and snarled, "Get your damn hand off me, bloodsucker."

The trace of warmth in Roger vanished, and he yanked on Zack's wrist, tugging him toward the master bedroom. Zack turned his wrist so he had leverage, but before he could pull free, Roger released him. A flash of joy sparked in him from the victory.

Roger spun to face him and, in a blurring motion, threw Zack over his shoulder and began to carry him across the room. The sudden change in position threatened the contents of Zack's stomach.

"Someone's in trouble with daddy," Carver crooned. And Kit laughed.

Zack pushed himself up enough that he could glare at Carver. "Fuck you, you fucking slut!"

Carver shot him an ice-cold glare and flipped him off. Zack flopped back down and used both hands to flip Carver off in return.

The world spun three times when Roger tossed him onto the bed. The troubling part was that physically, he'd only been flipped so that the extra spinning caused his stomach to roll. Zack managed to hold on instead of vomiting, but only barely. Acid was in the back of his throat.

Roger slammed the bedroom door shut. He kept his back to Zack for a long moment. When he turned to face Zack, his expressionless mask was gone, and a familiar warmth was in his brown eyes. He came over to sit on the end of the bed. "You've been off since last night. Please talk to me."

Zack clenched his fists. Because there was realization buried deep underneath the pain of the last day. One that had been growing. An obvious stumble in their routine that he'd noticed and tried to compensate for. The previous night had made his miscalculation plain to see. Tears burned hotter than the bile.

"If this is about Carver or Takashi—" Roger began.

"It's you!" Zack blurted out. The truth was supposed to feel good, but he only felt hollow. "You say you want to kill Seamus, but you don't know how. You don't talk about what you'll do as coven leader. What are you going to do if you can't get Quinn's money? What'll happen if you never get Seamus's accounts either? What are you going to do if someone doesn't follow your rules? What kind of rules are you even going to have?"

"We have time to figure that out," Roger said.

"You should already know!" Zack got onto his knees and crawled over to Roger. He grabbed his hand and held on tight. Touching him felt like brushing his hand against cold stone. Tears started to slip out. "Roger ... deep down, you care about others. I can tell! But I watched you turn it off tonight. You just threw a switch in your head. Those people were mindless slaves. How can you be okay with it?"

"I'm not, but we have to be. For now," Roger whispered hoarsely.

"For now," Zack mocked.

"Don't," Roger said. He had an edge in his voice, one of warning and mingled with exhaustion. "I have seen good people lose their minds and worse around this coven. And I am not innocent of misdeeds myself. But we can't help anyone if we don't exist. The idea that Anton or someone he knows has successfully created mind control bothers me deeply, but we do not have the luxury of throwing a fit whenever we see something we can't stand."

"You want me to swallow it and say nothing," Zack snapped.

Roger scanned him and said seriously, "I think you

already know that you must, or you would have done something on the plane."

Zack looked away. Roger was right. Of course he was.

Roger put his hand over Zack's. "This will be worth it. My rule will be nothing like his. I promise you."

"I want to believe in you," Zack said quietly.

"If you don't, why are you here?"

"Because if this doesn't work out, I'm nothing." Zack released Roger's hand. The alcoholic haze in his mind had led him to a mental cliff, and he teetered on the edge of the abyss of depression waiting to swallow him. "And this is about more than you and me. This is about the people he's hurting —that the coven's hurting. This is about making change. And I can find a way to handle the dark tunnel if I can see a fucking light at the end of it, but right now, it just feels like a fucking car coming at me."

Gently, Roger caressed Zack's cheek. He leaned in and caught Zack's gaze. "I have weathered this for centuries. You are so much stronger than you know, and together, we will make it through this."

"How?"

"Patience," Roger replied.

Zack blinked, and tears trailed down his face. Roger wiped them away before he could. "I don't have centuries to wait. Nell won't wait forever either."

"You won't have to." Roger kissed his forehead and then touched their foreheads together. "But we can't fix the world in a night. I need you to trust me."

The nagging voice that sounded like Cal was resurfacing, keeping him close to the abyss. *Vampires are the enemy. You're an idiot for going along with this.* The family would say that. Cal would.

Not Roger. Not Blake or Kit or any of his friends. The family had abandoned him, but he had new people in his life. And so what if Roger wasn't much of a planner—that was why he'd aligned with Zack, wasn't it? Together, they had a chance that they wouldn't have alone.

"I'll hold on," Zack said, and he managed a weak smile. He could do this. "Think I'm just overwhelmed still."

"And more than a little drunk."

"That too."

Roger kissed his forehead again. "Maybe don't drink that much in public."

"Mm. We'll see."

Roger chuckled softly and stroked Zack's cheek. "I'm certain tomorrow morning will provide enough motivation."

"Morning?" Zack scowled at him. "You don't have anything planned for the morning."

"It's been three hundred years, but I do remember what a mortal hangover feels like after a night of binge drinking." Roger kissed his temple, a quick brush of his cool lips that was refreshing. "Let's get you settled into bed."

And there was something to the way Roger was taking care of him that felt comforting, even though the abyss was lurking, waiting for his misstep. Zack stripped with Roger's help and shivered when Roger lightly traced the scar on his left shoulder. A sadness was in Roger's eyes, but he swept it away before he tucked Zack into bed.

Zack pushed that strange look out of his mind. He clung to Roger's words, to the thin line of hope he'd offered. Because otherwise, he'd tumble.

Half-asleep, he heard Roger wish him a good night, and he murmured something in reply. As the door shut, he drifted off to sleep.

CHAPTER 9

The hotel suite was massive, but the confines of glass and walls were high-end torture when Roger was restless. In Taliville, he'd walked the streets until dawn on nights like this. He could do that in Chicago, but he didn't want to leave the hotel while Zack was in his current state. He seemed fragile.

So Roger went to the balcony. The city beyond had changed over the course of his long, long life, but in the thirty years away, it hadn't changed dramatically enough to be unfamiliar. Lights still dotted the tall buildings, even late into the night. Past the skyscrapers were hints of the deep darkness of Lake Michigan. This far up, the chilly wind continuously rustled his shirt.

If he closed his eyes, he could ignore the cold metal railing under his hand and the outdoor furniture around him and imagine he was on the edge of a sailing ship. The only memory he had that made him long for his mortal days was bright sunlight on the endless blue waves. The seas at night weren't the same. Their depth was no longer a beautiful wonder but a foreboding nightmare.

"Because if this doesn't work out, I'm nothing." Zack's words

played through Roger's mind on a loop. The slight hitch in his voice, the clarity when all of his other words had slurred from the alcohol. Roger had dragged him off to the bedroom out of frustration, but as soon as he'd thrown Zack over his shoulder, he'd been able to grasp a clearer picture of Zack's fears and desires. Touch could enable him to reach past Zack's tattoo, and as drunk as he was, Zack had dropped his relentless guard.

And there was a fear festering deep in his soul, one that Roger had thought he was easing. He was terrified he was doing the wrong thing.

Roger hung his head. Zack's morality was a beacon for him. Before spending so much time with Zack, he would have never thought twice about the two gray-banded donors on the plane. *That's not true. There was a time I questioned. A time I thought to run.*

Attempting to flee Seamus hadn't worked. He'd believed that because Jamestown was as unfamiliar to Seamus as it was to him that he'd have an advantage, but he'd forgotten about the bond between sire and sireling. At the time, his vampiric life force had been connected to Seamus, and so his master had used it to hunt him down. As punishment, Seamus had left him on the deck of the ship during the midday. Roger had scrambled from sliver of shade to shade. His skin had burned, and he'd had deep blisters that took nights to heal since he wasn't allowed much blood.

And the gold ring had remained bright and shining.

Roger flexed his hand, unsure of when exactly he'd reopened his eyes. The memory had fully swept his attention. Out of an old habit, he went to spin his gold ring around his finger, but his finger was bare. Anton put a cursed ring on every vampire that Seamus held dominion over. The ring wouldn't fall off until one was strong enough to be their own master. It was a constant reminder of weakness and Seamus's claim.

Roger's had fallen off in 1989. He'd worn it anyway, but whoever had cursed him with the sleep spell had also taken the ring. Or perhaps it had just slipped off his finger and his captor hadn't noticed. He had a replica in his pocket, and he took it out to examine it. Anton might realize there was no magic in it, but he doubted Seamus would notice the difference. *This is our collar. If I don't begin to wear it, I'll never pass myself off as a devoted follower.*

"Do you think I like this?" he'd said.

And Zack had sounded so sure in his response. "You've been doing it for hundreds of years, so some part of you must."

But had he?

No. Doing nothing and liking what was happening were two different behaviors. *But I can't blame him for being angry.* Because Roger should have felt ... something. Looking over the past, he had a numbness where some emotions might have been. Even now, safe in the present, he pushed away the memories before the disgust and sadness could infiltrate his heart.

The sliding door to the suite opened with a soft woosh. No breathing or heartbeat accompanied the one stepping through the doorway.

Roger closed his hand around the ring and shoved it back into his pocket. Using his smoothest voice, he asked, "Is there something I can do for you, Takashi?"

"You have a visitor." Takashi had left his suit jacket behind, loosened his tie, and undone the top two buttons of his dress shirt. His black hair had broken free of the stranglehold gel on it, but only by a small measure, just enough to tempt Roger to run fingers through his hair. He had perfected the casual businessman look decades ago, and modern tailoring suited him better. He slid his hands into his pockets as he took another step out onto the balcony. "Dmitri would like a word."

Turning, Roger had a view of the hotel suite. The light of the room was bright against the midnight darkness. Kit and Carver were sitting on one of the black leather couches, watching some program on the television. Dmitri stood in the center of the living room in a stark suit without a trace of mirth in his features. Somber had always been Dmitri's default state. Becoming a vampire had only exaggerated his stoic, broody demeanor.

"Come out here," Roger said.

Dmitri scowled, then made his way out into the darkness. He stood beside the sliding glass door and motioned for Takashi to go inside.

"Anything you have to say can be said in front of him," Roger said.

A ripple went across Dmitri's features. The motion was quick and subtle, but Roger had seen that undercurrent of anger back when they were mortal men. He closed the door harsher than necessary. Completely disregarding Takashi, he said, "You told him?"

"Technically, Nell did." Roger leaned back against the railing. Around Dmitri, he had always been the casual one, and he slid into the old, comfortable habit of pretending not to give a shit. But he watched. He searched for details. Zack and his notebooks had stressed the importance of minutia, and while unlikely, Dmitri could have been the one who worked with the Unseelie who cursed him. "But consider him informed."

"I wouldn't mind a little more information, if I'm honest," Takashi said as he strode across the balcony to stand beside Roger.

"I could use some myself," Dmitri said, Russian accent thick. "We have been planning your return for two months, and the night before you arrive, you text that you're bringing another boy and Nell's lackey."

"Former lackey," Takashi replied.

Dmitri snorted in disbelief.

"I have the writ rescinding her claim to him," Roger said. "Signed in her blood and witnessed by myself and Zack."

"She released you?" Dmitri asked. "Has she lost her mind?"

Takashi leaned against the railing near Roger. "She has her concerns, of which I do not owe you an explanation. Depending on your point of view, I am here as either Roger's hostage against Nell's wrath or her assurance that Roger doesn't screw her over." He grinned coyly at Roger. "Though I'd be lying if I said being with you is a hardship. I have missed you."

"We have had good times." Roger smiled back at Takashi.

Dmitri shook his head. "But to excuse you from her coven—"

"Zack threatened to kill him if he was still politically bound to her," Roger said.

"I do admire him for that," Takashi said. "I was about to voice a concern that you would murder me once the deed was done, and then he issued his threat. Thankfully, that made my argument a piece of cake."

"You wanted to leave Nell?" Roger folded his arms over his chest.

"I love her, I do. Best sire in the world—and I have traveled far and wide enough to know. But to be stuck serving a master whose ambition is the status quo of her 'perfect' domain?" Takashi shuddered. "I have been seeking a way out that benefited both of us since that was the only way she'd grant permission for me to leave."

"Glad I could be of service," Roger replied.

"Don't be cross with me. I'm excited for this." Takashi grinned broadly and glanced between Roger and Dmitri. "A coup of this magnitude? It's been decades since anyone even considered."

"Someone tried to take out Seamus recently?" Roger asked.

"No, Parysatis in Cairo, 1977," Takashi replied. "They're still talking about her wrath the evening she smote the individuals attempting to take her place."

"This isn't a damn adventure," Dmitri snapped. "If we do not watch our every step, Seamus will catch on and murder the group of us."

"We're aware of the risks," Roger said. "Did you come to give anything besides grim warnings?"

"If you're asking about Quinn's accounts, I've told you it will take time to untangle them," Dmitri said. "I came because I had to ask, what the hell are you thinking?"

Roger rolled his eyes and relaxed against the railing again. Internally, he was running through what his potential answers could be. He needed Dmitri on his side, but he could be fussy. "Nell isn't happy about how long the money is taking, so Takashi is here to ensure that we aren't scamming her out of a few million and gathering enough intel to dismantle her empire."

"And the new boy?"

"He offered himself," Roger replied, "and made quite the spectacle doing so. I could hardly refuse him."

Dmitri muttered in Russian, "Always thinking with your dick."

"And my fangs," Roger replied in Russian. He flashed his fangs at Dmitri.

"Is there a reason we're switching languages?" Takashi said, also in Russian.

"You learned Russian!" Roger exclaimed and tapped Takashi on the shoulder. "You were stumbling over it in the '80s."

Takashi smiled, a smaller, more genuine gesture. "You were impressed I was aiming for my twelfth language. I'm learning my fourteenth."

"English, Japanese, French, Spanish, German, Arabic, Chinese, Hindi, Dutch, obviously Russian," Roger listed as he switched back to English. "Damn, I've forgotten the others."

"Farsi and Portuguese," Takashi replied. "I've learned Korean, and I'm studying Thai."

"Very impressive!" Dmitri blustered with clear frustration. "Can we get back to the matter at hand!"

"Which would be?" Roger asked coolly.

"What is the plan?" Dmitri said.

"I don't know," Roger replied.

"You don't ..." Dmitri shook his head and paced between the couches only to stop three steps into it. "Of course you don't have one. That would require *thinking*."

"Hold on," Takashi said.

Roger held up a hand toward Takashi to quiet him, then said, "I don't have a *specific* plan. I need to reestablish my position in the coven before I do anything. Once I can get a lay of the land, we'll be able to discuss a more thorough plan."

"Your *position*?" Dmitri said.

"I wouldn't have asked for your help in organizing my return so I could murder Seamus the first night," Roger replied. "If I am to lead, then I need to ensure I won't be stabbed in the back in the first ten minutes."

Dmitri was typically an emotionless vampire and careful with his expressions. But he became still as stone. "You want to lead the coven?"

"I do," Roger replied.

"What about Anton?"

"You want him in charge?" Roger asked incredulously.

"*No*. When do you plan on killing him?"

"Hopefully we'll devise an attack that will remove them both at the same time, but Anton is not my primary threat. I'm certain he'll come for me once Seamus is dead, but if I can rally the coven to my side, we will have an army to fight him," Roger said. "That's why I have to spend time with the coven before I strike."

"How long do you think it will take?" Dmitri asked.

"You're the one who has been here. Do people even remember me? Would they follow me?" Roger replied.

"I haven't been paying attention to whether or not they *like* you," Dmitri said, his tone cold as the grave. "But you've never been forgotten."

"That's something, then," Takashi said quietly.

"It will take a few weeks to gauge the others. Once we've taken the temperature, we can establish a timetable," Roger said. "We're going to Candide's new donor house in the suburbs tomorrow."

"It's popular," Takashi said. "Zack and I should be able to get a read on a few people."

"Where is the hunter?" Dmitri asked.

"Sleeping off a night of excessive alcohol," Roger replied.

"Of course you've chosen a party boy over someone useful. Your collection is always better for fucking than thinking," Dmitri snarled.

Using a burst of speed, Roger closed the distance between him and Dmitri. They were less than an inch from each other. Once upon a time, Roger would have pulled Dmitri to him, smiled, and kissed his neck until Dmitri relaxed. But they hadn't been like that in over a century, and wishing would never melt Dmitri's walls. "You will not insult Zackery or any of my people again if you know what is good for you. Do we have an understanding?"

"I suppose I should expect more of the same once you take over for Seamus," Dmitri growled under his breath. "Another violent tyrant."

The words were a blow, and Roger rocked onto his heels, taking a half step back.

"I believe we've had enough of a conference for the evening," Takashi said. He put his hand on Dmitri's chest and pushed him back toward the sliding glass door. "Do your part, Dmitri, and get Roger his money."

Dmitri kept his heated gaze locked on Roger. "He hasn't given me what I need to manipulate a few accounts in his favor. Otherwise, how do you explain this suite? The clothes? He dropped everything."

"*Me*," Takashi said fiercely. "Now that I've left Nell's coven, I can feel comfortable in publicly declaring my relationship to the captain of another coven. Which means no one will bat a fucking eye at our lifestyle or that I've been helping my beloved build a new fortune far from the prying eyes of mortals and immortals alike. If your firm is any good, then they won't gossip about not seeing his money. And if it isn't, then I have to wonder why Roger or any other vampire is trusting *you*."

By the time Takashi had finished, they were at the glass door. He opened it for Dmitri, but Dmitri didn't step through right away. Instead, he continued to glare at Roger with a heat that chilled Roger into his bones. How little did they know of each other that Dmitri thought Roger would be as cruel as Seamus? In a daze at the implication that he could be anything like his sire, Roger didn't bother to watch Takashi march Dmitri out of the hotel suite. He went back to the edge of the balcony and leaned on the railing, staring out into the night.

Takashi returned a minute later. He had a casual grace in his stance that must have been with him as a mortal. After a moment of watching the darkness, he brought his gaze back to Roger, but Roger continued to stare out at the night. Silence could be a conversation in itself. Over the course of their limited time together, they had developed the sort of bond that didn't need constant chatter to be understood.

Slowly, Roger glanced toward Takashi and took in his stance and expression. Now that the shock of Dmitri's insults had worn off, Roger could appreciate how quickly Takashi had jumped to his defense. He straightened and kept one hand on the rail. Takashi stepped in closer and gently put his hand on Roger's chest.

Kissing him would be a simple thing. He'd find reassurance there, and he'd provide some comfort for Takashi, too. Dmitri's presence had rattled him, and he could see traces of tension in Takashi from the encounter as well. Takashi's blue eyes had a low smolder in them, and he gently brushed his fingers down the line of Roger's buttons.

As Takashi tilted his head up, signaling for a kiss, Roger stepped back and let the contact between them drift off into the chill breeze. "I haven't spoken to Zack about our relationship."

Takashi chuckled softly and looked out into the night before regarding Roger again. He had kindness in his eyes, and it warmed his smile. "You should have that conversation with him. He's not sure you're even dating."

"How do you know that?" Roger asked.

Takashi had the decency to look away as he said, "I've read his journal."

"What?" Roger moved to his side.

"Don't be upset with me." Takashi sighed and slumped his shoulders. "Nell's known about his notebooks this whole time. She's been making copies for weeks. She's even carefully duplicated his leather journal. The flight from Cairo was decently long, and considering many of his notes are what I already know, I focused on his journal."

"Takashi—"

"It was a violation, I understand that," Takashi said quickly as he straightened. "I hope you won't tell him what I did, but Roger, you have to see things from my perspective." His smile faded to a worried frown. "You were *gone*. I know our closeness was somewhat transient, but you vanished. And suddenly, you are back, and there is this kid at your side. A Wright! And everything I could find online pointed to the same sort of vapid, selfish pets you prefer—don't make that face because you know if we argue that point, I will win—but when I read his journal, I discovered a caring, thoughtful young man. Do you have any idea how worried he is about *you*?"

"Me?" Roger frowned.

"He is one of the most intuitive people I've met," Takashi said. "Despite your attempts to dance around the topic, he suspects the sort of abuse Seamus has done to you."

Roger hung his head to avoid Takashi and the world. There were nights that clung to the edges of his mind, constantly shoved away from the light of observance. He had found a path to survival in being the playboy. Because if he couldn't escape, he could tell himself he enjoyed his life as a vampire.

And most nights, he actually did. The thrill of feeling another's desire, the taste of blood in his mouth, the ability to live long enough to see the world change over and over and over. He loved what he was. *Would I if I had another choice?* The easy answer was yes, but he'd never stopped to pick apart his existence and face the potential dread. In order to do that, he'd have to analyze the nights he'd rather forget.

As if he could forget when Seamus backhanded him at the farmhouse for letting the pregnant hunter flee. As if he could modify the memories of the two decades he'd spent on a pirate ship to be filled with the wonder of being a new vampire instead of dreading what Seamus would demand of him on the deck and in his cabin. As if he wasn't haunted by the memories of the vampires Anton and Seamus had drained of life in secret and then animated so they could execute them in public as traitors. As if there weren't a thousand other nights of pain that tainted every one of peace.

What had Takashi pieced together? What had Roger let slip?

I do not have time to fall apart. Roger quickly wiped the

bloody tears forming in the corners of his eyes and turned the motion into dramatically sweeping his hair back as he raised his chin. "He shouldn't worry. Neither should you."

"As you wish," Takashi said, though his expression and body language said he would worry anyway, and that was no trouble to him. "If he doesn't want to share you and you agree with that, I won't throw myself at your feet and beg you to change your mind. You'll at least be with someone decent who cares about you deeply. I can respect that."

"We'll need to continue the act like a couple in public," Roger said. He nodded to the living room. "That includes in front of Kit and Carver."

"You can only call things an act for so long before they become a reality." Takashi moved to sit on one of the couches. "I don't believe Kit or Carver will fall for it for a second. They'll likely wonder why we're trying to lie to them and everyone else."

"Fuck. I hadn't thought of that."

"Is there a reason you're keeping them in the dark about your intentions?"

Roger sat on the couch across from Takashi. "The fewer that know, the fewer potential leaks."

Takashi gave a nod of acknowledgment. "I'm sure we can spin things if we need to. Are we sharing them?"

"If they're amenable to it." Roger threaded his hand through his hair. The wind was starting to tangle it. "Why don't you have any pets of your own?"

"Masters of other covens believe they're handing off a spy if they allow me to borrow people, which they usually are." Takashi slumped and finally looked as if he was truly relaxing. "Life as an ambassador vampire is exhausting."

"Trust must be hard to have."

"Another reason I read Zack's journal," Takashi replied.

Roger started to play with where his ring should sit. When his fingers brushed nothing, he remembered the gold ring in his pocket. He was asking everyone else in his life to lie, and he wasn't carrying out the simplest one himself. But even thinking about reaching for it reminded him of the donors on the plane and their gray armbands.

If Zack can wear the collar, I can do this. Roger slipped the gold ring onto his finger.

Clearing his throat, he said, "I've caught up as much as I can about the GLC. What can you tell me about international affairs?"

"Plenty," Takashi said with a sly grin. "Where shall I start?"

"Cairo and what happened in 1977," Roger replied. "Let's not repeat anyone else's mistakes."

CHAPTER 10

Sunlight was both the bane of Zack's existence and the sweetest treat in all the world. He'd nabbed a pair of Roger's sunglasses, which made an incredible dent in the brightness. The balcony was a wonderful place to stretch out, though he'd picked lying on the cold concrete over one of the couches. The wind made wearing a hoodie pleasant, and he didn't have to wear one of his collars since he wasn't leaving the suite.

"All right, next part of the story," Blake said as she munched on a tortilla chip. After a few texts, she'd arrived with takeout and coffee. She was perhaps Zack's favorite person. "You got to the hotel, and then what?"

Zack groaned and put his arm over his head. "Could we stop?"

"Nope," Kit said sweetly. They nudged Zack with their foot. "Someone turns into an incredible ass when he's drunk."

Kit and Blake had been the ones to decorate his room with get-well presents after Cal's attack. Blake had brought him coffee from her aunt's shop on multiple occasions, and Kit had sat with him and watched movies and hadn't said shit when he'd sporadically cried in the first couple of weeks. The three of them had a group chat where they tossed memes back and forth.

If anyone was allowed to tease him for overdoing it, it was them.

And in the light of day, the previous night's drinking and ragey behavior made Zack's stomach churn. Ignoring everything in favor of the way the sunlight warmed his face was easier. *But is that the way you become dead to the world? Just shoving away the pain?* He lifted his arm off his face and said, "I was an asshole. And currently, my head is pounding, my taste buds are only accepting grease and coffee, and all I want to do is sleep, but we have to go out tonight. I. Am. Never. Drinking. Again."

"Okay, but what happened?" Blake plucked a chip from a bag.

"Zack and I took a tour of the suite, and then he went hunting for more alcohol. Got his hands on a bottle of vodka before Roger literally picked him up and carried him off to the bedroom," Kit said. "I am almost surprised he didn't vomit all over Roger's back."

"I wasn't going to vomit." Zack rolled over onto his stomach and repositioned the pillow that had been under his head. They had all cheated and brought some of the inside couch pillows out to the balcony to make the space more comfortable. "It all stayed in."

"Until this morning," Kit teased.

"I don't miss hangovers," Blake said. "Shifter constitution has its bonuses."

"Someone could've tried to cut me off last night," Zack complained.

Kit snorted. "Dude, you were in a psycho-hunter mindset until you got a few drinks in you. Then you at least had moments where you weren't angry."

Zack sat up quickly, which was a mistake. He managed to keep his lunch of tacos and chips from coming back up, but only barely. His hangover was diminishing but not gone. "You get that those 'donors' last night didn't have the mental capacity to be willing, right?"

Blake dropped her chip. "What? What are you talking about?"

"They came from Steward's Garden. I've read up on the place," Zack said, not bothering to hide the venom from his voice. He didn't have to with these two, even if Kit was still wearing their red collar when they didn't have to. "I'm pretty sure it's a hotspot for human trafficking. And they had these gray armbands that were clearly magical and these blank expressions. It looked like mind control to me."

"Oh my God, really?" Blake asked, horrified.

Kit set aside their taco. "Okay, I didn't look close, and I don't know shit about magic, all right?"

"I *do*," Zack said.

"It's not like I could do anything," Kit said.

"People thinking they're powerless is why this kind of shit persists!" Zack slapped his hand against the concrete underneath him. It stung, and he waved his hand, trying to shake off the pain.

"Maybe the system persists because of the overbearing power of the ones in control," Blake murmured. When Zack glanced her way, she pushed her sunglasses up. Over the last two months, she'd grown more confident. Instead of keeping her long dyed-purple hair over her face, she had her hair tuck into a messy bun and let it grow out to show natural brown. The long scars that ran across her face would always be obvious, but she wasn't hiding them as much anymore.

Unlike Kit, she wasn't a born shifter. She'd been attacked and contracted lycanthropy. She and Zack had bonded over researching more about werewolves and even a little about the packs of Chicago.

She leaned forward and spoke. "Consider how messed up America is. Rich white people have ruthlessly steered this country into countless atrocities, and some of them are *still* at it, no matter how much the public says no. They put the system in place that benefits them and don't give a rat's ass about anyone else. And they won't relinquish an ounce of that power, even if it would create them greater fortunes and save the goddamn world. They have this self-fulfilling bull-shit belief that the only way to feel powerful is to stand on others.

"Now, consider that the weakest supernatural is literally stronger than the above-average human. That vampires live forever and can twist a human's desires to their whims. That the fey can charm and bewitch them and fucking vanish from our realm instead of facing justice. That a werewolf can go on a murder spree in their wolf form, and no mortal authority would be the wiser because humans don't believe in the supernatural. You can't be surprised that the systems they've created don't even consider humans. They are preda-tors, and just like how humans don't consider the feelings of the cow in the herd, the supernatural see their food and nothing else."

"People *care*," Zack said defensively.

"*Individuals* care," Blake countered. "Just like how indi-vidual supernaturals don't like every aspect of their systems either."

She's right. And I hate that she's right. There has to be a way to make change.

After a silent staring contest between Zack and Blake went on for a minute, Kit grabbed their bottle of water and took a long drink. As they screwed the cap back on, they nudged Zack and Blake both. "Y'all are wrecking a beautiful after-noon and making me anxious about tonight. The world sucks. The best we can do is be kind. Let's move on."

"You want to just 'move on' from the fact that humans don't matter?" Zack demanded.

"I don't want to obsess over it constantly," Kit snapped.

"Is there anything wrong with taking a break and enjoying ourselves?"

Before Zack could answer, Blake piped up. "Nope. And I have the perfect idea."

"What?" Zack said.

Blake tapped Kit in the face with her pillow, and they whacked her with theirs in return. Lifting an eyebrow, Blake raised her pillow again and made a swipe at Zack. He leaned out of the way, and then Kit was swinging theirs at him.

A pillow fight was a ludicrous idea. But it was a better way to blow off steam than going through the same mental circles he'd been making. Zack scrambled to his feet and grabbed a cushion from the couch no one was sitting on. Wielding that as a shield and his pillow as his weapon, he said, "I've got two siblings and ten cousins. Bring it."

Mentioning his family, even offhanded, threatened to bring the anguish of their disownment to the surface, but Kit was swinging for his head, and there was no time to get caught in sadness. Zack pushed past the mental block and dived into the mock battle. He was with friends, and they were smiling and laughing, and he could do that too. Between the sunshine and the joy of catching them off guard and stepping around the mess they'd made with their lunch, he had no space for the dread that plagued him.

Mid-fight, he chucked his pillow at Kit's head. They dodged, and the pillow sailed over the balcony edge. All three of them hurried to the railing to watch it tumble to the ground forty floors below.

"Do you think they'll know where it came from?" Blake asked.

"I'm more worried it'll hurt someone," Zack muttered.

"It's a pillow," Kit replied. "How much damage could it do?"

"Has it hit? I lost track of it," Zack said.

Blake squinted. "I can't tell."

Kit rested their head on top of their hands on top of the railing. "Yup. Landed in the middle of the street. Doesn't seem to be screwing with the traffic."

"Ah, there it is!" Blake said. "Still getting used to super vision."

"What are we watching?" Carver asked.

All three of them jumped, though Zack was the first to spin around and face the hotel suite. Carver sauntered out onto the balcony and into the sunlight. He was wearing a pair of sunglasses, sweatpants, and a matching zip-up sweatshirt that he hadn't zipped. In one hand, he had a glass of water while the other he kept in his pocket. Though he seemed to be going for casual indifference, Zack spotted the tension in his lips and the way he held his shoulders.

Bits of the drunken night were playing over for him. Zack had been so wrapped up in his anger he'd ignored how Carver had ordered him shots based on insightful questions about what he'd liked. He'd been cruel when Roger was taking him out of the room just because he could.

Zack stepped away from the railing and toward Carver. This next step wouldn't be easy, but he'd been the asshole. He sucked in a deep breath. "Carver, I—"

Carver had closed a good distance. And when he came to a stop, he threw his glass of water in Zack's face. Kit and Blake gasped.

Cold water splashed all over his front, and Zack took his sleeve and wiped as much as he could off his face. "Yep. Deserved that. Uh, can you guys give Carver and I a minute?"

"Yup," Kit said and grabbed as much of the trash as they could.

Blake grabbed the rest and followed Kit. She whispered, "What did I miss?"

"I'll fill you in on what I know," Kit replied quietly.

Will they be able to hear us through the door? Zack cleared his throat. "I'm sorry for what I said last night. I was drunk, and that's a really bad excuse. I shouldn't have said what I said."

Carver took another step forward so they were less than two inches apart. He took off his sunglasses and glared down at Zack. With his broad shoulders and extra three inches, Zack wasn't sure if he was intimidated or slightly aroused by Carver's proximity. Carver growled, "If last night had been the first time you were a jackass, I'd write it off, but something tells me that's your true colors. Which is a fucking shame."

"Wait, what?" Zack said.

Carver used his sunglasses to accentuate his point by poking the end into Zack's chest as he talked. "You've been walking around Taliville with this chip on your shoulder, which I thought was because you're the head pet of a powerful vamp. Then I find out that you've got Roger wrapped around your finger and you're boyfriends. I'm okay with that. Vamps can get weird, so of course he's going to tell everyone his mortal boyfriend is his head pet. Makes sense."

"Roger said we're boyfriends?" Zack asked. His head was spinning, and he couldn't blame the hangover.

"Basically." Carver clenched his jaw. "He made it very clear that *your* happiness matters more than me. That if I pissed *you* off, I'd be out on my ass. And I made my arrangement with Roger because I am okay with that. He also made it clear that you've got some kind of panic hang-up with affection stuff, and I promised not to push it. I mean, before I assumed you froze up when I flirted with you because you were having a hard time being gay, so I was kicking myself. I thought if I just kept putting myself out there, you'd eventually come around.

"But it turns out you're a fucking insecure jerk who would rather throw insults and choke on the bile his family force-fed him than open his goddamn eyes and see that there's a whole fucking world out there for the taking if he just played the fucking cards he's been dealt." Carver lowered his sunglasses, and his frown grew deeper. "And you have been dealt a fucking amazing hand. Clever, intense, and sexy. You're a goddamn dream, except your fucking attitude turns you into a freaking nightmare, and I don't get how *you're* what Roger wants. Except, seeing you with Blake and Kit just now? I realize you're not an asshole to everyone. Just to *me*, and that fucking *sucks*."

In the middle of Carver's speech, Zack puffed up, ready to unleash his own rant at him about how off base he was and how he knew nothing about him. But as he watched Carver's face, he spotted the tears starting to form in the corners of his eyes and the deepening of his frown. He was holding back a sadness.

While Carver had come on strong, he'd never been mean. He was confident, or at least he seemed that way, but Zack had picked up crumbs of rumors. Another master had dropped him. He'd been working the donor house, but no one had claimed him, and Zack had never bothered to find out why. Reed had told him that people like Carver were always chasing their next meal ticket, and he'd written Carver off as a fang lover and a headache to endure.

But what had he seen Carver do? Flirt with him. Express interest in Roger. Ask how he could be part of Roger's group. Be open about his desires. Nothing that marked him as a bad guy. And here he was, upset that Zack had been cruel and almost crying about it. Either he was the best actor in the world or—*I've been such a jerk.*

"I'm sorry," Zack said gently, deflating as he did.

Carver blinked at him, but his frown eased a little. "That's all you got for me?"

Zack shoved his hand through his hair. "Come on, man. Can you cut me some slack?"

Carver folded his arms over his chest. The tears in his eyes seemed to be stopping before they actually started. "Maybe."

"We're not on a level where I'm going to bare my soul to you," Zack replied. "But I promise no more bullshit. And no more insults—did I say more than one? The night's a little blurry for me in some spots."

"You made a few comments under your breath," Carver said. "Most of them were too slurred to understand."

Zack rubbed the back of his neck. "I am never drinking again."

With a snort, Carver unfolded his arms and patted Zack on the shoulder. "You weren't that bad. I know you're the top of the pecking order, but I didn't want you to push me around. So I had to say something."

"I needed the reality check," Zack said. "Sorry we didn't include you in the tacos."

"Eh, I ordered room service. There's way too much of it since I got some for you guys. Didn't know you'd already ate. Thought I'd surprise you," Carver said.

"Aw, man. I'm just the biggest asshole ever."

Carver grinned and tousled Zack's hair. "I'm messing with you. I saw you guys out here before I ordered."

"Keep digging at me and I'm going to bite back," Zack joked.

"Promise to bite somewhere fun?" Carver teased.

Heat crawled up Zack's neck. "Not today."

As Carver walked backward toward the sliding glass door, he slid his sunglasses into a pocket and continued to smile at him. "But maybe someday, huh?"

Was there any harm in having a bit of fun? Everything else was shitty. Zack could try to relax just a little. He laughed and shook his head as he followed Carver into the suite. "Sure. *Maybe*. If you're lucky."

CHAPTER 11

Roger stretched one arm over his head and leaned against the doorframe leading into the master bathroom. His red silk shirt was coming untucked, but he could always fix it before they left. The way Zack's gaze darted to his hip to steal a glance of his bare skin was worth having to readjust his clothing later. When he'd woken, Zack was already out of bed and in the living room with Kit and Carver. He'd been freshly sweaty from a workout, which had sparked Roger's hunger.

Roger had gotten dressed, brushed his long black hair and pulled half of it into a loose ponytail to keep it out of his face, and changed his gold stud earring for a hoop. He'd taken his time with each step to allow his focus to distract him from his growing thirst and a burning desire to do more than taste Zack's skin in a kiss.

The humid air carried the lingering scents of Zack's sandalwood shampoo and soap. He stood at the sink, towel wrapped around his hips and shaving cream across his jaw and cheeks. After sneaking a peek at Roger, he stroked down his cheek with his razor.

"Why am I always the one waiting for you to finish getting ready?" Roger mused.

"Because it takes you like a decade to grow a beard," Zack replied.

"I would have stubble in a week."

"Yeah, well, I get it every day, and I haven't done this without a mirror before." Zack swore and dropped his razor into the sink. "Ow, fuck."

"Here." Roger strolled across the bathroom's marble floor and took his own straight razor from the second sink. He faced Zack and swung the blade out. "Let me."

"Sure you don't want to use mine?" Zack said nervously.

"The one you just managed to cut yourself with?" Roger leaned against the sink. "I could, but I've far more practice with this. When I first started shaving, I had to do it with the small knife I kept in case there was a rope I needed to cut in a hurry. Straight razors—what's the phrase? Right, they 'weren't a thing.'"

"You're *old*, got it." Zack sighed and closed his eyes. "All right. Do it."

"Don't purse your lips." Roger gently tilted Zack's face so he had a better angle and began to carefully shave his cheek. "You seem in a better mood than last night."

Zack squirmed. Luckily, Roger felt his tension before he moved and had a chance to move the blade away from his skin. "I let bullshit get to me."

"Oh?" Roger asked lightly. He glided the blade across Zack's skin and settled into a rhythm.

"Don't pretend you didn't notice," Zack replied between strokes. "Carver kind of let me know I was being an asshole to him."

"I did wonder what your problem with him was," Roger said evenly.

Zack opened his eyes, though from his angle, he could barely meet Roger's gaze. "I ... I know I'm not the kind of guy you usually go for. He is."

"Is he." Gingerly, Roger removed more of the shaving cream. "And what do you know about my love life?"

A tense silence closed Zack's lips. In such an intimate space, hints of Zack's desires were slipping out past his usual protections. The sensation Roger understood was an attempt to close a door. Zack didn't want to reveal something.

Which meant he *knew* something, and with Zack, that could be one thing or a million secrets. And he hadn't said a word about any of them to Roger. Had he written them down? Did Nell and Takashi know whatever Zack had discovered? What did he know anyway? Dmitri's crass remark about how Roger acted for sexual pleasure reverberated. Did Zack think like that? Why did every intelligent man that Roger adored believe he was a thoughtless sex fiend?

Roger continued shaving Zack's left jaw and cheek, moving on to the other side, but he had to pause when Zack shifted his weight from one leg to another. That wasn't a problem, until he did it again less than a second later.

"You know, maybe I can finish the whole shave thing because you've got to be getting hungry. You should do something about that," Zack said.

"This will take me less time than it would you. Though it would be easier if you stop squirming," Roger replied.

Zack sucked in a breath. "I wouldn't be squirming if you hadn't gotten all cold."

"I 'got all cold' because my boyfriend decided he preferred stalking me instead of asking me about my past relationships."

Zack caught Roger's wrist and guided his hand—and therefore, the straight razor—away from his face. With a serious voice, he said, "You're the one who asked me to investigate the GLC so I could be well-informed. It's not my fault that includes most of your former boyfriends." He swallowed hard. "And I caught that you just called me your boyfriend, and I want to talk about that. But I'm not in the mood to hear about how I'm a fuckup for doing what you asked."

Roger put the blade down on the counter and then gripped the edge of the red marble top. "I have never thought you were a fuckup."

"Then what's all this?" Zack motioned at Roger's face. "I thought I'd gotten pretty good at reading you, but this is the second time you've pulled out Master Vampire face, and I'm not a fan."

"This"—Roger pointed at his own face—"is because I *am* a master vampire in need of a domain, and I'm concerned that the man I'm trusting thinks I'm the fuckup!"

Zack glanced over his shoulder. The door was closed, but when he turned back toward Roger, he whispered, "My life is literally in your hands tonight and every night from here on out. I get to be fucking worried that we don't have a plan, okay?"

"We had a very basic plan at Nell's party to deal with Quinn, remember?" Roger snapped. "And how did that go for us?"

"Well, he's dead, and we're not, so that's a win," Zack replied.

"Yes. But it didn't happen according to plan, did it? And you were surrounded by a half dozen vampires."

"It went almost to plan. You got there in time."

Roger motioned at the living room. "I got there because Carver pointed me in the right direction, and he told Dmitri and Josefina to meet us in the garden."

"He did?"

"I didn't know his name at the time, but *yes*. It was him." Roger sighed and leaned backside against the counter, resting both his hands on the edge now. "I met him at the donor house while you were recovering. I've only ever had his blood, Zackery, despite the fact that he wants more and I'm interested."

Zack folded his arms over his chest. He dipped his head down for a heartbeat, which wasn't long because his pulse was thundering. Once Roger had tuned in to it, he was distracted until Zack raised his head and spoke. "Is this where we loop back around to you calling me your boyfriend?"

"If you can first admit that your research into my love life is incomplete data since we've never talked about it before," Roger replied.

"It's not *that* incomplete," Zack said sharply. When Roger started to glare, he added, "The emotional ins and outs, yeah, okay. I don't have the personal side of it. But you, yourself, have told me that you usually have multiple pets. You've told me that you usually have a special connection to them. And I know you well enough to figure out that you were dating a vampire or two while you kept pets and that, for you, keeping is basically dating. And I've seen enough pictures to know they're way hotter than me."

Roger rolled so that he was face-to-face with Zack and put a hand on the counter on either side of him. From this position, Zack couldn't hide while Roger spoke to him. "You are a terrible judge of hotness if you find nothing beautiful about yourself."

"Have you seen Dmitri? Takashi? Carver?" Zack bit his bottom lip, and he did try to avoid Roger's gaze, but they were too close together. After a slight rocking motion, he sighed heavily and dropped his shoulders. "Come on. Even Quinn was fucking hot."

"Stars have half the shine of your gray eyes, and the wind only pretends to have a measure of your boldness," Roger whispered. "A hundred poets could spend a hundred years, and yet they would not capture the subtle grace in the way you tilt your head before you laugh. They would fail to note how a pencil spins between your deft fingers like a ballerina's pirouette because they would be caught off guard with the way you grin when you've discovered a clue. They would be too drawn to how you wield your dagger as if it is a flawless extension of your arm to notice the line of your back leads perfectly to the round shape of your ass. And likely none of them would spot the flustered smile that dances across your lips in a moment whenever you're far too turned on to speak because it vanishes as you strangle that desire out of fear."

Zack hadn't looked away, and Roger had held his gaze through the entire makeshift poem. He sunk against the counter as Roger spoke. His breathing picked up slowly, and his heart continued in its steady, quickened race. Along with sandalwood and mortal iron, he began to smell of his want, a bubbling lust that was seeping upward.

Roger waited for Zack to put the lid on that want. He usually did, and all Roger could do was admire the control that took. They had been together more than a few times, but nothing had been like that first time, when Roger stroked Zack to completion and only watched him in his pleasure. As much as they could make each other come, that time had meant more than any of the others so far.

Because Zack had held back all those other times. He had fun—Roger had seen that—but there hadn't been the need in him like he'd needed to be touched the first time.

"I guess you have noticed me," Zack murmured.

Roger grinned at him. "Maybe a little."

Zack scoffed and managed a small laugh. He straightened, and Roger mimicked his motion, going to his full height, which was nearly half a foot taller. Zack leaned his head back to keep his gaze locked with Roger's. "How come you haven't slept with Carver?"

"Because," Roger said lightly, "we have an undefined thing going, and I would never dream of hurting you."

"So if I said you couldn't, that'd be it. You just wouldn't be with anyone else? Not even Takashi?"

"I wouldn't." Roger nudged in closer, sliding one leg

between Zack's. "If we agree otherwise, you could find other partners, too."

"And you would be okay with that?" Zack grinned impishly. "You'd be all right if someone else noticed how my eyes shine brighter than starlight?"

Roger took Zack's chin between his thumb and forefinger. "I'd hope he would be someone we share or that at the least I know them well. You deserve to be loved, Zack. I want you to have as many kinds of love and as many people that you can handle. I want you to have so much love in your life that you never feel alone in the dark again. Because you are worth *all* of it."

Luminous wonder filled Zack's steely eyes, but Roger tenderly held him in place and made him wait for the kiss he gently touched to his lips. Only then did he slide his hand along Zack's jaw and toward the back of his head to cup him. Zack's touch was warm, his mouth a pleasure to explore, and Roger wrapped his arms around him as their kiss deepened.

CHAPTER 12

No one had ever told Zack that he was handsome in that many words. A few people had flirted with him; the dating app he'd tried had been an inconsistent stream of "ur hot" before he deleted it out of annoyance. Previous girlfriends and boyfriends had thought he was cute, but none had expressed the kind of longing that Roger had. They had never been a partner like Roger was trying to be.

Zack threw his arms around Roger's shoulders and melded up against him. Roger's arm around him tightened, and that was amazing. Feeling the strength in his arms sparked a buzz in his groin, a building want that threatened to overwhelm him unless he gave in. Responsibilities and schedules and a thousand minutia pressed toward his consciousness, but for once, he could find a way to push them out rather than to build his walls out of them and keep himself from feeling *this*. Roger kissed him like the world had stopped spinning for them, as if there was nothing but time.

Roger lifted Zack up to sit on the counter, and the towel became a binding. Zack flung it open so he could spread his legs and wrap them around Roger to bring him closer. With a moan, Roger kissed his neck and slid his hands down. He caressed Zack's inner thighs and eagerly pressed his legs wider, thumbs seeking deeper, brushing along sensitive skin that made Zack groan and his cock thicken. A hint of fang ended one of Roger's kisses.

Zack slid his hand along Roger's cheek and then placed his thumb under his jaw to push him back a fraction. He didn't have to worry about cutting off Roger's air like he would a mortal—Roger didn't need it. Heat was in Roger's eyes, and they had turned a shade of deep red.

"Bite me," Zack whispered.

Roger moaned and started for Zack's neck.

But Zack used his grip to keep him from that. "Not there. Down there. If you want."

"Are you sure?" Roger murmured as he glided his hand along Zack's inner thigh.

Zack nodded.

Slowly, Roger sank to his knees and kissed the base of Zack's cock before kissing his thigh. The buzzing of lust inside Zack started to build, and his hunter's tattoo on his hip warmed.

"Don't use your magic," Zack said, breath catching in his throat. Seeing Roger on his knees was rare, and having this vantage point was a blessing. He leaned back for a better view, and his hand knocked the straight razor into the sink. "I want to feel it."

"It'll hurt," Roger said, his voice a cool caress against Zack's skin.

"I know." Zack licked his lips. "I'm ready for it."

Roger stroked Zack's skin, seemingly idly, but his focus said the movements were calculated. He adjusted Zack's leg, and Zack shifted his weight to accommodate the new position easier. Anatomy lessons flickered through Zack's mind. There were some important arteries and veins in the area that Roger was assessing. If he bit in the wrong place ... Zack lost his breath as Roger opened his mouth, upper and lower fangs on full display.

Then Roger's grip turned into an icy vise, and he bit Zack's inner mid-thigh. The jolt of pain drew a low groan out of Zack, but the low burn was nothing like the injuries he'd sustained in combat. This was intense in a different way he had trouble figuring out. Because pain wasn't supposed to be something he liked, but this ... this felt good.

Roger's fangs only remained in his skin for a moment. As soon as the wound was made, Roger latched his mouth around it. His fangs still pressed against tender flesh, but they didn't slice into Zack again. Blood was spilling, and Roger was drinking it down.

And feeling him suck and draw the blood only made Zack harder. He'd gotten glimpses the few times Roger had drank from his wrists, but not a view like this. The ache in his leg was nothing compared to the sheer hotness that was having Roger drink *there* from *him*. Zack leaned up a little and took the ponytail out of Roger's hair so he could run his fingers through his dark locks and hold on to him.

With that light touch, he could feel Roger swallowing. Shame tried to rear its ugly head, but Roger moaned, and that vibrated through his leg and up through his groin.

"Hurry up so you can fuck me," Zack groaned. He tried to press up against Roger, only Roger had his leg locked in place against the counter. With a whimper, he added, "Please, Roger."

Roger lapped at the wound, his tongue warmer than it had been, before he leaned back to gaze up at Zack. His eyes were fading from red into brown again, and he had a heart-melting smile on his lips, even if they did have a smidge of Zack's blood making them a brighter red. Quickly, he licked his lips clean of the blood. He stood with a fluid grace that Zack felt through the way he had his hand in Roger's hair.

"Since you asked so nicely," Roger murmured. He picked Zack up in his arms and left behind the towel.

Zack grabbed at the bottles, knocking things aside until his hand landed on the lubricant. Roger chuckled against his cheek. A flash of warmth moved through Zack, but there was nothing spiteful in Roger's laugh. Only happiness. *I make him happy.* Zack held on tightly, wrapping his legs and arms around Roger as he was carried, and kissed Roger's cheeks and jaw.

They landed on the bed together. The bite wound smarted, but Zack was too busy undoing the buttons of Roger's silk shirt to give a damn. Chest to chest felt good; Roger's lube-covered fingers in his hole were even better.

Roger's dick was always cool to the touch, and somehow, that chillness in his touch was pure bliss inside Zack. In a few long thrusts, he was deeper and deeper in. Zack locked his right, uninjured leg around Roger's waist so he could feel every movement.

"Harder," Zack panted. "*Harder.*" And he kept saying it with every breath until Roger was rocking him with every thrust, until their eyes locked and Roger's brown eyes burned bright red with want.

All of that was for *him.* Because of *him.* He'd managed to turn Roger on. And for the first time, the power of that coiled in him and banished the shame and the doubts. He'd want what he wanted.

Still bouncing to every thrust slamming into the place that drove him toward ecstasy, he needed more. Longed for something *more.* He held his wrist against Roger's mouth.

The guttural moan that slipped out of Roger as he opened his mouth nearly made Zack come. Anticipation made him hold out.

Then, Roger bit his wrist.

Pain morphed to pleasure and redoubled as Roger rocked against his prostate, and Zack was floating. Bright white bloomed into pure darkness as he poured out of himself and was a joy without form. Dimly, his body tried to inform his spirit of the slight shifts, of Roger's moans and cool come. Instead of caring, he drifted.

Eventually, the fuzzy feeling started to fade. He … he'd been in the shower again. With Roger, who'd cleaned him up. Now Roger was … was taping a bandage around his wrist.

Roger grinned at him, relief in his eyes. "I was beginning to think I'd have to leave you here for the night."

"No," Zack said, the word a mouthful.

Roger brushed Zack's hair back and frowned in concern. "Actually, I probably should."

Zack caught his hand and held on tight. Reality was driving the fuzziness away. "It's an hour drive to the Chateau. I'll be fine by then. Promise."

"At least that was a couple complete sentences I could understand." Roger leaned in and kissed Zack's temple. "Are you sure?"

Zack nuzzled Roger and drank in his scent. Besides the shower, he smelled of dirt and ocean. He hung on to Roger's purple silk shirt—apparently, he'd gotten dressed before coming back for Zack—and rubbed one of the buttons. "My head's clearing, and I'm not aching too bad."

"All right. I've dressed your wounds." Roger pulled away from him. "Stand for me."

Zack did, managing not to wobble. Roger relaxed, his shoulders loosening, and he nodded at the bedroom. Zack walked out to it and spotted an outfit laid out on the bed for him. A dark purple fishnet shirt and a pair of shiny black biker shorts were at the end of the bed, while a pair of black boots and a pair of socks were on the floor beside it.

"You forgot the collar," Zack murmured. He went to the dresser, where his collars were laid out like prizes. He picked up the onyx, which was beside his thin silver bracelet. No more than an eighth of an inch thick, he ought to get away with wearing the bracelet. He held it up. "And you're hovering. Why are you hovering?"

Roger kissed his cheek and plucked the collar from his hand. He fastened it around Zack's neck while Zack put on the silver bracelet. "Because you let me drink from a new place and then offered your wrist at climax. You've never done that before."

Zack leaned back into Roger and then winced as the first flare of embarrassment pushed past the fuzzy ecstasy. "And I was … uh. Loud?"

"Very," Roger said with a soft rumble of pleasure. He wrapped his arms around Zack and stroked down the center of his chest with one hand. "I'm still unsure if I came because of the taste of your blood or the way you sounded as you came."

"Everyone probably heard," Zack said.

Roger spun Zack around in his arms, and the adrenaline of the sudden movement chased the fuzziness to the edges of his mind. Zack grabbed onto Roger's shoulders as Roger held him close. A fierce scowl crossed Roger's lips, but his eyes only had a blaze of righteous care in them. "I won't let anyone make fun of you. Not even you, if I can help it."

"Thanks," Zack said with a soft chuckle. He let his hands glide down Roger's arms before extracting himself from his hold. He slid into the fishnet shirt. "I think … I think I want to try it."

"Try what?" Roger asked.

"Being poly."

"Zack …"

"I get if you're worried this is postorgasm bliss, but it's deeper than that." Zack put on the shorts, trying his best not to flinch as he put too much weight on his injured leg. The wound wasn't that deep, but between it and the fucking, he was stiffer than usual. He sat on the edge of the bed to put on his socks and boots. "What we just shared was amazing. And I know letting people in means more than sex. But I'm curious. And you have all this love, and I don't want to hog it or be the only source of it. You deserve as much love as you can handle too."

Roger swept in for a kiss.

Zack grabbed him by the shirt and kept him close, lingering in the kiss. Then he murmured, "We don't hide those relationships, though."

"Of course not," Roger said. He kissed Zack quickly again. "If someone breaks your heart, I need to know who they are so I can rip them to shreds."

"Roger, you can't plan on killing potential ex-partners," Zack complained, but he couldn't help grinning.

"I'm a vampire. I completely can." Roger gave him another quick kiss before standing and holding his hand out. "Ready?"

"I still need to do my hair and makeup." Zack rubbed his chin, then narrowed his eyes. "Did you ever finish that shave?"

"Damn it, I knew I forgot something." Roger groaned. "At least this time, you're dressed."

Zack stood and held out his arms as he twisted around. "This counts as *dressed*? I mean, my perfectly round ass is in freaking spandex."

Roger laughed and nudged Zack toward the bathroom. "Well, I, at least, will be able to contain myself. For now."

"I don't know," Zack teased as he led the way. "All I had to do last time was be depressing and kiss you."

"I'd suggest we get a third party to ensure we stay on task, but honestly, any of the three available witnesses would probably enjoy the show," Roger said. With a sigh, he added, "But I am serious. We're going to be later than we should, and we don't want to upset Candide."

"Fine, fine, fine. I'll stay on target." Zack started to clean up the disorganized mess the bottles and various toiletries had become in order to find his shaving cream. "Let's get the shave done. I'll have Kit help me with the makeup in the limo."

CHAPTER 13

Where the attitude in the limo the previous night had been
filled with caution and drunken apprehension, the
atmosphere was more akin to the impromptu intimate parties
Roger was known for. The driver was a shifter that Dmitri
had helped Roger hire, so the five of them had the back of the
limousine to themselves. Kit, Zack, and Carver were dressed
for display. Like Zack, Kit wore a fishnet shirt, though theirs
was red to match their collar and hair, and shorter, slicker
shorts. Carver had forgone a shirt and wore only a pair of
sturdy black briefs along with his red collar.

Takashi had dark charcoal pants and a red dress shirt that
coordinated in shade with Roger's purple silk. He'd been
wearing the matching suit jacket until Roger suggested he
loosen up and leave it behind. The collar of his shirt was
undone, and he had gold cufflinks of tiny anchors on his
sleeves.

Kit had brought their makeup bag, and they embellished
Zack's natural features. Carver found the bottle of bourbon
hiding in a compartment and poured some for himself.

After Kit was done with Zack, they asked if Carver
wanted any, which led to a rabbit hole of a discussion

between the three of them about whether or not Carver needed any makeup at all. The arguments back and forth were the type that Roger had heard dozens of different times from different people in different eras.

But the smiles Zack kept sneaking his way were breathtakingly new.

Takashi shared the back seat with him while the other three were closer to the driver's partition. The limo could fit another half dozen in the space easily, but Kit and Zack had slid to where Carver had found the compartment of alcohol. Kit had joined in the drinking, but Zack hadn't.

Takashi said quietly to Roger, "He seems in a better mood."

"We talked a few things out," Roger replied under his breath.

"'Talked'?" Takashi nudged Roger's leg subtly.

"Maybe a bit more than talked." Roger grinned slyly at Takashi.

"I'm glad you found a way to settle him."

"For now," Roger whispered. He leaned in to speak directly into Takashi's ear. He didn't need Zack to accidentally overhear him or Kit, who had the superior hearing. "Candide has always prided herself on her ability to control a tight donor house of pleasure. She hasn't resorted to using those gray bands on anyone, has she?"

Takashi faked a smile as he drifted back, and then he leaned in, using Roger as a shield from even potential lipreading. "You know her better than I. Do you think Zack will have the same reaction as last night when he sees them again?"

"No idea," Roger said. "We talked, but."

"But he's a hunter at heart."

"Not that." Roger glanced at the other three, but Zack was currently holding out a lip gloss applicator like he could waggle it enough and Carver would take it. Confident their conversation was still private enough, he told Takashi, "It's not the hunter in him. It's the hero."

"And that is more dangerous," Takashi murmured. He squeezed Roger's shoulder. "Hopefully he can keep it together and we can pull this off."

As Takashi started to back away, Roger put his arm on top of his and held him close. "You're not all right with the gray bands, are you?"

"With ridding someone of all sense of self and leaving them to be mindless puppets? *No*," Takashi said with a low snarl. "Are you?"

"No."

"Good."

"All right, all right, all right!" Carver said loudly as he took the lip gloss applicator from Zack. "Girlify me."

"It's not *girly* to care about your appearance and lip moisture," Zack replied.

Carver sloppily spread the lip gloss across his bottom lip. "Yeah, well, don't think I'll be doing any kissing tonight, so why's that matter?"

Zack shrugged one shoulder, but Roger could feel the spike of ice-cold fear emanating from him—a dread of rejection. Zack continued to play off the moment like he couldn't care, though. "You never know. You might."

"Oh?" Carver asked, raising an eyebrow.

"No promises," Zack replied.

Carver leaned forward. "You're a tease, huh?"

Zack snatched the applicator from Carver and tried to spread the lip gloss out better, but he wound up sticking it in Carver's mouth when the limo bounced.

Kit laughed and shook their head before taking it back. "Just wait, Carver. We'll have you with your own makeup bag inside a week."

"*Nope*," Carver replied.

"Bet we could," Zack joked.

The three of them made up a mock wager that Roger lost track of because the limo was turning onto the long drive heading for the Chateau de Vampire.

Candide had dreamed of building her own donor house away from the bustle of Chicago for over a century, and she'd finally built it during Roger's cursed coma. The building rivaled the splendor of a French palace, reminding Roger of centuries past. The structure was only three stories tall. A front garden had several topiaries of rabbits and birds. Red and purple lights cast illumination on the outside of the first floor, lending an element of dramatics to the impressive structure. All the lights were on in the first and second floor; no one seemed to be occupying the third floor.

Vehicles dropped their passengers off a good forty feet from the door, enough that a group of statues decorated the walkway. One was in the center, and crimson lights drew attention to it. The main figure was modeled after Seamus, though the statue made Seamus to be taller than he actually was. He was showing his fangs, about to go for a kill bite on the collapsed figure in his arms, a nude woman with her face blank in ecstasy.

Dotted around the walkway were four more statues. The two nearest to the circle drive had their backs to approaching guests so that they were facing the statue of Seamus. One was of Dmitri, standing solid and imposing in a suit styled from the 1930s—an era of dress he liked above others. The other was Anton, one foot on a chair that he was tipping backward. His marble was styled as if he had on a billowing shirt, open to his mid-torso and displaying his muscular pecs. Those had been exaggerated as well. His mouth was open, fangs long and lips grinning. Somehow, the artist had managed to capture a manic glee in the statue's eyes.

On the far-right side, nearer to the entrance of the Chateau, was a statue of Candide and one of her pets. She had her head high, her hand entangled in her pet's hair. The figure depicted beside her was on his knees and nude except for the collar around his throat. He had his face buried in Candide's long skirt. She'd chosen to have the artist display her in a mid-eighteenth-century French gown, the details nearly lost in the dim lighting on the statues.

Clearly, Seamus had demanded his statue remain the brightest focal point.

Yet Roger was drawn to the fifth and final statue, to the left of the entrance as they were heading in.

Someone had decided to depict *him*. Whether Seamus or Dmitri had insisted, or Candide chose him on her own, he wasn't sure. But he was standing in an early nineteenth-century outfit, something he recalled wearing for a painting back in the day. Candide had always liked him in that outfit, enjoyed when he was the Gentleman Thief and she had been the Faux Damsel in a highway robbery. He had his hand around the throat of a nude man, several holes replicating vampire bite wounds in the figure's neck, arms, and legs. His stone face had a pleased smile with a hint of fangs peeking out, made menacing by the red light thrown onto it.

"You're not forgotten," Takashi murmured in his ear as he stopped behind Roger.

Roger snapped out of his daze and glanced as subtly as he could to see the reactions of the others. Kit had been drawn closer to Candide's statue, staring up at her with something close to awe, while Zack was standing between Roger's and Seamus's. He was trying to cover up the glare he had fixed on Seamus's statue, but he hadn't managed to wipe it clean from his face yet.

Carver looped his arm around Zack's shoulders and tugged him to stand behind Roger and Takashi.

"Kit," Zack called.

Kit jumped and then rubbed the back of their head as they hurried over to Zack's side. "Sorry. And sorry, master. These statues are beautiful."

Other patrons were filing in and out, and Roger was suddenly self-conscious that he was standing before his own. He nodded and headed for the main door. "They are that."

"It certainly lives up to expectations," Takashi said as he strolled alongside Roger. "I'd heard she was trying to match the Europeans for style and lavishness."

"Ambition has always been one of Candide's strongest qualities." Roger pulled on a smile, his guise of the partying playboy.

On either side of the doors stood a man. Both wore black pants and a red jacket with a white collar on their throat. Without a word, they reached forward and opened the doors for Roger's group.

The foyer had an amber hue to it, the gentle gold highlighting a glittery vein in the tiles. Large vases held bouquets of flowers that were in palettes of red and gold. Their aroma almost overpowered the distinct aroma of death that happened when groups of vampires congregated.

Two portraits hung in dominant places. One was of Seamus, standing with his arm out like he was welcoming guests further into the Chateau. He had the hint of a smile and a devilish gleam in his red eyes. His charm was on full display in the portrait, and Roger couldn't help the way his heart tugged in longing that *this* was the true Seamus always was. That was far from the truth, but he could be wonderful when it suited him. And the reminder stung.

The other portrait was of a group. It was from the founding of the Great Lakes Coven in 1872, when they had finally settled and decided they weren't leaving a place. Roger stood alongside Dmitri and Candide. Anton sat in a chair, legs sprawled as if he simply didn't give a damn. Seamus sat in a chair slightly facing Anton but otherwise aimed toward the viewer. He had his hand in the hair of his favored pet of the time, a boy Roger couldn't remember the name of. They were all a version of themselves for the painting. Seamus, the charming, magmatic master. Dmitri, the serious one, Candide the cunning one, even in painted form. Roger had a casual air to him, while Anton seemed to be bored. Viewing the painting too long gave Roger a chill as if somehow Anton knew when someone was examining it.

Four men dressed in black were doing their best to not look like security despite the silver stakes and handguns on their hips. They had tan collars with Candide's crest tag, marking them as her employees and announcing that if one tried to eat them, they'd incur her wrath.

In the middle of the foyer was a reception desk, where a man and a woman were working. They wore a more revealing version of the uniform worn by the doormen. Instead of black slacks, they had shorts, and they had well-cut vests instead of blazers. Both wore white collars with the stag that was Candide's crest.

The woman stepped around the reception desk and bowed in the way pets traditionally did, one wrist out as an offering, head slightly tilted to reveal the long line of her neck, other hand behind her back. "Master Roger, Mistress is pleased you've chosen to visit her humble establishment this evening."

Humble. As if there was a single humble thing about the whole damn building. Upon hearing the word, he snapped out of his reverie for the place. It was what Candide had always wanted to build, but part of the problem had always been the price. Candide was frugal, but she'd been careful not to reveal to Seamus how much she was worth for fear he'd take that as an offense.

However, Roger's fortune suddenly joining the coffers had either directly given her the money to build such a place, or she'd used it as cover. *Probably the former. This is where my money went.*

But losing his temper on a subordinate wasn't only point-less but wrong. Roger pulled together his best charming vampire mask and said smoothly, "I've missed my dear friend. I assume that Takashi and I have feeding privileges?"

"Of course, master," the woman said as she straightened. She kept her gaze on Roger's feet. "What color chits would you like?"

"Two red apiece should do us," Roger replied. Red meant they might have more fun than simply drinking, but Roger only cared that they'd be able to have longer drinks from their hosts. They probably weren't going to have a chance to drink from anyone else that night except for Kit, Zack, and Carver, and Roger had already taken enough from Zack for the night.

"As you desire, master." The woman went behind the counter and came back with four red coins. Her high heels clicked with every step. She offered two coins in each hand out toward Roger and Takashi, slightly bowing as she did.

Takashi took his two and ran his thumb across the design, a single blood drop with the words *Chateau de Vampire* written around it. "No mistaking where we are."

Roger nodded. He said to the woman, "Candide will want to know we've arrived."

"My mistress is in on the property this evening. She planned on entertaining on the second floor. Allow me to give you a tour as you seek her out, master."

"That would be lovely."

"My pleasure, master." The receptionist motioned to the doorway on the left side of the long foyer. "This way, please."

Nell's donor house was a wealthy but cozy place. In many ways, it was just a converted house where vampires and mortals happened to hang out and amuse each other.

Chateau de Vampire had all the warmth of a deep freezer in the Arctic. The click of their guide's heels echoed down the hall. The first room they passed was a sitting room done up in reds and ambers. Patrons stood around, clustered in groups here and there, speaking softly to one another. Collared pets lounged together on one set of sofas while a few donors, denoted by their white collars and Candide's crest tag, sat on the floor.

The next room was another sitting room, this time in beige and gold, deep tans complementing the colors. The effect was rather monochromatic but impressive.

"The first floor hosts our general gathering rooms, masters," their guide said. "Your pets will also find basic facilities, including our caretaker's office toward the center. I'll be certain to point it out as I go. They are aware of what that can provide for them, yes?"

That hadn't been something Roger had thought to cover. Not every place bothered to have a caretaker, and there had never been one at a donor house in the GLC's territory before. Roger said, "Carver, you know, don't you, boy?"

"A donor house's caretaker tends to pets' injuries, master," Carver said in a quiet, deferential voice.

"Ours can assist in long-term care needs if a pet hasn't had the time to arrange a formal doctor's visit elsewhere," their guide said. "Or help a pet find care closer to home if that is preferred."

On their walk, they passed additional sitting rooms and one music room that alongside the usual harp and piano Roger was used to seeing also had a host of guitars. A mortal was strumming a soothing melody on a guitar while another sang. Everyone in the room was rapt with attention to the performers.

They came to a T-intersection deep in the building. Their guide motioned at the large glass doors before her. "The ballroom." Then she swept her hand to the right. "That way leads to additional general meeting areas, including an art gallery with a rotating collection. Our current display is 'Scenes of History' and features paintings from our newest coven captain, Dempsey."

Dempsey was one of Candide's sirelings. Roger tucked that mental note away and nodded.

Their guide motioned to the left. "The common library is that way, masters. In either direction, we would go past a bar, which offers modest delicacies as well. We add whatever your pets eat and drink to your account. If you would prefer your pets had no access to alcohol, or anything we provide for that matter, we can accommodate that desire."

"My pets know their limits and know not to overindulge," Roger said.

"Understood, master," their guide said. "There are a few illicit offerings at our bars as well. Mistress has even acquired fey rarities with the permission of our Master Seamus and is able to provide those as well."

"They know what would displease me," Roger said. "I see no reason to limit them."

Their guide nodded. "Would you like to see more of the first floor, masters, or would you prefer to move onto the second?"

"I think we can move on to the second," Takashi said.

"Agreed," Roger said.

"As you desire, masters." Their guide started down the left hall and continued explanations as she took another turn that led them to a grand staircase. She pointed out some of the finer furniture and art pieces as they traveled.

Some of them had been in Roger's homes once upon a time. He'd had his penthouse in the city, but his one in downstate Illinois that he rarely visited had been chockful of art. *She fucking stole from me.* Anger bubbled in him, and he had to curb it before it became a desire to cause pain. Others would be able to feel that impulse, and he needed to appear level-headed. *She thought I was dead. It's fine.*

Unless she's the one who made a deal with a fey to seal me away. Roger didn't pay much attention to what the guide had to say as they passed more rooms and doors. Apparently, one of them was an elevator. But fear and hurt were swirling. Keeping his jester's mask in place was tough, especially as their guide recited the history of a Manet piece that had been in *his* living room without a single mention of *him*.

While they continued down the hall, their guide said, "As you can see, this floor is for entertainment. A closed door signals a desire for intimacy. Access to the third floor and private rooms that are there is restricted unless you're a privileged member of the coven." She blushed, a hint of fear pulsing from her. "Which, of course, you are, Master Roger. You are a captain and should have such rights. I'm certain the staff would allow you anywhere you like, pardoning Mistress's private chambers."

His image might have been everywhere, but people had forgotten his importance. Roger said coldly, "And I'm certain they would allow me there if I had a need."

Their guide dipped her head. "I didn't mean to imply you wouldn't have our cooperation, master. Please forgive me."

Roger snorted. That was as much of a forgiveness as he ought to give.

"I love it when he oozes authority," Takashi said with a bright smile. He took Roger's hand and kissed it, then continued holding his hand. "Positively terrifying, isn't he?"

Their guide smiled politely, then motioned down the hallway. "My mistress is just a little farther this way, masters. At the end of the hall."

The rooms on the second floor were more crowded, though that could have been an illusion due to their smaller dimensions. Music played from speakers in a few places, and though sex and the stronger fantasies were played out behind closed doors, the subtle reek of lubricant mixed with the odor of the grave and the far more pleasurable scent of blood. Moans were an undercurrent to the general bubbles of conversations.

Still, Roger heard the crack of a whip twenty feet away

from the last room on the left. He stepped into old habits as they made their way. The GLC would be expecting Roger, an experienced vampire and occasional public Dom, and he didn't balk at dominance play of any level.

He'd always believed he found being the dominant in those scenarios was the most exciting, but with Zack, he was starting to wonder if he'd been stumbling along. Zack had been in control in the bathroom, directing Roger with every word and move. He'd been demanding, and that had been incredibly hot. Following instead of leading had been freeing, and he longed to know what would happen if he let Zack fully dominate him.

Seamus had been rough with him, and Roger had assumed that submission wasn't his thing. He'd made the best of out his times with Seamus, enjoying what he could, but being away from the GLC had made clear what he'd always known.

Seamus was not a good master, in any way.

What if he's changed while I was away? Roger forced his feet onward. *Dmitri hates him. Always has. If Seamus was better, Dmitri wouldn't even notice.*

A tiny, insidious whisper said, *Coward. You want an easy way out. There isn't one.*

The crack of leather against skin brought Roger out of his thoughts. He followed their guide to the open archway.

In the center of the room, a young man stood naked except for the pale red collar on his throat. His wrists were bound and attached to a chain that ran through a loop on the ceiling and back down to a hook on the floor, which was then held by a bored-looking man who lounged on the floor. That man had a deeper red collar and a crest tag marking him as Candide's.

The bound pet's back was to the archway, and his skin was red, with deeper slash marks striping him here and there. Many had been cuts at some point, trickles of blood decorated his skin, but most had already closed entirely. His long auburn hair was braided, with the braid hanging over his shoulder and onto his chest.

The floor beneath him was coated in what would look like silver glitter to the uninitiated, but Roger could smell the magic pouring off him. Crisp juniper was stronger than the smell of roses and death.

Candide had an Unseelie fey as a pet.

The mistress herself, Candide, had a long whip in her hand that she allowed to drag on the floor behind her as she walked around her bound pet. She made a hand motion, and the lounging pet tightened the tension of the chain and forced the bound one onto his tiptoes. Though she had at least two dozen for an audience, the click of her heels was distinct. Her blond hair was pulled back into a tight bun, the braiding of it exquisite. Similarly, her bloodred dress left no question about who was in charge of the room or the entire palace. As always, she exuded control and nobility above all else.

She only had eyes on her prize, and her eyes were ruby red instead of blue. She swished the whip and then brought it down on her pet's back. With each strike, she drew thin lines of blood from wounds that soon began to close. The young man didn't flinch. He'd dropped so far into subspace that he made guttural whimpers and moans begging for more or release—though knowing Candide, Roger suspected the poor boy had a cock cage on.

Roger had made shows of doing this sort of performance. Demonstrating his skills as a master had been a thrill ... hadn't it? The mere suggestion of displaying Kit or Zack or Carver in such a way—though without the blood drawing; Roger had never had interest in that—felt uncomfortable, like he was living in a shell of who he had been.

After a final crack of the whip, Candide whispered, "My good boy."

Her words brought a greater flush to her bound pet, and

long waves of natural want poured out from him. The other vampires basked in it; one in the back of the room undid his pants and coaxed his pet to suck on him.

Candide neared her pet and licked one thin trail of blood before tugging his head back and biting his neck. He whined with need, but she pulled away after the briefest of sips.

With a pleased smirk, she circled her boy again. She motioned to the pet on the floor, and the tension was released so the pet stood on his feet, though his arms remained nearly taut over his head. She lightly stroked his back, navigating the maze of marks and drawing a few drops of blood onto her fingertips. Daintily and quickly, she licked the blood.

Finally, she glanced Roger's way. Her smile grew. "Mon cher, it's wonderful to see you. Come, have a treat."

Turning down Candide's gift would be rude, and the boy smelled delicious. Roger returned her smile. "I'd be honored."

He neared the boy and looked over his wounds. The redness from Candide's attention was already starting to fade, leaving the appearance that the blood trails crisscrossed unblemished, pale skin. Roger licked one of the fresher trails.

The fey existed in their own plane of existence, a realm full of magic that infused its people. The boy's blood was ice-cool and brought to mind the winter wind under moonlight. Feeling cold was hard as a vampire, and the sensation was a rare pleasure.

After reigning in his impulsive want of the boy, Roger laughed gently and offered his arm out to Candide. "You have a knack for finding true treasures."

Candide took his arm, and they crossed the room together. All eyes were on them. "I see you have found some of your own. Hello, Takashi. Pleasure to see you again."

"The pleasure is mine, master," Takashi said. "I wasn't sure you'd remember me."

"Oh, come now! You were shy, but I do recall the way we

made you blush!" Candide laughed. She had always kept her French accent as a point of pride, refusing to blend her voice into an American accent. "And if you're going to remain formal, use mistress. I hate master. It makes me sound like a stodgy old man." Her attention turned to Kit. "Aren't you a delight? I love the hair. Is the color natural?"

"No, mistress," Kit said quietly.

"It's gorgeous on you. Well done." Candide moved on to Carver, raking her gaze over him before catching Roger's eye. "You'll have to watch him around Lucille. She'll want to take a bite out of him for certain."

"Lucille's home?" Roger asked. The vampire in question was one of Candide's sirelings, a girl barely sixteen when she was turned and from their time in New York City. She was to the GLC as Takashi had been to Nell's coven.

"She will be in a week." Candide squeezed his arm. "She's missed you, too. She said she can't wait to see her favorite uncle again."

Could Lucille have been the one to put him in a coma? Roger hadn't even considered her since she had been away at the time, but she was a vampire who made connections everywhere—did she want Roger's position?

Keep the paranoia under control. Save it for when you can think without everyone watching your face. Roger chuckled. "I'm still readjusting to phones. I went without them for a while, full detox of the modern world. But you'll have to give her my number. I would love to see her when she comes."

"I'll do that," Candide said. She gently tugged her hand free of Roger as she approached Zack. With one finger, she lifted Zack's chin. Protocol dictated that Zack keep his gaze on the floor, and he did, though it was a narrow thing. His heart was pounding, but his face remained smooth, no trace of fear or anger. "My, my. You've outdone yourself with this one. How tamed is he?"

"Plenty, and he's never for loan," Roger said sternly, more to the room than Candide.

He wasn't sure she was all that interested in Zack. Out of all the captains, Candide had the best poker face. She had bluffed her way into a conversation with a Seelie princess once, which had prevented her and Roger from dying by overexposure to magical sunlight.

Still, before she could set her heart on Zack, Roger took her hand again and folded her arm into his. "It's been decades. We should take a moment for ourselves."

"We do have lots to catch up on. I assume Takashi is able to watch over your pets?" Candide said.

"Naturally," Roger replied.

Candide held out her whip. Without looking over her shoulder, she said, "Darling."

A young black woman who wore a black leather collar with Candide's tag stepped forward from beside the archway and took the whip from her.

"I may be a while. Please see to my toy." Candide raised her voice. "My glorious audience is allowed to lick him clean. If you refuse to take turns and share, my darling has permission to use the whip on you and have security toss you in my dungeon, from which you will face judgment from Seamus." She brought her voice back down, oozing with charm and warmth. "You will do that for me, won't you, darling?"

"Yes, mistress," the woman replied.

Candide kissed her cheek and then led Roger out of the room. "Come along, mon cher. Allow me to show you my favorite place upstairs."

"I'll see you soon," Roger said to Takashi, but he made quick eye contact with Zack on his way. There was an edge in Zack's gray eyes, a wariness. But he couldn't pull free of Candide's enthusiastic grasp to check on him.

We can make it through this. He'll be fine.

Please. Be fine.

CHAPTER 14

Getting left in the middle of a donor house was a possibility that Zack had prepared for, but he didn't think Roger was going to ditch them within an hour of stepping into the largest donor house in North America. He stamped down on the building annoyance in his heart. Technically, he wasn't even in charge of their little group. Takashi was. Somehow, that irritated him *more*.

Matters weren't helped by Kit, who was staring at the mix of vampires and supernaturals and open displays of wealth like they'd just walked onto a movie set and seen an A-list celebrity smile at them, and Carver, who was starting to look queasy. Zack clenched his jaw. *He was supposed to be okay with this. He had to know what he was getting into. And this bothered him, but not the stuff last night?*

And worse, Candide had inspected Zack. Not like he was a piece of fruit on the verge of being too ripe—she'd had a calculating look in her eye. She'd been sizing him up. The question about how "tame" he was clearly aimed at his hunter heritage.

Had she bought the act? Was anyone going to believe Zack was a pet?

"We should go downstairs," Takashi said quietly.

"Yes, master," Zack said. He grabbed Kit's arm and started to pull them away from the archway.

"Come on," Kit whispered. They reluctantly tagged along with Zack while Carver brought up the rear of the group. "Can't we watch a little?"

"Try porn," Zack replied.

"Porn doesn't smell."

"Gross," Carver muttered.

"How can you say that?" Kit asked.

"Because to us, it smells like blood and lube up here," Zack whispered.

"Being human has got to suck," Kit replied.

They reached the first floor. Zack was hoping they'd walk past the library, but Takashi headed toward the front of the building. Every room felt full of people, but the one Takashi picked was fullest of all.

Before Takashi took a step inside, Zack said, "Master, wait."

Takashi whirled and caught Zack around the waist. He pulled him over to the side of the archway, which turned out to be useful to the group leaving the crowded room.

Still, Zack's hunter instincts screamed for him to knock Takashi aside and free himself from the unexpected touch. He managed to counter the desire to push, but that left his hands on Takashi's pecs. His very firm, very nice-feeling pecs. *Don't get horny. Don't get horny. Being pushed up against a wall isn't that hot.* Then he risked a glance up and saw the mild amusement in Takashi's blue eyes. He puffed up, ready to tell him off, only he shouldn't since Takashi was supposed to be Roger's boyfriend, and pets weren't supposed to get pissed at vampires in general.

So he held the breath in.

Which seemed to only amuse Takashi more.

Which made Zack want to explode, but he couldn't. And

life wasn't fair because while smug didn't work for most guys, it was working pretty well for Takashi. Even better than it ever did for Roger.

"I'd hope he'd be someone we could share," Roger had said.

Roger and Takashi had been together before. Was Roger already ... did he want Takashi back? Was there some sort of talk between them? Zack held in a groan. He hated not knowing everything.

Takashi leaned in. At first, Zack worried he was going for a kiss, and his mind spun. There were too many people watching, and he hadn't expected to be kissing anyone in public. Ever.

Instead, Takashi put his cheek against Zack's and whispered in his ear, "We can learn useful information while we wait for Roger. We don't have to poke our heads out far, but an empty room wouldn't do us any good."

Creatures that stuck out their heads tended to be the ones who got them bitten off, but Zack had to concede that Takashi had a point. He'd been so thrown off by Candide's display upstairs he'd forgotten what his mission should be that night. Recon.

"You're right, master," Zack said softly.

"Glad you approve," Takashi purred before stepping away.

Rather than letting his hormones absorb his focus like they were begging to do, Zack stowed the potential fantasies about Takashi and took in details of the room as they entered. It was another lavish sitting room with chairs and couches. An occasional coffee table broke up the space, though two pets were using one of the lower ones as additional seating. Beautiful, framed photographs of different locations around the world hung on the walls. Despite the crowd, the room had a stark feeling, a coldness that permeated the entirety of the Chateau.

Thankfully, there were two empty chairs in the back corner. Observing without having to socialize would be easier for Zack, and they wouldn't have to worry about people sneaking up behind them. He was grateful Takashi snaked his way through the room to those seats instead of trying for one of the few couch seats. After all, Zack, Kit, and Carver would be expected to sit on the floor if Takashi took one of those.

Takashi took the seat that had the best view of the room while Kit plopped into the other like they didn't have a care in the world. Zack couldn't tell if it was an artful act or if Kit really didn't care that they were in the devil's nest. Meanwhile, Carver looked a few shades paler than normal, and he sat on the floor between the seats.

Thrumming with too much nervous energy, Zack leaned against the wall beside Takashi's chair. Ten other vampires were hanging out in the sitting room. Judging from the collars, there were six other head pets, fifteen regular pets, and five donors making rounds through the room. Two servants, denoted with brown collars, were picking up empty glasses and taking the occasional order, usually from a vampire.

"Zackery," Takashi said lightly and then absentmindedly patted his lap.

Zack clenched his jaw and did a quick sweep of the nearby room. Had anyone else heard him? Kit and Carver must have. Even if no one else had, those two expected him to act like a pet.

Which meant he had to obey.

Fuck me. Zack pushed off the wall and sat on Takashi's lap, facing out into the room.

Takashi put his arms around Zack, his touch featherlight, and murmured in his ear, "There we go. Now we can share what we see."

Was there anything Takashi did that didn't have six motives behind it? Zack leaned his head back against Takashi's shoulder. "Who says I'm sharing?"

"Careful, I might think you don't like me," Takashi teased.

"Maybe I don't."

"I'm wounded. I adore you."

"You don't know me," Zack replied.

Takashi stroked Zack's arm. His touch was cool where the mesh was open, like he was dotting Zack's skin with ice as he moved. His voice was low and gentle in his ear, a continuing whisper. "I have had the opportunity to study you, and I find plenty to admire. I'd love the chance to sink my teeth into you and discover what you taste like. And if not your blood, perhaps something else."

The flirt made Zack blush, and he hated that anyone in the room would not only see his reddened cheeks but that the vampires might be able to feel that thin tendril of desire coiling in his stomach. Takashi could feel his every squirm, and he was having trouble sitting still.

And he accidentally made eye contact with Carver, who was suppressing a knowing grin.

Panic slithered through Zack's mind and started growing walls between the cracks in his thoughts. Anyone could see him on Takashi's lap. Anyone could see that he had a bandage on his thigh and another on his wrist. He kept searching the crowd for anyone who was judging him. Was that redhead staring? Was the guy with the dreads giggling at him?

"Hey," Takashi murmured. He was nudging Zack's hip.

Oh God, what does he want from me? He can't possibly want sex. Not here! Right? Startled, Zack jumped up from Takashi's lap. When Takashi grabbed for him, Zack instinctively slipped his grip. His lungs hurt. Why did his lungs hurt? They didn't have air. He wasn't breathing right. Why was he standing? Why was Kit staring at him like that?

Suddenly, Carver leapt to his feet, and he wrapped his beefy arms around him, instantly tucking Zack's against his shoulder, one hand on the back of his head. He muttered, "It's a hug. Just a hug. Nobody can see you."

The last sentence stuck out. *Nobody can see me.* In spite of having his face pushed up against Carver's muscular shoulder, he found breath again. He shook slightly, but he barely budged since he was in Carver's tight hug. Somehow, that helped, too. The sensation of being caught, being held, calmed the part of him that wanted to fight his way out. Because Carver was right—nobody could see him. They were in a corner, and Carver was just hugging him.

"Can someone tell me what happened?" Takashi asked carefully.

"He's shy, master," Carver said.

"Oh fuck, that's right," Kit whispered.

Zack closed his eyes. *Great. Now I've made a different kind of scene.* He eased away from Carver's embrace and quickly wiped his eyes. For some reason, he'd been on the brink of crying as well. *Fantastic.*

The job should be all that mattered. Instead, his freaking inability to get over his goddamn self had disrupted much-needed surveillance. He glanced out at the room, and people were definitely murmuring and paying attention to what was happening in their corner. Just exactly what he didn't want to happen.

"I'm okay," Zack whispered.

"Yeah?" Carver said.

"Yeah."

Slowly, Carver released him, and Zack managed a smile as he did. The curve of his lips felt fake, but he kept it and nodded to Carver. "Can I sit with you?"

Carver brightened with a grin. "'Course."

They sat on the floor, Carver leaning against Takashi's chair and Zack leaning against him. While the position wasn't exactly comfortable, no one else seemed to be paying close attention to them anymore, and Zack had a decent enough view of the room.

The conversations Zack picked up circled around

mundane topics. Someone griped about a movie they'd seen. Someone was in love with an old book. A group was debating whether the rise of fascism would mean the end of the human species or if vampires could use it to eliminate supernatural rivals and take full control of the livestock. Zack tried to hear as much as he could from that group, but they seemed to be running a thought experiment rather than concocting a scheme for world domination.

All conversations dipped into a lull as a new group came into the room. Zack recognized most of them from his social media research, but the young white guy at the center was the one that made Zack's heart lurch.

Vincent Talmadge couldn't be any older than Zack. His auburn hair was cut short, which only enhanced his delicate, waifish appearance. Bite marks were on his wrists, elbows, throat, and dotting his body in general. They were in various states of healing, but the one around his left nipple was fresh. He was attractive enough to be a supermodel, but he seemed thin and pale to the point where Zack wondered if he was actually healthy. Anemia was common among human pets, especially when their masters didn't care for their physical well-being.

In typical pet fashion, everything Vincent wore either clung to him or revealed places where he'd been bitten. His deep red vest hung open, and his low-cut, tight shorts hugged the sharp lines of his body. His black leather collar had a ruby at its center, and a platinum crest hung from it.

The four people who walked in with him were equally appealing and also had various bite marks. Their collars were shades of red, their crest tags steel, and they were dressed less conservatively than Vincent. All one man wore besides his collar was a thong and flip-flops.

When Vincent motioned at them, a set of pets on a central couch and their vampire vacated their spots. He took a seat in the middle and lounged. One of his entourage hurried to sit beside him as he was intentionally leaning over, like he expected someone to cuddle against. The other two with him sat on the floor, the man in the thong sprawling out.

"Shit," Zack whispered. "That's Seamus's prize pet. If he's here—"

"Then his master isn't far behind." Takashi swore softly. "You should find Roger."

"We should move," Zack said quietly.

"We can't look like we're running or hiding," Takashi replied quickly. "Go find Roger."

Damn it. He's right. Slowly, with his heart thundering in his ears, Zack stood. He nodded to Takashi in case anyone had heard him give the order and expected to see him "behaving" and then did his best not to run from the room. *There's nothing to be afraid of. This is just like when I had that late paper in high school.*

If that late paper could get up and slice my throat open.

He reached the hallway.

Cold preceded the man walking in his direction. Shadows were darker, the lights dimming ever so slightly as he strode past them. He had an ease in his gait, a swagger like he owned the place. His alabaster skin could have reflected light, only that light seemed to bend away from him.

Seamus had arrived.

At first glance, he wasn't an imposing man. He was close to Zack's height, maybe as tall as five foot ten at the most. His shoulders were only subtly wider than his hips, though his tailored clothing provided the illusion that he was broader in the shoulders than he actually was. His brown hair was cut to modern fashion, but he wore an old gold watch on his left wrist. He was … handsome. Maybe it was his attitude, maybe the shape of his jaw, but the man had a natural pull to him even without vampiric magic. He wouldn't be out of place at a family brunch, scolding his kids for misbehaving and looking ridiculously hot while doing so.

Except for the ice bath, he doesn't seem that tough.

Seamus smiled at him.

Shit. Zack was staring. A stone dropped into his gut. Staring at a vampire was against the rules, and staring at the coven master was a massive breach of protocol. Panic crackled up his spine, and he fought to keep his breathing normal. He couldn't afford for his fear to overtake him.

Zack dipped his head, spun toward the direction of the stairs, and managed three steps before he heard Seamus call out, "Wait."

There was no one else he could mean. *Fuck.* This was not how this was supposed to go. They were doing recon! They weren't supposed to deal with Seamus tonight. He was supposed to be busy at his club, Devil's Cove. *What the fuck is he doing in the suburbs?*

Seamus's steps were quiet, but the coldness that came with him set off Zack's internal alarms. His tattoo grew warm, flaring to life to shield his mind.

Two seconds into their meeting, Seamus was attempting to use mind tricks on him.

Zack laid his palms flat against his thighs. If he left them free, he might clench his fists, and that could be perceived as a challenge. He couldn't risk a fight.

Roger claimed each vampire had their own scent of the grave, but to Zack, Seamus was the first one to stand out. He smelled of dirt and blood—there was no mistaking the pungent coppery tang in the air around him. He strolled around Zack until they were face-to-face.

Seamus's good looks made Zack's skin crawl at this close distance. His smile was too practiced, the smoothness of his skin too flawless. His vibe passed from hot to monster-in-sheep's-clothing.

An itch to run worked up Zack's arms, but he had to stay put. No excuse to run away would be good enough if Seamus didn't want him to go. Not according to vampire rules.

"My, my, you're gorgeous." Seamus cupped Zack's jaw with an icy grip and tilted his head up until their gazes met. Red muddled Seamus's otherwise blue eyes. Older vampires had trouble fully shifting their eyes back to human color. Nell's were a beautiful shade of ruby brown. Seamus's irises looked infected.

Instinctively, Zack took a step back.

Seamus allowed his hand to slide off, and he chuckled. "I only want a better look at you. Did you know you have the prettiest gray eyes? And such long lashes for a man, though I suppose that could be mascara. Makeup is fashionable for men your age, isn't it?"

Holy fuck, are we seriously talking about trends? Zack struggled to find his voice and to keep it level. "Not exactly, master. And I'm not wearing any mascara."

"Wonderful. I wonder who's laid claim to you." Instead of waiting for an answer, Seamus grasped the crest tag on Zack's collar. He shouldn't have needed to—and Zack suspected it was an excuse to get close again—and he made a show of examining it. "I haven't seen that kraken in decades. Is this some deceit?"

"No, master," Zack said. "I was going to get my master for you."

"I could snatch this tag off and claim you for myself," Seamus mused, as if robbing another vampire meant nothing to him.

And the look in his eye said he didn't give a damn what Zack thought about becoming his. That if he wanted, he'd just *take* him.

Every single nerve in Zack longed to put his fist through Seamus's face. He had to fight the impulse to clench his fist and had to force himself to breathe so his jaw wouldn't continue to tense.

"I think you'd be disappointed in me, master," Zack whispered.

"I'm not sure I would be," Seamus replied. After a hint of silence that he was deadly serious, he chuckled and shook his head. "At least you have spirit, unlike his usual shrinking party favors. Go on, run and tell Roger that I'm here. I'm dying to see him again."

"Yes, master," Zack said and hurried for the nearest staircase.

He didn't escape Seamus's aura until he was halfway up to the second floor. The farther he was, the more his tattoo returned to normal. Had Seamus been actively using his power? Or had he just oozed that much magic? *How the fuck are we supposed to murder* that? No wonder Roger had said killing Seamus wouldn't be simple. A vampire with that magnitude of power could survive the basic staking. Zack's silver dagger would bypass that, but would it really be enough to kill him?

The sooner we obliterate him, the better. Zack sucked in a deep breath and let it out slowly. He'd survived his first encounter with the enemy. He had data. He could work with data. They could start making plans. *Assuming we make it through the rest of the night.*

CHAPTER 15

"You must tell me what you've been doing with yourself all these years, mon cher," Candide said as she hung on Roger's arm. Having just left Kit, Zack, and Takashi, she was leading the way to the third floor.

Roger kept his stride a slow saunter to match her pace. They had perfected walking in tandem centuries ago. Having her against him like this was a comforting motion in his step. "I've been naughty, of course."

"Naturally!" Candide squeezed his arm. "Your pets are delicious. You usually only keep boys, but that feels like an assumption with one of them. What gender is your fox?"

"Nonbinary," Roger replied. "Not my first to be so."

"That's right. You had that darling pet in … was it 1935?"

"'37."

"Yes! They were also gorgeous. You have the best taste." She leaned her head against his shoulder. "But you haven't said where you've been. You were missed."

"I needed a break," Roger said, subtly moving his shoulder so she had to straighten. She did. He still had no idea who could have set him up or if the Unseelies themselves had wanted him out of Chicago. Candide was an expert in guarding her emotions, but he was familiar with her expressions. He needed to see her reactions. "I admit I could have made a more graceful exit, but you seemed to have benefited from my absence."

A sharp glint lit Candide's smile for a brief second. They were walking past a few final rooms before the stairs. Several of them had lower lighting than the rest, adding an element of darkness that would hamper a mortal's sight but made no difference to a supernatural.

On a normal night, thirty years ago, Roger would have preferred to lose himself in one of those rooms. But he couldn't afford to fall into old patterns and seek distractions instead of the truth.

"I suppose I'm a touch guilty." Candide gestured at the hallway around them. "I wouldn't have been able to build this magnificent establishment if not for your generous, albeit unsolicited, donation to the coven."

"That seems to have included my art," Roger remarked.

"I was always jealous of a few pieces," Candide said with a mock pout. "You're not blaming me for keeping them safe. After all, you did abandon them."

"I'm glad to see them in good condition," Roger said smoothly.

They reached the bottom of the staircase, where two black-clad guards stood. They stepped out of Candide's way without a word. She continued holding Roger's arm as they made their way up, and the guards stepped back into place to prevent the random patron's admittance.

Once they reached the top, she unceremoniously released him. Her demeanor became cold and professional, and she quickened her pace. None of which surprised Roger. Like him, Candide wore many masks. Her pleasant socialite demeanor was least like her true self. Zack had taught him a phrase, "resting bitch face," and that best described Candide.

If she actually gave a damn about mortals or shifters,

Roger would have tried to prop her up as the leader of the coven. Candide was fifty years Roger's junior, though she'd been awake and might have gained an edge that would put her on level footing with him. However, everyone in the world around her was a pawn in her ambitious games.

She loved a few of those pawns. Roger was sure he was one of them.

"Seriously, Roger, where the fuck did you go?" Candide said shortly.

Roger had no problem keeping pace with her. Though he wished he could trust her, he continued his lie. "I meant what I told you. I took a break."

"Without your money? Without formally releasing your pets? You had many of us in a full panic."

"I didn't think anyone would mind," Roger said.

"It was chaos the first few weeks. We scoured every corner of Chicago and came up with nothing. We had to assume you were dead, though Dmitri insisted he'd feel it if you'd passed from the world."

And yet one of the worried vampires had likely been the one orchestrating Roger's disappearance. He took the puzzle piece Candide offered and set it in his mental picture with the others. He couldn't quite make things fit yet. "I had to make certain no one would forget me. I always planned to return."

"I'm glad you came back." Candide sighed and paused. She looked up to Roger, and a hint of the wistful girl Roger had seen when she was a fledgling broke through her otherwise cold nature. She put her hand on Roger's chest and touched the button of his shirt as if checking that he was standing before her. "It is a relief to see you, mon cher. While you've been gone, I've learned the truth of what our sire and his wretched lackey have been doing for centuries. Absorbing his own bloodline through a ritual is abhorrent. I was terrified you were a victim of theirs."

Roger put his hand over Candide's, lightly holding on to

her. She'd professed an attraction to him in her early days, but he'd never felt that same flicker of desire for her. She was feminine and lovely—and completely not what Roger sought in a lover.

But they had formed a friendship, and one that stood the test of time better than any of Roger's other relationships. He stepped closer to her. "I'm here."

"I missed you." Candide used her free hand to wipe a tear.

Was her sadness an act? Roger didn't think so. "I'm sorry to have been away so long."

She withdrew her hand. "Well, things are certainly going to be exciting with you around again."

"Apparently, if you're feeling bold enough to call Anton a 'wretched lackey.'"

"He's pissed me off. Again." Candide brushed a potential tear from the corner of her eye. "He attempted to seduce my pet, Dryden. Hence the punishment you saw downstairs. I have a very finely worded deal with the Princess of the Northern Shadow Glen about what may or may not happen to that boy while in our realm, and Anton nearly violated it."

"And yet you punish the boy?" Roger asked, raising an eyebrow.

"The boy knows the terms. He was *trying* to break the deal, and not for the first time. He enjoys playing the brat, and I enjoy punishing him. I'm simply furious with Anton because they were an inch away from trouble when I caught them." Candide gestured dismissively. "Talking about my randy, disobedient pet wasn't why I dragged you away. I have a surprise for you, though it's not nearly so grand as the one you had for me."

"It is hard to replicate the joy of having me back in your life," Roger said smugly.

Candide laughed and continued down the hall. "Still the jester—that's wonderful. I meant the surprise of dragging a tamed hunter into the heart of our empire. A Gladwell with your tag on him. His ancestors are rolling over in their graves."

Dread crawled down his back. *Gladwell*. Avoiding them had taken the better part of a century, and he still didn't dare return to England for fear they'd somehow know and cut his heart out. Roger forced a smile. "You must have misheard. He's a Wright."

Candide paused beside the door, her hand on the handle. She studied Roger's face. "You don't know?"

"I know he's a Wright. I've seen his driver's license, and he is my pet," Roger replied.

"You must have used your time away to forget about us and truly disconnect," Candide said, laughter lighting her eyes.

"I know I have a reputation for being the airhead of our little group, but I do have some intelligence. I would know if I was bedding a Gladwell."

Candide took her hand from the door handle and tilted her head. A second later, a mischievous smile crossed her lips. "You honestly haven't kept up. Thomas Wright married Carri Gladwell in 1995, uniting the two bloodlines. They have three children: Callum, also known as the Butcher, their youngest, Amber, who has recently earned a reputation as the Bolt. And then they have another boy, the middle child. *Zackery*."

Zack couldn't be a Gladwell. He *couldn't* be. He would have mentioned it. *Only when did I ever ask?* Roger put his hand over his face. The news was a sledgehammer to his psyche. Zack was from not one but *two* hunter bloodlines? No wonder he'd been raised with such biases against the supernatural.

Has he been conquering that? Or is he playing a deeper game? After all, if Zack could rid the world of Seamus, Anton, and Roger, he would be a legend among the Gladwells. Was every smile a lie? Every kiss a deception? Just another step to completing a long con? *No. Candide must be lying.*

"You've gotten it wrong," Roger said.

"I haven't."

"You have," Roger growled.

Candide's mirth faded away. "I do not mean to hurt your heart, mon cher, but if you don't believe me, there is some simple proof."

She opened the door.

The room had the thin veneer of a personal office, but the furniture was functional and overtly stable enough for fucking. Discreet metal loops were in the ceiling, dotting the walls, and adorned the furniture. It was a lush playroom designed for roleplay.

Ezra sat at the desk with a typewriter in front of him. He had his hands buried in his fiery red hair, and he glanced up from whatever on the page was preoccupying him. He had skin the color of pale moonlight and gray eyes the silver of steel. His delicate nose and cheekbones were offset by the noble demeanor he'd never lost.

The familiarity in Zack's features that Roger had never been able to place suddenly made sense. Ezra and Zack could have passed for brothers better than Zack's actual brother, Callum, did. The realization struck Roger hard enough that he was stunned into silence.

"When I said you should chain me to a desk and make me work, I didn't mean *literally*, mistress," Ezra said crossly, his English accent obvious. He lifted his wrists. Thick, heavy chains hung from them and went to an equally solid ring on the wall on either side of him.

Then he spotted Roger, and his mouth fell open. He stood, revealing that he wore only a pair of black briefs. He'd had a nipple ring when he was a mortal, and he had a sapphire in the piercing now. "Roger!"

"Down, boy." Candide strode into the room and put her

hand on Ezra's shoulder. When he didn't budge on his own, she pushed.

Ezra plopped down into his seat. "You're alive! He's alive!"

"I've been trying to contact you for two months." Roger managed to force himself into the room and close the door. He had had shocks to his system before. Perhaps Zack knew everything and simply didn't care. Maybe Zack was one of the few Gladwells who didn't know the story of the massacre and Roger could clear the air before anything awful happened.

Thankfully, Ezra didn't seem to note Roger's distress and carried on the conversation. He glared up at Candide. "Mistress has been keeping me from my computer and phone."

"Because we have a deal." Candide opened what looked like a bookcase, but it turned out to be a wardrobe full of domination toys and tools. She plucked a ball gag off a hook and approached Ezra. She seized him by his hair and yanked his head backward. "Now, tell Roger about our arrangement before he worries about his wayward noble brat."

"Candide, this is a little—" Ezra gasped as she tugged harder. "Mistress, please."

"Mon chien, I gave an order."

A thick roll of desire was mixing between them. Ezra trembled. "I made a deal with Mistress that I would be hers for six months if she could teach me manners and discipline. I didn't know that included keeping me from important messages!"

"Tch, tch. No one asked for commentary." Candide popped the ball gag into Ezra's mouth and secured it behind his head. She gave his head a push, and he kept his head dipped down. "You're worrying too much, Roger."

"Forgive me, I'm still becoming accustomed to socializing again." Roger sat in one of the chairs across from Ezra. The chair was wooden with scratches on its arms. He ran his fingers across one while trying to pull his mind back from the stream of memories that threatened to swell over him.

"Your boy has kept secrets from you." Candide moved over to a filing cabinet that turned out to be a liquor cabinet. She poured herself a drink, looked over Roger, and then poured him a rum. With a concerned frown, she handed him the drink and sat in the other chair beside him. "And you've been falling for him. Oh, Roger, why do you always have to love the pretty ones? They only ever break your heart."

Roger held the rum in his hand and leaned forward, resting his elbows on his knees. All the manners in the world didn't matter if he was going to get murdered by his lover. But Zack wasn't like that. He'd *saved* Roger.

Besides that, Candide was a viper. She might love him, but she might also use him. She'd clearly been doing well for herself. Convincing her to follow him could be difficult. How many might rally behind her? Was she the better choice to lead?

"I'm not in the mood for your patronizing tone," Roger said, for once dropping his own polished American accent for the rough poor Englishman's voice he'd been born to. He felt the ripple in Ezra's desires and Candide's. They'd always liked this side of him when everyone else had made him hide it away. *I should use that.* He swallowed the rum and set the empty glass on the desk. "Why didn't you tell him about me?"

"Honestly, I wasn't sure it was you until I held your arm this evening. There's no mistaking the flow of vampiric power within you."

"Dmitri verified me months back."

"Dmitri and I have been having problems lately. And we've had so many rumors proven false over the decades that I didn't want to raise my hopes, let alone Ezra's."

Roger wiped his mouth and shook his head.

"You're on edge," Candide said as she stood. She went to

the cabinet, took out the bottle of rum, and refilled his glass. "That's my fault."

"It's not you," Roger said as he took the glass. "Not entirely."

"I am in awe you chose to return at all. Had I been you, I might have stayed away."

"As if I could live in the open without *his* approval," Roger murmured.

"Too true." Candide leaned against the desk and sipped her drink. With a nod, she gestured over her shoulder. "If you like, we can bend Ezra over the desk, and you can redden his ass. I'll even let you fuck him. He's been longing to have something up his ass all evening."

"He hasn't wanted me since ..." Roger couldn't say the words.

"Since the manor?" Candide strolled around behind the desk. She ran her hand through Ezra's hair and pulled him up again. Stroking his cheek with her glass, she said, "That's a lie, isn't it, mon chien?"

Ezra closed his eyes.

Candide grinned to Roger. "He's been confessing all manner of sins to me. Wrath. Envy. Lust. Remember your sireling James?"

James *hated* Roger since he'd become a vampire. Roger rolled his drink, letting the swish of liquid settle him. "That's a rude question."

"It is since your heart broke when James fled for Alaska. Guess who convinced him that was a good idea?" Candide released Ezra's hair and strode around the desk to stand beside Roger. "You feel it, don't you? Or have your senses dimmed?"

Fully delving into another's fears or desires took concentration. A twinge of guilt didn't stop Roger from sifting through the ruckus pouring out of Ezra. His desire was high —pain and humiliation were strings that easily tugged Ezra into lust. He was a submissive through and through. Roger had explored that with him before he turned him, back when things were good between them.

Underneath that floating want was the sour taste of fear. Ezra was terrified ... of what? Reading emotions wasn't like reading a mind. The interpretations could be muddled.

"He's scared you'll hate him," Candide said.

"I could never hate him," Roger said quietly. "Not when everything is my fault."

"The both of you are so tragic," Candide chided. She ran her finger along the back of Roger's chair and went to the cabinet full of toys. After setting down her glass, she removed a flogger and ran the strips over her fingers. "We all know who is to blame, and it's neither of you. I don't want to discuss him, though. I want to clear the air between the two of you and remove this distraction from Ezra's mind."

Candide offered Roger the flogger; he thought about taking it. They'd disciplined pets together before. Though Ezra was a vampire, he was collared and chained like he belonged to her.

When Roger hesitated, Candide used the end of the flogger to lift his chin up. They locked gazes in another staring contest, but this time, shame and anguish caused him to break away in a matter of seconds.

But he'd cracked. The pieces of the masks he'd been wearing crumbled, and he had no clue how to weld them together again.

"Ah," Candide said gently. "You're sliding into one of those phases. You think you're the one who deserves the punishment."

Roger wiped a hand down his face. He didn't have time for this. He couldn't be ... *this*. This raw, hurt man would be the death of him, and he had to bury him down where he belonged. With a deep breath, he drew on the cloak of uncaring that he'd established for decades and a mask of indifference. Calmly, he said, adopting his usual American tone, "Perhaps. But I am not the one with your collar or chained to your walls."

"You could spend a night that way."

"Not this night, nor one anytime soon," Roger replied.

A knock on the door caught him off guard and seemed to disturb Candide, judging from the way she frowned. She strode over to the door and answered it.

One of her guards was on the other side. "Mistress, an insistent pet of Master Roger's demanded that I pass along the message that Seamus would like to speak to him."

"Seamus is here?" Candide asked.

"Yes, mistress. He arrived a few minutes ago."

"There go my plans for the evening." She sighed dramatically and walked out of the room.

Roger took a step to follow her, then paused. They were leaving Ezra chained and gagged in a fake office. Technically, he didn't breathe, so Roger didn't need to worry about his airway. Roger couldn't help thinking of Zack's questions. *What kind of rules will I have? What will I tolerate?*

Smothering his affections for others had been one of his many survival tactics. If no one knew he cared, then no one could be used against him.

Roger had never stopped to consider what that had done to those he cared for. The shame of what had happened at Gladwell Manor had tormented him for centuries. He'd believed that Ezra's anger at him was justified and used that to keep a distance between them so that Seamus would never hurt him.

But through all these years, Ezra had been hurting, too.

Quickly, Roger crossed the room to Ezra and tested the strength of the chains. They weren't silver, so they weren't eating into Ezra's skin. His cuffed wrists showed only the slightest sign of irritation. Tugging on the chains revealed that while they were secure, they weren't designed to withstand applied strength.

Roger pressed a kiss to Ezra's temple. "At some point, we need to talk, but know that I have never been angry with you."

Ezra trembled, then nodded.

"For the record," Candide said icily, "there is a key in the desk for the chains. He's capable of releasing himself at any point, and he knows it. My joy comes from stripping my submissives bare and giving them what they long for, not outright torturing them."

"Forgive me," Roger said as they started for the staircase downward. "I wasn't expecting Seamus tonight, and I'm rattled."

"I was hoping he'd stay away, but I'm not surprised. He has been growing anxious by your continued absence. He was debating who to send in order to compel you to come home."

"He could have called me," Roger said.

"And had the conversation overheard on Nell's landline?"

Roger frowned. "What?"

Candide paused at the top of the stairs and regarded Roger. "You're not aware?"

Suppressing the urge to growl, he replied, "Aware of *what*?"

"Dmitri said that you appointed him your representative and that all communication should run through him as you were not yet acquainted with new technologies. He made it sound as if you don't know what an email is. The only contact information he gave for you was a physical address and the telephone number to Nell's mansion."

Roger pulled his phone from his pocket and held the slim device up for Candide to see. "Would you like me to send you a selfie? An email full of emojis? How about a YouTube video of cats?"

"I *knew* he was up to something," Candide hissed.

Or she was. But her anger seemed genuine, and what she'd said made sense with Dmitri's attitude the night before. He hadn't wanted Roger to hesitate in his assassination plot. *What else has he lied about?*

"I don't have time to stall." Roger slid his phone into his pocket. "I have to repair whatever damage he's caused before Seamus believes that I'm the source of the problem."

Candide took Roger's arm. "At least one good thing about his moping for centuries is that you shouldn't have a hard time throwing him under the bus."

"I can't do that to him."

"All this guilt, mon cher," Candide murmured. "It will crush you one night."

"I have no idea what you mean," Roger said as he slipped into his habitual warm smile.

She matched him, bringing forth her charming persona again. Together, they descended the stairs.

Zack was waiting on the second floor for them. Though he was glaring at the floor, Roger spotted the familial similarities to Ezra that he had thought were a product of living too long. He should have noted that turn to his nose, the shape of his pout.

How did I miss that? Roger couldn't help the next thought. *Or did he hide it from me?*

As they passed, Zack fell in behind them. The three of them continued on to the first floor. Roger didn't need to search for Seamus on this floor; the air was cooler the closer they were to him. Seamus's scent of the grave was pungent, even from rooms away.

Bracing himself, Roger walked through the archway into one of the sitting rooms.

The first time Roger had seen Seamus, the vampire had been in the back corner of a tavern with his companion. He'd been just another stranger, but he had a beauty that Roger couldn't stop beholding. To this night, Roger wasn't sure if that was because Seamus had used his powers or because he was a handsome man. Throughout that night, Roger had caught Seamus watching him and drank and partied all the harder for it. Half the reason he'd dragged Dmitri out behind the tavern for a quick fuck was because he kept thinking about the stranger.

Roger hadn't known he was a vampire. He'd clocked that Seamus had seemed interested in him with a hunger that Roger thought he wouldn't mind. And in that moment, in that night, he wasn't sure what he'd hoped for.

And all the nights that followed? The pleasures had outweighed the problems for centuries.

Hadn't they?

Or had he just been powerless?

Memories faded away to the moment—the rush of seeing Seamus becoming a reality. He had found a simple wooden chair and sat on it in the center of the room as if he were a king holding court. There was nothing new about that. He was telling a story, engaging the audience by sweeping his gaze across the crowd and making eye contact with the vampires who would meet him. His voice was smooth with an ageless reverberation only the true masters gained with their centuries.

The warm feeling dropped from Roger when he realized that Takashi was sitting in close proximity to Seamus. His position wasn't the concern, but his careful attitude raised a flag. Takashi's expression was guarded. Kit and Carver were sitting on the floor beside him. Carver was not nearly a skilled enough actor. His brow was pinched in concern.

"And this one," Seamus said, pointing at Roger as he stood, "was in the middle of the room without a stitch of clothing on and a vodka martini in his hand. He didn't miss a beat. He strode across the room to the prohibition agents and kissed one! They, of course, were too stunned by his beauty to do anything but give in to him. Those that lived had the best night of their lives, and those that didn't, well, they made an excellent meal!"

Seamus had left out parts of the story. Like how Roger had known the lead agent and had been having an affair with him. Like the fact that Seamus and Roger had used their magic on the men to bring out their desire to fuck rather than destroy and those that couldn't handle their sudden attraction to men became the first course.

The part of Roger that loved the taste of blood and the feel of warm flesh in his hands loved that memory. Another part of him shrunk away from it. He'd always ignored the shrinking part because what else could he do but enjoy his life? Even now, he packaged away the guilt rising in his gut and turned on his charm to its highest level. *What will I tolerate?*

Roger laughed with the crowd in order to disguise the painful thorns in his mind.

The laughter died down when Seamus strode toward Roger. He held his arms out for an embrace. "You've finally come home!"

For a brief instant, hope fluttered, and Roger wished that he could believe Seamus was happy to see him. He made that wish another shield and met Seamus's embrace, hugging him in return. "Master, it's been entirely too long. Please forgive my absence."

"Of course," Seamus cooed. "We all take a break from time to time. You should have told me you needed it!"

"The urge came on rather suddenly." Roger had been planning his lies for months, and they tumbled from his lips. "You know how impulsive I can be."

"I do." Seamus's gaze flicked from Roger to a place over his shoulder.

Zack, Roger realized. He tightened his grip on Seamus's arm. "I have a gift for you."

"Oh?" Seamus was not subtle about sliding his attention toward Zack again.

With a touch of flair, Roger drew out the envelope holding Takashi's document and handed it to Seamus. "Forgive me for reappearing in Taliville, but I was trying to convince Nell to release my lover so that he could join us."

Raising an eyebrow, Seamus took the envelope and removed the parchment it contained. He read it, and a flash of surprise crossed his features. "This is genuine?"

"It is," Takashi said as he stood. He threaded his way through the crowd of pets sitting on the floor nearer to his couch and made his way over to Seamus and Roger. Closing the distance wasn't necessary to be heard—the room had fallen into complete silence—but Roger could have kissed him for the solidarity.

"What could you have done that convinced her to release you?" Seamus asked.

"Fallen in love with one of your captains and refuse to travel for her anymore." Takashi took Roger's hand in his. "We debated for a few years where the better home would be. I loved the mountains, but Roger missed the city."

The lie was a good one, and Roger could almost believe it himself. He smiled at Takashi. Bolstering his nerve, he swung his gaze back to Seamus.

Seamus regarded the two of them and then looked past them to Zack. "How does your hunter brat play into it?"

"Can you believe that Quinn tried to have me killed?" Roger said as if he didn't care. "I stopped the boy before he could finish the job. He was simply too beautiful to kill. I had to have him."

In his very long life, Roger had had to bullshit his way into Seamus's good graces too many times to count. But every time came down to the one instant, the fraction of a second where Seamus might turn angry instead of accepting. Trying to predict which way he would turn had been the challenge of centuries.

"He is a handsome one," Seamus mused. He folded the parchment and put it back into its envelope.

"Training him was one reason I delayed," Roger admitted. "I had to make certain he was tame."

"I could've helped with that," Seamus said.

"I wanted to ensure my skills hadn't gotten rusty."

"You wouldn't have taken months if you'd brought him to my garden," another voice said.

Roger had ignored the crowd in favor of appealing to Seamus, but there were at least a dozen other vampires in the room. He knew most of them, including the one rising to his feet.

Marcus had been dressed in a lieutenant's uniform the first time Roger had laid eyes on him. Despite loathing Quinn for his betrayal, Roger had been tasked with raising his sireling. Roughly a year had passed, and Quinn claimed to have trouble containing his impulses. When he spotted Marcus in the crowd, Quinn declared he was going to turn him.

Roger had warned Quinn not to do it. But Quinn had been upset that Roger refused to sleep with him. So he'd seduced Marcus, eventually turning an affair of a few weeks into an immortal drama. As fiercely as they could be in love, Marcus and Quinn would also delve into sabotaging behavior to ruin the other's good standing in the coven.

Seamus had confessed to Roger in 1939 that he found the whole thing rather amusing.

In the present, Marcus cruised between the other patrons and went to Seamus's abandoned chair. He'd grown his brown hair out to be shoulder length, and he'd used eyeshadow to encourage his hazel eyes to seem greener. His pants and vest were of the same black leather, molded to fit his body. The stark color was Marcus's attempt to make his skin seem more ethereally pale, but he remained the same pasty white he'd been the night he'd risen from the grave. Quinn hadn't had much power to bestow on him, and Marcus had never gained the strength other vampires his age should have.

That hadn't stopped him from becoming cocky and over-compensating with his bravado.

He took Seamus's chair and spun it around so the back was facing Seamus and Roger. Without breaking eye contact with Roger, he straddled the seat. "Candide's built a fancy house, but Steward's Garden is where the real fun is had. We could've had your boy broken in like that." He snapped his fingers.

"You know I admire your approach," Seamus said as he left Roger's side to drift toward Marcus. Then, he caught Marcus by the hair. "But you are a sledgehammer."

For his part, Marcus grinned.

Seamus smiled back at him, the predator gleam in his eye.

And they're fucking. Roger made a subtle motion to Zack, one they'd established as a "follow me" during training. He claimed Takashi's place on the couch, and the person beside him was good enough to scoot their pet off the couch so that Takashi could sit with him. Zack sat at Roger's feet.

"I prefer my pets' will intact." Roger threaded his hand through Zack's hair.

"How *mortal*," Marcus said with a sneer.

Seamus chuckled and released Marcus. He shook his head and motioned for the vampire on Roger's other side to move. Once the seat was empty, he sat. "You'd think being a vampire for two hundred years would give him some appreciation for the finer art of manipulation."

"Perhaps I just want a chance to wreck the brat that killed my sire," Marcus snapped.

Seamus shot him a warning glare.

Roger eased his arm around Takashi and sighed dramatically. "Quinn had a vendetta that was going to get him killed sooner or later. At least he didn't manage to start a war with the Wrights."

"And keeping your brat won't do that?" Marcus asked.

"Hasn't so far," Roger mused.

"Enough posturing," Seamus declared. "Roger has come home. Candide, you must have a few delicious ones you've been holding back for a special occasion. Pipe some sort of music in here. Let the celebration begin!"

Candide clapped her hands, and a dozen white-collared donors came into the room.

The worst of the tests was over, and Roger and Zack and the others weren't dead. Roger relaxed into the couch. *Now we just have to grin and pretend that we aren't sickened by whatever he decides to do tonight.*

CHAPTER 16

Zack had been prepared for the worst night of his life. He'd steadied his nerves for the disdainful and monstrous. Sitting by while vampires drank from donors was something he'd expected. Listening to them talk as if humans weren't in the room didn't surprise him in the least, even if some of the stories were about brutal murders told in a callous tone.

Watching Roger schmooze with Seamus was the gut punch. It shouldn't have been, but everything Roger did seemed to say that he *liked* Seamus.

Which made sense because Roger's mission for the night was to make a smooth transition back into the coven. He needed Seamus to like him. Zack couldn't fault him for doing what needed to be done.

But every minute in Seamus's presence only deepened the sense of wrongness Zack felt about him. Taking in the room around him wasn't the easiest since he couldn't risk accidentally making eye contact with a vampire, but he'd snuck glances. The vampires had laughed and smiled, only some of them didn't have any glee to it. Candide had excused herself after a few minutes, claiming she had a business to run. White-collared donors hung out near the walls, but most escaped from the room if no one called on them after ten minutes. Others alternated in.

No one *stayed* unless Seamus was holding court with them.

Roger was the center of that attention, with some of it splashing on Takashi. Seamus treated them to two additional donors apiece because he kept insisting that they try Candide's newest blood. And the more Seamus fawned over Roger, the more Marcus glared at them.

Eventually, Roger nudged Zack and made to stand up. "I'm glad to be back in your company, Seamus, but dawn is coming."

"I suppose I should let you go," Seamus murmured sadly. "Promise you'll be at my Halloween party."

"At Devil's Cove?" Roger asked.

"As always."

"We'll be there," Roger replied.

The relief that he, Kit, Carver, and Takashi were on their feet and their group was about to leave dropped into a cold flip-flop in Zack's stomach. Devil's Cove was Seamus's private club, where only the vampires he liked were allowed. The second floor of Chateau de Vampire was rumored to be the less extreme version of that club.

"The theme this year is deities," Seamus said.

"How wonderful," Roger said smoothly. "I can't wait to attend."

Just as Roger was about to finally stand, Seamus grabbed his shirt and pulled him into a kiss. Zack took an instinctive step forward, but Takashi caught him around the waist.

Sharing Roger wasn't supposed to mean *Seamus*. But this wasn't sharing, not really. This was another test. *The tests will never be over.*

The kiss was over in an instant. Seamus slid his gaze past Roger and met Zack's.

And Zack didn't look away. He should. He could feel the heat in his glare, and he was aiming it at Seamus.

"Your pet hunter certainly has spirit," Seamus murmured in Roger's ear, but Zack was close enough to hear. The chatter in the room was nearly nothing. With a downright evil grin, he continued. "Remind him what happens to disobedient vermin. I'd hate for you to lose such a pretty one so soon."

"Yes, master," Roger whispered. When he turned, his lighthearted demeanor shifted to a stern frown. He grabbed Zack by the arm and began to drag him from the room.

But Zack caught Seamus's expression. The bastard was damn near laughing. *He doesn't think we're a threat. He doesn't give a shit about us.*

By the time they reached the limo, Zack was ready to lay into Roger about the rough treatment.

Then he saw the terror peeking through the cracks of Roger's stern mask. The others must have picked up on it as well because the five of them silently climbed into the limo. Where the ride out had been anxious but joyful, the ride back to the hotel was deathly quiet. Breaking the silence felt sacrilegious, so Zack tucked himself against a window and watched the city creep back into view.

Zack had always pictured the streets of Chicago having bumper-to-bumper traffic no matter the hour. However, the streets were practically empty, and it took half the time to drive back than it had to make their way out.

Immediately, Zack went to the master bedroom while Kit and Carver split off to the bedroom they were sharing. Zack figured that Roger would be on his heels, but he headed for the balcony while Takashi took a seat on the couch and took out his phone.

Dawn was over an hour away. Zack couldn't blame Roger for wanting space, so instead of following him, he took off his collar, dropped it on the dresser, and then continued into their bathroom to wash off his makeup. He changed into a flannel pajama set and took his journal out from its hiding place under the bed. After writing his entry for the night, he added more data to his notebook.

There was a hint of gray in the sky. Roger wouldn't burn in sunlight—at least he wouldn't right away. Zack had seen him survive a few sparse minutes in daylight when he'd been thirty years starved of blood. And sometimes Roger stayed up a little past dawn while Zack went to sleep well before that.

But the bees and slithering worms that had crowded Zack's stomach while they were in Seamus's presence hadn't left.

Zack padded out to the living room. Takashi had a battered copy of an older HT Moss book in his hands. The author was the same one who wrote Zack's favorite book series, *From the Grave*.

Zack folded his arms over his chest, holding himself, and made his way across the room to look out the sliding glass door. Well, he tried. The light inside made it hard to see past the glass into the darkness. The gray hadn't really lightened the sky enough.

After a moment, Takashi put a bookmark in the novel and set it aside. "I'm sorry."

"For what?" Zack said with a frown as he glanced Takashi's way. Then, the night played back for him. "Oh. That. That's not your fault."

"I may not have known the harm I could cause, but that doesn't mean I can't regret causing it." Takashi stood and slid his hands in his pockets before crossing the room to stand beside Zack. "Won't happen again."

"Thanks." Zack sighed. "I'm more worried about him. He's been making this huge deal out of making me ready to be part of the coven, and I never really understood what coming back would mean for him. I could guess, but ..."

"But witnessing it firsthand has a way of providing clarity. You do realize that kiss wasn't something he wanted, right?"

"I know," Zack whispered. He clenched, his grasp on his arms tightening. "Seamus has demanded more than that from him, hasn't he?"

"It's not something he's ever talked about in the time I've known him," Takashi replied gently.

And life wasn't fair because Zack could imagine Takashi in a suit from the 1980s or in one from the 1920s. Jacket off, suspenders showing, dancing up close with Roger in a smoky speakeasy where no one cared two men were dancing together. A stolen moment, where the mistiness in Takashi's eyes wasn't filled with sorrow but wonder.

Candide had said that Takashi had been shy, but he wasn't like that now. Had Roger been part of that change? Did he love him? Had he loved him longer than Zack had been alive?

But he hasn't talked to Takashi either. He's hidden himself. Have I seen more than he has? That wasn't what mattered. Roger and the fact that he was hurting did.

Zack rubbed his arm and glanced out the sliding glass door. "I don't know what to do. It's not like people make greeting cards for 'Sorry you had to face your trauma.' Not that a greeting card would work, but …"

"I understand what you mean." Takashi dipped his head before half turning toward Zack. "I had a chance to speak with Josefina while I was home, and I spoke with Roger last night. It seems to me that he's only begun to face the real horror he's been living with."

"When we first met, he told me everyone had a sad monster of trauma inside them."

"He has a point. But I think he forgot something else while he was away."

"What?" Zack asked.

"It's amazing what you can get used to and astonishing

what you can begin to heal when it's not happening," Takashi replied.

There was a wisdom, which Zack immediately pushed away, but then he realized Roger wasn't the only one with deeper wounds. Cal, his mother—his whole fucking family. They'd been hypercritical, striking down things he loved. Living like them had made his social life wilt. Without them, he had friends. Blake, Kit, Reed. Carver. Takashi. He had Roger.

And if Cal walked through the hotel suite door, Zack wouldn't know what to do. Sure, he'd yell at him to get out. But if Cal tried to be nice?

Lucky for me, he never will. Did that really make him lucky? Zack bit his bottom lip.

"He's coming back inside," Takashi said.

A thousand potential greetings sat on the tip of Zack's tongue, but as Roger stepped into the light of the living room, each one crumbled into ash. Remnants of bloody tear trails clung to Roger's cheeks, reddening a track along his nose. He managed a weak, sad smile for Zack. "You're still awake."

"Been waiting for you," Zack whispered because anything louder felt like taking a sledgehammer to glass. "I was worried."

Roger stroked Zack's cheek. "Tonight was a lot."

"Yeah," Zack said. And the word was too little to encompass everything. Zack stepped forward and wrapped his arms around Roger.

"Give me something else to think about, hm?" Roger murmured. Then he gently kissed Zack.

If words wouldn't work, Zack could try other stuff with his mouth. He held on to Roger and kissed him in return.

"That's my cue to leave," Takashi said.

But letting him leave wouldn't be fair. Zack broke off the kiss and spun toward Takashi. He held on to Roger's hand as he reached out for him. "Wait."

Slowly, Takashi turned, a wariness in his deep blue eyes.

Zack took a deep breath and continued to hold his hand out. "Roger's poly. And I want that for him. For us. I've never done this before. I just … I just don't want you to walk away from him. Us. This moment. Be here. If you want to be."

"You're certain?" Takashi asked.

Zack nodded.

Takashi rushed forward, nearly zooming with supernatural speed, and wrapped his arms around Roger as he kissed him. Their mouths tangled together hungrily. Roger held Takashi closer with his free hand and held on to Zack's tightly with his other.

Seeing them together was like a key sliding into a lock and turning. Something marvelous in Zack was opening. He had a front-row seat to his boyfriend making out with another man, only Takashi wasn't some random other man. He was clever, and he shared a history with Roger. And he groaned in a soulful, satisfied way as their kiss came to a close. He pulled Roger down so their foreheads touched. "I have longed for that since I heard rumor you were dead. My heart has ached for your smile, and I have spent the last thirty years wishing I had said all I'd felt and held inside myself."

Zack had never said something so achingly beautiful. He was a stammering fool in comparison, and he had to swallow a knot of jealousy that he didn't know how to express himself so elegantly. *Takashi's had thirty years to think of what he'd say. Maybe with that much time, you'd think of something, too.*

"I've missed you, too," Roger murmured.

Takashi gave Roger another quick kiss. With heat in his eyes and a warm smile, he glanced at Zack. "Roger's not the only one I want."

Zack's mind blanked on the meaning of words for a moment. Then Takashi was stepping nearer. They were closer in height; Zack didn't have to tip his head up to reach his lips. Thankfully, Takashi was moving slowly, and Zack's mind had a chance to catch up to what was happening. He could back away from the kiss. He should. Roger was watching and …

And Roger had said that he wouldn't let anyone make fun of Zack for sexually enjoying himself. Not even himself.

He won't make fun of me. Takashi's giving me space just in case I panic. But this isn't a crowd. It's my boyfriend. Boyfriend and his boyfriend? My boyfriend and his boyfriend who might be my potential boyfriend?

Zack pressed his lips to Takashi's, surprised that his touch wasn't quite as cold as Roger's. A blush crawled across his cheeks, heating down his neck, and his heart thundered in his chest. He closed his eyes—he couldn't help it—and that narrowed the world to his sense of touch. Tenderly, Takashi slid his lips against Zack's and wrapped an arm around him. Zack leaned into him and licked the seam of his lips. When Takashi opened his mouth, Zack slipped in, exploring and mapping.

Slowly, Zack brought the kiss to an end. He managed to force his eyes open. The faintest blush painted Takashi's cheeks; the blood he'd drunk had given him more of a mortal reaction. And that wasn't the only part of him reacting. Pressed together like they were, Takashi's hardening erection nudged against Zack's thickening cock.

With a grin, Zack said, "Yeah, okay."

"Okay?" Takashi snorted.

"Well, as much as I think we should totally explore if that's the best kiss we could ever have, Roger's the one I want to focus on," Zack said. "He needs the distraction."

"I'm plenty distracted," Roger purred.

"Maybe." Zack took Takashi's hand. Holding on to Roger as well, he walked backward and tugged them toward the master bedroom. "I think we can do better."

CHAPTER 17

Threesomes were nothing new for Roger, but novelty sparked a blaze inside him as Zack dragged him and Takashi into the bedroom. His soul was scrubbed raw from the hours spent at the Chateau, and paranoid thoughts grew like ivy along a cracked wall. The insidious twists of his deeper thoughts were feasting on his fears. Why had Zack never mentioned he was a Gladwell? Was he preparing to stab Roger in the back? Was Takashi? Was Zack going along with a threesome as a subterfuge? He'd never suggested one before.

You're overthinking it. You know the difference. Did he? He thought he knew Dmitri, and yet the longer Roger spoke with the other vampires tonight, the more he'd realized that Dmitri had been lying to him and lying to others about him. What else had he lied about?

But Zack's hand was clasped in Roger's. Even if he could convince himself that Zack's warm smile was false or that his insistent kiss was a ploy, he had an insight into his emotions. Zack's wall was down. Liquid desire flowed through him, and the dread that was forever a hurdle was diminished. *And I know him. I know I matter to him. I know this isn't an act.*

And Takashi? Hundreds of other threads of ivy bloomed if

he allowed them. Takashi had been Nell's left hand. Her loyal ambassador. Her spy. Had he shifted his allegiance? Was he using Roger as a stepping stone?

The way he kissed said no.

Once they were in the bedroom, Roger pulled Takashi to him and kissed him. Takashi melted against him, wrapping an arm around his shoulders. Roger's tongue brushed against his fang and stroked the inside of his mouth. Kissing him brought back notes of the past, like elements of a wine, and flavored the present. The first time they had ever kissed had been in the back of a speakeasy, cigarettes, bootlegged gin, and blood on Takashi's tongue. But the one that had made Roger's heart soar had been in Nashville, in 1985, in a hotel room at dusk as they were just waking. That kiss had been the slow, waking exploration between two lovers who could have so much more—but Takashi was bound to follow Nell, and Roger had had to return to Chicago in less than a week.

And this kiss renewed that plea, that supplication for a hopeful beginning rather than the indulgence of a singular moment.

Zack approached him from behind and began untucking his shirt while Takashi nimbly undid the buttons of his shirt. With their guidance, Roger slipped out of the purple silk. Zack dropped it onto the dresser before planting small kisses on Roger's shoulder. The heat of his lips preceded the touch of them, a flash of promise before the act.

A needful groan vibrated out of Roger. Slowly, he spun around, caught Zack around the waist, and drew him into a deep kiss. Zack plunged his tongue past Roger's lips and ruthlessly took command of the kiss. He put a hand on the back of Roger's neck and locked him into place. Being pinned was typically a turnoff, but the desperation in the way Zack panted and coaxed him further into the kiss was charming.

Still, Roger broke off the kiss with a rumbling chuckle. "It's not a competition, sweetheart."

"Except who can get naked first," Takashi teased as he undid the buttons of his own shirt.

Zack stepped back with a boyish and beautiful grin. "Oh, well, *that* I can win."

Zack had already changed into his sleepwear. With a few quick movements, he flung off his shirt and dropped his underwear and flannel pants to the floor. Takashi had barely finished unbuttoning his shirt, and Roger had made no move to continue undressing, so Zack did easily win that.

Watching Takashi absorb and appreciate the freshly nude Zack was mesmerizing. Roger leaned back against the dresser and stayed out of the way as Takashi neared Zack. There was a magic in witnessing two partners discover what he liked and already knew about the other. Though Zack had been showing more skin earlier, the fishnet shirt had obscured his scar and tattoo.

Lightly, Takashi traced the scar on Zack's shoulder, and Zack fidgeted. Knowing the pain that lurked behind the story of the mark, Roger was drawn to him and slid around behind him to kiss the crook of his neck.

"Is that where …?" Takashi glanced up from the pink scar.

"My brother stabbed me? Yeah," Zack whispered hoarsely.

"To save me," Roger murmured. He planted another kiss, this one behind Zack's ear, and wrapped an arm around his waist. "I shouldn't have been so careless."

"I never should've let him near you in the first place."

"Let's not dwell on regrets right now," Takashi said.

"Agreed," Roger murmured. He continued pressing light kisses to Zack's jaw and neck.

Zack reached forward and undid Takashi's belt and pants. Then he slid his hands inside Takashi's open shirt, pushing aside fabric to reveal Takashi's muscular abdomen. Tentatively, he caressed him.

Roger sat on the end of the bed for a better view as Zack

explored Takashi while he undressed him. His long centuries had given Roger the opportunity to appreciate so many forms of stunning beauty, and yet, like Zack, Takashi stood out from the seas of men Roger had been with. No one aspect made him exceptional; rather, the combining of them into the whole made him unique. Zack and Takashi were close to the same height, so neither had to bend down into the kiss they shared. They continued at a leisurely pace, the testing and teasing bringing moans out from both of them.

Their kiss soothed a knot of tension that had festered into a ball of worry in Roger's mind. He could have been monogamous with Zack. He'd been so since they'd met because he didn't want to ruin the growing bond between them. And though Zack had said that he was willing to try, that didn't mean he'd be able to follow through.

Roger could sense the rising tempos of desire in both men before him. He opened his mind further, relying on the core of cold power inside him. As subtle as the drift of a caress, he brushed his ability against their lusts to gain a deeper understanding of them.

He could manipulate them, but why would he when they were so clearly enjoying themselves? Zack's wants were racing. He wanted to be touched, to be held, to fuck and feel wanted. Underneath them all was the desire Roger had always seen in him, even without using his powers. Zack longed to be *seen*, to belong and feel worthy.

Surprisingly, Takashi's surface desires shifted and pulsed with a speed that matched Zack's. Roger couldn't read minds, and Takashi's impulses were a blur of longing to chase the physical pleasures. His bloodlust was sated, but there was a yearning to taste Zack in the mix of his wants.

Plunging deeper, Roger delved beyond Takashi's guard. The sensation was a newer one for him. Rarely had he indulged his ability and pursued more than the lusts easily spotted and felt.

Takashi longed for a future of freedom. When he was mortal, he had soared on the trapeze, and the desire hidden toward the heart of him longed for his life to have some semblance of that. He had no massive terror of risk, only an ice-cold trickle of fear that he would never feel alive.

Takashi shivered and broke off his kiss with Zack to turn a wary glare at Roger. "What are you doing in there?"

The words brought Roger back to himself, back to the hotel room and the bed under him. Takashi's pants were halfway down his thighs, and Zack had his hand around his cock. During Roger's excursion into their emotions, the two of them had been getting along extremely well.

Zack was flushed, his cheeks a bright red that crawled down his neck to his chest, and he glanced bewildered between them. Slowly, he took his hand off Takashi's member and backed away by a step. "What's going on?"

"He was in my head," Takashi said.

Zack frowned. He ran a hand through his hair and then scowled more as he touched his tattoo. "Wait, were you in *my* head, too?"

"I'm sorry," Roger replied quickly. "I was only looking. You are both so beautiful I was drawn in. I was caught up in sharing the emotions with you."

"My tattoo would have gotten too hot to ignore if he'd tried to mess with me," Zack murmured to Takashi.

"I would never do such a thing to lovers without permission," Roger said. "You both know that."

"That's not what's worrying me," Takashi whispered. His glare eased to a worried frown, and he cupped Roger's cheeks in both hands.

Takashi was a younger vampire, but Roger thought he would have grasped a better control over his ability to sift through another's lusts and fears, given his long employment as Nell's ambassadorial international spy. Such a skill must have proved useful. Did he lack the talent?

No, no, Roger could feel Takashi slipping through his impulses and sinking into his depths. Roger put his hands on Takashi's wrists, ready to push him away. His fears were ridiculous, not worth noticing.

But as Takashi dove inward, Zack sat beside Roger on the bed. He lightly touched Roger's shoulder and asked, "What's going on?"

"I'm fine," Roger lied because now that they were both watching him, both observing him so closely, the fears he had pushed down were heading for the surface. If he let them reach much higher, Takashi would be able to feel them out. Zack was becoming distracted from pleasure and turning his attention to Roger in a way that threatened to push Roger's mental balance back toward the teetering edge he longed to put behind him.

Only I haven't been putting it behind me. I've simply been twirling on that edge. Roger softened his grip on Takashi's wrists. "I am sorry for the violation. I only meant to explore your passions. But please, let me speak instead of seeking my emotions."

And the wild, impulsive fear that Takashi would say no and continue scrutinizing him spiked so hard in Roger's mind that he thought his heart might beat again.

Slowly, Takashi withdrew his hands from Roger's cheeks and clasped his hands instead. He sat on Roger's left.

Now that Roger had the space and expectancy to speak, his voice fled. The words he needed would have to come from over the side of that edge he longed to run away from. But there was no escaping. There hadn't been for over three hundred years, no matter how much he had ignored his plight from time to time.

Unless, perhaps, *maybe* the men beside him could guide him away from the agony. Having delved into their emotions, he knew the fears he'd had about them were paranoia and not rooted in reality. Still, a few lingered. In the past, voicing concerns hadn't brought him peace. Seamus had always taken that as an insult; Dmitri had only grown more distant. The accusation had always been flipped back onto Roger.

Would Zack hate him? Would Takashi leave him?

Could Roger dare to love them? Or would he find himself dancing alone on the precipice, more unbalanced than ever?

Roger continued holding Takashi's hand with one of his and took the other and offered it to Zack. Without hesitation, Zack put his in Roger's. Roger had hoped that touching both of them might give him some sense of grounding. Instead, the fear tightened around his throat because he would have to speak. He couldn't keep putting it off.

"I learned something tonight. About you," Roger said to Zack. "You're a Gladwell."

"Yeah," Zack said slowly.

"I was afraid that you're playing at a deeper game. That you were planning on killing me in the end."

Zack narrowed his eyes. "*What*?"

Anger was predictable. After all Zack had gone through, he had the right. Yet Roger trembled before he could clamp down on the reflexive fear. He was too raw from the night. Being in Seamus's presence had been like scraping away the layers of healing he'd managed in Taliville and somehow reopening the worst of his mental wounds. *Not just seeing Seamus. Ezra, too. Not realizing that he and Zack were distantly related when I should have.*

Silence would only fuel Zack's anger. He prized information, and though the truth might damn him, the least Roger could do was reveal it. "I never thought another Gladwell would be able to stand my touch, not after what happened in the massacre."

"You were there," Zack said.

"I'm to blame for it."

Zack sprang to his feet and started to break away.

Before his hand slipped from Roger's, Takashi said, "Wait. I know this tale. Let him tell you what happened."

Zack hesitated, his gaze searching Roger's face. He must have found what he hoped to see because he nodded once.

"Our troupe, for we weren't the size of a full coven yet, fled from Paris with little more than the clothes on our backs. Seamus had a habit of pissing off the locals, and somehow a pack of hunters had caught onto us. So we landed in England with barely anything," Roger said. "Seamus's first order was to infiltrate the nobility, gain influence and money in any way possible. We'd had a taste of luxury, and Seamus wasn't willing to slide backward.

"I met Ezra at a ball, though we didn't truly connect until we found one another at a selective whorehouse." Roger tried for a grin, but the coyness he usually masked his history in was a brittle shell on the floor. He continued. "A demon was running the place, and I was one of the whores. There have always been humans willing to flirt and fuck the supernatural, and, well, we were in need of coin. Ezra became one of my clients.

"He seemed a perfect mark. Noble enough that he had plenty of money but with two older brothers, so he would never become a true man of influence. He already had three nephews as well, all of whom would see the title before him. His father was pressuring him to marry, but Ezra wanted nothing to do with that. I thought, given time, I'd help Ezra find the right wife who wouldn't give a damn that her husband had a man outside the marriage, that maybe he might even love her if we looked hard enough for the right woman. I let Ezra believe he was saving me from a whore's life when I was seducing him into being my pet.

"When I told Seamus about him, he demanded that I make Ezra one of us. I suggested we might be better off forming a generational relationship to the family." Roger dipped his head. He was so far into the telling, but the words were glass in his throat. "I was left to thirst, chained in a coffin, for the better part of a fortnight. Seamus made clear his … authority when he finally let me out, and I followed his orders. After a little more work, I had Ezra eating from the palm of my hand, and I convinced him to become a vampire.

"I introduced Ezra and Seamus on the night Ezra rose from the grave. Seamus was at his most charming to the point that even I was fooled by his good manners. He asked Ezra to write a letter extending an invitation to stay with his family. Eager to please me, Ezra did it. I should've known when Seamus allowed us to stay in London for another few weeks that something was wrong, but I thought he saw common sense. Ezra was new. Traveling so far without the proper precautions would only leave a trail of corpses for any enterprising vampire hunter to follow."

Zack sank down onto the bed beside Roger. "The stories say that Seamus turned him."

"I never discovered how that rumor began. Ezra might," Roger said. "It wasn't oft repeated in my circles. We knew the truth."

"The stories also say that Ezra was the architect of the massacre," Zack said. He frowned. "But from what you just said, it sounds like—"

"The manor was overrun with vampires before we reached it," Roger replied. "Seamus proudly declared that there would be no impediment to Ezra's lordship now. Ezra broke that night, and until tonight, I believed all his anger rested on me, and rightfully so."

For a long moment, Zack stared at his hand that clasped Roger's. He gave him a tight squeeze before looking up. "I can't absolve you, but I'm not entirely innocent either. Quinn might be the only supernatural I've actually killed, but I researched for my family. I have no idea if I sent them after the good or the bad. I've caused harm, too."

It wasn't the same, not by a long shot, but Roger couldn't

expect more from Zack. He was immortal and young. Life hadn't given him many opportunities for damning his soul. Roger raised Zack's hand to his lips and kissed the back of it.

"That would be why you dug around in Zack's mind," Takashi said. "That doesn't explain why you probed mine."

"Dmitri has painted me as this recluse unwilling to keep up with the modern era when he told me that he would pave the way for my return. I thought that meant my return to who I was. And Candide is as sharp as ever, and Seamus as corrosive. Even Nell has malice behind her good intentions," Roger said. He squeezed Takashi's hand. "Our kind is not known for their honesty."

"I suppose if we're being honest," Takashi grumbled. Roger's throat closed, but Takashi leaned around him to catch Zack's gaze. "Nell had a copy of your journal. I read the bulk of it before I ever met you."

Zack leapt up from the bed and circled to face Takashi. "What the *fuck*?"

Takashi stood and met Zack's glare. He tilted his head toward Roger. "As he said, our kind is mired in ploys and treachery. I had to know what sort of man had tied himself to Roger. I'm … well, I'm not sorry. And since you can't read my emotions to understand, let me give you a secret instead. Roger was the first man I ever kissed. My first lover."

Roger blinked. He hadn't known that.

"So I'm the one invading," Zack murmured and dropped his gaze to his navel.

Takashi tucked a finger under Zack's chin and nudged him to look up again. "I meant it when I said Roger isn't the only one I want. You are extraordinary."

The impulses that had been subdued while Roger spoke renewed. Holding on to Zack's hand, Roger could feel lust sparked and humming in him again.

Zack bit his bottom lip, shifted his weight from one leg to the other, and squirmed as he continued to meet Takashi's gaze.

The glares were gone, forgotten, and in their stead, warmth and yearning were reflected in Zack's steel gray eyes. Takashi smiled, and Roger was drawn into the beauty of how such a simple gesture could transform the man's face into perfection.

"Oh, screw it," Zack muttered. He lunged forward, wrapped an arm around Takashi's shoulders, and pulled him in for a deep kiss.

And there they picked up in their explorations. No residual anger at Roger tainted their desires. He did his best to keep from plunging into their emotions, but he couldn't help scanning the surface desires once more. Zack and Takashi only cared to feel good. They longed to escape through pleasure without a hint of wanting to punish Roger.

After their long kiss, Zack straddled Roger and kissed him. His lips were flush, his skin warm, and his tongue danced between Roger's fangs. Takashi took the opportunity to finish undressing before he climbed onto the bed behind Roger. Against Roger's skin, his touch was warm, but only a candle to the flame heat of Zack. Takashi's hands were calloused. Vampirism hadn't entirely smoothed the roughness he'd gained as a mortal trapeze artist.

Zack ended the kiss, breaking off with a panting breath, and Takashi pulled Roger backward into another. Roger moaned as he sank back against the bed, Takashi's mouth quickly meeting his again. Zack slid off his lap and worked to pull off the rest of his clothing. Then, they were three naked men in a king-sized bed.

Yet a cold, hard pearl in Roger's gut remained. He caught Takashi in a long kiss, marveled at how quick Zack was to sprawl against him, and every movement was a caress against his lovers. He delved his tongue between Zack's lips and then watched Zack lick and explore Takashi's chest while practically lying on top of him.

The weight of him became a restraint, and Roger slipped

out from under him. Takashi frowned at him, but his cheeks were flushed.

The desire and want in the air was thick, and Roger drew it into himself. He had ignored that pearl of fear for centuries, and it had no place in his love life. With his lovers, he would find solid ground to stand on.

He couldn't let this moment be tainted.

He reached for Takashi and rolled him onto his back. The glimmer of joy in Takashi's deep blue eyes eased the pearl deeper into the depths, and Roger spent a long moment gazing at them. Zack kissed his shoulder, and so Roger kissed Zack, then Takashi. His cock grew hard, and need chased the fears back to their deep shadows.

Takashi caressed his back, fingers tracing down his ass. "I have missed the feel of you." Then, he tugged, and Roger nudged against his hole.

"Eager," Roger chided. When he started to reach for the lube, Zack already had some spread on his fingers. Grinning, he moved aside, spreading Takashi's legs wider, and guided Zack's hand down between Takashi's legs. He kissed Zack's cheek as Zack began to work a finger in.

Takashi arched with a moan. "Fuck, I forgot how warm a mortal is in there."

"His fingers aren't his only warmth," Roger purred.

"I thought you wanted to do him," Zack said.

Roger nuzzled Zack's neck. He spread a little lube on his fingers and eased one into Takashi beside Zack's. "We'll both fit if we're careful."

"Screw careful," Takashi whined.

Zack laughed gently. "He got needy fast."

"This isn't needy yet," Roger chuckled. He pushed his finger deeper and rubbed, finding the place inside that made Takashi shudder with a moan.

With a wicked grin, Zack wrapped his hand around

Takashi's hard cock. He slowly stroked Takashi's length. Before Takashi could complain, Roger kissed him.

As much as lust pooled inside Roger and flowed out from Zack and Takashi, they continued to explore and prod and caress. Roger sprawled onto his back and coaxed Takashi to straddle him. They shared a spine-tingling kiss as Zack guided Roger's cock toward Takashi's hole. Takashi pushed down, and Roger moaned at the tight grip around his dick.

And then Zack was joining him, working his way in, and his cock rubbed against Roger's. He was all heat, and the air was pungent with coppery mortal scent. His breath came in quick pants, and his heart raced.

Roger took his hand and kissed the palm. Their gazes locked.

Zack began to *move*, and every fluctuation of his muscles rippled through Roger and Takashi. Following the heavy, now racing mortal tempo, Takashi leaned backward and rode them. His back was to Zack's chest. Both his lovers were in Roger's full view, and he drank in the sight of them. The sweetness of Zack's blood was a gasp compared to the trembling moan that filled him from their beauty.

Zack came first, though Takashi followed a heartbeat later. The warmth from Zack, the tightness as Takashi clenched around them, and then the coolness as Takashi unloaded across Roger's chest—all of it accompanied a symphony of their voices. Roger thrust upward and came.

The three of them lay together in the mess they'd made. An ache in the bones warned Roger that dawn was nearing. The night would be over. Hell would be waiting to draw him in again.

But for a while, he could remain sated and safe. What else could he want of the world?

CHAPTER 18

When Zack dropped by Blake's house, he thought they'd take a taxi or drive share to their destination. Instead, Blake had led the way out to the street, and they took the El—though she called it "the train"—a few stops before switching to another line, riding for a half dozen more, and then continuing their walk. They were near Darkworth, a private college that, as far as the general public knew, catered to an elite scholarly student base. In reality, the college provided a top-notch mundane education *and* taught some of the most proficient spellcasters in the world. The surrounding neighborhood had the hybrid feeling of a college town and a homey block where neighbors might actually know each other.

"So, how's your first week living in the lap of vamp luxury been?" Blake asked.

"Are you saying Nell's mansion isn't luxurious?" Zack replied.

"It's swanky, but the donor house is nothing like Chateau de Vampire or any of the other hot clubs you've been to." Blake nudged Zack with her shoulder as they continued down the street. "I know your posts and vids aren't the whole picture."

The collar around Zack's throat itched. His social media posts had to be uplifting and eye-catching for other pets and supernaturals. If he made videos about how he sat silent for hours on end every night, had to adjust to being up all night instead of during the day, or that Seamus creeped him out, then he'd break the scam he was trying to run on the coven.

"Uh-oh, I've accidentally caused your thinking face," Blake said.

Zack slid his hands into his hoodie pocket. The material was the softest Zack had ever felt for a hoodie, like a hug wrapping around him. Clothing in his family had been functional over soft or stylish. Having to care about style sucked, but there was an upside. His clothes were his. The few T-shirt hand-me-downs from Cal that he'd taken to Taliville were in the bottom of a drawer in the bedroom in Nell's mansion. He'd intentionally left them behind but hadn't been able to give them away.

"Thinking's not a bad thing," Zack said.

"Overthinking like we tend to do is." Blake slipped her arm into his and hugged his arm tight. "Come on. We made a vow during your recovery. We spill about the bad stuff and share a good thing."

"I don't want to get into the bad. It would take too long to explain. Josefina, Roger—everyone tried to warn me that Chicago would be different. There's a malice here. My family always taught me there was. But somehow, they didn't get it right." Zack cleared his throat. "But, ah. A good thing. Roger and I are officially boyfriends."

"Knew that already. You texted me."

"Right. Duh." Zack bit his inner cheek. Blake wasn't likely to poke fun at him or think he was gross. She'd been his most supportive friend. "We decided our relationship's poly."

"He didn't pressure you into it, did he?" Blake said.

"No. I know how he is with me, and I can see he and

Takashi have *something*. And he's always had multiple partners. I'm trying to be fair." Zack told his squirming stomach to knock it off and added, "I had a three-way with them."

"If you're happy, I'm happy for you." Blake squeezed his arm. "If either of them hurts you, I'll rip 'em to shreds."

She could, at least in her werewolf form. Zack grinned. "Thanks."

"And we're here!" Blake tugged on Zack's arm and led him through a shop door.

Magician's Brew had the wonderful scent of fresh-brewed coffee that vaguely disguised the tingle in the air. Magic was a kind of energy, and areas where spellcasters performed spells over and over could have a sort of latent static electricity in the air. Like with vampires, it could permeate a space, flavoring the energetic buzz. The vibe of the place was like a warm hug or finding the perfect corner to cozy up in.

In addition to the various tables and chairs scattered through the shop, there were booths along one wall and a small corner stage in the front. A sign currently dominated the stage and advertised a trivia night, a poetry night, and special late-night hours on the weekdays. Overhead, planters hung from wires, and a variety of flora filled them. A couple of the plants looked like they were of fey origin rather than a mortal version. Tiny multicolored lights dodged between the different leaves. To the untrained, they'd seem like fairy lights nestled in the plants, but Zack had spent hours watching the pixies in Nell's garden.

"Isn't it great?" Blake asked. "I came here once when I was still in school and had no clue how awesome it really is."

"It's a great breather from the vampire bullshit," Zack said quietly. He spotted that there were three people at a table not far from the entrance with pet collars on.

They ordered. Zack went for a black coffee with a touch of creamer while Blake bought a pumpkin spice latte. After they gathered their drinks, they slid into one of the booths near the back of the establishment. He sank into his seat. "I swear vampires don't know what a comfortable seat is. Not that I get to try many of them. I spend most of my time on the fucking floor."

"Careful how loud you say that." Blake tapped her ears.

He thought he'd kept his voice low enough, but anyone in the place could be a shifter or even a fey. Was supernatural hearing that good? "How do you keep from getting migraines all the time? All the stimulus you take in has to be murder on your brain."

"Definitely at first, but I'm getting used to tuning the unimportant stuff out." Blake hauled her purse onto the table and opened it. She tended to carry a bigger bag. Zack had no idea what she kept in it, but she seemed better prepared than Zack's family on a hunt. "Getting used to city life was an adjustment. It's kind of cool hearing things from a distance, but wow, I did not need to know that much about my parents. Or that the neighbors are planning on dumping their cat because she's pregnant."

"Yikes."

"Yeah. I'm making an argument that we should adopt the cat and her eventual kittens, but turns out my mom is super allergic. My job's not pulling in enough for a place of my own, and 'because I want to make sure kittens aren't abandoned to the streets' is sort of a thin excuse. Actually, it's hard to figure out if it's a 'hey, I think I'm feeling an animal kinship vibe' or 'any reason to move back out of the house will work.'" Blake rooted around in her bag.

"I have a question I'm dying to ask, but I recognize it's rude," Zack said.

Blake raised an eyebrow. "You know that's like the hallmark of something you should keep to yourself."

"Yeah."

"But now I need to know if your brain came up with a complete asshole question." Blake groaned. "Fine. Ask. But I reserve the right to glare."

"Family lore has it that supernaturals and domesticated animals don't get along," Zack said. "Does this cat like you?"

"I knew it was going to be something like that." Blake rolled her eyes. "Like any animal, even human beings, you can train them to do just about anything. According to Dr. Wolfe—and go ahead, have a poke at Dr. Wolfe, the werewolf psychologist researcher."

Zack held up his hands. "No poking. Promise. Go on."

"I've been reading these amazing research papers and books. She's been working with shifters, primarily wolves who have trouble controlling their forms, and pairing them with specially trained emotional support dogs. Typically, they use huskies or Akitas, not because they're closer to wolves or anything, but because they're bigger dogs and can keep pace with a shifted wolf. The dog is essentially a pack buddy who helps them realize they're in danger of shifting or guides them home if they do shift."

"That's incredible," Zack said.

"It's some pretty inspiring stuff. I'm thinking about going back to college and switching my major to psychology. I've been looking for supernatural therapists, and there's really so few compared to the huge community we have."

"That sounds like a great idea."

Blake narrowed her eyes. "But?"

"No buts," Zack said. And he meant it, at least so far as Blake's idea for herself. But he couldn't help wondering about his own future. He'd never had a plan for what happened outside of the family because he was supposed to be a hunter like the rest of them. Was he going to stay at Roger's side forever? Would Roger kick him to the curb when he got old? Would he be able to stomach his boyfriend staying young while he aged? Nothing he really wanted to think about. "What were you getting into your bag for?"

"Oh, right!" Blake withdrew a wrapped gift and a card envelope. She took her purse off the table before sliding them over to him. "I know it's tomorrow, but happy birthday."

"How did you know that?" Zack finished sliding the presents to his side of the table.

"Night Deets. And it's easy to remember since it's Halloween." Blake flashed a smile at him. "Mine isn't until May, but don't worry about it."

"Oh, I'm going to remember." Carefully, Zack opened the envelope and took out the card. Blake had gotten a funny one with a werewolf pun on it, which made him snort. Her gift turned out to be a vampire fiction book that was well-known and had recently been adapted for a streaming service.

"You haven't read it, have you?" Blake asked. "I know that stuff was banned in your house."

Zack ran his hand over the cover. "Only the first couple chapters. I borrowed a copy off my first boyfriend, but Mom threw it out."

His mother had been furious. She hadn't just thrown out the book; she'd grounded him for a month. After he released a vampire during the family hunt in Detroit, she'd scoured his room for any more of the "heretical vampire propaganda." He'd had a couple of books, a few comic books, and a set of Blu-Rays that weren't his, and they had all wound up in the garbage bin. His boyfriend had been pissed and broken up with him.

"You're making a face." Blake winced. "Sorry to bring up bad memories."

"Naw. It's fine." Zack slid the present off to the side, not out of sight but out of the center of the table, and brought his coffee to his lips. It'd cooled enough that he could risk taking a sip. "Seriously, Blake, this is great. Coffee, book, and time with my bestie. Perfect present. Don't stress."

"You know that's usually code for 'oh my God, I'm on the verge of a breakdown, but I don't want you to know,' right?" Blake said. "I think it's universal."

"Eh, more like 'please switch topics *before* my impending breakdown flares bright and ruins our afternoon,'" Zack replied.

Blake pursed her lips, then sighed. "Fine. But only because we are in a public place, and you *know* you can call me if you need to talk. Or you could drop by the house. We can steal a cat together."

"Deal," Zack said with a laugh he didn't feel.

"So, what's Takashi like?" Blake said around a sip of her coffee.

"He's … different." Zack slowly spun his coffee cup while he thought through what he wanted to say. "He's hot, sure. I haven't met a vampire who isn't ridiculously gorgeous. But he's more grounded than the other vampires I know. I wouldn't say he thinks like a human, but he's got this intelligence and experience, and that makes him incredibly intuitive. Roger's charming because he has this way of making you feel sexy. Takashi's charm is like he sees your whole package and likes it."

"You think Roger doesn't see the whole package?" Blake asked.

"I didn't say that. Roger gets me, most of the time. Or at least he tries to. It's not like I'm just a booty call." Zack sighed and drank his coffee. "Forget I said anything. Did you know Josefina offered to turn Reed?"

"No shit?" Blake's gaze drifted up to the nearest planter. After a second, she scrunched her nose and shook her head. "Nope. Don't see it happening."

"He seemed to be seriously considering it."

"Yeah, but it's Reed. He's too nice to be a vampire."

"Vampires can be nice," Zack replied. He was pretty sure his parents had felt a sudden chill, but he was sticking to it.

"*Some* vampires." Blake shrugged one shoulder when Zack narrowed his eyes. "I've been paying attention to supernatural social media. Vampires have an edge to them, and it's different than us shifters. We're like … like tap dancers or Irish dancing. Loud and exhilarating and just rawr! In your face. Vampires are like competitive prima ballerinas. Grace and curves and totally willing to plot your murder if you take their solo."

"More like figure skaters who get pissed if you copy their routines," Zack said.

"Oooh, that is better. Because of the sharp blades and the cold ice. I'm upgrading my analogy." Blake leaned in. "Now, Reed's been near vampires for like ever, but he's like the guy wearing a heavy coat on the sidelines of a hockey game and selling hot chocolate to other cold people in order to keep the ice rink open. He loves to watch, but do you really think he can withstand the freezing rink?"

Her analogy was ridiculous, but … *she has a point.* Reed genuinely cared about others. That didn't have to go away by becoming a vampire, but he would change. He'd have to feed on people, and newbie vampires tended to have accidents, which resulted in deaths. And Reed had wanted Zack to give him an outsider perspective, someone who would say no instead of an immediate yes.

"Where do I fit into your massive metaphor?" Zack asked.

Blake hummed a note, then leaned back. "You're the kid planning his big debut in a professional competition."

Zack choked on his coffee, sputtering and barely keeping stray droplets from landing on his present. When he could speak, he croaked out, "*What*?"

"You okay there?"

"No." Zack leaned in over the table and lowered his voice. "Because if I'm following you, it means you think I'm getting ready to become a freaking vampire."

"Aren't you at least considering it?"

"No!"

"Why not?" Blake started listing on her fingers. "Hot forever. Never gain weight. Heal crazy fast. Impossibly strong. And then there's the living for eternity. Imagine what you could do with it. And you'd be able to spend it with Roger."

"Roger and I have only known each other three months," Zack countered. "And I still have to figure out why all his past relationships failed."

"Look, I get that you're taught to stand at the edge rather than take a leap of faith," Blake said. "But I don't get why you're so upset at the mere suggestion that you might want to become an immortal badass someday."

Because my family would never take me back. Zack bit his tongue from saying the words. Blake had been there for him when he'd cried about being disowned. They'd shared coffees and brownies and pizzas and had their own book club where they reread all of HT Moss's *From the Grave* series. They were closer than he'd felt with any of his cousins in a long time, almost as close as he felt to his sister Amber.

And upon seeing the scars on her face, Cal had figured out she was a werewolf and wanted to kill her just for that.

And Cal wouldn't be the only one who felt that way in his family.

But becoming a vampire? That wouldn't just shut the door; that would make the people he still loved come after him. They'd want to hunt *him*. He couldn't slice the thin rope of hope that he had that maybe, someday, somehow, he could get them to care about him again.

"You read too many books," Zack said somberly. He put his hand on the novel she'd given him and was about to slide it toward her when the café door opened.

Striding in like he owned the place, Vincent Talmadge was surrounded by three other vampire pets. One of them took pics while Vincent primped and grinned for the camera. He and his companions were fully dressed for a change, and they wore attire that was slick and made each of them look devastatingly good.

The murmur of conversations in the shop had been pleasant but shifted to have a note of anxiety. The pixies hid among the leaves of their plants, soft tinkling their version of hurried conversations.

"Not him," Blake groaned.

"You know him?"

"He's an insufferable brute."

Zack frowned. Vincent was a lot of things, but brute didn't seem like a word that would fit him. *He's maybe a hundred pounds soaking wet.* "Who are you talking about?"

"Jeremy." Discreetly, Blake pointed to a man with a big grin. "I found this group meetup on Night Deets, and everyone was cool except that guy. Turns out he massively hits on all the new girls. Won't leave them alone. Who did you think I meant?"

"Vincent. The one with the black collar."

"Oh. Head pet rivalry?"

"Fuck no," Zack said quietly. "The guy's a total diva. Anyone I'd consider a rival would have to be way smarter."

"Should we go?"

"I can't afford to look like I'm running from him," Zack replied. "I'd seem weak."

"But you're not rivals?" Blake teased.

Zack rolled his eyes. He still had his hand on top of the book she'd given him. Before Vincent had walked in, he'd considered storming out, and the anger at Blake's suggestion that he was planning on becoming a vampire continued to simmer. But he couldn't leave, and with a moment to have a second thought, he didn't want to hurt Blake's feelings either.

Reed had said something like that, too. Did everyone assume a human in a relationship with a vampire would want to become one? *What kind of future are you expecting?*

Fuck, Zack had too much on his plate without worrying about this bullshit. He and Roger had a gajillion hurdles before he'd consider spending an eternity with him. He murmured to Blake, "We should keep talking until those guys settle, and then we can slip out."

Blake straightened. "Small problem with that."

Zack noticed it at the same moment. Vincent and the guy Blake had pointed out, Jeremy, were heading straight for their booth. Zack's inner voice strung together a list of swear words long enough to break the character limit on a microblog. He forced his frown into a smile. "Hey."

"Hey there," Vincent said. He had a silky voice that made him sound older than he looked. He put one hand on the back of the booth and leaned in a little while offering his hand to Zack. "Rules have kept us from an actual introduction. I'm Vincent."

Zack shook his hand. "I'm—"

"Zack Wright. We know," Jeremy said as he sat down beside Blake. He didn't seem to give a shit that she had to slide farther into the booth to accommodate him. "You're all our master has talked about for the last week."

Vincent's smile tensed. If he'd been an anime character, he would have gotten one of those stress marks over his temple.

"That so?" Zack said, equal parts terrified and interested by that fact.

"He's exaggerating," Vincent replied. His slick attitude was back, and he sat beside Zack. He was slim enough that Zack didn't have to move in order to give him space, but he did anyway. "Our master has a coven to run and other things to preoccupy him."

Vincent shot Zack a sly smile at the word *things*. He had to be dropping a hint that he'd been sleeping with Seamus and "preoccupying" him that way. But after seeing Roger exhausted every night and the tension everyone had when Seamus was in the room, Zack wasn't sure anyone could have sex with Seamus out of their own free will, especially not a pet. What would happen if Vincent said no? The guy had huge bags under his eyes and another fresh bite wound on his throat and looked like he was on the edge of collapse. All of that was buried under the style and smile, the makeup and the bravado.

But Roger was like that, too.

I haven't thought of Vincent as someone who might need help. I haven't thought about Seamus's pets at all. Zack pulled his coffee mug closer to him. If Vincent was suffering, then he could be a potential ally. The sudden intrusion upon his day might turn into an opportunity.

Blake was scowling. Zack wished he could banish Jeremy from the table or at least say something, but he didn't know how without offending Vincent. There had to be a balance he could strike. Some excuse he could make. She was getting dragged into this because she was sitting with him. He'd signed on to dive into the deep end of treachery and villainy. She hadn't.

"I've been following you," Vincent said. "Your Fang app profile, I mean. Love your vid about the suite. Looks amazing."

"I'll be happier when we move into a house," Zack replied.

"I don't know if my master is ever going to approve of that. Roger made him really upset by disappearing like that. Could take a while to earn forgiveness."

Well, shit. Zack forced a small grin. "Hopefully, my master will be able to prove himself loyal and our coven master will grant his permission."

"Who're you going as tomorrow night?"

"Still deciding," Zack lied. Thorough eavesdropping and social media research had revealed a wide array of the planned costumes. Rumor was that Seamus was planning on the costume of Hades, so Roger had settled on Dionysus.

Takashi had picked Hermes, and Zack, Kit, and Carver were going to be fauns. Well, Carver insisted they were satyrs, but Zack really didn't see the difference.

"You know, I can't figure out why you don't have more followers," Vincent said. "You're hot enough."

"Uh, thanks." Heat crept up Zack's neck. He shrugged with one shoulder. "I need a schtick. I didn't want to copy your vids, and I'm not much of a dancer. Coming up with content's tough."

"Eh, your content is fine. Most people on the Fang app are dying to see how the elite vampires live." Vincent's smile widened, and he perked up. "I know! We'll do a vid together."

"What do you have in mind?" Zack asked.

Vincent was already sliding his phone across to Jeremy and throwing his arm around Zack's shoulders. "I've got the perfect idea. Just smile."

Zack had an older brother and a dozen cousins he'd grown up with, so he could spot the red flag in Vincent's tone a mile away. This setup smelled worse than a bottle of milk left out in the summer sun. But other than jerking away, there wasn't much he could do. Jeremy already had Vincent's phone pointed at them.

So Zack smiled.

Vincent put an arm around his shoulders and dragged him closer until they were cheek to cheek. He flipped off the camera, the same move he made at the start of every video. "I've snagged a minute with GLC's newest black-collar elite. Isn't he precious?"

Holding a smile was hard to do, but Zack had been practicing.

"And people, he may look little, but he is *jacked*." Vincent ran his other hand across Zack's chest. His touch was aggressive and pulled the fabric tauter against Zack's skin. "He totally works out. You do, right?"

"Uh, yeah," Zack said. And he immediately bit his lip. When he filmed for his own page, he had time to edit them down. He doubted Vincent was going to give him that chance.

"'Uh, yeah,'" Vincent imitated. "Adorable. Am I right? He's absolutely adorable."

Whatever this was, Zack was done. He pulled away from Vincent and then reached for the phone.

Vincent slipped his finger through the loop on Zack's collar, the same one that the crest tag was attached to, and yanked him into a kiss.

Caught completely off guard, Zack froze. His mind raced through the outcomes. Roger had said he wouldn't let anyone mock him, but he couldn't control the *internet*. Vincent had thousands of followers, and they would be able to see this lackluster kiss. They'd know that Zack wasn't cool or sexy. They'd judge and decide that Zack was utterly unattractive. Then they'd whisper that there had to be another reason a party boy like Roger would want him around. Their cover would be blown. Seamus would suspect them and on and on and on. His mind circled, spiraling downward into a drain of paranoia.

In the back of his mind, he heard Cal's voice saying, *Serves you right, traitor.*

Vincent was working his lips against Zack's, but after a few seconds, he gave up. With a malicious laugh, he said, "I don't see you keeping that black collar for long, precious. At least you're pretty. Some dickwad will take you in."

And then Vincent and Jeremy were leaving the booth. They grabbed their coffees on the way out the door, and the other two pets that were with them followed behind. Three of them were snickering and whispering, but Vincent had a smug smile of victory.

Because it's all about sex and reputation. And I've just been trashed. I should have seen it coming. Zack clenched his fist. He hadn't given in to his instincts and backed off from the video because he'd been acting the way Roger and Josefina had taught him. He'd tried to keep pace instead of making his own path.

"What was that?" Blake whispered.

"Vampire pet bullshit," Zack muttered.

"Do you think he'll really post it?"

Zack's phone dinged. And then dinged. And then *kept* dinging. He closed his eyes. Ignoring the rash of notifications would be the smarter move, but there was a chance people were calling Vincent out on being a dick. After taking a deep breath, he glanced at his phone to sort through the chaos.

Vincent had already posted the video to the Fang app and tagged him. Comments were flooding in. "OMG what a loser." "How'd he bag a vampire that hot?" "GROSS." Zack's stomach churned with every insult. The vid played over and over while he skimmed further and further down the comments.

Notifications kept dinging his phone. People were finally watching his vids, but they were leaving slurs and insults. If there was anything positive, it was buried under the filth.

"Zack," Blake said.

"Thanks for the gift." Zack grabbed the book and the card. He tried muting the notifications, but now they were piling in on Night Deets, too. After arranging for a ride via an app, he put his phone on silent and shoved it into his back pocket. "I need to get going."

Blake reached for him as he slid out of the booth, but he dodged her touch out of instinct. "Zack, please. Sit back down."

"I'll be fine. Promise." Zack forced a smile. "We'll talk later."

"We better," Blake replied. "Otherwise, I'm storming the suite with tacos and Netflix while we plot that fucker's demise."

"Yeah, yeah, okay!" He knew he should be grateful that Blake was trying to make him feel better.

But all he could think as he ran out the door was that if he was a vampire, he could rip out Vincent's throat and have sweet revenge with blood.

CHAPTER 19

Carver had magnificent blood, and having an intimate audience was intoxicating in its own right. Roger had pinned Carver flat to the couch, the boy's wrists over his head and held in one of his, and he remained bent over him as he continued drinking down liquid heat. The touch of blood on his tongue and his throat brought a rush of power.

As part of the bite, Roger had twisted his metaphorical fingers through Carver's lust and brought it to the surface. He had his knee between Carver's legs, and he could feel Carver's length hardening. The boy's lust continued to build without Roger's magical influence.

His wasn't the only one. Takashi was seated across the way. From his chair, he would have a perfect view of Carver's slackened lips and fluttering eyes. They were in the living room of the suite. Though Roger had partaken of donors in public frequently since his return to the city, there was nothing quite like enjoying a feeding in privacy. Without the cloud of others, Roger could easily sense Takashi's growing desires as well.

Roger lifted his mouth from Carver's neck and smirked at Takashi. As he'd suspected, Takashi was sitting with his legs wide, his dick tenting his pants. Carver allowed his arm to drape over the side of the couch. Roger leaned down and coaxed him to straighten out his arm, his wrist pointed at Takashi. In a low, rumbling whisper, Roger said, "He has plenty, love."

Takashi slid off the chair and crawled over. He took Carver's wrist between his hands and skillfully bit where the blood wouldn't gush too quickly.

Roger returned to the wound on Carver's neck. With long, slow licks, he caught what blood was spilling without drawing more out of him.

Whimpering with want, Carver began to rut against Roger's leg. Takashi groaned a deep, hungry sound. Likely, he was tasting what Roger had enjoyed; Carver had a natural fire in his soul. Wound up like he was, the boy was liquid pleasure.

A sudden pang of cold preceded Zack into the room. Zack was drenched in sweat, oozing the acrid touch of fear. He smelled absolutely divine otherwise. And with his flushed skin and reddened cheeks, Roger longed to snap him up for a nibble.

Zack stopped short, watched Takashi continue to drink from Carver's wrist for a moment, and then met Roger's gaze. A week had passed since Roger had last tasted him, and he allowed that hunger for him to show in the way he drank in Zack's appearance.

Because Zack was *spectacular* in every way. Absentmindedly, Roger touched the open collar of his silk shirt and traced the fabric's edge down to the center of his chest, where he'd finally bothered to button it.

But when he locked gazes with Zack once more, Zack clenched his jaw and stomped off toward the master bedroom.

Smoothly, Roger stood and used a burst of speed to follow. Just as he reached for him, Zack grabbed him by the wrist and spun. Even with supernatural senses, Roger almost lost track of how quickly Zack had him pinned up against the wall.

Trapped between Zack and a wall wasn't a terrible place. Roger grinned. "Sweetheart, if you wanted to top, you only had to ask."

"This was reflex," Zack growled. He released Roger. "Never surprise a hunter."

"What's gotten into you tonight?" Roger asked carefully.

"Don't treat me like that." Zack yanked open a dresser drawer and rooted around in it. Eventually, he tossed some clothing onto the bed and shut the drawer with a thud.

Roger turned around and leaned against the wall. "Like what?"

"Like I'm some kind of bomb primed to go off."

"Slamming drawers isn't convincing of a calm attitude," Roger replied. "Were you jealous?"

"Of what? The impending vampire orgy in the living room? I don't give a shit." Zack stalked off toward the bathroom.

Roger grabbed him by the waist and hauled him up against the wall. "An orgy takes more than three people."

"Listen, if you want to go play hornball with Carver and Takashi, I don't give a flying fuck," Zack snapped. He pushed Roger's arm.

Roger didn't budge. Something had clearly gotten under Zack's skin. "What has you so riled up?"

"Don't you check the internet?" Zack shoved with more strength.

Not wanting to anger him further, Roger released him and let him head into the bathroom. He went back into the living room and drew out his phone. With the shower running in the distance, he opened a search browser but stopped. The internet was a wide, varied place. How the hell was Roger supposed to figure out which one thing was bothering Zack?

"What is it, love?" Takashi said lazily. He had his hand

around Carver's cock and was pumping him slowly. Carver was writhing against the couch.

A delightful moment, though Roger couldn't help being preoccupied with Zack's mood. His anger was a cloud on an otherwise starry night. Ignoring such a thing was Roger's usual reaction, but the notion of carrying on while Zack was hurting bothered him.

Roger frowned, his brow pinched. "Do either of you know why Zack would be pissed? And tell me to check the internet?"

"Yes, master," Carver moaned.

"Why?" Roger asked.

Carver only moaned more as Takashi stroked him.

Roger caught Takashi's eye and shook his head.

With a grin, Takashi slid his hand up to Carver's tip and then locked his hand in place. Carver whined and tried to buck into Takashi's hand, but that didn't work. "I was almost there!"

"I asked a question," Roger said.

"Vincent Talmadge posted something on the Fang app," Carver blurted out. He squirmed. "*Please.*"

"Hm, I suppose," Takashi said. Then he slowly began to slide his hand down Carver's length again.

As Carver was shuddering and nearing release, Roger ducked back into the master bedroom. The scent of blood and the powerful rocking of the desires emanating from Carver and Takashi almost sucked Roger back into a trance of his own lust. But there was something to be seen in order to understand one of his partners.

He didn't have the Fang app on his phone, but Zack did. Since Zack's phone wasn't in plain sight, Roger called it. Following the vibrations, he found it in a bedside drawer, which was an unusual place for it to be. Typically, Zack kept it on a surface or plugged in. With a few quick swipes and presses, he managed to open the Fang app.

Apps had clearly been invented by bored mages who wanted to siphon even more money from the general populace. That, or a brilliant inventor who had made a deal with a devil for eternal youth. Navigating took a little work, but Roger managed to open some sort of message bank. There were hundreds, and more were added as Roger attempted to read a few.

They were, almost without a break, slurs, insults, and outright threats. Zack couldn't know this many people, and there was no reason for them to suddenly turn on him. Had he been dealing with these kinds of remarks for months? Had his family set this off? No, that didn't make sense. The Wrights didn't have any access to the Fang app. Besides, Carver had told him to check Vincent Talmadge's post.

The shower turned off the same moment Roger finally found the video. Zack had been giving the camera his strained smile—the one he used when he was playing along but hated what was happening—and then the other boy *kissed* him. Then laughed at him.

And now, the internet seemed to be laughing at him in unison.

No wonder Zack was having trouble containing his temper.

"What are you doing?" Zack demanded.

Roger glanced up from the phone, an explanation ready on his lips, but was speechless at the sight of Zack next to nude. He had the towel around his shoulders, shaking the last of the water from his hair with it, and hadn't covered up his lithe, athletic frame. The temperature of the shower had brought a flush across his chest and downward toward his groin. His shoulder scar was a shade brighter. For the most part, the various bite marks Roger had given him had healed with little to no scarring, except for the one on his throat from the very first time.

Roger let his awe fill his voice. "How could anyone look at you and decide that mocking was the best approach?"

Zack blushed, and then his features hardened, and he glared. "You've been on my phone?"

"I don't have the app on mine," Roger said.

With a snarl, Zack ripped the phone out of Roger's hands and shoved it into the bedside drawer. "You shouldn't have bothered."

"You were upset. I had to know why," Roger replied.

"So you invaded my privacy?" Zack snapped.

Roger put his hands on his hips. "Were you going to tell me otherwise?"

"It doesn't fucking matter." Zack stalked over to his clothing and picked up his underwear.

"The fuck it doesn't," Roger returned.

"Vincent's right. This—" Zack motioned between them. "—won't last forever. You're going to replace me as black collar. Sooner, if you want to stay in Seamus's good graces, I'm sure."

"Screw Seamus. We're not talking about him right now."

"Fine. Then let's talk about the kind of rules you'd have as coven leader," Zack replied hotly. He threw the towel off to the side. His eyes were hard as he turned on Roger. "Would I have to wear a fucking collar to be your boyfriend? Are you going to expect me to carry on head pet duties when I don't have to pretend to be a pet anymore? What am I going to *be* in this new domain of yours?"

"Is that what you're worried about?"

"You know what? Forget it."

As Zack started to turn away, Roger caught him around the waist and made him return to face him. Zack was in his arms. Though the sounds and scents of the other room had begun to calm, Roger was still floating in that place between lustful need and forgoing pleasure. He longed to sink into

Zack's depths, but that wasn't for him alone to decide. And Zack, well, he was prickling even as Roger held him close.

"I am not going to 'forget it,'" Roger murmured. The quiet tone of his voice caused Zack to settle against him. He brushed a strand of Zack's hair back before tracing his hand down the length of his back. "That's the second time recently that you've doubted your place with me."

"More than the second," Zack grumbled. His gaze remained firmly on Roger's lips. "We've been here a week, and you haven't said anything about your plans."

"Because I am still making them."

"*Roger*." Zack wriggled out of his embrace. "I've been watching you kiss Seamus's ass and come home exhausted every night. You keep drinking from anyone Seamus puts in front of you, including the victims of the gray band mind control. What's your plan? Like him to death?"

"We haven't caught sight nor heard of what Anton is doing," Roger replied.

"Fine. We don't know where the big bad vampire warlock is. But what about what you plan to do as the coven leader?" Zack demanded. He motioned to himself. "Do all humans have to be pets? Is there some place at your side for me? Or will I have to keep wearing your damn collar and pretending my life doesn't fucking matter?"

"You *matter*," Roger growled.

"Not according to anyone but you." Zack blinked. Tears were forming in the corners of his eyes, but they weren't spilling just yet.

"To Takashi, Blake, Kit, and Carver as well," Roger replied. "And easily a dozen others in Taliville."

"This isn't Taliville!" Zack shoved his hands through his hair and stalked away to the curtain-covered window. With his back to Roger, he quickly wiped his eyes.

Roger didn't have to rely on his powers to sense Zack's

deepest desire. Since their meeting, that part of Zack remained unchanged. He longed to do the right thing. He believed in making a difference. In order for him to matter to the world, he would struggle to make it better than how he found it. Zack's family may have narrowed their focus to destroying supernaturals, but Zack held to the foundational principle. He would fight cruel and vicious beings with every fiber of his soul.

Vincent's video had exposed Zack to the worst side of the coven's underbelly, but wasn't that the nature of the beast Seamus continued to feed? Roger had witnessed pets tear each other down, mock and belittle one another, and worse— all in order to appease their vampiric masters. When Roger was young, he'd even encouraged it. Having others fight over him had been a thrill.

These nights, however, he found such bullshit distasteful. Love was better than rampant jealousy. Peace greater than any entertainment. And though he had been sitting on the edge of his seat, waiting for the moment Seamus might lose his temper, he had forgotten that those under Seamus could be just as cruel. Monstrosity wasn't limited to vampires. Callum Wright was plain evidence of that.

Slowly, Roger neared Zack. He put his hands on his shoulders. When Zack didn't pull away, he wrapped his arms around him and held him close. He rested his chin on Zack's shoulder. "I would find a place for you at my side. Not as a pet, but ... but there will be humans and shifters that would seek asylum from their abusive masters. They would need someone. I would be too intimidating. But you might not be."

"You want me to shepherd the broken," Zack said.

"I want you to find a *home*. Preferably one with me in it," Roger replied. "If you want no responsibilities, we could make that happen. Short of giving you the throne itself, I'd give you whatever power you want."

"Wouldn't I have to be a vampire for some of that?"

Roger was glad he didn't have to breathe, otherwise his

lungs might have stopped. He had only shortly considered turning Zack, for the briefest flash of a moment while he was on the operating table. But Zack was a monster hunter. What would he have thought if he woke as a vampire?

Gently, Roger eased his way around to face Zack. He searched Zack's feelings, but they were closed off behind the shield of his mind and fortified by the magic of his hunter's tattoo. Likewise, Zack had donned a careful, blank expression.

"Is that something you want?" Roger asked.

"No." A glint of steel hardened Zack's eyes. "Never."

That affirmation hadn't been a surprise, but to hear it uttered tilted something in Roger's soul or whatever passed for one. Zack was mortal, that was obvious, but Zack was *mortal*. He would age. Eventually die. He would never be the same as he was in this moment, and though Roger had the chance to see him through decades upon decades, there would be a time *without him*.

But he could never force vampirism on another. All the times he'd made sirelings had already failed horribly, and each of them had *wanted* to become an immortal. All his fledglings hated him, and he wasn't sure he'd be able to withstand the amazing man in front of him turning on him like the others had.

Roger cupped Zack's cheek and met his gaze. "All right then. I won't ask the question again, but if you change your mind—"

"I *won't*," Zack insisted.

Of course he wouldn't. This was Zackery Wright that Roger had in his arms, and though he may doubt what he was becoming and his function in the world, he'd always known what he wanted.

"You always have a place with me," Roger murmured. He pressed his forehead against Zack's and caressed his back.

"We have to get going."

"Do we?"

"You can't ignore the rest of the world," Zack muttered.

"Watch me." Roger kissed Zack's cheek, then his jaw, then just under that.

"Roger," Zack groaned.

The complaining note was obvious, but Zack didn't push him away, didn't tell him to stop kissing him. Roger lingered over the place where he'd first bitten Zack. Some nights, he hated seeing that scar. He had not been in his right mind, hadn't been careful in the least, when he'd bitten Zack so viciously.

This night, however, he deftly ran his tongue along the seams of the scar. Zack shivered and pressed up against him. The mark wasn't just an ugly reminder of Roger's bloodlust but where he had first touched Zack. Their initial fight could have ended either of them. Only Roger had seen a brilliant boy hoping to prove himself, and Zack had stayed his hand and trusted a vampire. They'd been forging this path together, and though Roger wasn't sure where it would lead, he knew he needed Zack and Takashi at his side. Others as well, but the three of them could change the world. He was certain of it.

Roger guided Zack over to the bed, kissing and caressing him the whole way. Zack's skin was wonderfully warm, and a hint of sweat kicked up. Roger licked the first place he found a drop, though that turned out to be mostly water from the shower.

"Roger," Zack whined, "we're supposed to go to the Chateau."

"The Chateau doesn't exist. Don't you know? The world ends at the suite door," Roger whispered.

"That's going to be tough when we run out of food." Zack squirmed, slipping a bit from Roger's embrace. "You're blood-fueled horny."

"That's not it."

"I saw your huge fucking boner when you got done feeding from Carver." Zack pushed away.

Roger caught him by the wrists, only allowing Zack to get so far away from him. His grip wasn't terribly tight but firm. "He may have started the dance, but that isn't why I've remained on the floor. Dance with me."

"Look, if this is some attempt to make me feel better about the stupid video, I get it. You think I'm sexy."

Roger tugged Zack closer and caught him in his arms again. With one hand, he traced the edge of Zack's cheek and jaw. "I love you. And you have confessed that you are painfully temporary compared to me and will remain so."

"You want me to become a vampire?" Zack asked. The hardness in his eyes flattened his expression.

Roger cupped Zack's cheek. "I want happiness. I want *you*. And if I can only have you for a mortal lifetime, then I will adjust. The reality of time threatens to overcast tonight, so forgive me if all I long to do is cherish you."

Zack melted against him. "When you put it like that …"

Grinning, Roger kissed him. Then kissed him again. And longer. Zack wrapped his arms around Roger's shoulders and leaned up into the kiss. His underwear was a thin veil for his hardening member. The press of it was a delight, and Roger moaned into their continued kiss.

"Okay. Roger—we … *ah* … Roger, we really should—" Zack groaned as Roger tugged his underwear down.

Roger gripped Zack's ass with both hands and held him flush against him. With a growl in his voice, he whispered in his ear, "I am going to ensure that you never forget that you are loved and desired before we even *consider* leaving this bedroom."

"You're going to pound my ass until the doubt's gone?" Zack smirked.

"If that's what it takes." Roger nibbled on his bottom lip until Zack gasped.

Zack put a hand on his chest and nudged a bit of distance between them. "I appreciate this. I do. And I wish we could fuck away the night, but you're still avoiding the subject."

"I'm trying to fuck you, and you're attempting to bring me back on mission." Roger squeezed one of Zack's asscheeks with his hand. "Have I mentioned I love your determination?"

"Trust me, I'm on the brink of failing that. But we—Roger, touching my hole is cheating."

The lust had fled Zack's tone. With a sigh, Roger put his hands on more innocent places on Zack's bare body.

Zack cupped Roger's cheeks and leaned up for a kiss. "I get it. I do. *You* have to start making decisions, and that's terrifying. But no one's going to follow you if you keep sitting in Seamus's shadow, just like no one's going to respect me if I hide from Vincent's stupid video. We have to get out there. That's the plan, right? Get other people to like us? See where you stand in the coven?"

"Fine. Fine." Roger kissed the tip of Zack's nose. "Are you certain we couldn't share a quick moment?"

"*Yes.*" Zack pushed away from Roger and pulled his underwear back in place. "I want to be able to walk straight."

"I could be gentle."

"*Roger.*"

Holding up his hands, Roger chuckled. "All right. I'll let the subject go."

"Thank you," Zack said primly. Then, he continued dressing for the evening. He chose a pair of gold shorts and a matching vest, along with one of the duller black collars. He strode toward the bathroom with purpose.

Roger watched him. Drank in every detail. Because though there had been a time before him, he was too painfully aware that there would be a time *after* him.

Every night with Seamus in charge was a torture to him but was more so for Zack. Roger had made his way through the centuries. He could last another several if he had to. Not Zack, though. While Roger had never intended to drag out his plans for a takeover, he'd never considered the limitations. Zack wouldn't age into an old man overnight, but Roger couldn't waste his precious youth and kind heart.

He'd need to talk to Candide. If anyone in the coven could help him find his footing faster and better, she would be able to. Roger changed into a wine-red suit that would complement the color of Zack's outfit and leaned against the doorframe to watch Zack apply the final touches of his makeup.

CHAPTER 20

Never. Zack rested his head back against Roger's knee and dared to close his eyes as Roger absently brushed his fingers through his hair. The Cal voice tried to rear its ugly head, but Zack had enough going on in his mind. So what if closing his eyes around vampires was dangerous? Every breath he took was a risk. He pushed those thoughts away and recentered on the moment Roger had asked him if he wanted to become a vampire. The sincerity in Roger's brown eyes had been tempting for a split second.

That had been weakness. Zack *couldn't* become a vampire. An immortality feeding on people? Without the sun? And who would want to live forever, anyway? Plus, vampires weren't *humans*. He wouldn't be the same. Unless that was another myth his family had ingrained in him. How much did vampirism change a person?

Zack opened his eyes to take in his surroundings again. Roger and Takashi had settled into a room on the second floor of Chateau de Vampire. The room had a gold theme to it. Roger and Takashi stood out among the furnishings and even the other vampires since Roger's wine-red suit and Takashi's gray suit with baby blue shirt both complemented each other and made them seem artfully dressed for the space. Kit wore a gold skirt and vest that matched Zack's outfit, and they sat on the floor on the other side of Takashi. Carver had been exhausted and stayed home.

Zack was probably blending into the couch he sat beside, but he didn't mind. Just being out was the challenge. He kept trying to shake the notion that the other pets were a breath away from laughing at him or mocking him. Getting rid of the anxiety wasn't easy, though.

And unfortunately, he couldn't raise his gaze far enough from the floor to see what the other vampires were like. Sure, the vampires he knew liked being what they were, but was that true of everyone?

Didn't matter. He'd said no and meant it. He wasn't going to change his answer. Ever.

Roger was carrying on conversation with a handful of others. There'd been some chatter among them about the "lesser" vampires, which Zack figured out meant the ones who weren't living in penthouses with a view of Lake Michigan and spending every night in an expensive donor house like the Chateau. One of them had the audacity to sound like she pitied the fact that a vampire around two hundred years old ran a bar and was little more than a stereotypical grouchy bartender.

"Nathaniel still has his place, then?" Roger asked. "The Last Deal?"

"An abhorrent name," the other vampire said. "That's for demons, not our kind. It should be something like the Last Kiss."

"You're annoyed because you've been banned permanently," one of her vampire companions said. "Honestly, Roger, it's a disgrace that a captain should see to. Nathaniel doesn't allow any feeding in his bar. There isn't a private feeding room at all! One can hardly call it one of our establishments at all."

Nathaniel. Zack knew the name. If he had the right vampire, then Ezra was his sire, making Roger his grand-sire. The vamp had been one of the few that emerged from the Wright Base back in 1947. Zack's great-grandfather had tortured him in hopes of "understanding the evil coursing in the veins of the Devil's most beautiful lure." Zack had swallowed that line of shit for years, but it had never sat right with him. After digging into the history of what had happened, he was sort of glad there were some of his cousins who would probably never speak to him again.

"Those were the same rules he had when he opened his bar in the '80s," Roger said. "As I understood it, his argument was that it was a place for the younger ones to learn control. Though I don't mind a good feast—" Roger stroked Zack's neck.

Right. Zack had a part to play. He arched up into Roger's touch like he wouldn't mind dying in Roger's embrace and closed his eyes so he wouldn't have to see anyone else's judgment.

"—there is something to be said for blending in among the masses. We don't want ferals ruining things and enticing the hunters to stalk our territory, do we?" Roger finished.

"I hadn't thought of that," the first vampire said stiffly.

Zack clamped his jaw shut and fought the urge to make a sarcastic remark at the fucking asshole vampire.

A young white guy strode into the room, though he dropped to his hands and knees and crawled his way over toward Zack. The behavior wasn't *completely* uncommon. Some vampires never wanted their pets to walk in public, which led to a lot of crawling. But no one had been clearly heading for Zack before.

The guy wore a pink collar with Candide's crest tag dangling from it. His skin was porcelain pale, not the sickly of an unwell, pasty mortal. His eyes were bright purple without any sign of a contact changing the color. Across his cheeks was an iridescent glitter that glimmered silver with deep blues, reds, and purples. His long, auburn hair was tied up into a messy bun. The closer he came, the heavier the scent of pine trees filled Zack's nose.

He had to be the Unseelie fey that Candide had been whipping the first night they were at the Chateau.

He slinked/crawled his way up to Zack and crooked his finger at him. Zack sat up a little, which was apparently all the invitation the guy needed to invade his personal space. He pressed his cheek against Zack's and whispered, "My mistress longs to see your master upstairs in her private chambers. He is to bring his loves and his pet."

The phrasing raised a red flag. *Loves?* And *pet?* What did Candide know about the nature of his relationship with Roger? Did she *know* know? Would she turn them over to Seamus?

Zack locked the growing fears behind a door. Though his tattoo would protect him, the magic wasn't one hundred percent. If he allowed too much fear into his heart, then it'd show on his face. Vampires wouldn't have to rely on their magic if he couldn't stop himself from obvious clues.

So, Zack languidly put his arm over the guy's shoulder and kissed his cheek instead. He wouldn't have to tell Roger what was said. Roger had already heard every word.

"Seems I have somewhere to be," Roger said with a sigh. He rose with fluid grace. "Another time."

"Until then," the first vampire said.

Zack waited until Takashi stood. Kit joined him, and then three of them followed Roger out of the room. Candide's pet walked in step with Zack until they reached the staircase to the third floor. He slid to the front and led them toward the end of a hall. He opened a door, then stepped out of their way.

Like everywhere else in the Chateau, the room breathed high-end luxury. However, there were plenty of pillows and low-to-the-floor seating. Everyone in the room had a collar, most with some shade of red but a few white and three black. There were three additional doors; one was a set of double doors.

But what Zack's gaze settled on was a pale young man standing in the center of the room. He had a red collar on, but he wore a loose shirt and pants. His flame-red hair would probably have caught anyone's attention. However, Zack was stuck on the shape of his nose. The color of his gray eyes. The general shape of him.

Because he'd seen that color, those shapes, in the mirror. He'd seen that gray in his mother's eyes.

The young man had to be the vampire Ezra Gladwell. Zack sought the signs and saw the hint of fang when he moved his lips to greet Roger, even though he didn't hear the words. The high-pitched whine in his ears was too distracting.

All his life, he'd believed that Ezra Gladwell had to be a larger-than-life monster. Family lore said he was the cause of everything. While Roger had revealed what had happened centuries ago, the meaning of it hadn't sunk in. Ezra couldn't have been any older than Zack when he became a vampire. And Roger could be incredibly persuasive.

You know that from personal experience, the Cal voice whispered.

Not the same. He's been honest with me.

Has he?

Zack swallowed.

When Roger and Takashi started to head for the double doors, Zack took a step to follow. Kit grabbed his arm and guided him over toward a floor cushion instead. They whispered, "It's just vamps in the next room."

"Oh."

"Are you okay?"

"Yeah." Zack sat down beside them and glanced over his

shoulder. The double doors were already closing behind Roger and Takashi. Ezra Gladwell was gone, too. He must have disappeared into the room with them.

"You look like you're going to faint," a young woman said as she sat on the low couch across from Kit and Zack. Her skin was a shade of medium brown with a healthy glow. She had her hair pulled back into a low puff. She wore a black collar with Candide's crest tag and a flowy, sleeveless, green jumpsuit. "Do you need water? Or the caretaker?"

Zack's brain had to catch up. A caretaker? *Oh, right.* That was the word for the on-staff doctor for the donor house. He swallowed, and his throat had too much in it. He cleared his throat and shook his head.

He'd seen the woman before. She'd been the one Candide had given the whip to. The fey boy who had led them up to the rooms sat down beside her like they were old friends, though she didn't give him the slightest bit of attention.

"I'm fine," Zack said. "Just shocked. I'm Zack, by the way."

"Oh, I know." She smiled. "I'm Mara. Pronouns she/her. The brat beside me is Dryden, using he/him. And you?"

"I'm Kit. They/them." Kit nudged Zack. "He uses he/him, when his mouth's working right."

"It's working *fine*," Zack said shortly. "I've had a long day."

"Don't tell me you're letting that annoying pissant Vincent get to you," Dryden said. The fey stretched out and nudged Zack's knee with his foot. "He's not worth the trouble, sweetie."

"I appreciate the support, but—"

"It's not support. It's facts." Dryden waggled his foot.

Zack batted his foot away and rolled his eyes. "I get it. Vincent's a pissant."

"Vincent's practically *dead*."

Kit frowned, and despite his best effort, Zack mirrored

their confusion. He said, "What?"

Gleefully, Dryden sat up and leaned toward Zack. He motioned for Zack to come closer. "Why don't you tell me why you froze in that little video, and I'll tell you why you don't have to worry about the pest?"

Mara put her hand on Dryden's chest and pushed him back against the couch. "He's not allowed to make any deals. Our mistress has forbidden him from doing so."

"That's like telling a kitten not to scratch the furniture," Dryden pouted. "Deals are what I *do*."

"I thought that was a demon thing," Kit said.

"They took it from us!" Dryden declared.

"And demons will say the fey took it from them," Mara replied. "Look, don't worry about Vincent, and don't listen to Dryden. Vincent's desperate, that's all. I didn't sit down here to gossip about the little things. I was hoping Zack and I might discuss what our masters are considering for upcoming events."

"Like hosting?" Zack asked.

Mara motioned dismissively. "Your master won't be hosting anything for a while. However, my mistress would hate if his outfits clashed with her ensemble, particularly for the Winter's Grand Ball."

"That's almost two months away," Zack said.

"We've been planning since New Year's for it," Mara replied. "Mistress hasn't hosted it for seven years, and she's thrilled to have it at the Chateau. Everything must be *perfect*."

Great. I'm stuck out here talking wardrobe, and Roger's probably planning world domination with his fellow vampires. Zack pressed his lips into a smile because he couldn't let the others see how badly he wanted to bolt from the room. "Of course. Why don't you tell me what your mistress has in mind?"

"For starters, she has plans for these amazing ice statues." Mara grinned broadly. "I can't *wait* to see the mages work their magic."

CHAPTER 21

Candide's private chambers inside the Chateau were exactly the sort of rooms Roger had envisioned for her. They were reminiscent of their original lavish house in Chicago. They'd shared a home for a short while—less than a decade—when they were settling into their new city. This room was much like their living room had been.

Most of the furniture had likely been in it. A good portion of it was in the style of the early twentieth century and had the sort of well-cared-for appearance that was hard to replicate. A deep red rug covered the hardwood floor from corner to corner, and Roger recognized it as the one that they'd had. It'd been in his penthouse before his coma.

The walls were bare except for the paintings. Each was of a different locale that Candide had once called home: a stately manor in the French countryside, a Parisian house of the early 1700s, a London home in the mid-1700s, a Brooklyn townhome, and the three different places she'd had in Chicago. Roger knew every building.

Candide sat on a chaise. She wore a stunning gown that was tight through the bodice and spread into a wide skirt. She lounged as if she didn't have a care in the world, only moving a hand to beckon Ezra to come closer to her. After Ezra knelt on the floor beside her, she lazily carded her fingers through his hair.

And for once, Ezra seemed at peace. Roger hadn't seen him so relaxed in … well, over a century at least.

Upon the room's singular love seat was Lucille and Dempsey, two of Candide's sirelings. Lucille could have been Candide's younger sister in life. She was fair-skinned and blond. Her teenage appearance had long been underestimated. Other vampires assumed that because she looked like a sixteen-year-old, she must have the mind of one. As the eras changed, ignorant vampires began to assume she was less and less mature like the modern mortal teens they encountered. They failed to see that behind Lucille's pale sea-green eyes was a mind as devious and calculating as Candide's. After all, she was the first vampire Candide had ever made and was among the ten oldest in the coven.

Dempsey was the second-youngest vampire in the room, older only than Takashi. Not long after arriving in Chicago, Candide had fallen in love with the musician. Dempsey was skilled with a violin and flute and, since he'd been turned, had studied various instruments and musical styles the way Takashi studied languages and Roger collected art. His pale blue suit was a striking contrast to his deep brown skin. He appeared relaxed, but he had a wariness in his dark brown eyes. When Roger met his gaze, Dempsey flitted his attention to the final vampire in the room.

Across the room from Candide was Dmitri. He wore a black suit and a stark white dress shirt. His dark hair had the slightest curl at the ends, and his sharp features threatened to slice through Roger's memory and drag his heart out onto the floor for all to see.

Perhaps falling in love again had opened the wounds of broken loves. Roger slid his hands into his pockets and kept the slightest grin on his lips. A leader wouldn't show subordinates any sign of weakness.

"You called, we've come, mon cher," Candide said.

"To be fair, I texted you and Dmitri," Roger said amicably. "You didn't mention you already had company."

"She invited them." Dmitri gestured with his chin at Lucille and Dempsey. "Though you aren't above bringing children into this mess yourself."

"What mess would that be?" Roger asked.

"Don't be boring or dense," Candide said with a sigh. "I had other plans tonight."

"As did I. I was planning to sink into a warm bath and listen to my new vinyls," Lucille complained with a pout. "They've been stacking up while I was away. Taylor's set to release another one soon, and I haven't listened to her latest rerecord yet."

Or perhaps she does have things in common with the modern youth because I'll have to ask Zack what that meant. Roger tried to observe Dmitri and the others the way that Zack might. A tension was threaded through the room, creating an invisible wall around Roger and the others. Each vampire was holding themselves perfectly still apart from Candide running her fingers through Ezra's hair. They were all old enough to have dropped the habit of breathing to keep up a pretense of mortality.

Out of all the beings in the world, they were the few that might understand Roger's inner agony intimately. They had been bearing the weight of the same monsters in their lives night after night. But had Dmitri ever revealed to them the terrible magic that Anton performed? Did they know what had happened to many of the vampires they'd once called friends? Lovers? Did they give a damn? A conscience wasn't required to be a vampire. In the GLC, the damn thing could lead to one's demise.

And Roger found his footing and his first rule. *Doing the*

right thing shouldn't be a death sentence. Of course, that would have to spiral into what was "right," but there were some things that should be sacred. They shouldn't fear that their loved ones would be ripped away from them. They shouldn't have to endlessly dance to Seamus's amusement to a wretched tempo that left them exhausted and terrified.

They should have a goddamn *choice* in their lives.

Roger lifted his chin and scanned each of them. Takashi had adopted a pose similar to his own, a patient look in his blue eyes. Dmitri was ever the brooding one in the corner. Lucille and Dempsey held themselves like Candide did, and she was a statue of poise and grace except for her hand in Ezra's hair.

And he realized that Ezra and Candide must have found a fragment of peace in each other, the same sort of peace he was coming to know when he was with Zack or Takashi.

In a clear voice, Roger said, "I intend to rid us of our vile masters and claim the seat of master of the Great Lakes Coven."

Silence stretched. The room must have been soundproofed because Roger didn't hear a trace of sound from the parlor.

Dempsey sagged in his seat and sprawled his long legs out. "About time one of you old bastards got your shit together."

"I'd love to believe this isn't some foul plot of Seamus's. Some attempt to rile us into a conspiracy and turn on us, perhaps?" Lucille said sharply.

"It isn't." Candide ruffled Ezra's hair.

Because of course, Ezra had shared his burning passion to rid the world of Anton and Seamus with his lover. Roger met Candide's gaze and saw steadiness in her. Knowing one another so long, he could tell she was on board with his dream.

She gave him a small smile, then said, "I was hoping you had a greater plan than murder the monsters."

"He doesn't have a *plan*," Dmitri scoffed. "He simply wants the power."

"What exactly did you envision would happen to the coven once Seamus was dead? That everyone would peacefully carry on with their lives?" Roger asked.

Snarling, Dmitri stalked toward Roger. Every word dripped with hate, and he pulsed with a desire for violence like a roll of thunder preceding an oncoming storm. "We didn't meet in 1989 to discuss killing Seamus. *Anton* was our target, but *you* have hardly mentioned his name. No, it's been about Seamus. Seamus. Seamus! And I have to wonder how long you might have hoped for a chance to overthrow him. Because you can lie and pretend to have all these fucking airs of gentility, but I know you. I can imagine what you would do with the leadership. You'll fuck. You'll feed. You'll run it into the ground because you don't actually give a damn about anything besides your own desires."

Roger could retaliate with all the tiny things he had done for others. His mind was already flitting with indignant responses.

But a memory rose into place as he stared into Dmitri's eyes. He'd seen hate and despair in him before.

Roger had been pretty in his youth and handsome as a man. He'd never been short of partners, never balked at using his body to get what he needed. A bed. Food. A ship to sail on. Steady work. But he'd grown tired of his bosun's demands and left the ship, walking along the docks until he found another that would take him on. He'd spotted Dmitri on the deck, and a piece of him had clicked into place. The crew had been surly and turned out to be pirates, but Roger had never cared whether his work was deemed legal. Governments were merely thieves with better organizational skills.

And it hadn't taken Roger long to fall into Dmitri's orbit. Half a dozen languages were spoken on board the ship, but

Dmitri was the only Russian. Roger had taken the time to learn from him, and they'd had their own language.

The moment that was making his heart ache in the present was from one of the longest nights of his life. He'd woken, and Dmitri hadn't been in his hammock. Later on, he'd convince himself it was destiny, but he wandered out to the deck. Dmitri had been at the side of the ship, staring into the waters under the full moonlight. The bits of conversation were erased from his mind, but the intent and hatred in Dmitri's eyes was there.

He'd intended to throw himself overboard, the depths of his self-hate had gone that far.

Roger had stopped him. Stayed with him. Done it again and again any other night Dmitri thought the hatred would finally claim him. They hadn't dared to give that mood a name, but Roger recognized it now: depression. Vampirism hadn't erased it, but Dmitri had become busy. He never kept pets for long. He had a habit of killing them, but then he had a habit of picking assholes, so Roger had never given it much thought.

Dmitri still hated himself. And he had plenty of hate to spread. He had it for Anton, who'd made him.

And he clearly had it for Roger.

Our love never stood a chance. Roger braced against that thought. It wasn't a fair one, but it felt true in its sting.

Dmitri expected him to be cruel in his response. That's what vampires were.

That wasn't all Roger was.

Remaining calm, Roger said, "Seamus won't stand by while Anton is assassinated. He would route us and burn the world to ash."

"And what is the problem with that?" Dmitri hissed.

"I, for one, like the world. And I adore being in it," Takashi said.

"Same," Lucille said.

Roger held his hand up as Ezra opened his mouth to speak. The others fell silent once more, which was reassuring though a tad surprising. The only time he had commanded a room like this had been a demonstration of how well one of his pets could take a spanking.

I don't have what it takes. Roger steadied his nerves. Zack believed in him, even if he did have his doubts. Takashi did, too. He could move forward. He didn't have to remain locked in his position.

"Anton will have to die as well," Roger said. "I don't see where he would let the world rest, either. But he terrifies the coven. They would scatter from him. If we kill him first, Seamus would bend four hundred vampires in the direction of my destruction and then systematically tear it from the inside out for any other traitors while building himself a new army of fledglings to unleash upon the world. We have to be careful. You agreed to that in 1989."

"I have been careful another thirty-two years, and it has gotten me *nothing* other than agony," Dmitri snapped.

"Perhaps we can destroy them the same night, but I haven't seen Anton since I came back." Roger glanced to the others. "Does anyone know what he's been doing? Where he is?"

"He lives with Seamus," Dmitri replied. "Always has."

"And we both know there are *years* where he won't leave the mansion if he's distracted with some spell or creation," Roger said. "I'm not assaulting Seamus's fortress. That is utter madness and a certain way to die."

"I have seen him plenty."

"Having seen him isn't actionable intelligence, unless you know where and when he'll be."

"He's never bothered sharing his schedule with anyone, not even Seamus!"

Candide stood and gently put her hand on Dmitri's shoulder. When he jerked away from her, she pressed her lips into a thin line. "I truly believed I'd witnessed every version of every argument the two of you could ever have before we ever moved to this city, mes chers, but this is a new one. Roger has the right idea, Dmitri. We can't plunge daggers into the darkness and hope to strike the target. Failing would be worse than never striking at all."

"You will make excuse after excuse until the sun burns us all to ash," Dmitri said. He gestured between them. "The two of you can fuck yourselves."

As Dmitri spun toward the exit and stalked toward the door, one of his sentences clicked into place for Roger. *I have seen him plenty.* Zack's notes had lacked information of where Anton had been, what he had been up to. None of the vampires in the room with Roger had answered the question either.

But the first few years Roger and Dmitri had been vampires had been rough ones. Always starving. Always the fledglings, the youngest. Always doing Seamus's and Anton's bidding. Roger had convinced himself that he might have loved Seamus in those early years, but with the lens of experience, that wasn't what had happened.

There were cracks in those lies that formed scars in his mind. Though the seams were faint, they were traceable.

Though Roger had desperately ignored his scars, Dmitri's wounds had never closed. Roger saw that now. Saw the pain and suffering still carving into Dmitri's soul with mirrored shards.

Because *I have seen him plenty* meant *He's been visiting me.*

Dmitri had never chosen Anton for anything in his life. But Anton chose him for many things.

Roger reached for Dmitri. An invitation to stay with him in the hotel was on his lips. His hand was about to touch Dmitri's shoulder.

In a liquid blur, Dmitri spun and moved to strike Roger's jaw.

Instinct kicked in, and Roger quickly blocked the blow. His training had paid off. He whispered, "You don't have to be alone."

"I've never been anything else," Dmitri said icily.

And those words were sharper than a blade's edge and hamstrung the sympathy that had nestled in Roger's heart. He stepped away and continued to hold Dmitri's gaze. But all he saw in his brown eyes was the anger, and all that he emanated was a desire for destruction, a fear of what may come.

Roger couldn't mend Dmitri. He retreated another step.

After the door slammed behind Dmitri, the tension slowly bled from the room. The others were watching him. He and Dmitri had had public arguments before. Seamus had once said they were his favorite form of entertainment. But he had to hold himself together. He had to do what no one seemed to believe he could do. Lead.

Immortal coldness came too naturally, but he embraced the numbness and turned it to his advantage. He slid his hands into his pockets once more and faced those that remained. "I can't afford for the coven to have a similar reaction. None of us can. I need them to accept me as the best path forward."

"Few would act like our dear Dmitri, though you will need to establish yourself." Candide folded her hands together. "Right now, the coven may assume that you would unleash them from any rules, and I feel that is not what you intend."

"Hardly," Roger said.

"I hope you don't plan to follow a hunter's mentality," Lucille said. "You won't find any love for a puritanical morality among us."

"Hear, hear," Dempsey said.

"A hunter's mentality would burn us all in our beds before allowing another night of existence," Roger said.

"You would know, wouldn't you?" Lucille said smugly. "However did you convince your little Ezra clone to be your pet?"

"He's far from a duplicate," Takashi said. His tone was diplomatic, but he had a stillness in his manner that demanded an end to the discussion of Zack.

Which Roger embraced. If he had been alone with Takashi and Candide, he wouldn't have minded talking about him. Dempsey and Lucille weren't in his heart and shouldn't be given free access to his feelings. "The practice of the gray bands will die with Seamus and Anton. In addition to being cruel, they could be interpreted as a breach of the Chicago Pact. Their existence puts our standing with other supernatural powerhouses at risk."

"I completely concur," Candide replied. "I do have a few ideas of what you could do to win the coven's heart."

Roger motioned to the nearest empty seats. "I reached out because I wanted to hear them."

And though they settled in and began to discuss new paths for the coven, Roger couldn't help wondering how many might hold the same anger in their hearts that Dmitri did. Each one of them carried wounds too deep for him to trace their entirety.

He pushed that aside. He had to lead, and a leader moved forward. The past would need to become nothing more than a memory, and Seamus needed to become less than that.

CHAPTER 22

The night at the Chateau had been boring as hell, but it'd been exactly the kind of shit Reed had been preparing Zack for, so Zack hadn't been surprised that he wound up talking about banal crap like color schemes and attire. The other two head pets, who belonged with Dempsey and Lucille, had eventually joined Zack and Mara's conversation. Throughout the evening, Zack watched her and how others reacted to her. He built a hypothesis.

And the evidence began to pile up, especially as all of them, vampires and pets, eventually went down into the general areas of the Chateau and spent time with the other coven members. While the vampires carried on pretend niceties and played their mind games, Mara was on the move. She was subtle, never hurried but never in the same place for longer than she had to be. Following her around the Chateau would've been too obvious, but Zack kept an eye out for her. She escorted donors who had been bled out of rooms and into the company of a brown-collared employee who saw them off to the caretaker. She spent time with a nervous pet who was struggling not to cry. All with grace and command.

Vincent Talmadge wasn't the head pet of the GLC. Mara was.

That wasn't how it should be, and Dryden's dismissive attitude about Vincent launched a series of questions. Why shouldn't Zack worry about his cruel prank? Why did Mara treat Zack like he mattered but didn't care about Vincent? Were they only pretending to get along with Zack?

Zack managed to get some sleep, but he was up by noon. With hours to kill, he tucked into the suite's office with his notebooks and laptop and settled in to research. First, he updated his notes and journal with what he'd overheard and experienced over the last week. He'd put down bits here and there, but he hadn't taken the time for a full inventory of what he'd learned. Doing that ate up valuable time, but the gained knowledge might be useful. He should've been writing down more instead of getting caught up in life.

With his notes in order, Zack flipped through to what he'd already learned about his current nemesis.

Vincent Talmadge was a little over eighteen years old, though his social media profiles had him as Seamus's pet almost three years ago. He never talked about family, and he rarely mentioned his friends. His posts were almost entirely about this party or that, showing off how good he looked in his outfits, and basically creating a fiction of how wonderful his life as Seamus's head pet was.

The best information would be on Night Deets, so Zack hopped onto his computer and rooted around the website. He ignored the dozens of notifications. People might've been wishing him a happy birthday, but he didn't need the sea of crap that was inevitably piling up in his inbox. He went back as far as he could in Vincent's profile.

In an early pic, nearly three years old, Vincent was wearing a red collar and was sitting on another teen's lap. The teen had on a black collar. Zack zoomed in and spotted hints of a crowned serpent on the crest tag. Seamus's head pet when Vincent had joined the collection. Luckily, the guy was tagged, so Zack scooted over to that profile.

The guy hadn't aged in between. In his bio info, he had Marcus listed as his sire. His undead life didn't seem to be as glamorous as his life while he was Seamus's pet, and he had far fewer posts and updates. But his Night Deets profile went back six years, so Zack chased down the early posts and discovered another name. Another link in the chain.

The most recent post was a memorial message from a guy named Arturo, but other than that, there hadn't been anything for the last six years because that teen was dead.

Zack had been so focused on the vampires that he'd only looked at the mortals in relation to them. But as he continued hunting the truth sickening his stomach, he knew he'd learned something horrible.

He wouldn't have to worry about Vincent because Vincent would be dead within six months. Chances were slim that he'd get turned into a vampire. While Night Deets only went back about sixteen years, Zack couldn't find another of Seamus's head pets that had been turned instead of dearly departed.

The office door swung open slowly. Zack shut his laptop and brought his attention out of his notes and his own head as Takashi came into the room.

"Researching on your birthday? Don't you ever take a break?" Takashi asked.

"I, uh, this is actually what I normally end up doing for my birthday." Zack hurried to close his notebooks. If he kept moving, he might avoid the slight shake that was threatening to overtake his hand.

"What's happened?" Takashi said.

So much for trying to play it cool. Zack sighed and sat back in his chair. "Reality."

"How do you mean?"

"Look, I *know* Seamus is a bastard." Zack leaned forward

again and gestured across the desk at his half dozen note-books. "This is a trail of his destruction. I know what Roger meant when he said Seamus demonstrated his 'authority.' And it probably wasn't the only time he was raped. And he's not the only one Seamus hurt like that. And that's just one way he's inflicting trauma on others. He strangles every room he walks into."

"All of which you had warning for." Takashi neared Zack and leaned his butt against the desk in order to face him. "Where is reality kicking in?"

"Vincent." Zack deflated against the desk. He avoided looking at Takashi. "I feel like an idiot for not catching on. Vincent's not the head pet of the GLC. He's a prized fuckdoll —which is gross considering he's been that for a couple years and he only turned eighteen last month. He's slowly dying in front of everyone's eyes, and nobody seems to give a shit, or they're too busy saving their own asses from this monster."

"Ah," Takashi said. "It's no longer a matter of paper and memory but witnessed."

"Yeah. And it's making me more nervous that he went out of his way to throw me under the bus." Zack bit his bottom lip, then sighed. "Seamus has shown some weird interest in me. I noticed it the first time I ran into him. One of his pets said something about how he's been talking about me. And considering Vincent scowled and then pranked me, it's got to be true. I really don't want to think about what that means."

"Then let me provide a welcome distraction." Takashi pulled a small jewelry box from his pocket and laid it on the desk in front of Zack. "Happy birthday."

With a confused frown, Zack opened the little box. A beautiful white-gold pendant shaped like a dagger hung from a matching white-gold chain. The pommel of the dagger had a pink tourmaline gem, and little diamonds decorated either side of the hilt and then a line down the center of the blade. It was a gorgeous piece that was a touch less than two inches long. Cal would've mocked it for having pink, but that was technically Zack's birthstone. Well, that and opals, but Zack liked the pink tourmaline better.

And he liked it. And it was a perfect present. Probably one of the most expensive he'd ever gotten.

"We, uh, we've never really talked about you and me," Zack said.

Takashi raised an eyebrow. "Not exactly what I expected you to say."

"Ah, fuck! I mean, *thank you*. It's gorgeous. I love it. I do. I just." Zack took a deep breath. "I don't know if this is a 'I'm a rich guy and I wanted to get my boyfriend's boyfriend a nice gift' or if it's a 'I'm ridiculously into my new boyfriend' gift."

"Which would you prefer it to be?" Takashi asked.

That wasn't an answer at all. Out of everyone Zack had met, Takashi had a poker face that rivaled Nell's. And he had to. He'd been to so many places and had to deal with so many volatile vampires the only way he'd been able to survive was to keep stuff close to his chest.

He'd read Zack's journal, and though that should've upset Zack more, he could see the logic behind it. Given a reverse of their situation, Zack would've devoured any information he could've had on Takashi before he walked into their lives. Well, he had, actually. However, the internet didn't provide a whole picture, and Zack had been limited to that and rumors.

Yet when the three of them were together, Takashi had insisted that Roger wasn't the only one he wanted. He'd gotten a glimpse of all the crap Zack had to say about the bullshit he went through and decided he was worthwhile. And nobody, not even immortal millionaires, bought diamonds for someone they didn't have some kind of feelings for. Those feelings didn't have to be romantic, but as Zack tried to weigh Takashi's overt attempt to remain casual, he realized he wasn't the only one terrified of rejection.

The idea was such a simple basic notion. He'd known

academically that of course no one wanted rejection. And he'd had tender moments with Roger. But in this moment, the knowledge was a new dawn. The epiphany worked a tiny magic all its own. His intuition could be wrong, but he was willing to gamble that he'd reached the right conclusion.

Takashi was hoping he'd say they were boyfriends. He was scared Zack would reject him.

And this wasn't about Roger; this was about how he felt for Takashi. *That's how this should work, right? Being poly? There's me and Roger, him and Roger, him and me, and the three of us? And maybe we get casual with others on occasion, maybe we don't. But that doesn't change how I want him in my life.*

Zack stood so he and Takashi would've been sharing breath if Takashi had to breathe. Takashi's aura was a cool touch, a light reminder of his vampiric nature. The woodsy cologne he used covered up his scent of the grave for the most part.

Zack brushed his lips against Takashi's in a slow and tender kiss. He held off from trying to deepen it, choosing to draw it to a languid close instead. With a smile, he said, "Thank you for the necklace, *boyfriend*."

Takashi had a brilliant, beautiful, shy smile for a heartbeat before the slick, amazing immortal confidence returned. "I'm glad you like it."

"I wish I could get away with wearing it tonight," Zack said.

"Pity that you can't." Takashi kissed Zack's cheek. "I did have another reason for coming in here. Everyone else is getting ready for the party."

"Fuck. I'm going to wind up last again."

Takashi laughed and nudged him toward the master bedroom.

CHAPTER 23

The original Devil's Cove had been an island in the Caribbean Sea, but Seamus had so loved the name that Roger had endured several clubs named after it over the centuries. The first one in Chicago had burned in the early 1970s as part of a conflict with the Seelie princess of Chicago. By the end of the decade, Seamus had rebuilt his private club and named it, once again, Devil's Cove.

The outside of the building had aged gracefully and blended into the surrounding neighborhood. On a street with other bars, the occasional bubble of activity as vampires had to wait their turn to make their way past bouncers went unnoticed. Fortunately, there had been no line outside when Roger and the others had been dropped off. They'd made their way inside without difficulty.

Devil's Cove hadn't majorly changed since the rebuilding. The main floor had a large recess in the center that dipped down a half flight of stairs. That butted up against the stage on the far side of the room. The second floor was a balcony that curved around the first, except for the wall with the stage. The booths on the first floor and balcony had been replaced with various couches and heavy chairs. Other than that, the only updates Roger could spot were that the bars—two on the first floor and one on the second—had a slick industrial chic to them rather than the heavy glass monstrosities Seamus had been convinced were stylish in the 1970s.

A few of Roger's nightmares began in his memories of Devil's Cove from the '80s. As he wrapped his arm around Zack, he hoped nothing new would join that bank of terror. His outfit for the party was a suit of deep purple that had embroidered golden grapes. He'd asked Kit to provide a bit of makeup so that he had trails of gold glitter across his eyelids and then lightly fading off toward his hairline. A dangling gold earring replaced the gold stud he had been wearing. He was shirtless, and the suit jacket had a wide, low cut before the buttons just above his navel.

Takashi's suit was a pale blue, and he had a sheer white dress shirt on with it. When Roger first saw the wide-brimmed cap with wings, he thought it'd been ridiculous, but Takashi had an impish glee in his eyes while wearing it, and that made him too darling to think that he was anything other than handsome. His dress shoes had wings embroidered on them.

Kit, Zack, and Carver were dressed in satyr costumes. Their chests were bare, though they'd each adorned some manner of glitter across their torsos that matched their makeup. All three wore custom horns. The same was true of their furry trousers. Zack's was a light brown, Kit's reddish, and Carver's a dark brown with spots of white.

Zack leaned in and pressed a kiss against Roger's cheek, near his ear. He whispered, "This place smells weird."

Upon entering, Roger had become nose blind to the scents, but he took measure of them again. Old blood, entrenched fear, and the constant presence of vampires made for a dulling smell. It was musty, like a disused building, despite the activity.

"You'll get used to it," Roger replied. "Come on, we need to say hello to him."

Zack gave a tight nod in response, something Roger felt more from the brush of their cheeks so near each other rather than saw.

The party was in full swing. Alongside vampires and their pets, faeries revealed their true nature and celebrated. Without their glamours, the Unseelie faeries tended to appear as elongated humanoids. Some had wings, some didn't. Some had long, spindly fingers, while others were far shorter all over. A pack of pixies assaulted a gray-banded server and stole the empty glasses on their tray in order to smash them against the floor at the server's feet. Nothing changed in the server's expression, which exasperated the pixies and caused them to flit away to annoy someone else.

Roger led the way to the balcony floor. Seamus had a wide, open booth without a table at the center of it that was a step up from the floor. Subtle enchantments were worked into the ends, but the lack of glow meant they were likely disabled for the time being. If they were the same as his usual, then Seamus would be able to soundproof the booth upon a command.

Given the theme of deities, Roger wasn't the least bit surprised that Seamus had gone with attire alluding to the Devil. His bloodred suit was flashy, and the little red horns on his head added mischief to his demeanor. Other vampires hanging around him had chosen other deities. Some of them had gone Greek like Roger and some from other beliefs across the world. Marcus was dressed similarly to Roger, apparently choosing Dionysus as his inspiration as well.

I wear it better. Roger made a small bow to Seamus. "Lovely party, master."

"Stop that master nonsense," Seamus said with a grin. Something he'd said without meaning before and likely didn't mean it this time either. "Join me and send your pets below to the pit."

Roger nodded, then glanced over his shoulder to Zack. The others had bowed when he had, but he managed to catch Zack's eye. Zack gave him a small nod of confirmation, then whisked Kit and Carver back down toward the first floor.

Seamus leaned forward, his focus on Takashi. "You too, *boy.*"

Sending Takashi away would please Seamus, but there was a note in his tone that Roger had heard too many times. Seamus didn't appreciate Takashi—hell, he never appreciated anyone. But there was a disrespect that had corroded Roger's relationships before.

Seamus couldn't stand for anyone to grow close to Roger, and the story was that he and Takashi had already been together for thirty years. Seamus didn't know that was a lie, or at least Roger had no reason to believe the ruse had fallen through yet.

Insisting that Takashi remain with him would be a direct defiance, but letting Seamus get away with banishing him below to where the lesser vampires and pets were would mean that Roger saw Takashi the same way. As much as Takashi knew he cared, everyone else would only see Roger treating Takashi poorly. Seamus would be stomping all over him.

And a nagging little thought popped up in Roger's mind. Takashi had said it first. *How long can you pretend something before it becomes real?*

Roger couldn't continue to stand by.

A buzzing in his throat and stomach threatened to overcome every nerve. No one stood up to Seamus. Ever.

But he had. In little ways. He had pulled Seamus's attention and distracted him from others. He'd persuaded and seduced him. This turn of the dance would be bolder, more obvious, but he could manage it.

Because otherwise, what was the point? Why was he making Zack and the others suffer through the bullshit if he couldn't finally stand on his own two feet? Who would follow a spineless bastard who did nothing but suck up to the sire he eventually staked?

He still had to disguise the move to throw Seamus off the scent. With a quick tug, he pulled Takashi to his side and kissed his cheek. Afterward, he said loud enough for the other vampires to hear, "I saw Lucille in a booth near the stairs. I'll catch up to you soon, love."

Takashi squeezed his arm in reply, then headed for Lucille's booth.

Roger smoothed his features into a courtesan's smile as he steeled himself for whatever reaction Seamus might have. In moments like this, Roger's fear tended to grasp the better of him, and he always waited to see which version of Seamus greeted him.

But he'd spent months with Zack at his side and long nights reading through the notes that he had made. He had his own experience to rely upon as well. If he swallowed the fear, he could take in Seamus like Zack might and use all that information to form a conclusion and a course of action.

Seamus stretched and put his arms out along the back of the low seat. Though the benches were crowded, no one had dared to take up the few feet to either side of him.

Since he hadn't been invited to sit, Roger slid his hands into his pockets. The gold ring on his finger was a heavy weight.

As Seamus was sitting in the middle of the booth's bench in a position that was lording his presence over the entire party, he clearly was angling to be the center of attention. His grin didn't meet his eyes, but his gaze had the spark of a lazy predator rather than a monster on the prowl. Midnight was close, and the club was filling with guests.

He's in a good mood but wary. Roger gave a quick glance

over the other vampires sitting in the booth. He didn't know most of them, and they reeked like the freshly dead. Newer vampires, less than a few decades old. Seamus had always surrounded himself with a few prized "students" that eventually disappointed him. This latest crop seemed to be the same sort of sycophants as Marcus was. Malice twisted their smiles, and several had spots of blood on them.

Would Roger's efforts be lost on them? Was there one among them that wanted to break free from the violent path Seamus demanded of them?

And then he realized far more than the dozen vampires before him could see him. He was close enough to the balcony edge that others on the floor below could spot him as well as the other groups of vampires in other booths on the second floor.

He had to dance a waltz in tap shoes without making a sound. *I can do this. For Zack. For Takashi.*

For me.

Roger smiled broadly and gestured to the floor below with one shoulder. "I love what you've done with the place."

And then he turned to gaze below at the pit, that sunken area of the first floor where the mortals were dancing. A band was playing lively music on the stage. He strangled the fear of turning his back on Seamus because nothing was wrong. He threw himself into the belief like he had every time he needed to fool his mind into a place of calm, and he fell into the trick in a second. He wrapped it around him like a cloak and kept gathering information. Zack and Takashi would want to know everything.

Many of the vampires had chosen subdued costume-inspired attire for the party like Roger and Seamus had. Some had props like Takashi's hat. Roger spotted more than one hammer among the crowd. The name of that god didn't spring to mind, and he didn't recognize every deity that was represented. The vampires remained at the edge of the pit, which was an old tactic Seamus had implemented during parties. He enjoyed having the weak penned in, and the mortals were always the weakest, in his opinion.

Unlike their vampire masters, the mortals in the pit were in full costumes. They were dressed as nymphs, satyrs, spirits, demigods, and other creatures from mythology. Zack, Kit, and Carver had wound their way into the middle.

Seamus joined Roger at the railing, and Roger fought to keep his shoulders relaxed, especially as Seamus put his hand between his shoulder blades. After a second, Seamus slid his hand up to Roger's shoulder so that he had an arm wrapped around him as they stood together. "Was Nell's party for you anything like this?"

Nell's party had been a pirate-themed costume party, and no one had been forced to wear a collar. Roger had given Zack a gold medallion of his crest to wear, but that had been an overabundance of caution than necessity. Other than the fight with Quinn, it had been delightful. Seamus would hate to hear that.

"The band wasn't nearly as good," Roger said and meant it. Though this band wasn't playing the same sort of music, he preferred the sound of electric instruments to the strings that had been at Nell's party. "I hope you're not upset about Quinn."

"Why would I be? He was your progeny," Seamus replied. "And he was becoming *annoying*."

"Let me guess, he bothered you about starting a war over his murdered pets?" Roger knew the answer to that. Quinn had explained his reasoning for wanting to kill Zack before attacking him for what became the final time. Having met Callum Wright, Roger was certain those innocents weren't the only ones the hunter had killed. He saw no difference between a vampire and someone who chose to be with them.

"He peddled that crap to you, too?" Seamus snorted softly and leaned against Roger. "I never understood why you went through with turning him into one of us. He was always such a pest."

Roger forced his smile to stay in place. Seamus had been the one to pay Quinn to seduce him, and he had lorded that fact over Quinn's grave while Roger waited for him to rise. If not for Quinn pressuring him, Roger never would have offered him the chance to become a vampire. In the end, Quinn had begged for Roger's blood for money and immortality, not for love like he had claimed.

Seamus knew all of that. Yet he was choosing to revise history to one that suited him.

Like he always did.

"I was young and foolish," Roger said, though he'd been about the same age as Takashi was now. "And you did find him amusing."

"Only for your sake."

The music shifted, and a thrum floated on the air. Magic of any sort had a potency that played against the body's five senses. Typically, Roger shoved his awareness off, but he began to note the way the power of the spell registered. Data was at the core of a good plan, so he opened his mind to the sensations.

And something *shifted* in him. The difference was like streetlights illuminating a darkened street. Sensing the lust or fear in an individual was like brushing his fingers across their skin, but the touch of this spell went past the five senses. He struggled to keep pace with the experience. The spell slithered out from the music and became a weight on his chest. At the same time, the magic had a magnetic pull that attempted to pull him under its sway.

The band was glittering, and their glamours faded away to reveal their true forms. A pack of Unseelies controlled the instruments, and at the front was their singer, a siren. He was handsome, and Roger was certain they'd fucked at some point in the past, but that wasn't the danger of the moment.

The first problem was the goddamn spell. Roger was strong enough to resist the urge building in his loins, but others weren't. The mortals in the pit, who the spell was aimed at, certainly weren't. While Kit's and Carver's motions were becoming more suggestive, Zack was growing tense. His hunter's tattoo was likely protecting him from the siren's song just as it blocked Roger's abilities.

Vampires from the edges began to thread their way into the pit where the mortals danced. That didn't bother him much.

But he finally spotted Anton below. Dressed entirely in black, he blended into the shadows and the in-between places as he slid through the crowd. He grabbed a mortal that started to dance up against him and sunk his teeth into their neck. They dropped to the floor. Anton's lips and chin were covered in blood.

This was the trap. Roger had been in it before, in 1845. Seamus had pulled him close during a party, kept an arm around him, and murmured into his ear while Anton slaughtered the mortals he'd brought. The threat of what Seamus could do had kept Roger in place, and he'd watched his mortal lovers drop one by one.

Anton was going after Zack. After Kit. After Carver. He would kill other innocents along the way.

Roger started for the stairs, but Seamus seized his arm and yanked him to a stop. Once, during training with Nell, Roger had asked Zack how he was so slippery, and his response had been, "Physics."

You can't grasp a shadow. Instead of drawing the shadows around him, Roger imagined his arm melting into the shadows, joining them. A burst of darkness spotted his vision, but when he blinked, he'd propelled himself a step backward, free of Seamus.

The look of shock on Seamus's features spoke to a truth that something had happened, but Roger was too cold and dazed to sort through the particulars. He had to get to Zack, had to save him.

Since walking past Seamus would only cause more trouble, Roger jumped up to the balcony railing. The ceiling was high enough that he didn't have to bend. Instead, he was where everyone in the club could see him. He caught sight of Takashi struggling to get past the vampires at the top of the staircase. He must have realized the trouble and was attempting to get down to their mortals.

And Takashi wasn't the only one who was worried. The second-floor vampires were that touch farther from the spell, were able to resist it that fraction better. They were a mix of older and younger, and Roger saw among the older ones the same realization he'd come to. Anton and Seamus were playing with all of them. A few weren't as quick to hide their helplessness.

Then, they spotted him standing on the railing.

No one would follow a shadow. Roger had to step into the light.

But he had to keep Seamus from ripping their throats out as soon as the crowd looked away.

Roger unbuttoned his suit jacket, then hissed out at the rest of them. Not as a threat but to show them his fangs, trying to infuse in them the same urge he had. He spread the desire with his own ability and pushed it out farther than he ever had before. *Protect.*

He dropped to the floor below. The mortals had quickly cleared for him, but then they surged around him, drawing closer. Delicately, he threaded his way between them and made for Zack and the other two. Without his vantage point, the pit was a sea of bodies. The spell crashed over him, but he shoved it out of his mind. He had his desires in control. No influence would distract him.

Moments were an eternity, but Roger spotted Zack, Kit,

and Carver dancing. He moved with the currents, across them where he had to, and reached them.

Just as Anton came from another direction.

Roger pivoted Zack so that he took his place and became the center of their tiny knot. Carver rolled up against him, grinding against his leg. Roger wrapped an arm around him, touched Kit's cheek, and kissed Zack before leveling a glare at Anton.

He mouthed the word "Mine."

Anton smiled brightly, as if he didn't have a care in the world, then melted into the crowd around him.

The knot in Roger's chest didn't ease until Takashi emerged beside them. The pit was descending into chaos. Blood drinking and magic-fueled sex were quickly overcoming the dancing. Roger steered his group toward the exit. "Let's get the fuck out of here."

CHAPTER 24

Thud. Beat. Thud. Thud. Zack punched the combo into the bag and watched the long swing. The weight carried it out, momentum tugging and pulling it, and he stepped toward it as its pendulum movement brought it back. He caught it on his good shoulder and threw a few punches up close. Then he backed off and danced around to the side of it.

The suite's workout room was just large enough to hold the bag, the treadmill, a weight machine, and an elliptical. Having a private room for it in the suite was ridiculous. *Vampires probably don't want their pets getting sweaty in front of anyone else.*

He concentrated on his pace. Light steps, quick movements, and bringing in the punch to precision points. He wasn't aiming to build his strength at the moment but working on his endurance. Even a vampire could overblow their stamina. Surviving came down to taking out the enemy in the first blow or outlasting them.

Certainly been working on the second one lately. The thought was grim and kicked off the slow cycle of events that had occupied him the last three weeks. Thanksgiving was a week away, and picking apart the data was easier than thinking about how he wouldn't taste his Grandma Bonnie's pumpkin pie or nab a bread roll fresh out of the oven rather than waiting for dinner. Processing the vampire politics and thinking about the slowing but continuing crap filling his inbox was preferable to reliving the family flag football game and wondering if anyone would even miss him from their team. He'd always been picked near last. Cal and Denny were almost always the captains once the older cousins decided they were too old or had too many injuries to play.

No, the timeline of what had happened was more important. He could push away what could've been and focus. He drove another punch home, and the bag rocked harder. Breathing and moving, he shifted around to the other side, waited for the swing to reach the right point, then delivered another combo punch.

The Halloween party had been fucked-up. From his research, Zack had expected the vampires inside of Devil's Cove to be among the poorer side of the coven. A bullshit mentality his family had instilled in him, he realized. The vampires that the Wrights and Gladwells tended to hunt created nests and practically lived as a hive. Those groups never had a vampire more than a few decades old and had little in common with the covens.

The attendees of the Devil's Cove party had been decked out in wealth. Every costume that the pets wore had been a custom job, and the outfits the vampires had worn were high-end quality. Devil's Cove seemed a more functional version of the Chateau de Vampire, but it'd been dripping with the same wealth.

The fact that the rich could be monsters, or that the monsters could be rich, shouldn't have been a surprise after his months with Roger. Zack had let himself get caught up in the way "nice" vampires behaved and been swept away with the luxuries his new life was affording him. Money could provide, but it couldn't protect. And plenty of monsters, both human and not, were wealthy assholes. The concept just hadn't struck home until he'd seen it in person.

Punching the bag didn't alleviate the growing chasm in his heart, but he continued working it. He tried to fall into the rhythm of the punches. His mind plunged through memories.

They'd bounced between a few parties that night, none of them as extravagant as Devil's Cove, and they'd been against theme everywhere else. Roger had glided through on his natural and unnatural charms. *No. That hadn't been magic.* When Roger was at his most charismatic, he was irresistible, and constantly, others flocked to him. Zack had become a speck. And that shouldn't have bothered him, shouldn't have dug into his skin weeks later.

Except it just kept happening.

The next night, Roger had given him his birthday present with a belated, though loving, "happy birthday." Zack had received a first-edition *A Study of the Vampyre and Its Allies* by Rudolph Hagen, which dated back to the early 1800s. The text had been one of the fundamental training books the family had used, so it seemed like a really weird present. But Zack had read a few chapters, and it wasn't the same one that he remembered. Somewhere in the editions, the care Hagen used to define vampires as complex individuals had faded away to make them a homogenous monster.

Just another lie of the family, he guessed. Just more bull-shit he had been fed.

Zack's shoulder was growing sore, so he stripped off the boxing gloves and moved over to the treadmill. He turned it on to a brisk jog.

Vincent's smear campaign raged on to the point that Zack had ditched his phone in a dresser drawer and hadn't looked at it in three days. He'd picked up a cheaper one with a fresh number to text Blake. She was appalled that Vincent hadn't let up and nudged him to take a swing back. But Zack was torn between an exhaustion of going out every night and looking like a piece of arm candy and a growing pity for the position that Vincent was in. Few vampires seemed to give a shit about the mortals they had with them, and none seemed to care about how another vampire treated their pets. Vincent wasn't the only one who looked like he was on the verge of collapse almost every night.

And Zack could only take notes and plot.

And be stuck in a waiting pattern. He kicked the treadmill up another setting.

Roger promised he was working on a plan. Promised that he'd started taking the steps necessary to finally take power. That was why he was laying on the charm. More invitations to more parties and gatherings poured in every night. Going to the Chateau had become routine. The glimmering spectacle was working. Zack had overheard vampires complimenting him on a "brilliant show" at the Devil's Cove Halloween party. As if, somehow, jumping over a railing and encouraging a hundred other vampires to go prey on mortals was a good idea.

You know it was more than that, his practical mental voice chided. He had seen the wisdom in it, especially since he had glimpsed Anton in the crowd. The blond, white vampire had cropped up here and there in the throngs of people. He'd been moving in a hunting pattern. And Zack had longed for his dagger, but he hadn't had it. Then Roger had been at his side and scooped him, Kit, and Carver out of the mess.

And for three weeks, Zack had remained fucking helpless.

He increased the treadmill speed.

Because no matter what Roger said, he was still human. He would always be weaker than vampires. Always frailer. He could train his body into peak physical form, and he'd have to rely on luck and Roger to get a fatal blow in on a vampire.

Roger didn't need him.

Nobody did.

That's not true, his practical voice proclaimed.

Isn't it? the Cal voice replied. *You're a blip to him. You don't matter to anybody.*

That wasn't how Roger treated him. Wasn't how Takashi looked at him. Wasn't how Blake spoke to him.

Zack pressed the button on the treadmill. He'd nearly missed it, but he got his hand on it and notched the speed up again. His lungs and legs were burning.

There wasn't energy to think. He had to focus on putting one foot in front of another. Finally, he found some peace.

For a glorious minute, he was nothing but muscle and bone.

Then his right ankle gave out, and the world tilted. He slammed, left knee first, onto the treadmill and rocketed backward. Instinct kicked in, and he brought his arms up in time to protect his face, and then he hit the floor beyond the treadmill with a thud that went soul-deep.

"Holy shit!" Carver said. He rushed to Zack's side.

Zack batted away Carver's attempt to help him up and sat on his ass instead. With a glare and a deep sucking breath, he said, "I'm *fine*."

Carver was dressed in those ridiculous tight bicycle shorts and a tank top that he'd worn to the yoga studio in Taliville all the time. He held up his hands and avoided Zack on his way to turn off the treadmill. Dryly, he said, "Yeah, you seem fine with a bleeding knee."

Zack was taking stock of his injuries while Carver spoke and hated that Carver had noticed his hurts before he'd had a chance. His left knee was bright red but only bleeding a little, his right ankle was throbbing, and his arms ached from the workout and the fall. And with the adrenaline starting to wane, his left shoulder complained more. *Every hunter has their battle wounds. And mine came from fighting my brother. What does that make me?*

"I overdid it," Zack said.

"You had this thing pushed up over eight miles an hour," Carver said. "Overdoing it's an understatement."

"I don't need any more crap thrown my way, all right!" Zack snapped.

Carver gave him a flat glare.

"Fuck off," Zack said between gritted teeth. "I'm allowed to have a goddamn emotion!"

"You're doing that thing again."

"What thing?"

"Where you're angry and decide to lash out at me. I don't know why you're suddenly pissed off, but I know it's not because I tried to help you get up from a fall. And if it is, then *you're* the one that can fuck off," Carver said coolly.

And a terrible gnawing anger clawed its way up Zack's throat, heading for his mouth. The trickle of pure rage slipped down from his mind and raced to meet it. But then he had a flash of his father. Thomas Wright was always patient. Because observation and waiting out the moment often led to greater clarity. With that thought, Zack seized control of his urge to spew a slew of vicious words.

Carver had a point. Zack was hurt and angry at the fucking world, but Carver hadn't done anything worth becoming the focal point of the rage building in Zack's soul.

"I think I'm done working out," Zack said tersely.

"Thought I heard Roger and Takashi waking up."

"I'll go see." Zack struggled to his feet. Though his knee ached, his ankle wasn't reinjured, so he could walk. Whatever weakness had overcome the joint had passed.

"You know, it's a little unfair," Carver said, his tone off-handed as he stepped onto the treadmill and began a brisk walk pace.

Zack paused at the door. "What is?"

"You have two immortal hotties wrapped around your little finger, and you never crack a smile."

"You think I should be happy because I've got

boyfriends?" Zack scoffed. "Why are you coming at me for that? You're involved with them, too."

Carver hopped off the treadmill and approached Zack. "You and I both know that they're not into me the way they are with you. Takashi and I have a little fun. Roger's nice, but we haven't connected on a physical level like I thought we would. And all that's fine. Because I get to brush elbows with some amazing people, and I get to party and eat great and not have a care in the goddamn world. You have all of that *plus* romance, and all you do is piss and moan every night."

"I do not," Zack replied.

"Fine, you never *say* it, but it's obvious that you only see the problems."

"Oh, is it?" Zack snapped.

Carver raised an eyebrow. "Well, you're taking out your anger on me, for starters."

"Maybe this time I have a fucking reason to be angry with you," Zack replied. "Unlike you, I'm not seeing a dime for any of this. And how're your parents? Got any siblings? Do they answer your texts? Calls?"

"When are you going to stop moping over what you lost and appreciate what you've got?" Carver returned.

There was no getting through to him. Zack huffed and stormed off for the master bedroom. His sore knee made his walk less dramatic than he'd been hoping for, but Carver didn't follow him.

Every detail of the living room was new to him again. The modern-styled furniture was sleek and extravagant. The flat-screen television was massive. And what sort of suite typically had a full bar? A well-stocked kitchenette in a corner? Then, there was the view of Lake Michigan out beyond the balcony. The world sucked, but he was comfortable.

Money wasn't the point. The suite could burn for all Zack cared. He whipped open the door to the master bedroom.

Roger and Takashi were kissing, a slow and gentle push

and pull between the two of them. Both of them slept in pajama pants. Where Roger was stacked with muscles, Takashi was more lithe but no less muscular. A thin trail of dark hair was a whisper of a line from Takashi's navel and toward his groin, disappearing from sight beneath his plaid sleepwear. Takashi had his long fingers threaded through Roger's long, black hair.

And the picture before Zack was beautiful. Stunning. Literally better than any porn or fantasy he'd ever had. They finished their kiss, and Roger turned toward Zack with a lazy smile on his lips. Takashi nipped at Roger's chin, then leaned against him as he regarded Zack as well.

They were happy to see him, though that was quickly becoming confusion and worry.

Because he was the problem. The angry, stupid mortal who couldn't deal with his shit.

"I need a shower," Zack said, unwanted sharpness coloring his voice.

Roger left the bed. "Zack—"

"It's not you." Zack hurried into the bathroom.

"You're hurt," Roger said.

"I fell."

"How?"

"I was stupid."

Soundlessly, Roger followed Zack into the bathroom. Rather than shutting the door behind him, he continued trailing Zack. Takashi slipped out of the bed, shut the door between the bedroom and the rest of the suite, and then lingered in the bathroom doorway.

So I've got two boyfriends trying to handle me now. Great. Zack stripped off his tank top and tossed it onto the floor. He kicked off his sneakers. When the two of them continued to watch him, he snapped, "Can I *help* you?"

Roger folded his arms over his chest. "You're lashing out. What's really bothering you?"

"Nothing." Zack winced as he dragged his shorts over his wounded knee. He hadn't been careful, but he wasn't about to slow down now that he was on a roll again.

Roger cheated and used his vampire speed to zip in front of Zack before he could get into the shower. His black hair framed his face, gently brushing his shoulders, and the set of his shoulders created a perfect triangle to his hips. Even with a stern expression, he had the ability to worm into Zack's heart and open gates.

Zack slammed those gates shut, though he could feel them catching, like Roger still had a foot through them. He met Roger's gaze in another of their long staring contests, but he was crumbling every second. The gates might have closed, but the walls around them fell away into dust. Roger and Takashi were everything.

And I'm a blip. Zack brushed at the itchiness on his face, and tears escaped from his eyes.

Slowly, Roger unfolded his arms and cupped Zack's cheeks. He brushed his thumbs through the forming trails. In a soft voice, he begged, "What is wrong?"

"Nothing new," Zack whispered. "It's the same shit night after night after night. We go out. You feed. You schmooze with other vampires. And I just *sit*. I sit and I watch and I wait. And then I get told I should be appreciating my fucking life the way it is."

Roger frowned. "Who said that?"

"Doesn't matter. It's what everyone's thinking, isn't it? I should be able to hold out. Be happier. But how can I be happy when everything's a fucking nightmare and there's nothing I can do?"

While Zack spoke, Takashi approached him. He kissed Zack's temple and then wrapped an arm around his shoulders.

Their touch was too much because it meant that both of them were trying to understand him. That they cared. And if they cared that much, that meant the Cal voice in his head was wrong again. As much as the rest of him knew that was the better way, that the part of him that took on his brother's voice was a piece of self-doubting shit, he hated that any bit of him could be wrong.

So he slithered out from between them. "I want to shower. Alone."

"All right," Roger said gently.

Mercifully, they listened, and within a moment, Zack was alone in the bathroom. He stepped into the shower and turned on the faucets to a near-scalding degree. At least there he could pretend all the water on his face was from the showerhead.

Cleaning up did its unique brand of magic. The steam seemed to penetrate him and exfoliate his mind, clearing away the sadness that had manifested so poorly. Still sore, his overworked muscles complained lightly, but nothing so bad that a little rest and water wouldn't fix. But he took his time toweling off. Roger and Takashi were probably waiting on him to emerge.

And they'd want to help him. And that might set the whole spiral off again.

Zack clutched the towel to his chest, but he was reasonably dry. He couldn't put off getting dressed. Besides, there wasn't another exit from the bathroom. If he waited too long, they'd probably come back in.

Sucking in a deep breath and lifting his chin, Zack walked back into the master bedroom.

Roger and Takashi were sitting on the edge of the bed facing the door. Their conversation drifted to a pause as they turned their heads to look at him.

"Did you know," Roger said, voice caring but not too gentle, "that Takashi has never seen the *Twilight* movies? I thought the five of us might stay in tonight. Have a marathon."

Zack had shared those movies with Roger when they were first connecting in Taliville, and he'd watched them over and over while he was recovering. They were a tie to his past, a rebellion against his mother, who didn't want him to watch "vampire propaganda."

"A movie marathon sounds great. But not *Twilight*."

"How about *The Covenant*? The one with that Sebastian Stan fellow," Takashi said.

"Never seen it," Zack said. "I'm not sure I've even heard of it."

"Really? I could've sworn it came out this century."

Zack grinned weakly. They were trying to make him feel better; he could, too. "Is this where I remind you that I turned twenty a couple weeks ago? So, like, half of this current century happened before I was ten?"

"If you're attempting to make me feel old, I already knew I was when sock hops became a thing."

"That makes me ancient," Roger replied. "Considering I was growing old when thirteen colonies decided to revolt."

"Jesus, you are *old*," Zack teased.

Roger chuckled and pulled Zack onto his lap. "Worth it to have met you."

They shared a quick, sweet kiss. Zack wrapped his arms around Roger's shoulders and leaned his forehead against his. "We can really stay in tonight?"

"Yes."

Tension uncoiled, and Zack rested against Roger. "Awesome."

"I'll tell the others," Takashi said. He poked Roger. "You should ask him."

"I plan on it."

"Ask me what?" Zack asked as Takashi quietly left the room.

Roger stroked Zack's back slowly. "Takashi and I were discussing when I should strike. My place in the coven seems on solid ground, but is four weeks enough information?"

"It is." Zack slipped off Roger's lap and pulled out a notebook from under the bed.

"How many of those do you have?" Roger asked.

"Never enough." Zack flipped open to the pages of timetables he'd been creating over the last week. He had marked locations, events, and what nights they took place. Along with that, he'd thrown in the average attendance for the location and any key players he was pretty sure would show. "Honestly, you could do it any night."

"No." Roger sprawled atop the bed and drew Zack's notebook closer. He examined the data. "Slipping your dagger and Cal's knife through the security of any location will be difficult."

"We don't need Cal's."

"Two silver blades are better than one. Contingency."

"Fine. Then any night we go to the Chateau. Candide's on our side, right? She'd help us get them through."

"If it doesn't put her in danger, yes," Roger replied. "She doesn't want to compromise her position inside the coven."

"Coward," Zack grumbled.

"We didn't live this long by being brave." Roger ran his fingers over the coarse ink. "We want witnesses, but not ones that will interfere."

"Can't you just challenge him?" Zack asked.

"That gives him warning, and he'll cheat. I've seen him do it before, though no one's dared to try in over a century. Besides, in one-on-one, I wouldn't have you. A stealthy, witnessed assassination is our best shot."

"You're not wrong." Zack sighed as he sat on the bed. "But a straight-out assassination would be so much easier."

"We can't leave any questions about who killed him. With four hundred vampires in the coven, I *have* to make my claim clear to as many as possible."

"Then what about the Winter's Grand Ball?" Zack asked. "It's at the Chateau, lots of guests."

"Too many." Roger tapped to the list of Unseelie Court members Zack had identified on the guest list. That had taken a bit of fishing around on Night Deets to find and plenty of listening to rumors. "One of these bastards might be the one to put me in a coma. No one's made another attempt, but we'll need to be careful ourselves."

"Then New Year's," Zack suggested. "The party's happening at the Chateau, though it seems to be Seamus's event. He's made silver part of the color scheme. That should give us some kind of advantage, right?"

"So long as the blade doesn't glow," Roger remarked. "Why does it do that, by the way?"

"Magic," Zack replied.

"Yes, but sometimes it's bright, and others, it's rather dim."

Zack closed the notebook and rolled it into his hands. The enchanted blades of the Wright family were one of the close-guarded secrets. In truth, the blades responded to the threat their owners felt while in the presence of a supernatural. Zack's had dimmed around Roger because he wasn't a danger to him.

But giving away such a secret wasn't his place.

But the family had disowned him while Roger had been with him every step.

But how much would his family would forgive him?

Would they ever?

Zack released the notebook. The world was too much, and he couldn't take on thinking through every consequence. "I'll tell you. Some night. Just … not right now."

"All right," Roger said softly.

"I just need this Netflix and chill night, you know?"

Roger grinned salaciously. "I have figured out what that slang means."

Heat flared across Zack's cheeks. "I meant it *literally*, not as an offer for sex."

"I know, but perhaps?"

Zack pushed Roger's shoulder playfully, then hopped off the bed. He had a pair of pajamas that was silkier and made him feel sexier than the flannels he often wore. He tugged them out of the drawer and started putting them on. "Eh, we'll see."

CHAPTER 25

The couch was theoretically big enough for the five of them since Kit decided to sit in Carver's lap. Zack insisted on sitting on the far side from them, putting Roger and Takashi in the middle. They'd ordered pizza for the mortals, though Roger stole a slice to taste it, and he refilled the drinks whenever someone's had run out. The film slipped in and out of Roger's attention. After the first one, discussion broke out over what should follow it. Despite Roger's attempts to catch up to recent media, names of actors and movies flew past without tugging any recollection from him.

A knock on the door disrupted their conversation. As Roger rose, he glanced to the others. "Did anyone order something else?"

"No, but if they have carrot cake, I would not turn it down," Kit said.

"Carrot cake? All the deserts in the world, and you come up with *carrot cake*?" Carver said with a short laugh.

"What? My dad hates raisins. Carrot cake's like what I always order." Kit puffed up. "I suppose your taste is so much more sophisticated?"

"Red velvet."

Zack snorted. "Red velvet's basic anymore."

Roger made his way to the door while the others continued.

Dressed in black, Dmitri had a haunted look in his brown eyes as he scanned over Roger and then glanced into the room beyond. "I need to speak with you. Alone."

The light in the room didn't seem to reach Dmitri. The joy of the conversation seemed a million miles away from the place where he stood.

"Balcony?" Roger suggested.

Dmitri gave a short nod, then led the way outside. Late-fall darkness had swept in hours before, and the wind had chilled with it. Roger had barely closed the sliding glass door before Dmitri shoved a piece of paper in his direction. As soon as Roger took it, Dmitri crossed the balcony toward the railing. He kept his back turned.

"What's this?" Roger asked slowly. He read through the names and numbers.

"Quinn's stash and a little extra," Dmitri replied.

"Thank you." Roger slid the paper into his pocket and strode to join Dmitri at the railing. Wind whipped at his hair, pulling and tugging it from his face. "You're not in a good place."

"Not all of us can carve merriment into existence at a whim." Dmitri jerked his head toward the sliding glass door and the room beyond.

"This took work," Roger replied.

"If you say so."

The urge to bristle and argue with Dmitri bubbled to the surface, but Roger sought the trouble beneath the waves. A gulf was between them, and perhaps he'd had something to do with its creation. But then, the thirty years he'd been gone may have lengthened it, and there was nothing he could to reclaim that time. He could only move forward.

"You have to know that taking the coven for myself isn't

about the power," Roger said quietly. "Four hundred vampires can't be left to their own devices."

"I don't care about them."

"You don't have to. I do."

"*Why?*"

Roger stepped closer. "Because many of them didn't choose to become this any more than we did. Many of them had no idea what bargain they were accepting like Ezra. And some few wanted the bloodthirst to excuse their perverse natures like Marcus. And the very rare ones like Candide would turn Chicago into a gilded cage for humanity and spread that outward until the planet was under the control of the vicious."

"Wake up, Roger. The world is already under the sway of the damned and the wretchedly ambitious," Dmitri replied, exhaustion plain.

"Maybe. But if I can keep these vampires in check, then there might be a little less pain in the world," Roger said.

Dmitri closed his eyes and leaned forward to grasp the rail. After taking a ragged breath, he said, "God, I forgot what an idealist you can be."

"Sometimes. They tend to bring it out in me."

"Your mortals?"

"And Takashi."

Dmitri opened his eyes and turned to look at the hotel suite. The light made seeing inside possible. Carver was standing, the remote control high in his other hand. Kit was latched onto his shoulder while Zack was clearly trying to figure out the best way to tackle Carver without hurting him. Takashi lifted Kit by the waist and raised them up. The struggle continued.

"He's been smitten with you since the '20s," Dmitri said. "I hated him then."

"You were through with me, remember? Why were you jealous of a fledgling who wanted to be with me when you had left my home screaming you wish you'd never seen my face?"

"Love and hate tend to mingle until it recedes beyond meaning. I am damned without salvation, and you belong in this hell with me. Any alternative is … maddening."

That far-off tone in Dmitri's voice rang alarm bells in Roger's mind. He lightly grasped Dmitri's arm. "What are you planning?"

"Nothing," Dmitri said.

But Dmitri wouldn't meet his gaze. Roger tightened his hold on Dmitri's arm. "Don't lie to me, love."

"I haven't been that for you in ages."

"Because you chose to leave me," Roger replied.

"You always chose another." Dmitri motioned at the suite.

"I have a place for you in my heart." Roger turned to face Dmitri and held on to both his arms. "You don't have to leave. Stay with us."

Dmitri took a step back, then another, and slowly pulled away from Roger's touch. "I'm due elsewhere."

"Then you are planning something. Please, Dmitri, whatever it is, come inside and share it with me," Roger said.

"You've made your position clear. You wish to kill the king and take his throne. I plan to burn the devil from my life."

Before Roger could reach for him again, Dmitri skipped to the top of the railing and then dropped into the darkness. Roger spun and clasped the railing. He hunted for Dmitri in the air below and spotted him drifting downward, eventually landing on a building across the street. Dmitri dashed across that rooftop and jumped from the next.

Not quite flight but close. I'm not the only one gaining strength with age. Roger watched the night, but he had lost sight of Dmitri after he jumped from the second building.

The sliding glass door opened, and Takashi emerged onto the balcony. He pushed the door shut and held it closed.

There was a hint of laughter on his lips, and he held the controller to his chest. Carver began to bang on the glass between attempts to force the door open. Takashi said, "Sorry if I'm interrupting. Where is Dmitri?"

"Gone," Roger said.

Takashi opened the door and tossed the controller at Carver. Before he closed the door again, Roger heard Zack's voice. "Is everything—"

"Five minutes," Takashi promised and finished shutting the door.

"I don't know if I can pull myself together that quickly," Roger murmured.

Takashi joined him at the railing, one hand resting on it as he surveyed the empty air below. "Did he jump?"

"More drifted from rooftop to rooftop."

"Flight is rare among our kind."

"Any true power seems to be." Roger reached for the shadows around him, and he could feel the presence of the darkness like a cloth waiting for him to fold and manipulate. He released his hold and stared out into the night. "I don't know what he's gone to do, but he suddenly gave me the money."

"That feels strange," Takashi said.

"I thought his nights of wishing for death were far behind him," Roger whispered. His throat burned with a pain that he hadn't truly felt since he was mortal. "He's been hiding it. Three hundred years, and he's hidden it from me." He scoffed at himself. "Who am I fooling? I never bothered to look for it."

Takashi put a hand on his shoulder. "You weren't looking for it because you were in the midst of your own pain. He isn't your burden."

"*I* am the reason he's a vampire. That Anton tortures him through the years. If I hadn't ..." Roger dipped his head before taking a breath and raising his chin again. Bloody tears colored his vision red. "I was the one who didn't give a damn about drinking late into the night. I was the one who felt the odd surge of desire roll over me and gave in to it. I was the one who dragged Dmitri into the dark with me. It's my fault the sun was ripped from him along with his life. And what have I done with my time? Party. Drink. Fuck. No wonder he hates me."

"Turn around," Takashi whispered.

Roger shook his head and planned to stare off into the night, but Takashi nudged him. He gave in and faced the hotel suite.

Zack had nabbed the room service menu, and he pored over it with Kit. Meanwhile, Carver had settled into a chair and was scanning through a streaming service.

Up until Dmitri's interruption, Roger had been cozy with them. He'd meant to distract Zack from his troubles and had gotten comfortable, too. But the whole reason Zack needed a break was Roger's fault. Without him, Zack would've remained an ignorant hunter, but he might've been happier.

"I'm dragging him down," Roger said quietly. "You, as well."

"I am finally free." Takashi leaned against Roger.

"Not once Seamus accepts your coven application," Roger said.

"Eh, that's temporary." Takashi wrapped his arm around Roger. "Kit and Carver seem to be having the time of their lives. And you can't torment yourself about Zack."

"If not for me—"

Takashi squeezed Roger. "I know it's cheating referencing the journal, but he never fit. He was out of place long before he met you."

Roger had guessed that might be true long before. Zack had his morals, but he'd been eager to prove himself. Years ago, he'd made a "mistake," according to the family, yet all he'd done was release a vampire too young to have committed any sins. Compassion had been his fault. What sort of family would discard him for that?

"Choosing to focus on glimpses of joy doesn't make you an uncaring fool," Takashi said firmly.

"You'd be surprised how often I've been told it does," Roger replied.

"I wouldn't. The world isn't known for its kindness. That only makes those who try more beautiful." Gently, Takashi reached up and put one finger to Roger's jaw to nudge him into a kiss.

Kissing him was one of those pleasures that eased the razor pain in Roger's soul. He lingered in the slow slide of their lips and light touches. Afterward, he pressed his forehead to Takashi's. "I am glad you're here and grateful for this."

"It's not entirely altruistic," Takashi said with a grin. "I would've accepted it if I was told no, but I jumped at this opportunity because I've wanted you for a century, and tiny tastes weren't enough."

"You might find the taste of me sours over time."

"And you might decide to spit me away," Takashi said. "That's not the future I see, but we'll deal with changes when they come."

Roger hugged him and found comfort in their embrace. Though the wind promised winter, he found new hope blooming in his soul. "Please tell me you have another movie picked out. I fear whatever our mortals will find."

Takashi laughed and slipped out of the hug. He held onto Roger's hand. "Do you think they've seen *The Lost Boys*?"

"I'm not sure I have." Roger followed Takashi into the hotel suite.

But a piece of him lingered out in the dark and the shadows, and he wondered if light would heal the broken pieces of his spirit or shatter him further.

CHAPTER 26

Knowing the date that they would finally dispense of Seamus made the next few nights far easier to handle. Zack didn't relax, but he could carry on the pretense easier. He continued absorbing information, making small talk when he absolutely had to, and ignoring his social media notifications. Carver was keeping tabs on it, apparently, and he'd made a couple of comments about Vincent's new video. Zack had replied that he'd rather sit through a twelve-hour marathon of a reality TV show about home improvement instead of watching another two-minute video of whatever Vincent had to say. He made a few posts about food and watching *The Covenant*, and that was it.

At least, for his regular phone.

Since the figurative trolls had found Zack's number, he took out his secondary phone as he debated reaching out to his family again. He wasn't just thinking about them. Seamus was a vampire older than any that Zack had heard of besides Nell. Though he was researching the best he could, he was certain that there was more information just out of reach. Would the silver truly work? Would the enchantment on his dagger be enough to dismantle Seamus? Quinn had been a quarter of Seamus's age, and Zack had had to keep his dagger deep in his chest for seconds before he perished.

He told himself he didn't care if the family didn't message him back. He simply needed to try to gain that smidge of insight someone else might have. Anything might help them gain an upper hand, and they needed every advantage. Unfortunately, he'd only memorized a few phone numbers, and his journal with his hard copy directory was back at his parents' house. But he knew his immediate family's, the landlines for his grandparents, one aunt's, and three cousins.

Rather than sending one to all the ones he could remember, he only sent a message to his father, his sister, his aunt, and his cousin Lacey. They were all long shots, especially Lacey since he hadn't spoken to her in almost a year.

Somehow, checking his secondary phone and seeing no messages was worse than having a stream of notifications from Night Deets and the Fang app. He sat on the end of the bed and tried to will a message to pop up, but nothing happened.

Takashi stirred, and then Roger moved. Sunset was coming sooner and sooner every night. Zack hopped up from the bed and shoved his phone into a drawer. He was about to slam the drawer shut, but that might wake them faster. Carefully, he guided it closed and then crawled onto the bed.

Roger reached for him, so Zack slithered up between them, staying on top of the covers. When they first woke, Roger and Takashi were like ice. Hints of chilliness were all right, but he preferred a layer between them until they warmed up.

"Evening," Roger murmured, his voice deep and husky.

"Hey there," Zack said with a small smile. He kissed Roger, then turned to Takashi. "Hey to you, too."

Takashi nuzzled him, pressing his lips to Zack's neck. He brushed another kiss against his pulse.

Zack poked Takashi's leg. "You're awake, right?"

"I'm awake," Takashi said, grogginess in his voice. "You smell like oranges."

"My soap ran out. That's the hotel's."

"I like it." Takashi licked Zack's neck. His tongue wasn't as cold as his lips, and he didn't have the same deep chill that clung to Roger. He lazily put an arm over Zack's chest.

"It's an interesting change from that woodsy stuff." Roger slid an arm across Zack's hips.

The Cal voice proclaimed, *You're stuck between two bloodsuckers, idiot.* The rational voice, the one Zack liked and listened to more and more, was quiet, but a different one that was all his own mind whispered, *This is so fucking hot.*

"I'll have to buy some, then," Zack managed. His cheeks felt hot, and every breath reminded him of the weight of Takashi's arm on him.

"Mmhmm," Takashi moaned against Zack's skin as he planted another kiss on his neck. He pressed closer and continued exploring Zack's neck.

Roger absentmindedly teased the skin just above Zack's pant line as he drew Zack's earlobe between his lips.

Zack groaned. "If you two keep going—"

"You might have a problem?" Roger palmed Zack's dick through his jeans.

Zack arched into Roger's touch. His shoulders were still pinned to the bed by Takashi. "Fuck, that's not fair."

"It's not fair that you smell this fucking good," Takashi whispered. He kissed behind Zack's ear, then trailed his kisses down to the crook of his neck.

"He more than smells it. Touch him," Roger murmured. He slid his hand under Zack's shirt, pushing it up.

For a moment, Takashi seemed too enthralled to notice, but then he lifted his arm, and Roger was able to finish tugging Zack's shirt off. Zack sank back onto the bed and gasped at Takashi's cool touch against his warm skin. Roger was already toying with the button of Zack's jeans and managed to pop them open. He kissed Zack's cheek and his neck.

"So warm," Takashi said against Zack's neck.

"Delightful," Roger said.

"I can't tell if you're hungry or horny," Zack teased.

"Both," Takashi whispered. He dragged his finger along Zack's jaw, coaxing him to turn toward him.

They kissed, and Zack reached up to cup the back of Takashi's head as they did. Their tongues slid forth and back, dancing between Takashi's lips before parrying one another in Zack's mouth. All the while, Roger kissed Zack's shoulder and eased the zipper of his jeans downward. Breaking off the kiss, Zack panted, and his breath clouded the space with a hint of coffee. He nipped Takashi's bottom lip and sucked on it a little as he ran his hands through Takashi's hair.

Roger finally sprang Zack's cock free of his jeans and underwear by tugging the material down. Zack groaned as Roger grasped him but only caressed the end of his length with slow circles of his thumb. When he tried to rock into Roger's hand, Roger loosened his grip.

"*Fuck*," Zack hissed. "Not fair."

"Not fair is not touching all of you." Takashi slipped from underneath the covers and joined Zack to lie on top of them. As he settled in again, his hard, silk-covered cock pressed against Zack.

"You still have pants on," Zack said. "We all do."

"Let's change that," Roger said. His husky voice reverberated through Zack.

What would have taken only a few seconds became a slow caress and tease as Zack helped Takashi strip and then Roger. They both took hold of his jeans and underwear and slid them down his legs. The socks went, too, and Zack fought an urge to kick and giggle when Roger accidentally tickled the arch of his right foot.

Takashi claimed his lips again and latched a leg over his as their kiss deepened. Zack was careful to avoid the sharp points of Takashi's fangs, twirling to either side of them instead. A needful groan vibrated through Takashi, felt more than heard, and he pinned Zack to the bed.

"I want a taste," Takashi muttered in his ear.

"Go for it," Zack replied.

Takashi moaned, and his lips moved down Zack's cheek, toward his jaw, to his neck.

Roger kissed him while Takashi sought a place to bite, and Zack caressed his cheek, then rested his hand on his shoulder. When Takashi bit his shoulder, Zack gasped into Roger's lips. Roger returned his hand to Zack's cock, wrapping it around so only a hint of friction came any time Zack attempted to seek more.

With a wicked, gorgeous smile, Roger kissed the palm of Zack's hand, then wrapped his free hand around his wrist. He nuzzled over one of his previous bite marks.

"Yeah," Zack panted. "Do it."

Roger sank his teeth into Zack's wrist.

The heady rush pounded in Zack's ear. His pulse raced, but for once, his mind didn't cloud with worries and concerns. He stayed in the moment with them. Roger placed his palm flat against Zack's lower abdomen and kept his hips pinned. At first, their bites were a sharp pain, but that dulled. Their lips and tongues worked the wounds, and they drank his blood. Takashi was too close to watch, but Zack could keep his gaze locked on Roger. Lust and wonder danced across his features, a sort of rapture playing out.

Takashi broke off first, though Roger quickly followed. Blood continued to slip from the wounds, but Zack checked his wrist and saw that it'd slowed to a trickle.

"Fucking exquisite," Takashi said into Zack's ear. Then he caressed down Zack's chest, skipping over Roger's hand, and gently stroked his cock. After sliding up and down once, he continued his drifting exploration as far as his hand could reach.

Roger grasped Takashi's chin and pulled him up into a kiss. Their mouths were coated in blood, somehow artfully messy with it. And Zack's cock stirred, his own internal engines revving because they had his blood on his lips. They were making out over him and chasing every last drop of his blood from the other. Roger groaned and pressed closer, only Zack was in the way of him reaching Takashi, so his hardened cock nudged roughly into Zack's side. The moan that escaped from Takashi seemed to come from his core.

Zack couldn't get his hand on his cock through the tangle of limbs, and neither of them was touching him there. Choking back a whine, he attempted to pump up into the air and find something, anything, to touch with his dick, but Roger and Takashi held him down. He was theirs.

And they're mine. Zack reached up between them with his bleeding wrist. The scent of his blood seemed to startle Takashi, and he broke away from kissing Roger to licking the thin stream that slid down Zack's arm.

"We haven't forgotten you, sweetheart," Roger murmured. His irises were a faint red rim around the wide darkness of his pupils.

"You've forgotten something." Zack lifted an eyebrow and then did his best to glance down at his cock.

Roger laughed, and the sound was so relaxed and free that something in Zack uncoiled and stretched. He stroked Zack's inner thigh and coaxed his legs farther apart. The chill of his hand was less but still there, and Zack shivered. The reaction was electric, coursing up his spine and to his toes and fingertips.

"Whatever should we do?" Roger teased Zack's thigh, so near to his balls and not quite close to his hole.

"Come on," Zack whined.

Takashi was the one who chuckled this time, and he nuzzled Zack's ear. "Are we being cruel?"

"You're being incredibly fucking hot, and I'm going to explode if we keep messing around with foreplay."

"You're not the only one," Takashi replied. He rolled his hips against Zack's side, and his cock pressed harder.

"I can do something about that." Zack grinned and pushed Takashi onto his back. Pressing quick, feverish kisses to Takashi's cool skin, he made a line to Takashi's hard cock. Doing so scooted him out from between them. Somehow, the room's air was chillier than the two of them. Zack grasped Takashi's member at the root and lightly kissed his tip.

Takashi groaned, and the sound only deepened as Zack slid his mouth over him. Soon, Takashi's hand flew to the back of Zack's head, and he slid his fingers through his hair, unable to find purchase in the short length in the back.

"My gorgeous loves," Roger said. His voice sounded distant and yet in Zack's ear at the same time. He pressed a kiss to the center of Zack's back, then gently nudged him into a position with his ass in the air. At first, Zack thought he pressed a finger into his hole, but wetness was left behind.

Roger was tonguing his hole. Zack shivered and moaned and sucked Takashi. Working his way down, he took more and more of Takashi's length in his mouth. But as much as he pushed backward toward him, Roger's tongue just couldn't reach deep enough to satisfy. With a frustrated groan, he pulled off Takashi with a wet pop and glanced over his shoulder.

"Fuck me," he pleaded.

By the time Zack had returned his lips to Takashi's dick, Roger had shifted position and nudged his tip against Zack's hole. A moan shuddered out of Zack, and he rocked between them, taking in more of Roger or Takashi in turn. His own heavy cock swayed with the movement.

Deeper and deeper they reached, and Zack lost himself to

the fill and absence they brought. He was never totally empty; he was never actually full, caught between moaning, yearning, and panting.

And somewhere in the rocking, their positions started to shift. The rhythm hurried on, and Zack moaned as Roger was fully seated, but the sound was muffled around Takashi's cock. Takashi cupped the back of his head and brought him farther down. Zack took him far in, his throat catching and closing around him.

Roger wrapped his hand around Zack's dripping cock first, but Takashi joined him, and both of them were stroking him. A whine in Zack erupted into a moan and then a muffled, long shout. Ecstasy started in the base of his spine and spilled upward and through him. The darkness behind his eyelids became an electric white burst that faded to an oblivion too sweet to perceive.

When he finally drifted back into his body, he was cuddled between them. Roger at his back, Takashi at his front. There was some kind of conversation going on, but Zack needed a moment to understand what words were.

"You can't get him a book for Christmas," Takashi said quietly. "You just got him one for his birthday."

"It's hard to think of anything. He's not interested in material things," Roger murmured.

"Surely you can think of *something*."

"Everything else feels too cheap."

Takashi stroked Zack's hair, a sort of gentle petting that made Zack wonder if he realized that he was awake. "Come on, Roger. Appeal to his heart. You ought to know it."

"I do." Roger kissed Zack's shoulder. "Maybe a cozy sweatshirt and tickets to an event of his choice. Something daytime he can take Blake and Kit to."

Zack squeezed Takashi's hand. With a light chuckle, Takashi said, "I think that's a good idea."

Something buzzed, and Roger moved. The bed dipped and settled as he went to the edge of it.

"What is it?" Takashi asked.

The alertness in his tone woke Zack the rest of the way. He rolled onto his back to regard Roger, but he could only see Roger's back. His head was dipped, his face out of view.

Then Roger sighed and lifted his head up enough that his hair fell past his shoulders. He ran his hand through it. "Playtime is over. Seamus has summoned us to Devil's Cove. Tonight."

CHAPTER 27

Roger buttoned his suit jacket and smoothed his hands down the length of it. He'd chosen a midnight black with a deep blue base and a royal purple dress shirt. The top three buttons were undone, and he had a gold chain on and diamond cufflinks. He was in style without being too flashy. He was back; this was *him*.

But Seamus hadn't asked to see him since the Halloween party, and Roger had hardly spotted him during the ensuing weeks. Getting summoned churned in Roger's gut. Matters weren't helped by the fact that he'd attempted to reach out to Dmitri and hadn't heard back from him. His strange behavior the other night and Seamus's sudden demand to see him were spinning Roger's mind to frantic corners. Zack and Takashi hadn't shared any hypothesis of what Seamus could want, and Roger had been too afraid to ask them. If what they could guess was worse than what he imagined, he didn't want to know.

As far as Seamus knew, Roger was the same as he'd always been. *Time to carry on.*

Inside the three steps across the pavement, Roger locked his fears into a chest and tossed them to the bottom of his mental sea. He pulled on his old, reliable persona. By the time he knocked on the door to Devil's Cove, he had his sly, charming smile fixed in place. Takashi, Zack, Kit, and Carver fell in behind him.

A small hatch opened, and a moment later, the door opened. Roger's group was admitted into the short hall that led into the club proper. Zack, Kit, and Carver checked their coats, and then the five of them moved into the main club.

The entire atmosphere had changed from the party energy to the slink and shadow Roger was accustomed to. The lighting was dim, soft yellow glows. Each fixture seemed incapable of reaching its light to the pool of the next. Rather than teeming with the undead and choked with crowds of mortals, there was ample seating and free space at the bars. The vampires were still displaying their full plumage with fine clothing and half-naked collared pets. Instrumental music played over the speakers and had a menacing flair, which Roger would've enjoyed if he wasn't scanning the area for possible attacks.

No one seemed to particularly mind that he and his had come into the club. Roger drifted forward, ignoring the scent of old fear and fresh death. Mortals, naked except for the gray bands on their arms, ferried drinks and empty glasses between the patrons and the bar. Two larger, muscular men dressed in the simple blacks of the bouncers dragged a sobbing, beautiful young man between them. His words were lost to a gag, and he struggled in vain against the men carting him over to a booth.

A vampire with dark, curly hair and an olive complexion ran his thumb across his lip as the bouncers drew close. Roger recognized the vampire: Xenofon, a vampire sired by one of Seamus's now-dead fledglings during their crossing to the new world in 1800. With a hungry grin, Xenofon welcomed the captive mortal into his arms. "You look delicious."

Roger continued moving forward. He didn't need to look

to understand the sounds. In a matter of seconds, the mortal's cries turned to whimpers. No doubt he'd be dead close to dawn, assuming Xenofon still preferred to play with his food rather than outright kill.

Nearby conversations didn't even shift their pitch. A few passing glances went toward the booth where Xenofon and his friends were, but not a glimmer of concern showed on a vampire's face. Few mortals showed anything other than a primal fear that might happen to them.

Because this was the sort of place Seamus had sculpted over the centuries. Before spending time in Taliville, Roger had grown numb to the ongoings. This was nothing new. Roger himself had had food brought to him on numerous occasions. Because he was expected to feed like that. Because he couldn't show that he was any different from the rest of them. *Don't fool yourself. You've enjoyed it, too.*

He had. And a part of him hungered for blood, especially upon smelling a fresh spill in the air from another booth. Dmitri's words returned. *I am damned without salvation, and you belong in this hell with me.* And there was a piece of truth in that, wasn't there? Hunters were blind in their hatred of the supernatural, but it stemmed from what the supernatural could do to the helpless. The power, the magic, the control they could effortlessly wield in the matters of a human's life and death terrified hunters, and for good reason.

This is no place for a crisis of conscience. The pit, which had been cleared of furniture for the party, hosted several pods of booths. Toward the center was a large one, and Seamus sat in the center of it, his back to the door and face toward the stage. Roger had the opportunity to continue glancing around the club. Reflexively, he nodded greetings to the vampires he knew.

Which was a good portion of them. Roger spotted at least a dozen vampires over a century old out among the crowd. Lucille and Dempsey had a booth, each had a mortal pet, and another two vampires were with them. Their sirelings, Roger realized. Every branch traced back to Seamus, but the vampires sharing a booth tended to be closely connected.

Some few, like Nathaniel, remained solitary. Nathaniel was Ezra's first sireling and someone that Roger had had to save from that wretched farmhouse in 1947. He had a wary look in his good eye, the other an unfocused milky white. It had never fully healed from what the hunters had done to him.

The older coven members did not turn out like this unless there was a celebration or a summoning. And Seamus never casually summoned them.

Centuries of practice aided Roger in keeping his easygoing demeanor. His smile felt natural, even as part of his mind screamed for him to run. As he approached Seamus's low-backed booth, he put an arm around Zack's shoulders and kept him pressed close.

"You called, I answered, master," Roger said with a purr in his voice.

Seamus showed him one of his unreadable smiles. He had drops of blood that almost blended into his dark red shirt. Though he had dark slacks, he'd foregone any suit jacket. His cuffs were rolled once, and his brown hair was ruffled, as if he was attempting a casual attitude. But the sharpness of his eyes betrayed his otherwise relaxed appearance. He was after *something*, but whether that was to punish Roger or to orchestrate a vampiric bacchanal, Roger wasn't sure.

Several of Seamus's pets sat on the floor near him. They leaned against each other, cuddling in a pile, except for Vincent, who sat on the couch beside Seamus and remained curled up against his side.

Candide occupied one side of the U-shaped seating arrangement. Her sleeveless dress was a crisp black with a plunging neckline. She had a gorgeous ruby necklace that caught glints of light and dazzled with a bloodred color.

Alongside her, Ezra leaned into one side while her black-collared pet had her head in Candide's lap. Ezra was clothed, wearing a matching black shirt and pants to Candide's dress, and he was without his collar.

Three more of Candide's pets were on the floor. One was the fey boy, Dryden, and he was bound in a kneeling position. Rope crisscrossed his body with intricate knots, and he had a ball gag in his mouth. He shimmered faintly with fey dust, particularly at his temple, and his cock was locked in a cage. One pet beside him plucked at one of the ropes, causing Dryden to shiver.

Roger lifted an eyebrow and glanced at Candide.

Candide rolled her eyes. "Honestly, when the brat's lord said that disciplining him would be a challenge, I thought he was bluffing."

"I'd offer to take him off your hands, but I've no time to break in someone new," Seamus said. "I am pleased you came so early, Roger. I was afraid you'd show at midnight and then bolt again."

"Forgive my quick exit from the party, master." Roger undid the button of his suit jacket and took a seat. Takashi sat between him and Seamus while Zack sat closer to the outside edge and up against Roger. Kit and Carver curled up together on the floor, using the couch to support their backs. "My collection is very new, and I couldn't stand to see them lost in the sea of others' pleasures."

"A worthy excuse, I suppose," Seamus replied. "You brought them again, which I was hoping you'd do. Hello, Takashi."

Takashi nodded to Seamus.

"Neither of you have been pressing me about Takashi's application," Seamus said.

Roger slouched against the couch. "We have all eternity, don't we? I'm hoping you'll accept him sooner rather than later. We've held off on house hunting until you do."

"You should start!" Seamus said. "We've missed you dearly, Roger, and it's so good to have you home. I've been thinking of investing in an additional building. Plenty of condos, all for our kind, naturally."

"I'm not sure." Roger put his hand on Takashi's thigh and nuzzled Zack's cheek. "I do adore my privacy at times."

After giving Zack a quick kiss on the cheek, Roger swiveled his gaze to Seamus. Each word and action were steps in the delicate balance between them, a chance to stub a toe or accidentally slam his foot on Seamus and draw his wrath. His genial demeanor had been a façade leading to a trigger of violence before.

Seamus flashed a broader smile. "I suppose I can't blame you for that. And you'll want space to grow your collection?"

"Naturally." Roger draped his arm around Zack. *Happy-to-be-here is the name of the dance.* "We fill our suite too well, and three hardly meets our needs."

"I've not taken any for myself, technically," Takashi said. He slid his hand over Roger's and then linked their fingers together. "I've longed to pick out a Midwest wolf. There's a pack of absolutely gorgeous men that seem to be dying to be matched with a vampire, but I haven't arranged a meeting with any of them yet."

"Mm," Seamus said. He pivoted his attention toward Candide. "I hear that you've added something unique to your collection lately, darling."

"Dryden?" Candide caught Dryden by the braid and forced him to tilt his head back. The boy gave a performative moan that made Roger snort. She glared coolly down at him, and Dryden settled from his light squirming to an awed stillness. "He's hardly special."

Dryden blinked rapidly. When Candide released his hair, he hung his head forward. The emotions drifting from him shifted dramatically from impish lust to a lingering need. Roger had seen Candide discipline pets before. If he had to guess at the boy's thoughts, she'd finally punished him for his latest transgression in a memorable way. Candide made a gesture, and a pet beside Dryden undid the gag. After an initial gasp and breath, Dryden bit his lip.

"Fey brats are as common as mortal spawn these days," Seamus said dismissively. With a hungry gaze, he turned his focus to Ezra. "Come now, don't tell me she let you out without any collar at all."

Roger could've sworn the air dropped a degree around them, and Candide went entirely still, not a single motion in her limbs.

She really does love him, and no one was supposed to know about his deal with her. Roger extracted himself from Takashi and Zack in order to lean forward in a smooth gesture. He chuckled and shook his head. "Ezra? With a collar? You're listening to too much gossip, old man."

"If you wanted to continue your stupid act, you shouldn't have vanished for three decades and then brought home Nell's brightest fledgling and a Gladwell-Wright spawn," Seamus said harshly. Any hint of mirth was gone. "Don't take this as a request: Shut up, Roger."

There it was. Seamus was pissed. His anger wasn't just beneath the surface; he was a volcano primed to burn his enemies to ash. How many of the vampires would take his side? Why hadn't Roger insisted on bringing Zack's dagger and just doing the damn deed tonight? *Because I'm a coward.*

Roger closed his mouth, and though he slowly relaxed against the couch once more, he didn't slouch.

"Taking another vampire as a pet is highly unorthodox, Candide," Seamus said, ice in his voice.

Ezra, who had always been fueled with his own fire and rage, moved with cool precision. He sat up and drew a deep red collar from his pocket. Instead of the usual circular crest tag, his was shaped like a heart. As he went to put it on himself, Candide gently took it from him and fastened it around his neck. She stroked just underneath it at the base of his neck in a quick, intimate gesture.

"He's less my pet and more my submissive," Candide said quietly, not meeting Seamus's intense glare. "At least, for a while longer. He wanted to learn from me, and I have plenty more to teach him."

Then she lifted her chin, a smile gracing her lips as she donned her mask of the polite socialite. She caressed Ezra's back and kissed his cheek. "Can you blame me? A beautiful boy like him begging for a firm hand—how could I resist? Roger's attempted to meet his needs, and so have dozens of others. I'm simply being thorough with him and finally scratching his itch."

"I always found him too dull to bother with," Seamus said dismissively.

That was a lie. As far as Roger knew, Ezra had never been to Seamus's bed because he refused to go, and Seamus hadn't coerced him into it. As much as Seamus manipulated the emotions of others, he either couldn't do so to Ezra or for some reason had wanted Ezra to choose him. Roger tucked away the questions that sprung to mind. *Maybe if I wrote everything out like Zack does, I could finally see the patterns.*

"Perhaps I just enjoy the way he lets me dress him. He is so very pretty," Candide said.

"Isn't he wearing a bit much, though?" Seamus's grin returned but with the edge of malice that made Roger's memories stir with sinkholes of despair. "Come, come. Have him stand up a moment so he can strip."

Candide kept her hand on Ezra's shoulder and met Seamus's stare. Her smile would have seemed perfectly in place for anyone who hadn't known her. Her calm was hiding the raging beast within her. Of all the vampires Roger knew, she could control her temper the best.

But Seamus's attitude and demands were wearing her patience to its breaking point.

If I am to crawl out of this hell, I can't let this shit continue unchecked. Roger put his arm around Takashi and said nonchalantly, "Surely Ezra isn't the only submissive vampire. I bet there are covens out there where such a thing has been common. Collar and all."

"I can think of a half dozen," Takashi said.

Seamus slid his glare toward them, but his words were measured and playing at polite. "I would wager they follow the dress code of other pets."

"Only in Hong Kong," Takashi said brightly. "The master there, Meredith—I believe you know of him—is a terrible brute. Forces all his sirelings to serve as his pets for at least a decade and treats them awfully. And he's always churning out new vampires. I don't know how he's held on to the territory for a century, except that he empowered the British there for the decades, and those few mortals in the know aided his continued existence. Now, his vampires are so weak and demoralized I've heard whispers of other covens coming to claim his territory."

Takashi's delivery was perfect, and Roger had to suppress his urge for a smug smile. His speech had nabbed Seamus's full attention long enough that Candide's tension relaxed. And the information had been perfect as well. Roger knew Meredith. The vampire had been in the UK when the coven had lived there. He was only half as old as Seamus, but somehow, the two behaved as if they were equal rivals.

"All right then," Seamus said with a gentle grumble. "Stand anyway. I want to see this fashion Candide's fixed for you, Ezra."

Ezra stood and did a slow spin. His clothes were impeccably tailored, and he had a hint of makeup that brought out his steely eyes. His hair had always been a fiery disaster that stuck up at odd angles after too many hours, but the cut of it accented that feature and made use of it. He was charming and handsome, the pinnacle of noble youth caught in a vampire's immortality.

"I suppose I've seen worse," Seamus remarked. "He is allowed to fetch us refreshments, isn't he? That's not too menial of a task for him?"

"He'd be happy to do so," Candide said.

"Fantastic." Seamus glanced down at Vincent, who was still curled up against him. "You and the hunter spawn should go to the bar and bring back drinks for the other pets. Run along now, scoot."

Vincent quickly stood, glared at Zack as soon as his back was to Seamus, and then nodded in the direction of one of the bars. Subtly, Zack looked to Roger for permission. Roger gave the slightest nod, so Zack rose and followed Vincent away. Ezra headed off on his errand as well.

"It's been a while so many of us old ones enjoyed an evening together," Roger said casually. Outright asking why Seamus had summoned them, especially in his current mood, was a bad idea. Roger drifted his hand along Takashi's shoulder. "Did you want to talk about the application?"

"I'm happy that Takashi will be part of our coven. I'll make an announcement about it tonight." Seamus checked his gold watch, an old one that he'd taken off a mobster in the 1920s. "We have some time before the show, though."

"Show?" Candide asked.

"Ah, it's a surprise," Seamus said with a gleeful smile that froze Roger's soul. "I promised Anton I wouldn't say anything, but it will be *glorious*."

Dmitri had been out to kill his devil—Anton. And now, a few nights later, Anton had planned some sort of show. Roger dipped his head, letting his hair provide a curtain. He couldn't contain the worry. *Fuck it all, Dmitri. What did you do?*

CHAPTER 28

A creeping chill had settled into Zack's bones, and it had nothing to do with the cold-ass club or the vampires' auras. A whole conversation had happened in front of him, and Zack couldn't do anything besides watch. Seamus had been clearly digging deep, trying to get a reaction out of Roger or Candide, and they just sat there and took it. Zack knew why in theory, but seeing the practice of it was torture. He was glad for the protection of his tattoo because he'd wanted to tell Seamus to fuck off to hell. He'd wanted to lose his whole temper on every vile thing that was happening inside the club.

The party had been bad enough. But someone screamed in the near distance. It was cut short, and there was the terrible sound of sucking and moaning floating underneath the general murmur of conversation.

And all Zack could do was put one foot after another. He focused on Vincent's back. That served as a distraction for only a second because Vincent was wearing very little. His shorts were deep red and didn't entirely cover the bottom of his ass. Though his shirt had long sleeves, the material was sheer to the point of transparency. Even in the dim lighting,

Zack could trace bruises, wounds, and scars on Vincent's back. He was covered in them.

"Holy shit," Zack whispered.

Vincent sneered at him over his shoulder. "I thought hunters didn't have weak stomachs. I guess that explains why you never earned a moniker. Your brother's the *Butcher*, and you're *nothing*."

Zack grabbed Vincent's arm and twisted him around to face him. A pent-up breath caught in his lungs and burned with the anger he'd been shoving down while Roger and Takashi suffered sitting near Seamus. Months had been compounding inside him. No, *years*, because shit with the family had always been boiling underneath the surface. And protocol demanded that he show Vincent some measure of respect since he was the coven master's head pet, but Seamus didn't give a damn about his pets. Touching Vincent was like grabbing a ghost. His complexion was pale, his body too thin.

Those details caught a cog in Zack's mind, and it reversed the spin of his thoughts. Because Roger had buried his hurts and shared only a fraction of that pain to him and Takashi. Every vampire acted like a living porcelain doll around Seamus, as if they were terrified that Seamus would take them off the shelf and slam them onto a concrete slab and dance on the pieces.

And if the life of a *vampire* was like that, the humans in Seamus's collection had it a million times worse. The other high-ranking pets of the coven didn't give a shit about what happened to Vincent. Instead of leading like Reed did, Vincent was a spectacle to everyone. Because Seamus never kept anyone more than three years, and Vincent's time was almost up.

He has to be alone. Terrified. Another cog caught and spun. Terror could easily display itself as anger. That was why Zack had lashed out, wasn't it? He'd been scared that his family really had given up on him and terrified that nothing he did would make a difference. Not knowing if he and Roger were actually a couple had made him act horribly toward Carver, who didn't deserve it. Because Carver had been a safe target, someone of seemingly strong armor.

That's what I am for Vincent. He's helpless and angry. I'm the safe target to attack. Sure, Vincent had trashed him on the internet, but Zack would recover from that, especially since his friends and lovers didn't give a damn about what others said on social media about him.

Zack had been mocked by Cal and his cousins his whole life. Not until this precise instant, when everything seemed to run through his mind in lightning-flash equations and evaluations, did he truly appreciate how free he'd been the last few months. Carver had been right. He had a lot of good going on in his life. Roger cherished him. Takashi adored him. Kit and Blake were loyal friends. He had Nell counting on him to slay Seamus, and he'd earned Josefina's respect. And in addition to all of that, he had a lush bed to sleep in and whatever he wanted to eat. Though he wasn't safe outside the hotel suite, he was safe inside it.

Vincent didn't have any luxuries except his anger.

And he didn't have the endless supply of hurtful, soul-scathing barbs that Cal did. He didn't know Zack that well.

So Zack grinned at Vincent. "Come on, is that the best you got? Calling me nothing?"

Vincent narrowed his eyes, obviously seeking out some trick.

"You've had weeks to think of shit," Zack said. Technically, they weren't supposed to talk without permission, but vampires also loved their dramas. Zack didn't care how many watched. "Or has it been months? How long have you been creeping on my Night Deets?"

"I had to find out what the big deal about Taliville was," Vincent replied, his haughty attitude rising. "Still haven't figured it out. There's like, what, four stores?"

"Eh, I forgot to count," Zack said.

Vincent puffed up. "And what is *with* the bandages? Do your masters not know how to bite you? Are the wounds still bleeding? Or are you too embarrassed to be seen with fresh bite marks?" He gave a mock gasp. "Wait, do they turn you on? Are you afraid you'll choke up and get a hard-on where everyone can see? Or are you scared that you will and no one will be able to see your dick anyway?"

"Wow, a small-dick insult." Zack made a "keep going" gesture with his hands. "You can do better than that."

A wild look filled Vincent's blue eyes. For a heartbeat, Zack thought he was going to go for a slap. Instead, Vincent grinned broadly, and the fire in his gaze diminished to a flicker of amusement. He straightened his shoulders. "You are, without a doubt, the *worst* excuse for a head pet I've ever seen. Your wardrobe looks like it was picked up off a sales rack three years ago, your masters coddle your injuries, you can't stand to be around other pets, and you've been here weeks without a public feeding. Oh! Maybe that's what the bandages are hiding! You only want us to *think* your masters actually like your blood. Are these scars makeup? Let's see."

Zack let Vincent grab his arm roughly and fiercely rub at one of the scars on his wrist. Doing so gave him the opportunity to attempt to count the marks on Vincent's arms. He got to six before Vincent rotated his arm in a way that he lost count.

Ripping the bandage off was a step too far, but Vincent moved faster than Zack could get his arm free. Fresh droplets of blood seeped from the deeper corners of the wound. Zack hissed, "Shit!"

"I guess they are real," Vincent said patronizingly. He slapped the bandage back in place.

A favorite game among the Wright cousins was "rescue the damsel." It involved a "damsel" getting tied up and some cousins pretending to be monsters while the others were the valiant hunters who were going to save the hostage. Zack had been picked for damsel more often than most. It was how he'd learned to slip knots and ropes.

He'd also taught himself how to turn off his tears.

And to turn them on.

"Of course they are," Zack cried. Pinpricks of tears became shallow drops that spilled down his cheeks. He bit his lip and dipped his head.

"Well, perhaps you aren't entirely useless to your master," Vincent said snidely. Then he spun on his heels and headed for the bar.

Carefully, Zack did his best to secure the medical tape that had held the bandage in place. He'd need to change it when he got back to the hotel, but it'd stay if he was cautious. Holding in a grumble, he trailed Vincent to the bar. They reached it together. The bartender was busy at the other end with a group of vampires.

Under his breath, Vincent demanded, "Okay, what kind of game was that?"

"What do you mean?" Zack whispered. He quickly wiped his tears from his cheeks and the residual tears before they could fall.

Vincent rolled his eyes. "I've been at this long enough to know when someone's up to something. So spill."

"Look, I don't think anyone would want to be with a certain vicious vampire, and you probably don't want to die. That makes your choices limited," Zack replied quickly. "Your master is … ugh. You need all the wins you can get."

"Why?" Vincent hissed. "Why would you want to help me?"

"Maybe I can't stand to see someone in need without doing something."

"I don't need charity from hunter spawn."

"Then next time, think of something better than some basic-ass insults," Zack returned.

A brief smile graced Vincent's lips before it faded to his haughty grin. "I will."

"You know, I have no idea what to order here," Zack said.

"We don't, unless it's for our masters. They've got one drink they make up for us here," Vincent replied hurriedly. The bartender was finally finishing at the other end and making his way toward them. "Don't make eye contact with the bartender. I'll order for Mistress Candide's pets as well as mine, got it?"

"Okay." Zack managed to fix his gaze to the bar just before the vampire reached them.

"What?" the bartender demanded.

Vincent raised nine fingers, then made a small prayer gesture.

"And you?" the bartender said to Zack.

Zack mimicked Vincent. He held up three fingers, then made the prayer gesture.

"Yeah? Who for? I don't recognize that." The bartender grabbed Zack by the collar and hauled him forward. The bastard would've been able to see the crest tag just fine from the other side of the bar.

Zack was hauled off his feet. He scrambled to get his arms under him and support himself against the bar. "Let me *go*."

The vampire twisted his hand and forced Zack's head against the bar by using the collar as a handhold. "What was that, *boy*?"

A whoosh moved past Zack. It was a burst of cold greater than Takashi's aura but less than Roger's. A hint of lilacs mingled with the overwhelming scent of the grave for just a moment. The blur solidified into a vampire, but Zack couldn't get a good look from his position.

The bartender yelped, then released Zack. As Zack slid off and stood on his own, the vampire who'd come to his rescue grabbed the bartender by the back of the head and slammed it down onto the bar. His rescuer was a white guy who had a sharp scar through one eye, and that eye was milky white. Nathaniel, Zack's mind supplied, thanks to his copious research.

"Apologize," Nathaniel demanded of the bartender.

"Fuck you!" the bartender hissed as he squirmed.

Nathaniel knocked the bartender's head against the surface again.

"I'm not going to say sor—"

With a quick movement, Nathaniel broke the bartender's neck and let him fall to the floor. It wasn't a killing move against a vampire but did put an end to the conversation.

Others were definitely staring at them. Zack scanned the nearby area, doing his best to avoid eye contact, and everyone within ten feet was openly watching them. He checked Vincent for a reaction, but Vincent was unreadably calm.

Should he thank his savior? What was the protocol for this?

"He was manhandling another's property," Nathaniel said loudly.

"Thank you, master," Zack said in a whisper.

A chilling, bone-deep cold brushed against Zack's back and then enveloped him. A voice smooth as silk said, "Come now, you can do better than that, little one."

Zack spun toward the source of the cold and the voice. His fists clenched; he couldn't stop the instinct to protect himself.

The vampire was roughly six feet tall, and his eyes were bloodred. Drifting down to his shoulders, his pale blond hair seemed almost colorless against his porcelain white skin. He had the sort of beauty that was hard to hold in one's mind, a startling level of perfection that hurt to behold. Maybe that was because of the predator's edge in his smile or the unnatural grace with which he moved. He wore a billowing white shirt, the lace that would have held it shut across his chest was practically undone, and tight, black leather pants with matching heeled boots that came up to his knee.

As the vampire stepped forward, Zack took a step back and slammed up against the bar. That brought a chuckle out of the predator. He shouldn't have been meeting the vampire's gaze, but now that he had, he didn't dare look away.

"Foolish, little one," the vampire seemed to say. Zack wasn't entirely sure the bastard's lips had moved. "To stare into the eyes of one's better."

But then the vampire seemed to laugh like that was a fucking joke.

Seamus had made Zack's skin crawl.

Anton made his heart freeze.

No wonder Roger has been terrified for centuries.

With slender fingers, Anton hooked two under Zack's chin and tilted his head upward. Gently, he twisted Zack's head this way and that, and though Zack didn't take his eyes away from Anton, Anton examined him. "My, my. I am beginning to see what the fuss is about. A pleasure to meet you at last, Zackery."

Zack kept his mouth shut. His hand threatened to tremble, so he clasped one wrist with the other hand.

At his side, Vincent had performed the kind of bow that Zack should've done upon spotting Anton. Nearly bent in half, he had one arm behind his back with his other wrist out as an offering. His head was tilted to the side, exposing his neck.

Anton ignored Vincent and took a step back to rake his gaze over Zack anew. He brought a hand to his own lips and trailed his index finger along his lower lip. "If I only had the time ... and the right, I suppose. Nathaniel, you did well. That little pissant shouldn't have been marring Roger's treasured pet."

"Thank you, master," Nathaniel said with a grumble.

"This will leave us without a bartender for the evening."

Anton finally looked away from Zack. He sighed dramatically, then brightened. "Wait. You'll do it."

"The bastard's already starting to stir, master," Nathaniel said.

"He won't be completing his duties this evening." Anton snapped his fingers.

Two black-clad bouncers zipped around the bar and grabbed the bartender. They hauled him out from behind the bar and started to drag him off toward a distant door deeper in the club.

"Oh, I have a better idea!" Anton declared with glee. The bouncers stopped in their tracks and pivoted to face Anton. Putting his hand on Zack's shoulder, Anton continued/ "You *must* show us how it's done."

"How what's done, master?" Zack asked carefully.

"You are a Wright, aren't you? And a Gladwell? I surely don't have to explain your purpose to you." Anton grinned manically. "What am I thinking, you don't have a weapon! One moment."

Anton grabbed the nearest barstool and cracked it against the floor. Pieces broke off from it, but he took one of the legs and snapped it across his knee. Then he handed the fragment of wood to Zack. "Go on, then. Show us."

Zack took the piece of wood. It technically had a sharp end, but it was far from a stake. The pit of his stomach hardened. Anton *wanted* him to kill a vampire. This was clearly some sick game for him, but this was a chance to put down one of the undead. And could he even say no to Anton?

You can do this, the Cal voice in his mind said. And this time, it was repeating a memory. Every great once in a while, he'd shown he could be a big brother. They'd been training out in the yard. Zack had been twelve, Cal seventeen. After watching him, Cal had shaken his head and guided Zack through the best forms for staking a vamp. *Power doesn't come from the arm. Comes from the core. Silver gets the job done easy for you, but wood'll work. Harder, though. You got to feel the movement coming up from your soul. And once you see the blow, do it. Strike. Never hesitate, little bro.*

Anton wanted a dead vampire? Fine. As he stalked toward the vampire, Zack twirled the piece of wood in his hand until he found the better balance. The vampire hadn't recovered, but that only made Zack's job easier. He put one hand on the vamp's shoulder and shoved the piece of wood in. Though he'd certainly pierced the heart, he regripped the makeshift stake farther down and shoved it another three inches into the vamp. Then he stepped away.

Everyone was watching, particularly Anton.

Zack made a sweeping bow, but not like a pet would. He stretched both arms out wide, one foot behind for support, and bowed at the waist with a dramatic flair.

"Marvelous!" Anton clapped enthusiastically, though he stopped nearly as soon as he started. "What a wonderful opening act. Oh, I should be on my way. First things first."

With a sudden burst of speed, Anton grasped Vincent by the hair and pulled him up. There was nothing gentle in the way Anton bit into Vincent's neck just below his collar. Vincent cried out, then bit his bottom lip.

Before Zack finished running the math on whether he could grab the makeshift stake from the vampire and shove it into Anton's back, Anton released Vincent and walked away from him. He plucked a handkerchief from his billowy sleeve and handed it to Zack as he continued past. "You have blood on your hand, deary."

The bouncers carried off the vampire body, and Anton trailed after them.

Zack had managed to take the handkerchief with his clean hand. He hurried over to Vincent, who had clamped his hand over the fresh wound. Blood dripped down his chest. Zack offered him the handkerchief.

"That won't do it," Nathaniel said. He was looking behind

the bar, opening cabinets. A snappy comeback flew to Zack's lips, but he quashed it as Nathaniel held out a clean rag.

"Thank you, master," Vincent managed.

"Suppose I am the bartender tonight. Hold on a second. I'll get what you boys need."

"Left-hand fridge usually has it made up, master," Vincent said.

"I'm not giving you that drugged shit," Nathaniel said in a low volume. With the general chatter of the other vampires, Zack wondered if anyone else had heard him. "Won't take me long."

With professional flair, Nathaniel made eleven vodka cranberries. For the twelfth one, he poured the cranberry juice first, then added the barest touch of vodka on top.

That way, it smells like it's alcoholic, especially to a vampire, but it's not really. Zack motioned at the glass and then to Vincent.

"That's right," Nathaniel said with a ghost of a grin. "Can you carry the lot?"

"Yes, master," Zack said. Though it was kind of an impressive number of drinks to have on one tray, even if it was big enough.

"All right, get going."

Zack nodded. Quickly, he wiped the small amount of blood on his hand off with the handkerchief. When he realized he had nowhere to stash the damn thing, he frowned. Nathaniel offered to take it, so he passed it off. Then he took the tray of drinks and carefully followed Vincent.

CHAPTER 29

Watching from across the room was utter agony. Ensuring that no emotion flickered across his face made Roger wish for a stiff drink. Or three dozen. Hearing the slam across the room initially drew Roger's attention, but he quickly lost track of the action as he spotted Anton emerging from another area of the club.

As unnerving as he was, Anton did have style and grace. Another slam happened at the bar, but Roger kept his gaze trained on the ancient vampire. Though he was technically younger than Seamus, Anton had the ethereal quality rare to the older ones. Nell cultivated an air of it, but Anton seemed to manifest an entire atmosphere around him.

As Anton approached the bar, every patron in the club seemed to quiet. Though he never raised his voice, Roger could hear him perfectly. The shock of seeing him had thrown Roger's sense of spatial awareness. Only when he spoke did Roger realize he was talking to *Zack*.

Takashi clamped a hand on Roger's leg. The tight, subtle movement prevented Roger from standing, which he'd been about to do. He'd begun moving on instinct. Because Seamus was dangerous, but Anton was lethally unpredictable.

Case in point: Anton handed Zack a stake and clearly expected him to use it.

Which Zack did without hesitation.

"Quite the killer you have there," Seamus said smoothly as the vampire's body was dragged away. "However did you tame him?"

The playboy's jest, the way Roger used to handle such a question, dried in his throat. Anton was drifting after the bouncers carrying the body, but once Roger accidentally made eye contact, he sauntered toward them. *The devil's not dead. What happened to you, Dmitri?*

Memories flickered past. The Gladwell Manor, bodies strewn about the rooms, but the horror had been what Anton had done behind closed doors. The heavy presence of dreadful magic and the smell worse than death itself. Anton's cheerful laugh that always came when blood was spilled in gruesome ways. In the early decades of his immortality, Roger had done his best to impress his sire and his lover. Seamus and Anton had seemed too big for words. Ancient and powerful.

And monsters. Roger hadn't had any choice but to be like them. His hunger and their demands left him no choice.

But in Taliville, he'd had a choice. With Zack and Takashi, he wasn't the stupid playboy or the soldier or the unreliable friend. Kit and Carver didn't treat him like an unknowable vampire master. He was becoming someone new.

Someone he liked far better.

Someone who didn't stand a chance in hell of surviving Seamus and Anton if he couldn't hide his fear and disgust and pretend nothing had changed.

"My usual way," Roger murmured as he finally tore his gaze away from Anton. "Pretty words and long kisses."

"Hello, love." Anton looped his arms around Seamus from behind and nuzzled his cheek. "I am nearly ready."

"Are you? You seem to be dawdling," Seamus remarked.

"I wanted a nip before I began. Do you think enough are here?"

Seamus put his hand on top of Anton's arm and appeared perfectly content to be held by his lover. "Seems everyone was eager to please me this evening. Except for Ezra, who's disappeared. He was supposed to bring us a few morsels."

"I passed him in the hall on my way out. He caught sight of my surprise and lost his temper." Anton frowned childishly, but in the next moment, he grinned, the glow of his joy reaching his bloodred eyes. "Luckily, I had an extra cage."

"What did you do to him?" Candide demanded as she stood.

"I saw your mark of ownership, so I didn't touch him," Anton said with an eye roll. "Well, except to throw him in the cage. I'll let him out after the show." His grin turned malicious. "Unless you'd like me to add him to it?"

Like a king gazing upon a lesser, Seamus turned his head to regard Candide. He appeared thoughtful, but both Candide and Roger knew what he wanted. An ego stroke.

Begging was not Candide's way and would only spur Anton on. Instead, Candide lowered her gaze and said calmly, "I would like him returned, master."

Seamus shot a smug grin at her, then leaned back to speak with Anton. "I think she's actually in love with the brat. Keep him comfortable back there if he's being a nuisance and let him out without harm afterwards, love."

"Oh, all right. Anything for you." Anton kissed Seamus briefly and deeply.

Together for over half a millennium. Their love would be inspirational if they weren't both power-hungry murderers. Roger checked the bar and saw that Vincent was leading the way, his hand to his neck, while Zack was carrying the full tray. Rather than fall back into her practiced politeness, Candide continued to regard Seamus and Anton with hostile suspicion. If that bothered them, they gave no indication.

"I should get going," Anton said sadly as he ended the kiss.

Seamus kissed his hands and let go of him. "Half an hour, then you can begin."

"Fine," Anton said petulantly. Then he drifted away toward the door he'd initially emerged from. That area of the club was reserved for private events, which usually resulted in at least one mortal's death. It connected to the backstage area as well.

The last show Roger had seen in this club was the night Ezra's lover had been paraded out as a traitor and killed onstage. The young vampire had already been dead—his body reanimated by Anton's magic—because Anton and Seamus had stolen his life force. The general public of the coven didn't know that, however.

Did they finally consume Dmitri? Would they be able to do that to me after all this time? Roger clutched Takashi's hand. Some potential leader he was turning out to be. He was panicking in the presence of the coven's most powerful.

Even though his mind raced, his body fell into old habits, feigning a relaxed pose. He could keep the carefully neutral expression affixed to his features while his mind spun ever-worsening tales about what had happened to Dmitri in the few nights since they last saw one another.

Before long, Vincent and Zack had returned. With one hand still holding a rag to his neck, Vincent passed out the drinks among the other pets. Only at this point did Roger remember how often the mortals' drinks were drugged in Seamus's club.

Once Zack sat down, Roger leaned in and murmured into his ear, "I don't know if it's safe."

After a quick glance to see if Seamus was distracted, Zack winked at Roger and took a long sip. As subtly as he could, Roger looked over to the bartender and saw Nathaniel rather than the one who had been there earlier. Nathaniel had always been the quiet subversive of the coven. Had he been closer to Seamus, his unwillingness to victimize mortals might have led to his undoing. But Nathaniel had kept his distance, and after the hunters had maimed him, Seamus gave up his attempt to pull him closer. Nathaniel was an example of how strong someone in Seamus's bloodline could be but a reminder that even vampires might not be as unchangeable as they believed.

Seamus had been carrying on some quiet conversation with Vincent, something that was giving Seamus a reason to grin.

Candide had her mortal woman lying up against her, and she silently drummed her fingers along her pet's arm. The motion was subtle, quick. When she caught Roger's gaze, she had more than a trace of fear in her eyes. She had had ideas about how to win the coven's heart, but each had boiled down to a single point: proving worth.

Seamus was strong. Whoever came after him would have to be just as powerful, or the coven's respect would fall apart. If no one believed Roger could keep them safe, then they wouldn't follow him. Because as much as they feared what Seamus could do to them, as long as they kept in step to the dance he led them through, they and what they loved were safe.

Or at least they could tell themselves they were. Seamus's good mood could turn sour in an instant, and then anything might become ash and smoke.

Candide was frightened for Ezra. She'd demonstrated an ounce of love, and Seamus was already using it against her.

And Roger wanted to reach across, grab her hands, and tell her that everything would be all right. But that could be a lie, and suggesting it might be truth would turn it into a lie even faster. Seamus had to have the superiority.

"I'm not sure I've ever seen that look on your face before, Roger," Seamus said coolly.

The vapid playboy act had been called out already. Roger found himself falling into a new role, but he would have to dance a waltz along a high wire above a pit of silver stakes to see this through. Smooth words came to mind, and he fixed Seamus with a bored stare. "I'm wondering what drama you've concocted tonight."

"Anton is the architect behind this evening's entertainment, though I've found a portion of it illuminating already."

Roger caught, in the corner of his eye, that Zack had a flash of a calculating frown.

"Whatever did that poor bastard do to deserve such a public death?" Roger asked lightly.

Seamus grinned. "Nothing. He was given an instruction, so he carried it out. Like a good boy does. Like your Zackery did as well. I must say, your precision could use a little work."

Zack clenched his jaw and stared at his glass.

"You *have* managed to train him. Astonishing." Seamus slid to the edge of his seat. "How did you break the spirit of a Wright?"

"I never had to break him," Roger said casually. "I plucked up the seed the Wrights had so carelessly thrown to the trash and nurtured him."

Zack went still.

I said something a little too true, a little too much like a master vampire. Roger refused to give in to the impulse to glance at Zack. Because he had to keep his head, he had to remain aloof and in control, or the proverbial shit would hit the fan and be set on fire, and then Seamus would make them choke on the ashes.

"Is it possible I've been underestimating your gifts this whole time?" Seamus said.

A trick question. It had to be. Roger smiled the slickest, most wicked way he could. "I think you've always had a perfect measure of me, Seamus."

"Perhaps, but it has been so long since you reached for your potential I thought it withered away."

Before Roger could parse out any underlying meanings to that statement, the lights around the club dimmed further. Seamus rose from his seat. He began to thread his way through the club to the stage. There were no stairs to climb, so he merely leapt, the movement as quick and natural as breathing for a mortal.

A spotlight illuminated Seamus. His dark red shirt glimmered underneath the brightness. The crowd had been murmuring, but upon his taking of the stage, the club became quiet as a tomb. Standing above the others, smiling broadly, he was the handsome specter of Roger's nightmares and the charismatic con man of his hopes. Seamus would never be kind, never change for the better.

A cold stone dropped in Roger's stomach. Some part of him had still held out hope, hadn't it? That somehow everything would be simple and fall into place for him. But dread was weighing down every fiber of his being. Seamus never did anything so showy without bringing hell down upon someone.

"How wonderful that all of you accepted my invitation this evening," Seamus said. With silence dominating the atmosphere, he easily projected his voice without a microphone. "It has been some time since we gathered like this. Halloween isn't a gathering, is it? It's a party! And we deserve those. They aren't the time for business.

"Tonight, we need to deal with a few small matters. First, we have a new vampire to welcome into our coven." Seamus motioned out toward the crowd. As he spoke, a light shone down on the pod where they were sitting, and Takashi stood. "Takashi Sato, formerly ambassador of the Ancient Nell. That title will have to drop, obviously. He'll remain the Slick Polyglot. Did you have another one? No? Ah, well, we'll find one with time."

The light dimmed, and Takashi sat beside Roger again.

"I hope by now that you're all aware that one of our lost captains has returned home," Seamus said. "Roger, Gentleman Pirate of the Seven Seas, Highwayman of the Unwatched Roads, and Tempter of Forbidden Desires. Please, join me."

There was a perfunctory clapping of hands as Roger made his way to the stage. He was grateful his heart didn't beat. At least he didn't have to worry if it was beating too quickly or loudly. Instead, he only had to keep his fear smothered in the depths of his mental oceans. The chest he had thrown it into continued to bob closer and closer to the surface. *Stay in the moment. Stay vigilant.*

Roger hopped onto the stage, his motion as liquid as a cat's. As he stepped closer to Seamus and shared the light, he waved out to the crowd with a single gesture.

Seamus threw an arm around his shoulders, tugging Roger down a bit as he did. Until moments like that, Roger continuously forgot Seamus was technically shorter than him. Seamus put a hand on Roger's chest as well. "This bastard has been at my side longer than anyone besides Anton. When he vanished, I was beside myself. Roger, your return couldn't have been better timed. Our coven is striding into the future, and you have always been one of my loyal followers."

"Thank you, master," Roger said smoothly.

After a quick kiss to Roger's cheek, Seamus released him. "I have another announcement before we move on to my love's spectacle. I believe it's time to name another captain. After decades strengthening our bonds with other covens, I've asked Lucille home to take on a leadership role among us." He motioned out in the crowd.

Lucille zipped to the front of the stage. The beam of light widened a fraction so there was space for her underneath it as well. She'd never seemed less like a teenager than she did with the wicked grin she shot toward the crowd of Devil's Cove.

Roger attempted to meet Candide's gaze, but the light made seeing the crowd difficult. Any step to shade his eyes would be obvious, and he had to smother any surprise. *Did Lucille turn on us? How much do they know?*

"Thank you, master," Lucille said cheerfully.

Seamus kissed her cheek as polite applause bubbled up from the crowd. Then he motioned for silence. Once the crowd had settled down, he ushered Roger and Lucille to the far-right side of the stage. "If the two of you wait a few moments over here. Yes, there we go."

The light left them, centering on Seamus as he reclaimed the middle of the stage. "What is it the mortals say these days? Ah, yes, I'm the warm-up act, though we've already had one this evening. We know that we vampires have that killer instinct, but discovering that mortals have such a visceral edge to them is always a delight, isn't it?"

There was movement on the opposite side of the stage. Seamus carried on a monologue with an air of charming patience. His words were anchors, locked around Roger's feet, and plummeted him to new depths. He wasn't smothering his fears below the waves but drowning with them now. His smile remained, strained but there, and he fought the urge to race across the stage and discover what was happening before anyone else knew.

Because he was seeking shapes in the darkness, he spotted Anton emerging onto the side stage and nearing the proper stage. He had a rope in his hands. He caught Roger gazing is his direction and gave him a smile that would make an angel weep.

"Most of all," Seamus was saying, his voice dripping with a level of seriousness that would've chilled Roger if he wasn't already frozen, "I have called you together to remind you of what we all are. *Vampires. A coven.* When a vampire betrays one of us, they betray all of us. And that betrayal must be punished accordingly."

Roger's throat closed. *Dmitri, what the fuck happened?*

Another spotlight illuminated a pale circle on the far left stage. Anton strode into it, and the light followed him as he made his way toward Seamus. He yanked on the rope trailing behind him, and a figure tumbled out into view.

Dmitri hit his knees. His arms were bound against his chest as if he were praying. Every stitch of clothing had been removed. His eyes were bloodshot, and his jaw was at an odd angle. Roger watched him begin to heal, but the distant look in his eyes said that he'd suffered worse horrors.

Roger's feet remained rooted to the spot. He didn't dare shift his focus. Were they going to kill Dmitri? Of course they were. What else would be the point of this pageantry?

"Hello, love," Anton said to Seamus as if they hadn't seen each other minutes before. They kissed.

The stage lights turned up, though the brightest spot remained on Anton and Seamus. Roger slid his hands into his pockets to keep from making fists. *They're expecting me to react.*

Though Anton spoke toward Seamus, his voice carried out into the room. He was putting on a performance; he might've gone as far as writing a script that he was now reciting. "Look what I discovered poking around our gardens."

"What have you found, lover?" Seamus asked.

"A rabbit that thinks it's a wolf. Isn't that hilarious?" Anton yanked on the rope.

Dmitri was already on his knees. Though he struggled, he couldn't catch his balance and fell onto his face. Anton glanced over his shoulder, then sighed as if he was the one being put out and strode over to Dmitri. With a single hand, he lifted him from the floor and waited for him to get his feet under him.

As soon as Dmitri stood, Anton delivered a sharp kick to his knee. A sickening pop preceded Dmitri's pained scream.

"Oops," Anton said with a grin. "I forgot to do something first."

He slapped Dmitri hard enough that his jaw broke anew.

Roger had seen torture before, and he'd administered some himself. Moments from the Gladwell Manor flickered into view once more. Of all the horrors he'd seen, that one was troubling him most. *Because that was when I knew what monsters we can be. I buried that. Devoted myself to becoming the vapid one because if you don't look, you can't see. And Dmitri has always paid the price of that chosen ignorance.*

But Dmitri wouldn't be the one to suffer if Roger attempted to alter the course of Anton's production. Zack, Kit, Carver, and Takashi were essentially helpless in the center of a crowd. Even if some portion of the vampires of the coven agreed with him, if they didn't immediately follow him, his people would be the first to suffer. He had to hold himself together and remain passionless as a rock upon a shore. He had to play into the farce before him. What other choice did he have? *None.*

Yet to stand by while Dmitri was hurt made him a coward. *I should have stopped him from whatever madness led to this. He should have waited for me to strike.* Then another thought struck. *Is he even alive? Or is this some cruel trick of Anton's? He's reanimated corpses before.*

But corpses never cried out in pain, and Dmitri had done so once already.

Anton dragged Dmitri across the stage and deposited him at Seamus's feet. "I'm afraid this rabbit isn't suitable for dinner, but I did find him with some others."

"Oh?" Seamus asked.

Anton clapped his hands.

Four more bound individuals were dragged out onto the stage. Like Dmitri, they were naked, but they also had gags in their mouths. Each of them had a few cuts and bruises, but nothing that looked like they'd truly suffered yet. Three were men, one a woman. The oldest of the men had a tattoo on his left shoulder identical to Zack's.

Hunters.

Dmitri tried to do the job himself and failed. Roger fought the urge to glance out to the crowd. He had to figure out and act his role.

"I do see that you have guests, love." Anton kissed Seamus's cheek. "Shall we offer them first choice for dinner?"

"I think that's only fair," Seamus replied. He spoke to Lucille. "Go and take your pick, darling."

"Why, thank you, sir," Lucille said sweetly. She made a show of examining each potential victim, but Roger knew which one she had her heart set on. As long as he'd known her, she had a type.

She chose the oldest man and stared him down with intensity. Likely, she was attempting to overcome his mental shield and tattoo in order to use her powers over him, but he continued to glare in her direction.

"No need to soften him up," Anton said. "Enjoy yourself!"

Lucille lunged forward and grabbed the man by the shoulders. She hauled him down and tore into his throat. The pure and wonderful coppery scent of fresh blood hit the air, and despite the stress plaguing Roger's mind, his hunger burned his throat, longing for a taste. When she finished, she let the man's body drop to the stage floor, then grabbed him by the bindings and dragged him out to lie beside Dmitri.

Dmitri closed his eyes. Roger felt no emotions flowing from him other than a desperate desire for everything to end. Before he delved too deeply into that, Roger walled Dmitri's psyche from his mind. There was nothing he could do to help him out of that sinkhole, and he couldn't afford to tumble into it after him.

"I always expect hunters to be tastier than they are," Lucille commented. "You'd think people steeped in magic and exercise would be divine, but that one was just lacking."

Anton put his arm around Lucille's shoulders, leaning on her. "Perhaps it was just that one, not the whole lot of them."

"Roger, you've been having hunter blood lately," Seamus remarked. "Has it been worth it?"

"Blood is always worth the effort," Roger replied smoothly. "The only drops I didn't enjoy were when we fed on rats."

"I'd nearly forgotten about that. Now I wish I had." Seamus put his hand on Roger's shoulder. "Go on now, take your pick."

Denying a gift like this in front of the coven would make a statement and would likely put him on the stage floor beside Dmitri. Hoping his smile didn't show the strain compounding in his mind, he nodded to Seamus. He strode slowly over to the remaining three hunters and took his time evaluating them.

All three bore the same tattoo as Zack: the woman had it on the back of her left shoulder, a man closer to thirty had it on his upper right arm, and the youngest man—at most a few years older than Zack—had it on his left leg, near to his hip. Though the tattoo was in different places on each, the magic was similar to the one that protected Zack.

Roger had been intimate with the perpetual spell's power for months. The shielding was magnificent but not impenetrable. The easiest way through was with permission. That was the only way he'd ever slid through Zack's mental defenses.

But that wasn't the only route. Roger gauged each of his potential choices. The woman and the older man both had their chins raised, a defiant look in their eyes. What little Roger gleaned from them was a desire to make their last moments count. Roger had seen their like before. If they were tortured, their hollow lives would crack into pieces. Anton liked to play with his food, but these two would bore him quickly. He'd kill them within an hour, as would any other vampire who got their hands on them.

But the younger man struggled to contain his fear. *That's the one*. Subtly, Roger slid his ring off inside his pocket and left it there.

He stepped closer to the boy and put a hand on his cheek. Tears had soddened the gag, though he wasn't currently crying. He shivered from Roger's touch. Skin contact made access to the boy's fear simple. *God, does it run deep*. He was exactly the sort that Anton and Seamus might take months to kill, possibly years if they felt like it. They'd age the boy's fear like wine and drink from him in sips until they finally, *finally* tired of him.

Unless Roger claimed and killed him.

Gently, Roger guided the boy toward the front of the stage. The crowd of vampires in the audience was the coven's most influential. They were the ones he had to seduce. They had to see that he was not beholden to hunters or to Seamus.

The energy onstage shifted as Roger claimed the attention. He'd been the center of focus before such a crowd many times, though usually under his own making. He and Candide used to lecture on the craft of dominating a pet with and without the use of vampiric magic. How many of the vampires that had answered Seamus's summons remembered those demonstrations?

No matter. His focus had to be on the boy. Carefully, he undid the gag and drew it out of the boy's mouth.

The boy's tears began anew. Hands still bound to his chest like a supplicant praying, he sobbed, "Please."

Roger put his thumb over the boy's lips. He couldn't stand to hear more begging. In theory, he could take this boy home. But if the boy wouldn't stay, if the others thought that made him weak, then every step he'd taken to protect the ones he cared about would be washed away.

Death was coming, and Roger would rather deliver it than receive.

Relying on his vampiric power, he slithered his control

through the cracks of the boy's mental armor. Fear rocked the boy's mind, but he reached into the turbulence and offered balance. He stepped to the side so the audience could witness how the boy's tremors stilled. Those with an observant eye would be able to see his own red eyes and the boy's hunter tattoo. They'd notice that Roger was able to overcome a magic that should have rebuked him.

From balance, Roger guided the boy's mind away from fear, settling him into a calm peace, for all mortals craved calm deep in their souls. The boy's shoulders relaxed, and tension melted from his posture. Keeping a hand on him, Roger strolled around his backside. As he went, he let the distance between them grow until, by the time he reached his other side, he only brushed him with his fingertips.

The boy's head naturally turned toward him. The wide-eyed fear was replaced with a spark of intelligence. With his panic dulled, perhaps he was thinking through the situation clearly, taking stock. He glanced from Roger out to the audience.

Roger removed his hand. He still had his hooks in the boy's mind. He could rip him open and dig for desires to morph and twist into his whims, but he refused.

When the boy finally looked at Roger again, recognition filled his deep blue eyes. He had figured out his situation and knew his future had run out. Despair was quickly turning to a middling acceptance.

His voice cracked from dryness. "Please?"

So many different requests could be bundled into that word, but Roger knew which ones he meant. *Please don't draw it out. Please don't make it hurt. Please make it quick.*

"Of course, darling," Roger said quietly, confident that the entire room was caught on his every motion.

He swept in close from behind because he had to make a show of this for the room and tilted the boy's head to the side. He wrapped one around his waist and held tightly onto his jaw. The boy's heart thundered in Roger's ears, and the twitch of his pulse caught Roger's full attention. Blood moving, pumping, rushing—all of it a kind of magic unique to mortals.

When he caught the rhythm of it, when he felt the sway pulling his hunger further and further up from the depths where he kept it at bay, he bared his fangs. The dramatics and the hiss were for the crowd.

Sinking his fangs into the boy's neck was entirely for him.

Wondrous, beautiful, life-extending, power-blending blood struck his tongue, and he swallowed. Striking a quick bleed point meant more and more of the blood gushed toward him. Rather than suckling a wound, he was drinking as quickly as he could, and it wasn't enough. Streams of warmth were slipping past his lips, coursing down the boy's chest to be caught on the ropes and the way his arms were bound to him. The boy moaned, and the vibration through his throat echoed through Roger.

He had held back this portion of himself. The one that truly enjoyed the feed. And God was the blood *divine*.

There was a moment, just before death, when the blood of a victim was at its peak. Roger had chased too many past that threshold, and the souring of the taste ruined the rest of the feed. He pulled his mouth away from the wound and held the boy in his arms as the life fled his body.

Death didn't necessarily bring peace and beauty with it, but the boy's body was the sort of shell that made poets wistful. Roger picked him up in his arms. A momentary confusion flared across his thoughts. He wasn't about to torture Dmitri by laying the boy beside him. His actions had been about mitigating pain, not bringing more of it.

A bouncer stepped forward and silently offered to take the corpse. Roger handed the boy over, taking a second to smooth his hair.

As the bouncer carried the boy's body away, Seamus

joined Roger and gently put a hand on his shoulder. "I forgot what a joy watching you feast can be."

The words were said with such genuine compliment that Roger smiled at his sire despite himself. His defenses were down, and he could feel Seamus attempting to tug on his desires. That sharpened his mental barriers, but the rush of taking a life still infused Roger's grin. Nothing could replicate the last few swallows of a life's blood, and nothing tasted as precious as a human's. When Seamus leaned in, Roger pressed his forehead against his.

After all, without Seamus, he would've been dead centuries ago. Some forgotten pirate beneath some crushing wave. He wouldn't have the world to taste.

An applause was resounding, vibrating. Roger rolled his head to the side, keeping lightly in touch with Seamus's forehead. "You're in my mind."

"Are you mine, Roger?" Seamus whispered. "My captain? My beloved rake?"

No honest word would pacify him. With Seamus so deeply in his mind, he'd feel the urge for dishonesty. Roger's loyalty had been tested before. There was one way he could lie with his tongue.

He kissed Seamus, gentle and careful. Too much passion would infuriate Anton and cause the madman to throw a fit. Seamus sought the taste of the blood on Roger's tongue and lips, and he let him have it.

Fuck, a monster shouldn't be able to kiss like this.

For a moment, the briefest glimmer of an infinity, memory swept into the place of reality. The first night Roger had been a vampire, they'd shared a kiss. It'd been nothing like this, some mix of heat and greedy touch, but Seamus's meaning had been clear. He had been claiming some piece of Roger's soul, and his claws had scratched at him ever since, digging and scraping to claim more and more of it.

This kiss was freeing. Roger could hear the applause

around them, and he could rebuff Seamus's attempts to sink into his psyche. As Roger slowly pulled back from the kiss, Seamus had a dazzle in his mottled red and blue eyes.

Because this was how he'd survived the centuries. When he was very, *very* good, he could seduce the devil himself. Roger smiled and began to retreat toward the back of the stage. "Thank you, master."

He was determined for that to be their last kiss.

CHAPTER 30

An invisible band tightened around Zack's chest. He couldn't draw a deep breath. The whole thing was perverted to a level that he'd never truly contemplated as possible. Roger sank his fangs into the young hunter's neck like he was creating some sort of art performance piece. And there was a strange sort of beauty to it.

The part of him that took on Cal's voice berated him for the mere thought, aided by memory. *I always knew you were into some vile shit.*

I'm not into this, the rational part of his mind responded. *This is shock. I'm in shock.*

And that was solid ground he could stand on. The world continued to spin around him, but he could take in the pieces and slot them into place. Reality wasn't beyond his grasp, merely fuzzy around the edges.

Because if he looked too closely, he'd scream.

Especially when Roger kissed Seamus like they were old lovers.

Were they? Roger had always sounded like anything that had happened with Seamus hadn't been by choice. Was that kiss part of an act to keep Seamus happy? Or was everything he'd ever said to Zack the lie? Was Roger a sociopathic mastermind who was stringing Zack along?

You know that isn't true, the practical voice declared. But numbed as he was, Zack couldn't help wondering if he had dug far enough into Roger's past.

The horrific show didn't end with Roger's kill. Seamus and Anton picked one of the two remaining hunters to share. They ripped into her neck, blood spraying from their bites, and the audience fucking loved that too. When Seamus promised that the vampires who made the most noise would have the scraps, meaning the fourth hunter, the bastards started making a thunderous amount of noise. A wave of disappointment sounded when Seamus picked a close knot of vampires.

All of this happened while Roger stood onstage. He was off to the side now, but he had that sly grin on his lips that twisted Zack's stomach into knots. Zack had liked that grin, but he wasn't sure he could stand it anymore. *Have I killed? Yes. Have I enjoyed it? Not every time*, Roger had said when they met.

I know him.

Don't I?

Eventually, and yet all too soon, Anton dragged Dmitri offstage, Lucille departed for her corner, and Roger and Seamus rejoined their group. After a few minutes, Ezra came back, and though he looked extra pale, he seemed all right as he sat beside Candide. The lights in the club returned to that dim murkiness that provided more shadows than illumination. The sounds … Zack put those out of his mind. Other vampires were claiming their victims or amusing themselves with their pets. Either way, there was nothing Zack could do for another mortal.

What would these vampires be like under Roger's

command? Roger was going to demand they stop killing people, right? But then he'd just murdered someone in front of all of them, so how could he make that demand?

Roger's aura was colder than it'd ever been, and a chill settled into Zack. There was a quality to him, a liveliness, that was hard to pinpoint, but once Zack spotted it, he couldn't stop noticing the subtle change. In the pale light, Roger almost had a glow to his pale skin, and his eyes were maroon. Specks of blood dotted his clothing.

If there was conversation, Zack didn't hear it past the high-pitched whine in his ears. Candide, Takashi, Roger, Seamus—the four of them were chatting like they'd just met for fucking drinks after a long day of work. The casual camaraderie was a strange melody with the background percussion of the occasional scream, laugh, or erotic moan.

"Is he all right?" Seamus asked suddenly.

"I'm afraid tonight has been rather intense," Roger said. "I should get him and the others home, don't you think, Takashi?"

"Am I terrible if I admit that I'm longing to get back to this book I'm reading?" Takashi said.

"I don't think so," Candide replied.

"Zackery," Seamus said.

The mental warnings to keep his gaze low came a fraction too late. Upon hearing his name, Zack automatically turned his attention to Seamus. His mottled blue eyes lacked warmth to a degree that Zack wondered if he'd ever been human at all. The cold, sharp intelligence felt as piercing as a dagger.

"Don't tell me that spirit of yours is withering, Zackery. I'd be disappointed," Seamus replied.

Because that was what everyone around Seamus did, Zack realized. They cut themselves down to fit into tiny boxes or stayed out of the light long enough that they forgot how to grow. The other pets sitting in this nest of vampires were doing their best to pretend they didn't even exist, and the conversation Roger, Takashi, and Candide had carried on had had such an element of falsehood to it that Zack wanted to puke.

Hunters had to work with their fear, not give in to it. *Hunter.* That's what he was, deep down in his soul. His family couldn't take that away from him, and he couldn't pretend that wasn't a part of him.

And a predator was watching his every movement, waiting for him to expose a weakness in order to pounce.

Surviving Seamus wasn't about shriveling away from the nurturing light but stretching toward it despite the bastard. After all, Roger had shown incredible power circumventing the young hunter's tattoo. Zack wasn't sure how far Roger had gone with it, but the guy had been shaking so hard he could hardly stand. By the end, he was standing straight enough that Zack could tell his fear was gone. Roger and Seamus had kissed like equals. Seamus wasn't tolerating their presence; he was entertaining them.

Zack slid to the edge of his seat. Clever words were failing him. Holding Seamus's gaze seemed to sap his courage because there was some hunger in his eyes that bothered Zack. Like Seamus was waiting to devour him. *No, he's got something else in mind. But why show any interest in me? What would he want from me?*

And a tiny, irrepressible part of him thought he recognized that hunger in Seamus, that he'd seen some glimmer of that monster before.

In the mirror.

That wasn't possible. It couldn't be. Seamus was a millennium-old vampire. There was nothing Zack could have in common with such a creature.

Recoiling from the thought, Zack pressed into Roger's side. "I think I'm tired, master."

Roger kissed the top of his head. "I will take them home, then, if that's all right, Seamus."

"I'm surprised you've stayed this long," Seamus mused. His gaze continued to burrow into Zack. "Go on. Take care of yourselves. I'll see you again soon."

Returning to the hotel suite happened in a blur. Zack went through the motions with the others, but no one said anything more than necessary between leaving, the ride back, and walking through the hotel lobby. Zack passed under the chandelier without raising his gaze. He couldn't stand it if this would be the night that he finally figured out whether or not pixies had died in the making of the glowing glass.

Without the constant press of new horrors, Zack was left to spin his mind around what he had witnessed. Roger leading the hunter out, ungagging him, treating him like he'd done with Zack. Kind. Thoughtful.

And he'd bled him dry.

No one said anything on the elevator ride up.

No one said anything as they entered the suite.

Zack hesitated just inside the door. The clang of it shutting behind him rattled speech from him finally. "That was fucked-up, right?"

Everyone was in mid-retreat. Takashi had headed toward the bar in the corner while Kit had plopped onto the leather sofa in front of the massive television. Carver had a foot on the stairs that led to the two other bedrooms. Roger was halfway to the balcony.

"I'm not the only one thinking it, am I?" Zack asked.

"Which part?" Carver said. "When Roger killed a hunter or when you staked a vampire?"

A boulder slammed into Zack's lungs. "What?"

Carver continued plodding up the stairs.

"You think that what happened on that stage is the same as what I did?" Zack demanded.

Kit left the sofa and wandered over to the bar. "Is there a bottle of fey wine back there? Something Seelie?"

Takashi glanced through the bottles. "Midsummer Glow."

"Perfect." Kit took it and headed for the stairs.

"Really? You're just going to grab some booze and hide in your room?" Zack said.

"You're going to turn this into a thing," Kit said. "You've got your 'priority humanity' voice on. And it's clear that you think you didn't do anything wrong. You *killed someone*, and you think it's nothing like what Roger did. All I see are bodies."

"That guy attacked me," Zack said. "And Anton put a stake in my hand."

"Yeah, well, Seamus sired the fangs in Roger's mouth, and who knows what that guy did. Maybe he was a fascist asshole who deserved it. Doesn't matter. He's fucking dead, and we're alive." Carver said from the top of the stairs. "Think we can split that wine, Kit?"

"Your room or mine?"

"Yours smells nicer."

Zack was speechless until the door clicked shut behind them upstairs. A clink sound at the bar drew his attention. Takashi was putting ice in a glass, and he took a bottle of whiskey from the cabinet and poured himself a drink.

"Do one up for me," Roger said dryly.

Takashi slid the drink across the bar to indicate Roger could nab that one, and he took out another two glasses.

"After what just happened, everyone's going to get drunk and pretend nothing's wrong?" Zack said.

"What do you have us do, Zack?" Takashi asked as he dropped ice cubes into the fresh glasses. He gestured at the glass with the bottle. "Do you want one?"

"No," Zack said.

"The first question remains." Takashi poured whiskey like a

punctuation. "We're *vampires*. You've asked Roger what his long-term plans are. At least, I imagine you have. I know I have. But what about you? We slay the monster, we take the coven. Does your vision of the future include your vampire boyfriends?"

Takashi rounded the bar and leaned against it beside Roger. The two of them, standing motionless next to each other, were the manifestation of Zack's wildest dreams. They were gorgeous. Incredible. Dangerous.

And he wanted all of that. He wanted what he had with them to go on forever.

But what did wanting them turn him into? They were killers. Both of them were elegant, beautiful beacons of death. His family had already disowned him for sleeping with one vampire. Did they know about Takashi? Would it make a difference if he killed Seamus? Could he ever talk to them again? Why was he caring so deeply about them in the first place?

Zack shoved a hand through his hair. The crest tag on his collar tinkled against the ring. He'd forgotten he had it on. He scrambled to get the damn thing off and tossed it to the floor. *They got you used to it, little bro. You belong to them. The blood-suckers.*

"Zack," Roger said softly, gently, as if he were the torch in a darkening forest.

Zack glanced up. Roger had concern in his deep brown eyes, and he stepped forward with an unnatural grace.

The terrible thought, the one Zack had banished as soon as he'd had it, returned. Because something had happened on that stage that twisted the wires in his mind. Somehow, he must have gotten things crossed. The atmosphere. Maybe it had chewed through his hunter's tattoo and caused him to long for things he shouldn't want. Made him jealous when he should've been sickened.

"I'm fine," Zack said. And he was panting. Why was he

panting? He put a hand to his chest, then slid it up to rub through his hair.

"Zack," Roger said again. "You need to breathe."

Roger was slowly walking toward him. And if they touched, in that moment, Zack would lose the rest of his soul, he was sure of it. Because he'd already sold off pieces of it. He'd never truly hated vampires like he should; that was why his mother had put him on the bench instead of letting him join the family in the field. Maybe he'd been born without one altogether. Maybe that was why he didn't see the world the way his family did.

Compassion isn't a weakness. Roger had said that.

Zack put a hand to his forehead. What would his future hold? Sitting on the sidelines while Roger ruled and Takashi offered advice? Aging while they remained hot and dangerous forever? Never talking to his dad or sister or brother or mother or cousins or grandparents ever again? Protecting Roger and Takashi from *them*, the people who had been his family but had discarded him?

A tiny bit of him knew. Knew where the power was. Knew who had it. Knew that it would damn him.

So he couldn't want it.

But he did.

I've spent too long with them, the first thought proclaimed.

"I need some air," Zack said. He twisted and grabbed the door handle.

Roger cheated and put his hand on the door, preventing him from opening it. He whispered, "Talk to me. *Please.*"

Please. That had been the hunter's last word. That had been what Zack had said to Roger more than one time when he was begging for sex or for him to bite him. And that had been all him. Roger hadn't toyed with his mind. He'd simply been there for him. Seen him in a way no one else had.

Except Takashi. Zack's gaze drifted to him. Worry was in his blue eyes, but so was confusion.

And there would be a time where they would have each other, but not him. He'd be gone. Unless. Unless … he became … *No. I'm not like them. I don't like it.*

Only he'd killed. He'd killed two vampires without giving a shit. He'd given out countless details on how to destroy various supernaturals over and over and over, and he'd thought he'd done a good job.

He was a monster, too. That's what Seamus saw in him. What Anton had freaking clapped for.

I saved someone. Two someones. That girl in Detroit and Roger.

Two vampires, the Cal voice in his head countered.

"Did you enjoy it?" Zack asked. "Killing that guy tonight? Did you like it?"

Carefully, Roger slipped his fingers through strands of Zack's hair. "What's gotten into you?"

Zack dodged out of Roger's touch and straightened. "Answer me."

"You still haven't answered Takashi's question," Roger replied.

"Maybe I'll get to that. Maybe I don't know what to fucking do anymore." Zack stumbled as he took a few steps backward. The makeup on his face was a mask he wished he could tear off his skin. "I didn't have a choice. But you did. You could have said no. You could have just torn his throat open. Or you could've brought him back here. But you killed him. Why? Why do that? Why not spare him?"

"Everything that happened tonight was a test," Roger said seriously. "Had I spared him in any way, that would've meant I agreed with what Dmitri was doing."

"And what was he doing?" Zack asked.

"I believe Dmitri attempted to kill Anton."

"Is that why he was here the other night? To recruit us?"

"He might have thought about it, but he didn't make his intentions clear."

"Why did he wait this long to take a shot at the throne if he wanted it?" Zack said.

"Because Dmitri doesn't care if the coven collapses," Roger said. "I think he'd prefer it. He hates what we are. He believes we're all damned. I think he was just hoping to take out Anton before he couldn't stand living any longer."

"Before he ..." Zack frowned. "He's been a vampire for hundreds of years."

"And all this time, he's been holding one hate deeper than his self-loathing. The one for Anton." Roger paced away from the door. "He should be diagnosed with chronic depression. He's had rare times where life wasn't a burden for him, but he's been hiding more of himself than I realized until the other night. He told me he was off to kill the devil, something he's always called Anton."

"You should've told me," Zack said. "We could've helped him."

"If we had, then Seamus would be burning everything to the ground," Roger said. "Those two may consider everything else in the world a toy to break, but they love each other to madness. You must have realized that tonight."

Zack had spotted the devotion in the two ancient vampires. "And you think Anton's going to leave us in peace when we kill Seamus?"

"Probably not, but the coven as a whole is terrified of him," Roger said. "They would help Seamus. Anton, they'd run from. Don't you think that's true?"

"Yeah," Zack admitted. *More likely we'll meet a swift death, but I can't give him a reason to back out.* "What are they going to do to Dmitri? Do you think he'll tell them what you're planning?"

"I think it's a safe assumption he has," Takashi said.

"No. Dmitri won't talk. That's why Anton put on his little show tonight," Roger replied. "He was attempting to draw us out. Make anyone who sympathized or could have been working with Dmitri react."

"Don't call it a little show. Don't minimize the death of four people like that," Zack growled.

"Five," Takashi corrected. "Unless you aren't counting a vampire as a person, and then we have my original question to consider once more."

"I don't know what I want my future to look like," Zack exclaimed. "I have been hanging on by a thread for months, okay? And when I stop to think about anything, it hurts. The only thing that doesn't hurt is being with the two of you. But I can't count vampires as people. You're … you're not playing by the same rules."

"Zack," Roger said with compassion and heart.

And something snapped inside Zack. Like a switch, but deeper in his soul. As if somehow, someway, the universe had *clicked*. "The supernatural world—no, the *world* isn't black-and-white. It's not even shades of gray. It's bloodred and infected green and starlight blue and comforting brown. It's a beautiful rainbow, and there is something *wrong* with me, okay? Because I can drive a stake through some guy, and I don't care. I don't! He was rude and a vampire, and honestly, I think Anton would've snapped my neck if I said no. So I didn't even stop to think about it. I just did it.

"And I watch the two of you, and I get sad. Not because I'm jealous or feeling left out but because you two will get to be together forever if you want. If you can survive the crazy bullshit and the inevitable humans fucking up the globe, you get *forever*. And I get another twenty really good years? *Maybe*. And then *maybe* I get another forty after that.

"But all I can think about is how badly we need to kill Seamus. About how that applause keeps ringing in my head. How deep down, I know you did that guy a favor because he wasn't a screaming mess, but all I can see is a dead boy. And you're probably right. Seamus is probably looking for an excuse to kill us because he enjoys lording this perpetual threat over our heads. He gets off on being in charge. But we keep twirling and spinning and hoping that he's too busy with someone else to notice the daggers in our hands.

"And I train. And I train. And I *train*. I am stronger than I've ever been, and I am so fucking terrified that I will never be enough. I won't get the job done. I won't live long enough to see any real change happen. That something is already dead in me, and I can't love the two of you the way I should." Tears were streaming down Zack's cheeks. "And now that I've said all of this, you're going to think I'm weak and sideline me, and everything I've been working for will be for *nothing*. I'll be *nothing*."

In a blur of speed, Roger caught Zack's arms. When Zack instinctually twisted away, Roger moved with him and embraced him tightly. "You will never be nothing, Zackery."

Zack choked on his sobs. They were flooding out of him. As much as he wanted to believe Roger, a portion of him couldn't. Because the only thing besides nothing he could be was a monster. And he hated that any part of him wanted the power being a vampire could give him. He hated that some tiny hope in his heart burned for the day he'd have the balls to ask Roger to turn him. Because he hadn't wanted that.

Come on, little bro. You have, the Cal voice taunted. *You've climbed in bed with them, and you like it.*

Abandoning his drink at the bar, Takashi crossed over to them. He cupped Zack's cheeks and wiped his tears away, even though they kept coming. Softly, he said, "Roger is right, lover. Some night, you will see how special you are."

"How can you say that? How can you believe that? When I killed somebody and I'm not even sorry? When Seamus … when he sees …"

Roger spun Zack around in his arms. "When he sees what?"

Words choked him fiercer than the tears. If he said it, he

was either wrong or right, and both were miserable outcomes. But if he said nothing, he was left dangling in pain. "He sees a monster in me. You have before, too. Right? It's why you wanted me along. Because I am a killer. Nell thinks I can do it. Everyone does. Even my family wanted me to be one."

Roger brushed his hands through Zack's hair and then pulled him in for a tight hug. "Monsters never cry about what they are."

"What did you even see in me?" Zack asked. "Why? Why spare me when you killed that hunter? Why didn't you kill me when we met? What made me different than him?"

"Beyond circumstance, likely what I've seen," Takashi whispered. Roger shifted to Zack's left side, and Takashi stood closer to his right. "You have been bent out of shape and flipped upside down, and I know that leads to questions. I know how that can hurt. But you have the strength to survive, you have an intelligence that can be too sharp for your mind to find peace, and we will see this through. You have to start thinking of what you want your future to be, Zack, because it could be anything."

If I become like them, my family will hunt me. They'll hunt them. Everyone will hurt.

But I can be with them. Fight with them. Love them. Let them love me.

What else can I do?

I can't breathe.

"I think tonight's been a lot," Zack managed. He held his arms tight against his chest. "I think … I think I just need some sleep. Alone, if that's okay."

"Are you certain?" Roger asked seriously. "We can lay with you."

"Naw. It's middle of the day for you guys. I'll … I'll come back out here if I need you."

As Zack started to slip away from them, Roger caught his

arm. Another of their staring contests began, but Zack quickly ducked his head. Slowly, Roger let him go. "All right."

Takashi kissed his temple, then Roger did, and finally, Zack went away to the dark master bedroom. He shucked off the clothing and took a moment in the bathroom to wash the makeup from his face. His soul still felt raw, but nothing but time could do anything about that. He crawled into bed with the rainbow teddy bear Josefina had gotten him as a get-well present and wished for a dreamless sleep.

Anything else would be too cruel.

CHAPTER 31

"Should we leave him alone?" Takashi asked.

"I don't like it, but it's what he wants," Roger said with a sigh. He slunk over to the bar and sat on one of the stools. His whiskey was waiting, and he took a long drink of it. The smoothness gave way to a burn, not entirely unlike the current agony rumbling in the back of his mind.

A lot was a pale summary of what the night had been. Now that they were out of the club and a relative measure of safety wrapped around him, Roger sank into the terrible what-ifs of what might be happening to Dmitri.

Slowly, Takashi joined him. "Should we talk about what happened?"

"Just now or at that hellhole?" Roger finished his drink and poured another.

"Either. Both." Takashi lightly dragged his glass closer to him and half spun it. "Roger, I have no idea what to say."

"Come on, that can't be the worst you've seen," Roger muttered.

"Anton has Dmitri. Aren't you worried about that?"

"I'm not worried that he'll talk. If what Anton wants is answers, then Dmitri will deprive him to the grave and beyond." Roger took a sip of his whiskey. It wasn't strong enough to numb him, not with his supernatural counterbalances. If he kept drinking, perhaps that would work. Anything to banish the sound of Zack's sobs or the sight of Dmitri hitting the stage floor.

"He'll torture him," Takashi said.

"He's been doing so since the night he was made, some way or another." Roger couldn't look away from the glass, and he closed his mind to Takashi's radiating emotions. The truth was painful enough without knowing whether or not he was striking fear in his lover. "I was encouraged to make sirelings, you know. Everyone in the coven is. Not Dmitri. Not a word has ever been said about his lack of sirelings. I thought, well, Dmitri didn't choose this. He wouldn't choose to make anyone.

"But tonight. God. Tonight. Anton had the whole thing orchestrated, didn't he? From the moment he stepped out from behind that stage. Probably whatever else he was doing beforehand." Roger knocked back half his glass. "Anyone else who'd attempted to kill Anton would've been dead already, or they'd have died on that stage. But Anton continues to hold on to him. I can't help thinking that Anton didn't want Dmitri to make sirelings. Makes me wonder if he interfered in other ways, too."

"Like with your relationship with him?" Takashi asked.

"Dmitri was hot and cold when we were mortals. I thought the way we were as immortals was just an extension. But that last time. Just before I met you. He ... the change was sudden, and I ... fuck, why didn't we ever talk?" Roger was whispering by the end. Too much had happened. That night, the centuries, the pain, Zack's crisis, everything was mixing into a toxic sludge that trapped his heart.

"We can use this to our advantage," Takashi said quietly.

The words were so brutal, the sentiment so foreign that an extremely old instinct kicked in, and Roger thought his heart skipped a beat. But he hadn't had a beating heart in centuries. *Takashi's has long been silent as well, and it shows*. But that cold thought wasn't fair. Takashi had the benefit of distance. Zack would likely wake and consider something similar.

"You think Anton will be distracted," Roger said.

"We could move up our timetable on Seamus."

"No."

Takashi pivoted to face Roger. "You saw the way he was looking at Zack tonight, didn't you?"

Roger filled both their whiskey glasses and refused to look at Takashi. "I did."

"I don't know what his interest in Zack is, but you know nothing good will come of it. We have to strike."

"We have to wait," Roger said.

Takashi grabbed his arm roughly, and the barstool swung so that they faced one another. "What the hell *for*?"

"I have to be certain they will follow me." Roger slid off the stool and walked over to the double glass doors, whiskey in hand. He rotated it slowly and watched what remained of the ice cubes continue to dwindle. "None of us will be safe if the coven decides that I'm too weak for the role of leadership. Halloween and tonight were steps to secure my position. But I also can't be seen to be just like Seamus. I won't allow what he does. I can't ... I can't stomach the killing, Takashi. They were dragging in innocents and slaughtering them tonight. And the gray bands, that can't persist. But these vampires are used to that sort of violence."

"You're worried that you can't change them," Takashi said.

"Of course I can't. For better or worse, we're killers." Roger took a long sip of his drink. "And drinking that boy dry tonight was ... I wish I felt greater shame for it. If any part of me was still mortal, I might. But that final moment is intoxicating. How do you handle it?"

"It?" Takashi relaxed against the bar.

He was putting on a front. Roger was sure of it. With a roll of his eyes, he said, "You know what I mean."

"The draw to kill?" Takashi swished his whiskey back and forth. "Mostly, I lure racists and bigots into a place of my choosing. The internet's made stalking them so much easier."

"Killing those you find wicked," Roger said.

Takashi finished his drink and then stood. "I'm doing humanity and the world a favor."

Slowly, Roger crossed the room back over to him. He stroked Takashi's cheek. "I remember when we met. Your mortal self clung to you. Wide-eyed. Beautiful."

Takashi straightened. "There is nothing wrong with having a little morality."

"There isn't. But until you and Zack, I have been pretending mine was adaptable." Roger pressed his forehead against Takashi. "I had to. You understand that, don't you?"

Takashi put his hands on Roger's shoulders and whispered, "I do."

"I am rediscovering those lines I won't cross, but I'm going to be shit at keeping the bastards in order if I don't truly understand what I will and won't allow. How will I even punish those who disobey me? I don't want to kill them, Takashi. I don't want any more blood on my hands than I need to have. But what else is there?" Roger sighed and moved away. He poured himself another drink. "I promised you and Zack that we would claim the coven on New Year's, and we will. But I need the time before then to figure everything out. That way, I'm not leaping into this thing without any idea of my goals."

"You won't be doing this alone."

"I know." Roger kissed Takashi's cheek.

Takashi stepped in close so that they were chest to chest and drew him into a gentle embrace.

"Are you all right?" Roger stroked Takashi's back in a long, soothing movement. "I realized I haven't asked."

"I've seen far worse."

"That wasn't the question."

"I only need a bit of time to process what I saw."

"Seamus and Anton can be … a lot."

"They're exactly the sort of creatures I thought they were, but you surprised me. I could feel the power on that stage." Takashi moved back just enough to be able to look Roger in the eye. "You pushed through a hunter's tattoo. I didn't think that was possible."

"The things aren't impervious."

"To the common vampire, they *are*." Takashi ran his fingers through Roger's hair and lightly played with the end of a lock when he reached it. "You have no idea how powerful you are, do you?"

"I've had the benefit of studying one up close. That's all."

Takashi shook his head. "No, Roger. You have this untapped potential. I can see it in you, waiting to step into the spotlight. Embrace that power. We need it."

"I will," Roger murmured. He kissed Takashi. Then he picked up the bottle of whiskey. "Now, I intend to perfect my brooding vampire face out on the balcony. You're welcome to join me in silent contemplation of how the last several centuries have had a pain I refused to recognize."

"Roger—"

"I will be fine," Roger said with a half-hearted grin. "But I think, for a change, I need to sit and mull things over. Perhaps start a journal or something."

"You don't have a journal," Takashi said.

"Well, maybe I'll go down to the gift shop and buy one or something."

Takashi laughed and held up a hand. "Hold on." He went off to their bedroom and reemerged a minute later. In his hand, he had a leather journal, and he offered it to Roger. "This was almost my birthday gift to Zack, but he has such a nice one he's already using."

"The necklace was far better. He's been wearing it every chance he gets." Roger took the journal and kissed Takashi again. "Thank you."

Takashi caressed Roger's cheek, teased another kiss, then gently pressed their lips together for a moment. "I'll be here if you decide you want to talk."

Roger squeezed his hand, then stepped away. He found a pen, grabbed the bottle, and headed out to the balcony. The light from the suite was enough for him to write by, especially as he took a seat on the couch rather than stand at the edge. The cold night air was bracing but of course lacked that quality of salt he found himself missing. At some point, he'd have to find an excuse to take his lovers to see the ocean.

The journal was a beautiful dark leather and supple to the touch. Embossed on the cover was a set of fangs, the stylized sort that tended to represent a set of vampire's teeth, and the fangs had a dagger set between them. Roger snorted and rubbed his finger across the embossing.

Then he uncorked the bottle of whiskey, opened to the first page, and wrote, *I have no idea what year I was born, mortal or vampire …*

CHAPTER 32

Zack's phone was ringing.

He was closer to the edge of the bed for a change, so he rolled over and nuzzled up against Takashi. Cool side of the pillow found, he started slipping back down into the wonderful bliss of sleep.

Then his phone began to ring again.

And he realized that *his phone was ringing*. It never did that. Somehow, spam calls hadn't found either of his new cell numbers yet. Either something was up with Blake and she needed him. Or … or … He scrambled to grab his phone.

His parents weren't calling him, but Zack lost his breath anyway.

Because his caller ID said his sister was.

The shock threw him so hard that he missed the second call. Just as he was attempting to call her back, his phone rang for the third time. He answered, "Amber?"

"Zack?" she said. "Zack? It's you, right?"

"Yeah, yeah, it's me." Zack glanced at the bed. Neither Roger nor Takashi had moved. Somehow, talking while they were sleeping felt rude, even if they weren't likely to wake up. "Hold on."

Quietly, Zack padded out to the living room, but the space was too big, and his voice might echo. He whispered another quick "one minute" and crept into the office and shut the door. After listening for anyone else moving around in the suite, he let out a sigh of relief and said, "Okay. Hi, Amber. It's amazing to hear your voice."

"Now I realized I should have FaceTimed. Can we do that? I need to see your face."

"Yeah, sure."

The call switched over, and for the first time in months, Zack saw his sister's face. She had a long piece of her auburn hair hanging in front of her left eye, though she nervously played with it. In his head, Zack knew his sister was young. She was only fifteen. But somehow, the memory of her seemed older, and now that he could see her again, she seemed *young*.

She also looked like she was crying and was currently attempting to hold back tears.

"Amber, what's wrong?" Zack asked.

"Don't get mad at me, okay? But. Gah. Is there like. A window?"

She's asking me to step out into the sunlight. Zack swallowed. "It's too freaking cold outside. I'm not doing that. Here." He opened his mouth wide and brought the camera close enough to get a good look at his teeth. "No fangs. See?"

"Okay." Amber nodded and took in a deep sniff. "It's been months and Mom keeps saying stuff and the parents are talking about how hunters died last night in Chicago and I had to know if one of them was you."

Zack sat down with his back against the door. "I'm alive."

"Okay."

"I don't know what Cal told you—"

"He said you got brainwashed, but I didn't think that sounded like you," Amber replied. "Everything's been awful since you left."

"How?"

Amber shrugged, then sighed and raked her hand through her hair. "Lots of fighting. Mom keeps taking hunts, and Dad's still recovering. You know he took a piece of rebar to the stomach, right?"

"Yeah," Zack said softly. "Cal mentioned it. But since no one's been answering my texts or calls, I couldn't find out if he was okay."

"You could've come *home*," Amber replied.

"Mom and Dad made it pretty clear that they wanted nothing to do with me anymore when they fucked with my social media and cut off my phone."

"That was just Mom. Dad has been super pissed since that happened. It's what like half their fights have been about," Amber said.

His parents were fighting? Zack couldn't remember the last time they'd had an argument. "Wait, really?"

"Yeah."

"Amber, sweetie, who're you talking to?" Dad said off camera.

"Oh, shit. Glad you're alive, Zack. I miss you."

Before Zack could say anything, she ended the video call, and he was left to stare at the wallpaper on his phone. He'd picked a picture that he'd managed to snag of him and Roger in the early nights of their relationship. Roger had barely known anything about modern smartphones, and Zack had been showing him the ins and outs of taking a semi-decent selfie.

His family thought about him. Amber had actually been worried about him. A nagging sense of guilt kicked in when he realized he was happy that they weren't happy without him, but his heart felt a million times lighter. Mom was upset with him, and that wasn't a surprise. She'd been the one that saw him let a vampire go in Detroit, and she'd been the one that refused to let him go on another hunt. She'd always acted like he had a thing for vampires.

Because you do, the Cal voice said.

Maybe because everyone's a monster, deep down, and vampires at least don't hide it.

As Zack started to stand, his phone rang with another FaceTime. He answered it, expecting Amber.

But his father appeared on-screen instead.

"Dad?" Zack said.

The strain in Dad's face flooded into relief upon seeing Zack's face. Thomas Wright was an experienced hunter. He'd been doing the job since his teens like most Wrights, and yet Zack had never seen him look that worried before. And had he gotten more gray hair in the last four months?

"Hey buddy," Dad said slowly. "Good to see your face. You holding up okay?"

"Yeah. Yeah." Reflexively, Zack rubbed his shoulder. "Cal said you got hurt. How're you doing?"

"Too long sitting on my ass, but I'm fine." Dad had stubble, which was unusual for him, and he scratched at his jaw. "I got a million things to ask and no easy way to do it."

And Zack could practically hear the questions now. *Is the vampire controlling you? Is it feeding from you too much? What did you tell him about the family? Are you sure you're not brainwashed?* Zack let out a breath through his nostrils, trying to keep his temper in check. "I got a few myself. Like why'd you let Mom cut me off?"

Dad winced. "It's not like that, Zack."

"Then what's it like?"

"What's happening between your mother and I should stay between her and I. We don't have a lot of time before they get home, so we need to keep this short."

"Before they ... you don't want to be caught talking to me, huh?" Zack snapped.

"Zack, buddy, you have every right to be angry with me."

"I know I do!"

"*Zackery*," Dad said with a blend of authority unique to parental units. "The situation at home is complicated. I don't want to waste time dragging you into it when you're clear from it for the time being."

"Amber said you and Mom are arguing because of me," Zack said.

"We're arguing for a lot of reasons. What you did ... it kicked a hornet's nest into an angry bear and then set the bear on fire, all right?"

"What *I* did?" Zack demanded. Reason said he should listen to his father and keep him calm, but he had been hoping and waiting for months to hear from his family. He should've known that any reunion with them would lay at least a part of the blame on his doorstep. "What about what Cal fucking did?"

"We gave him permission to drive to Taliville," Dad said. "We needed someone to see what was going on, and I wasn't in any shape. Your mother stayed back to take care of me."

Zack stood and paced as he spoke. "If all Cal had done was drive into town and berate me, maybe I'd forgive that ... that *bastard*!"

"Zack, he's your—"

"I will actually throw my phone off the balcony if you say brother right now, Dad. And our balcony is very, *very* high up." Zack thrust a hand through his hair. "Brothers aren't supposed to tie you up and ditch you in a bathroom while they attempt to murder the guy you're sleeping with. Brothers are supposed to listen to you when you've got an amazing idea instead of assume that you're only thinking with your dick. Brothers are supposed to give a shit if you call them out on slaughtering innocent people. And brothers aren't supposed to fucking stab you and leave you for dead!"

Dad grew paler with every sentence Zack said. "Wait, *what*?"

"Which part did he forget to mention? The fact that he kept trying to kill Roger even after Roger clearly wasn't going to kill him *because I asked him not to* or that Cal killed a couple of sleeping humans in Texas just because they were sleeping with a vampire. He said some absolute fucking bullshit about them being cannibals because the vampire made them that way, but I honestly can't believe anything he fucking says anymore." Zack sucked in a breath. Dad was too stunned to stop him, apparently. "He threw a stake at me, Dad, and told me I had to kill Roger, and he doesn't even *know* him. And he wanted to kill Blake, and Blake, she's ... she's fucking *sweet*, Dad. She didn't choose to become a werewolf. But she's trying to make the best out of it. Did you know that like emotional support animals for shifters are a thing somebody's working on? To help people? Because supernaturals are *people*, Dad. They're not all fucking monsters that should be ash and dust."

"Zack, buddy, I need you to breathe," Dad said, though he sounded like he had a sob caught in his throat.

"Code for calm down. No. Fuck that. *Fuck that*. I have been lashing out at all the wrong people, and guess what, Dad? You're one of the right people. I have tried calling you and Mom and Amber and Grandpa and Grandma and even Cousin Denny once, and I fucking hate Cousin Denny. And nobody's answered. Everyone's just believed Cal. Everyone's been saying he did the right thing leaving me behind, haven't they?"

"Zack, let me talk," Dad said.

At that, Zack finally paused to look at his phone again. He'd been waving it around some while he spoke, but he settled long enough to hold it up. That invisible band had cinched around his chest again, and taking a deep breath was a challenge. Because he didn't want to. Some part of him just didn't want to breathe because breathing meant living, and living meant dealing with the pain, and if he let in the pain his family had inflicted over the last couple of months, then he'd let in the trauma of the last several years. Mom's coldness ever since Zack had "failed" in Detroit. Dad's distance. Amber siding with Cal and teasing Zack.

And though Dad had asked to speak, he seemed to be waiting.

And Zack had waited too long to ask one question. "Dad, did you know that the vampire I let go was a girl Amber's age? She'd been missing for two weeks. Only two weeks. I was a kid, and she was a kid, and I let her go because she didn't choose to become a vampire. She wasn't evil."

Dad ran his hand through his hair, holding on to the back of it for a long moment before releasing it and a long sigh. "I didn't know, Zack. I didn't know most of what you just said. I thought … Cal has always had a habit of exaggerating his exploits, but I thought I could spot the lies. I won't tell you what he's said because it's clearly not the truth. And I'll be honest with you because you deserve it—I'm not sure how much of this will make a difference with your mother or the rest of the family, but knowing makes a difference for me, Zack."

"And me!" Amber said from the background.

Dad wiped his hand down his face. He clearly hadn't known Amber could hear everything.

Though he should've. Amber had always had a talent for sticking her nose in where she wasn't supposed to have it. Zack sorely missed that suddenly.

"What were you doing in Taliville in the first place?" Dad asked.

"We got a hunt. I thought I could prove myself." Zack leaned against the desk. "But I hesitated, and Roger … he didn't have to give me a chance, Dad. But he went out of his way to give me a chance to think for myself. And we're after … I'm not going to tell you who because you'll try to talk me out of it. But I'm going to make a difference, Dad."

"Zack, he's a vampire. Are you sure you can trust him?"

"He's my boyfriend. I trust him."

"Vampires can play games better than anyone."

Zack picked at a piece of lint on his pants. "Cal seems to be able to run a good one."

"He's got you there, Dad," Amber said off camera.

"Teenagers," Dad muttered under his breath.

"I'm twenty now. Officially not a teenager," Zack replied.

Dad wiped a hand down his face again. "Zack. I don't know if we have time to get into everything you're up to, but you can come home. You don't have to go through with it."

Dad's offer was genuine. And home would be full of crap. There was no way Cal or Mom would be happy to see him, even if he carted all of his notebooks full of information back to them. They might be able to figure out how to kill Seamus from everything he'd learned without Roger's help. With Dad on his side, maybe the family would listen to him, or at least be divided. He might start a real conversation in the hunter community about their impact on supernaturals. He might be able to stop Cal from hurting more innocent people and put an effort into stopping the family and community from creating more hunters *like* Cal.

But that would mean turning his back on Roger and Takashi, on Blake and Kit, on his promise to Nell. Reed, Josefina, Carver—they'd all be disappointed in him.

And he had never truly fit in with his family. That was the real reason Mom had benched him, why he'd never earned a nickname like Bolt or Butcher like his siblings. Mom had started shutting him out years ago, and Dad had stopped asking questions. Five minutes of interest didn't make up for the long weeks at home alone over the last summer or the weeks he'd helped take care of Amber when his parents and Cal were out hunting the years before that.

And Dad could've reached out before, but he hadn't. He

hadn't even done it now. Amber had. If anyone in his family deserved a real shot, she did.

Zack was where he needed to be. *No. Where I want to be.* He took a deep breath and straightened. "I'm not coming home, Dad."

"Zack—"

"Look, you're the one who said you're short on time, so let me tell you things you need to know. Four hunters died last night. They were dragged into Devil's Cove. Dmitri was one of the coven captains, and he wanted to kill his sire, Anton. The five of them failed, and Dmitri's the only one left alive."

"Were any of them turned?"

"No. At least three of the four weren't. I doubt the last one was. It went pretty quick for all of them."

Dad nodded.

Zack cleared his throat. "And, uh. Completely different note, but I have two vampire boyfriends now."

"Two?" Amber grabbed the phone, and she appeared on-screen again. "I can't get one human boyfriend, and you've got two immortal ones?"

"Amber," Dad said, voice straining to contain order.

"I'm trusting Zack's judgment. He's not going to date murderers, Dad."

"I've killed two vampires, Amber. My hands aren't clean either," Zack said quietly.

"Yeah, but they were *vampires*."

Zack tilted his head back and slapped his hand to his forehead. "Fuck, no wonder everyone got pissed at me last night. I sounded just like that. Fuck."

"Killing vampires is our raison d'être," Amber replied.

"And killing humans is kind of what vampires are supposed to do," Zack said. When Amber sucked in a breath, he said, "Wait, wait, wait. They're not like that, like that. They've just both been alive a really long time, and some- times there are reasons."

Dad took the phone back. "Zack, maybe you should come home."

"Dad, look, if you want to stay in contact with me and try to make this work, this is what it is. Vampires kill on occasion. Some of them are evil bastards that I would gladly run my stake through. My boyfriends aren't evil. And if they turn out to be evil, then I'll burn their hearts out, and you can tell me, 'I told you so.' But some part of you *has* to know that every-thing the family's taught us is through their narrow little filter, right?"

"You can't let them lure you into a false sense of security."

"Trust me, security's not something I'm feeling huge on lately." Zack ran his hand through his hair. "Roger got me an original copy of Rudolph Hagen's book, the one that practi-cally everyone has a copy of. But the reprints are nothing like the original, Dad. There's all this juicy stuff about how vampires and humans can actually coexist in it."

Dad frowned. "Really?"

"Yeah."

Amber darted up into the camera. "Uh, I think Mom just got home. So we should go. I love you, Zack. I'm glad you're not dead."

"Love you, son," Dad said.

Zack was almost too choked up to say "Love you" in return before hanging up. The tears were stupid. He shouldn't have been crying. But the relief that the people he'd spent so long loving didn't actually hate him was too great. He wiped his eyes. Mom and Cal sounded like they were worse, but Dad and Amber cared about him. *I'll take what love I can.*

After another long minute, he emerged from the office. Kit and Carver had come down from their rooms. Carver had his sunglasses on and his feet kicked up on the coffee table. Kit had the room service menu in their lap.

"Hey," Kit said quietly. "We were about to order food. Carver needs protein."

"And to never drink again," Carver muttered. "Fey wine is not something to fuck around with."

"Duh, it has literal magic in it." Zack sat down beside Kit and snagged the menu. "Do you want to split a pizza?"

"Full moon's coming up. I need to stack on the carbs and protein, so sure. As long as we can get some wings and breadsticks," Kit said.

"And no deep dish. Too much cheese."

"Now I know you're weird," Carver said. "Chicago deep dish is the best."

"Dude, gross," Zack said.

"That means you haven't had a good one."

"I don't think I've had one ever," Kit replied.

"That's right! First time in the area for you," Zack said. "We've got to go out. We're not going to get the good shit from the hotel restaurant."

"The hotel restaurant is five stars," Carver said. "And delivers up to the room."

The three of them tumbled into an argument about whether or not trekking out for the pizza would be worth the while. Kit and Zack eventually won, and they headed out into the afternoon on a mission for food.

Carver's right. Life doesn't always suck.

CHAPTER 33

November slid into December in that peculiar way that time could run away with itself. Though the nights stretched in length, they had a habit of becoming dawn sooner and sooner. Roger stayed alert for some indication of Dmitri's fate, but on the few occasions he was in Seamus's presence, he made no mention of him. Anton was absent from gatherings and the donor houses, and no one spoke of him either. That wasn't unusual for him but left Roger grasping at the void for any hint of his former lover.

Invitations flooded their social calendar. Roger did his best to dazzle new and old acquaintances alike. His smiles felt less and less forced. Not in the way they had in the past, though. Instead of becoming the color of butterfly he believed they wanted of him, he remained more calm, constant. The inevitable creep of the tide upon the shore, missed more in its absence than noted for its sparkle.

The suite remained their makeshift home, though Roger had begun the research to buy a house. The damn things never seemed to stay on the market long, and he hadn't found the right one to jump into the fracas for.

The week before the Winter's Grand Ball, they pushed the

furniture in the living room to the edges each night and practiced their ballroom dancing. Zack had been in contact with Candide's head pet, and their outfits for the ball were ordered and tailored.

New Year's was less than two weeks away, and though Roger had the ball to worry about that evening, the minutes counting down to when he would finally strike out against Seamus seemed to etch themselves in Roger's skin. He had plenty of time; he had none of it left.

But at least tonight there's a party. Roger knocked on Kit's bedroom door.

In a robe, Kit opened the door. They were freshly showered, and their natural musk mixed with the scent of strawberries.

"I know we're all getting ready," Roger said.

"But you're looking for a nibble," Kit said.

"If you don't mind."

Kit let Roger into their bedroom. Clothes were strewn about the room in the sort of chaos unique to haphazard youth. Roger hadn't entered Kit's room often during their stay in the hotel, but he knew their scent. And there was a pair of underwear that didn't belong to them. Roger stood beside the pair, looking down at it, then glanced over at Kit with a raised eyebrow.

Kit was sitting on their bed. When they spotted what Roger had noticed, they blushed, though they tried to act cool about it. "Carver and I hook up sometimes. You said our bodies are our own."

"They are." Roger joined Kit on the bed. "It's fine that you keep each other company."

"Is it?" Kit demanded. They got onto their knees and faced Roger. "Other masters would have a problem with their pets hooking up without permission."

"That wasn't the deal that we struck," Roger said.

"Yeah, but what if I wanted that out of you?" Kit said.

Roger leaned back and sifted through Kit's desires. There was something familiar they were emitting, something that Roger hadn't paid much attention to. "Ah. You want to be someone's submissive."

"I thought that was how vamps and their pets operated," Kit said.

"Being a dominant vampire takes a certain mindset," Roger said. "I've never held to it twenty-four seven. Was that what you were hoping I would provide?"

"Zack's not the only one who can keep their ears open." Kit sat cross-legged and picked at the comforter. "People say you're one of the better coven masters. That you have a firm hand."

"What I seem in public isn't how I am in private." Roger hooked his finger under Kit's chin and made them look up. "And I'm not exactly how I used to be. Vampires can change."

"Oh."

"I'm disappointing you."

"Yeah. Kind of. But this is kind of new for me. People were a little more private about some of the displays in Taliville. You had to get invited to watch a flogging; you didn't just walk past it almost every night."

"That's true." Roger glanced to Kit's neck. They were already wearing their collar. They'd made more of a habit of it than necessary. *How am I only just realizing this?* "You want to feel the ownership a collar should provide."

Kit's hand went to their throat, touching the crest tag and then drifting to the side. "I think I do. I used to have these fantasies that I thought were wacky but only scratched the surface of what I've seen. But it's also obvious. You really only have eyes for Zack and Takashi. I don't blip your radar."

"Should I be apologizing?" Roger asked.

"Nope. You made it clear from the get-go. This was trans-actional. I'll be fine." Kit held out their wrist.

Roger took hold of their offered wrist. There wasn't much

more he could say, so he used a thread of his power to soothe Kit's nerves and then bit them. Their blood held a trace of their werefox magic and eased the itch building in Roger's skin. He only drank enough to ease his hunger rather than sate it.

"Thank you," Roger said.

Kit held their wrist upward, and the wound began to close. It would be another minute or so before the minor injury was completely closed and a little longer than that before it disappeared entirely.

"You do matter to me, Kit," Roger said.

"Yeah, but only kind of."

"Kit."

Rather than look at him, they shook their head and kept their gaze on their wound. "The money's good, you've always been up-front with what you want, and I got out of Taliville. What more could I really want?"

"It isn't awful to want more," Roger replied. He ducked down so that he was in their eyeline. "You should have someone to guard your heart, if that's what you want. But you're right. That's not me."

"Ugh. You're going to make me cry, and that's going to wreck my makeup."

"I should be getting dressed myself," Roger said. "I'll see you in a few minutes?"

"Of course," Kit said.

Roger left their bedroom and slowly walked down the stairs. The open staircase lent him too much vision of the suite, and his gaze was drawn toward the darkness past the glass doors leading to the balcony. With the lights on in the suite, seeing anything of their small portion of the Chicago skyline or Lake Michigan beyond was impossible. But the world was out there. Waiting.

Maybe journaling is miserable for me. I'm falling too easily into this brooding mood. Only the conversation that he'd had with

Kit sounded very close to the dozens he'd had in the past. Pets left, for one reason or another. Some few he'd actually dismissed, but most seemed to grow tired of him or tired of how he behaved toward them and left.

Roger let his hand drift along the length of the railing until he finally reached the first floor. They had practiced a little at dusk and hadn't bothered to move the couches back. Carver had pushed one of the couches a few inches out of his way and was behind the bar.

"What are you looking for?" Roger asked.

"Can you believe everything is top-shelf? I'm looking for some lower-brand stuff so I can feel the burn, but it's all expensive shit. Ah! This'll work." Carver straightened with a bottle of rum in his hands. He was dressed for the night. His deep blue tuxedo had a double-breasted jacket. The velvet had the lightest shimmer to the fabric, and he had a nearly translucent silver shirt on with it. Instead of the usual collar, he had a bow tie made from a custom fabric with Roger's crest. Either Kit or Zack had convinced him to try a little makeup again, and the hint of eyeliner brought attention to the sparkle in his eyes.

"You look amazing," Roger said.

"Yeah, but who wears it better?" Zack asked.

Zack was leaning against the doorframe leading to the master bedroom. He had an identical tuxedo and bow tie to Carver's, though fitted to his slimmer form. In addition to the silver cufflinks—of which Roger had made certain they were pure silver and outfitted Carver with matching ones—Zack wore the white-gold dagger necklace that Takashi had given him for his birthday. With his hair styled and light makeup on, he had the full swagger of a man ready for an evening of refined entertainment.

Roger had gotten hard more than a few times while looking at Zack, but he wasn't sure he'd ever had such a quick reaction to seeing his lover dressed.

"Ha, ready before you for a change," Zack teased.

"You are," Roger said breathlessly.

"I think I win the contest," Zack said to Carver.

"Okay, one, I didn't agree to a contest. Two, he's madly in love with you, so biased win at best," Carver said.

"Yeah. You're right. We both look smoking hot."

"Could someone give me a little help?" Kit called from upstairs. "My dress is being annoying."

"I got it," Zack said when Carver started for the stairs. He shot a grin at Roger as he went. "I think I better get out of eyeline before someone messes up my clothes."

Roger laughed at the remark, but Zack hadn't been entirely wrong. He definitely wanted to make a mess of him. *Maybe when we get back.* Still chuckling, he headed into the master bedroom while Zack went for Kit's bedroom.

The flurry of movement continued in the master bedroom. Takashi was mid-preparations, nearly dressed. As Roger entered the room, he was fussing with his cufflinks. All of their tuxedos had been made by an Unseelie tailor newer to the city, though Roger was quickly falling in love with the tailor's keen sense of style. Takashi's black silk shirt perfectly matched the shade of his fine wool pants, and the cut accented every inch of his body, making him absolutely delicious. His jacket was of the same wool, only there was a glimmering silver pattern in the weave. It lay on the bed, and the curving loops and scrolling accents seemed coiled, ready for action.

"I might be the last one ready for once," Roger remarked as he started shedding the clothes he'd been lounging in.

"You had plenty of warning," Takashi replied.

"I was distracted, then hungry." Roger pulled his tuxedo out from the closet. His was silver in color, nearly metallic in its sheen. Across the back of it, in a fine black weave, was a kraken, its long tentacles reaching out from the center and wrapping around his upper arms. The fabric itself was custom and had cost an extravagant amount of money to have made in time, but that was the luck of dealing with fey merchants. They could manipulate their realm to give them the time, if necessary. And the touch of it was comforting, though a touch slick, and left the slightest buzz to the skin. His shirt was a shade of midnight blue, so dark it was black.

"I was thinking of wearing my hair tied back tonight," Roger said.

"Seems criminal," Takashi replied. "I love it down."

Roger grinned at him and stole a kiss. "I'll leave it for you to undo later that way."

"That's tempting in itself," Takashi murmured.

"And I have a ribbon that matches the tux. Seems a waste not to use it."

"Did you have an earring?" Takashi asked.

"Been debating between a few." Roger opened the jewelry case on the dresser. He'd added to his small collection of earrings. Many were simple hoops, and some few were more complicated and had jewels or pendants that dangled.

"I do have something." Takashi took a jewelry box out of a drawer and handed it to Roger.

"What's this?" Roger asked with a grin.

"Something that I thought would fit."

Roger opened it to find a platinum stud earring with four dangling tiny sapphires in the shade of Zack's and Carver's suits. Kit would be wearing a dress featuring the same color as well. Roger's smile grew, and he kissed Takashi again. "Perfect."

"I should go before I'm tempted to keep you out of the clothing," Takashi said.

"Have you seen Zack? You might be less tempted if you stay here," Roger joked.

"Perhaps I'll just have to close my eyes until everyone's ready to leave, then." Takashi picked up his jacket and draped it over his shoulder as he left the bedroom.

Delaying wouldn't stop the world from turning. Roger freshened up, fixed his hair, and then dressed in his tuxedo. Wearing it was like slipping into a glove, cozy yet utterly smooth. He left the bedroom just as Kit was coming down the staircase.

They had a tuxedo half-jacket that match Zack's and Carver's while the dress itself was a silver ballroom-length gown. The glimmer of it sparkled in rainbows rather than the colder silver light that came from the boys' shirts and Roger's tux. The sheer top layer of the skirt had tiny diamonds sewn here and there, adding to the prismatic rainbow glint. They'd leaned into cooler colors for their makeup, embracing a wintery theme. Rather than a bow tie, they wore a silvery collar with Roger's crest tag on it.

"You look stunning," Roger said.

Kit grinned. "Thanks."

"The sooner we get to the formal event, the sooner we get back and out of these suits, right?" Carver said.

"You've been getting too used to walking around half-naked," Zack commented as he headed for the door.

"Didn't you ever notice what he wore in Taliville?" Kit asked. "He's like always been half-naked."

"Spandex is clothing," Carver replied.

Roger lingered, the last to reach the door. Part of him wanted to call the whole thing off. The Winter's Grand Ball would be an event for the city's supernatural elite. The wealthy and magically gifted would be out in full finery for the evening. The five of them would be under scrutiny from other leaders and important beings, and there was every chance they wouldn't measure up.

We'll be fine. Roger touched his new earring, repeated the sentiment to himself, and left the suite.

CHAPTER 34

Chateau de Vampire was decked out in deep evergreen, light blue, and a brilliant shade of white, from the lights that adorned the walkway into the building to small Christmas trees decorating the hallways. Zack had believed he'd seen the place crowded before, but as they made their way through the halls to the magnificent ballroom, they must have passed hundreds of people. Everyone was dressed to impress, and some supernaturals had dispensed with their human guises. In addition to the myriad of fey who had revealed themselves, shifters who had control of their abilities had adopted their hybrid forms. Some had the kind of control where they'd only changed their ears and hands, while others had a full animal face but could still manage human speech.

"I wish I'd known they'd be doing that!" Kit whispered to Zack.

"Can't you pop it out?" Zack asked.

"If I go partial, I get a tail, which would not work with this dress. Plus, the ecto-shed ruins clothing."

"So these people have been holding their forms for hours?"

"This much magic in the air? It's almost more of a challenge keeping my human skin," Kit replied.

"Huh. Did not know that."

Kit looped their arm in Zack's. "And somehow, I'm not surprised, hunter boy."

"Did the whole city turn out for this?" Carver asked.

"There are millions of people in Chicago," Zack countered.

Carver gave him a flat, unamused look. "Fine. The whole *supernatural* community?"

"Anyone who matters, from what Mara said."

"Awesome," Carver muttered. "I hate crowds."

With Roger and Takashi in the lead, they entered the queue to be announced into the ballroom. Idle conversation floated through the hall, though the line moved fairly quickly. Zack fought to keep from fidgeting with his clothes or his hair or from rubbing his eye as he had the lightest bit of silver eyeshadow on. Kit had insisted that it brought out the steely quality of his eyes, but without a mirror, he hadn't been able to see for himself.

Just before them in line were two young white guys, roughly in their mid-twenties. One had dark brown hair, and the other had a lighter shade, and their tuxedos were in a deep blue color with hints of gold. The whole length of the wait, they had a quiet tango of words bouncing between them, but they'd perfected the art of couple speak, and Zack couldn't hear them. The taller, darker-haired one handed his card over to the announcer as they reached the podium.

The announcer nodded to them, then proclaimed as they continued forward, "Benjamin Clarke-Coldwell, Mage of the Circle of the Enduring, and his husband, Noah Clarke-Coldwell, Warlock."

The couple bled into the larger group, and then it was time for Roger to hand over his card.

"Roger, Gentleman Pirate of the Seven Seas, Captain of the

Great Lakes Coven," the announcer said, "and his partner, Takashi, the Sly Polyglot, and their collection."

Roger and Takashi paused long enough for the announcer to finish, and then they led the way toward the right side of the ballroom. Zack kept back from the spotlight, though he couldn't help watching them in the moment the rest of the room was taking them in. The kraken woven into Roger's tuxedo jacket seemed to writhe, though Roger stood in place.

Then they were in the party.

The ballroom was three times the size of Nell's. Throughout the room were large ice sculptures of various wintertime figures. One was of Jack Frost, complete with puffs of cold air slipping out from between his lips. Another was of the Queen of Darkness, done in purple ice rather than the pale blue many of the others were done in. And then there were the Santa Clauses of various cultures. A zing of brisk air had infiltrated the party, but whether that was the ice statues or the presence of so much magic in one place, Zack wasn't sure.

On a balcony to the left was a full orchestra. Their current song was a brighter medley of several Christmas classics. The far end of the first floor had large glass windows that revealed the dark skies outside. Three massive chandeliers glimmered, the large brass fixtures having a graceful flow to each of its seven arms.

Waitstaff dressed in black-and-white outfits circled the outer rim of the room, offering drinks and small appetizers. Zack snagged what he thought would be some kind of sweet but turned out to be a spinach turnover. It tasted all right, but he was glad for a passing tray of champagne to wash the thing down with.

"Is that a buffet?" Kit asked excitedly.

"Those are the tiniest sandwiches I've ever seen," Carver remarked.

"They're meant to be finger food," Zack replied. "You

know, one bite so you don't have a chance to get it on your clothes or have your hands full while making introductions."

Kit clutched Carver's arm and looked to Roger. "Can we check it out?"

"Stay together," Roger said. "I don't want any of you on our own unless necessary."

"Yes, master," Kit and Carver said before zooming off toward the buffet.

"You're not going with them?" Takashi asked Zack.

"I'm trying to convince my stomach that I didn't make a mistake having the snack I just ate, master," Zack said quietly.

Roger put a hand in the center of his back and leaned in to kiss his temple. "You look fantastic."

"So does everyone else," Zack whispered.

"My God, it *is* you," a man with a nasally voice said. He was a white guy on the older side, though Zack was pretty sure he wasn't elderly yet. With a broad grin, he angled into their cluster. "Nicholas Snyder. It has been decades since I've seen you. Of course, you haven't changed, but alas, time takes its toll on us mere mortals."

"Ah, how true," Roger said politely. "Excuse me for not recognizing you. It has been ages. How have you been?"

"Married. Kids, they're grown," Snyder replied. "Have you seen Elias around? Elias Coldwell? He's a Magus on the Council these days."

"You don't say," Roger said.

"There he is. Come along, you must talk to him again. Elias, Elias, look who I found. *Roger*."

Caught in the current, Zack followed along behind Roger. He muttered, "Who the hell are these guys?"

"Mages I used to party with," Roger murmured to him.

Roger made a show of acknowledging Elias, who was an older guy as well. Conversation bubbled and brewed between them. Others joined in, and soon, Roger had a tight knot of people around him. Takashi was clever and charming, and the little gathering seemed to take them as a couple and completely disregard Zack. Despite his best attempt, he was soon on the outside of the group.

Not like I had anything to say anyway. Zack began doing what he'd been doing for the last few months. He made mental notes and correlated what data he already had with the new facts. Most of what was spoken was entirely gossip, but that could be useful down the line. The mages seemed entirely unimpressed with warlocks. They kept poking Roger for his opinions on what side Seamus would take when the "inevitable conflict" occurred.

"It's bullshit, you know," Dryden whispered.

Zack had seen him approaching but had decided not to turn toward him. He kept his focus forward, which apparently encouraged Dryden to invade his personal space.

Dryden's long, auburn hair was in an extravagant braid, and he wore a forest-green suit with silver accents. He had an impish grin as he stood at Zack's shoulder, mouth close to Zack's ear. "Aren't you going to ask 'what's bullshit?'"

"I already know," Zack replied in a low voice. "The mages have been worried the warlocks are going to strike for a decade. They never do."

"Oh, they're worried about more than that. The warlocks are the ones actually bothering to push magic these days," Dryden said. "Witches, too, and the odd sorcerer, but their magic has different roots than the mage and warlock. Want to know the difference between them?"

"Between mages and warlocks, it's the acceptance into a secret society or independent learning," Zack said.

"Clever boy."

"You don't get to call me that."

"I do when I'm fifty years older than you." When Zack frowned at him, Dryden smiled at him. "I'm fey, remember?"

"Right," Zack replied.

Dryden held out his hand. "Dance with me?"

Turning someone down would be rude, and Zack was standing around, attempting to invent some reason to pay attention. He caught Roger's gaze for a moment and motioned to Dryden. After signaling that he would be going with Dryden, he took his hand and let Dryden lead him out onto the dance floor.

As a new song began, Dryden stepped into the pattern of the dance and drew Zack along with him. The waltz had a lighthearted air to it, and Zack easily stayed in pace with him. Dryden's smile was probably how he charmed people so he wouldn't get in trouble. With delight, he said, "You have no problem following."

"I honestly wouldn't know how to lead," Zack replied.

"I doubt that's true." They danced another few moments before Dryden continued. "We have the same saying that mortals do. Look out for the quiet ones."

"I was raised a hunter, and we have a saying about your kind," Zack said. "The more you sparkle, the more dangerous you are."

"Moi? Dangerous?" Dryden faked a gasp and then laughed.

The motion of their dance caused a light blurring of their surroundings. The music kept a brighter tempo alongside the click of heels and the swish of fabric. Voices murmured, dancers talking to one another the way that Dryden was carrying on a conversation with Zack.

Zack kept his chin up, his poise as naturally perfect as he could. "Anyone in the coven or adjacent to it could be dangerous. Hell, everyone in this room is."

"Except one of the flutists. She is an absolute doll." Dryden snickered at that.

Zack glanced up at the orchestra, scanning the various musicians. Among them was a doll, sitting on a chair with a flute to her lips. "Is that ..." But then he realized that dolls wouldn't be able to make a flute work correctly and that his hip, where his tattoo was, grew warm. Between one blink and the next, the "doll" was revealed to be a young woman.

"An illusion," Zack drawled. "How original."

"I don't see you casting any," Dryden replied.

"Fair. I guess."

"How did you see through it so quickly?"

"It wasn't logical. Should have had her playing the drums."

"Oh! That would be better." Dryden spun Zack. "You know, I think I'm beginning to like you. And this has been a wonderful dance."

"Yeah. This has been ... weird but fun," Zack said cautiously.

"I don't mind that," Dryden said with another grin. When the song came to an end, he bowed to Zack.

Zack returned the bow. As he straightened, Ezra Gladwell approached him and offered his hand the same way that Dryden had. Zack swallowed. Looking at Ezra was like staring at a multiverse version of himself, only with fiery red hair. He took Ezra's hand and started another spin around the dance floor with him.

Ezra took the lead. "If anybody notices us, they're going to talk about this little pairing. Sorry."

My look-alike has a British accent. Or his has an American one. At least we're not completely identical in appearance. Zack kept his steely, calm expression. "Because they'd think the last person I'd ever touch would be the infamous Ezra Gladwell?"

"That, and we could be brothers. It's a bit odd," Ezra said. "Has Roger been honest with you?"

"About what?" Zack asked.

"You must know by now that he's my sire, not Seamus," Ezra replied.

"That came up, yeah. How did the family get it wrong?"

Ezra glanced off to the mid-distance. Zack followed his eyeline and spotted that Roger had stepped onto the dance floor with Candide, while Takashi was dancing with one of the mages. In a voice that made him sound more ancient than anyone else Zack knew, Ezra said, "I found Mary a few years after our family died. My twin. I'd shared everything with her until Roger. He was my first real secret. My vampire. My immortality. It all sounded so romantic. And because of that, she didn't know about him. I tried to beg forgiveness, but all she wanted was the name of the vampire who had 'corrupted' me, as she put it. So I said Seamus. Because as wicked and sinful as Roger can be, he isn't evil."

And so began the rumor and a legacy. Zack turned his head back toward Ezra, but the question forming in his mind slipped into shadow. Intensity could come in many forms, and Zack recognized the spark in Ezra's eyes. He'd seen that same quality in pictures of himself. Joy could be as fiercely felt as anger. Looking at Candide and Roger dancing, Ezra had that utter happiness in his gaze.

"You still love him," Zack whispered.

"I've always loved him, but not the way I love her now," Ezra replied as he brought his attention back to Zack. "You must have noticed. People fall for him easily, but he never lets them in."

He's let me in. And Takashi. Zack kept that thought for himself, and they finished out the dance.

The next song was livelier, and Zack was about to make his way off the dance floor when a fey woman stepped forward. She had a long gown of deep greens and purples. Her skin was a pale blue, her hair ice white, her eyes a solid black, and she had a pair of long ebony antlers. She was taller than him by at least a foot. With a smile that was a bit too wide, she said, "I would adore a partner for this next song."

"I'll admit I don't know how to lead, my lady," Zack said.

"Oh, I can do that," the woman replied. Her voice had a strange melodic quality to it, like ice breaking upon concrete, but in a musically gifted way.

So Zack was whisked back out to the dance floor by his strange new partner. The other dancers gave them a wider berth. She had a grace that Zack found easy to match, and she gave a delighted laugh as they swept out toward the center of the floor.

When their song ended, she put a long finger under Zack's chin and tilted his head farther up. Though he was still on his feet, he felt like he'd been drawn up onto his tiptoes. Her smile grew wider. "Oh," she breathed, nearly a moan, "oh, you are simply magnificent. I can't wait to see what you become. Do remember to call on me."

She kissed his forehead—or she *might* have kissed his forehead. The moment was so quick, like seeing a figure in the corner of one's eye and then turning to find a shadow. Before Zack could make sense of the sensation, she was across the dance floor, picking out her next partner.

Luckily, Takashi stepped in next. He brought Zack closer to the edge of the dancing rather than the center. He teased, "You are allowed to say no to people."

"I think saying no to a polite request from a fey is a good way to get cursed," Zack said.

"Especially her," Takashi replied. "I meant, going forward, that you don't have to dance with everyone."

"I don't know. Josefina spent hours teaching me how to do this. And I'm kind of having fun. Even with my last partner."

Takashi raised an eyebrow. "Do you know who that was?"

"Uh, an archfey?"

"Lady Belladonna of the Chicago Court of Shadows," Takashi said. "So not just *an* archfey, but one of *the* archfey of the city."

In a hurried whisper, Zack said, "She told me to call on her."

"What?"

"Yeah. That's weird, right?"

"It could be good. Very good for us."

Zack wanted to ask how, but the music came to an abrupt stop. Though the announcer had been continuing to introduce guests, the whole of the party seemed to turn to witness the newest arrivals.

"Seamus, Terror of the Isles, Devil Pirate of the Seven Seas, Dread Noble of the Countryside, Architect of the Shadowborn Rail, Patron of the City's Rebirth, and Master of the Great Lakes Coven," the announcer proclaimed. "His partner of centuries, Anton, Warlock of the Midnight Hour, Captain of the Great Lakes Coven. And their collection."

A round of applause complimented Seamus and Anton as they stepped into the party. Seamus's tux was a midnight black that seemed to absorb light. Anton wore a bloodred tux with a brilliant white shirt. They'd brought eight mortals with them; Vincent was at the front of the well-dressed group coming in behind Seamus and Anton. Each one was decked out in a different color so that the group of them looked like a clustered rainbow.

A ripple flowed through the party. The ice statues had left the room cooler, but Seamus's arrival chilled conversations to whispers. As the music began anew, the whispers became murmurs and recovered a measure of their earlier delight.

"Shall we continue?" Takashi asked.

"Yeah," Zack said.

They danced. Falling into the fun of it, Zack found keeping his balance and poise was second nature. All too soon, the song was over.

"Maybe another one?" Zack asked.

"I was hoping for a turn," Roger said smoothly.

Zack spun to face him.

After having the opportunity to gaze upon him for months, Roger should have been ordinary for Zack to behold. Yet seeing his smile carved into Zack's heart like he'd never looked upon him before while tracing familiar patterns in his soul. Roger had tied his raven-black hair into a low ponytail, but the simplicity accentuated his beauty rather than detracted. The earring with its four tiny sapphires was new; the roguish quality it lent him wasn't. When Roger had said his tux would be silver, Zack thought he'd stand out. Instead, Roger seemed to be the living embodiment of the party—handsome, stylish, ethereal, and yet entirely real.

Roger offered his hand, and Zack took it without breaking eye contact. The swell of violins proceeded a waltz, and Roger guided Zack through the first few steps before taking bolder ones. Soon, they were gliding. Zack could feel the touch of the floor, but only briefly. He wouldn't look down; he didn't want to break the magic if they were somehow floating.

A bracing cold swept across the dance floor, and Zack fought the instinctual urge to look behind him. Instead, he measured that aura, felt the press of the too-familiar wintery blast. As he and Roger naturally turned with the movement of their dance, he caught sight of Seamus dancing with Vincent. Like they had for Lady Belladonna, the others started to clear a bubble of space around Seamus. And Seamus was pressing that bubble ever closer to where Roger and Zack were dancing.

Roger pressed his cheek to Zack's, his words a quick tumble. "Are you comfortable showing off?"

"Definitely."

Roger's steps had been an elegant balance, and while that remained at the core, the shift in his stance lent more power to his movements. Knowing him, knowing the touch of him, Zack let himself be carried away and trusted his body to follow Roger. The first spin was a blur; the second brought a genuine smile to Zack's lips.

Box step was too clunky of a descriptor for the way they crossed the floor. Zack eased through the long strides and movements. As their rotations continued, Zack realized that the floor had practically cleared except for Seamus and

Vincent, the mage and warlock pair, and Candide with Lady Belladonna.

The tattoo on Zack's hip began to warm. With a quick frown, he caught Roger's gaze.

"Not me," Roger whispered. "He's throwing off an intense aura."

The crowd had shuffled another few feet back from the main dancing area but remained to watch. Several of the faces —Zack didn't have time to truly evaluate them—were slack, as if caught in a loop.

Seamus was attempting another manipulation. These were the preeminent members of the supernatural community of Chicago, and Seamus was asserting his authority as a badass vampire. No, he was marking his territory.

And that dug under Zack's skin and festered in an instant. The party had been lovely, even if it was full of people who could snap him in half with a thought, and he'd been having fun. *Seamus can't help pissing on everything.*

"Can you do anything to counter him?" Zack asked.

"I can try."

Zack squeezed Roger's arm. "Then do it."

"I may need a little blood," Roger murmured.

"Lucky for you, I've got plenty," Zack said with a wink.

Roger smiled at him as if he were made of magic. As they continued to revolve around the dance floor, Roger navigated them closer to the edge. His eyes flared ruby red. He brought Zack's wrist to his mouth like it was a natural step in the waltz and sank his fangs into his flesh.

It had to be one of the sexiest moves Zack had ever seen in his entire life. He could feel a flush in his cheeks. People were watching. More than watching. Zack gave himself over to the touch of Roger's power. Desire emanated from him. A want of joy, a touch of love. Basking in Roger's ability was like being spooned between him and Takashi. Not overtly sexual, but the promise that anything was possible.

Roger was sharing the desire to *live*, to truly appreciate all of life's tiny joys along with the epic ones.

Muscle memory made keeping in step with Roger possible as Zack strove to see the effect Roger was having on others. Gentle smiles greeted him. He and Roger were the crest of a wave, and where there was tension, the crowd itself seemed to sigh as they made their way past. Roger stopped drinking before they made the full circle, but his magic continued to flow. Though Seamus's cold fear continued to claw the air in the center of the dance floor, Roger had formed a barrier. And as the song drew to a close, and the audience clapped, that barrier flooded into the center and dissipated the chill that Seamus had been laying out.

With a bit of blood and a smooth application of will, Roger had countered a vampire three times his age.

Roger wasn't just some vampire. He hadn't been that to Zack in a long time. Yet, in the moment, Zack was taking him in, and beyond the bias love gave him, he saw how special he was. And he tumbled head over heels for him all over again. As the crowd swept in to dance, Zack looked for Takashi and found him nearing them.

Vampires couldn't cast reflections, but Zack was certain he saw the same sort of light in his soul mirrored in Takashi's gaze. *And that's not just for Roger. He's falling in love with both of us.*

"You were wonderful," Takashi said as he offered Zack a napkin.

One boyfriend had already had a taste. Trying not to let the blood spill onto the floor, Zack exposed his wrist again for Takashi. "Want some?"

Takashi's eyes shifted from deep blue to a vibrant red. "If you wouldn't mind."

"Go ahead."

Takashi sealed his lips around the wound Roger had created and gently lapped the blood spilling from it. The slide of his tongue along the tender flesh made Zack tingle from his toes to his cheeks, the sensation evolving into a warmth that pooled through him. That longing to get his boyfriends back to their bed and naked remained as Takashi took one last lick and then put the napkin he had brought over Zack's wrist.

Anyone might be watching, but Zack didn't give a damn. He belonged to Roger and Takashi, and they belonged to him. *The rest of the world can fuck off for five minutes.*

Unfortunately, their little bubble didn't last that long. They'd managed to slip away from the dancing, but that meant people felt comfortable approaching Roger and engaging him in conversation. Compliments flew in, ranging from his grace to his magical prowess.

But there was bound to be someone who wouldn't want to compliment them. The crowd gathering around Roger seemed to forget Zack existed, which suited him all right. He scanned the party for the real problem.

Long minutes dragged past before Zack finally caught sight of Seamus emerging from a hallway and reentering the party. Other partygoers parted the path for him until he stopped beside an Unseelie man. His pets in their rainbow attire swirled up beside him.

A color was missing. Purple.

Vincent.

The warm, cozy cloak that had wrapped around Zack's mind fell away to the stark cold. His gut didn't sink, but his resolve hardened. There was nothing he could do against Seamus at the party; they'd left the enchanted daggers in the safe in the suite. But he couldn't simply stand by. He had to know what had happened.

Even if what I find is a corpse. Zack leaned up to kiss Roger's cheek and squeezed his shoulder. He murmured, "I'll be back."

Then he threaded his way through the crowd toward that hallway.

CHAPTER 35

"Bold little thing," the mage Snyder said.

The man had been an insufferable prick in the 1980s. The son of a Magus, spoiled so thoroughly in childhood, he continued to spread rot throughout his adult life. And after witnessing Zack express tenderness, he was perpetuating the crass ideology that pets were pieces of tinsel to watch glitter and nothing more.

That's how the outsiders see what we do in the coven. Roger kept a polite smile on his lips, one that had a brief second of genuine emotion as Takashi handed him a flute of champagne. He held Takashi's hand. *He asked me, when does pretending become reality?*

"For a pet, don't you agree?" Snyder said, flailing in an attempt to keep the conversation going.

I don't want to continue that cycle. Roger chuckled and shook his head. "I'm hoping with the new year, we'll finally move away from such archaic behavior in the coven. I think of Zack as one of my boyfriends, and my other 'pets' are truly donors. After all, I pay them handsomely, and I am not the keeper of their lives."

"An attitude they're sharing in New York these days," Takashi added.

"I think it's brilliant," a woman replied. She shivered for emphasis. "The whole collection thing seems so ghoulish."

"Don't let the ghouls hear you say that. They'll be thoroughly wounded by that idea. Keeping living flesh instead of devouring? Absolutely revolting to them," Anton said. He threaded his way through the others clustered around Roger. "Darling, you were magnificent. I was wondering, might I have a go?"

Anton made a slight bow and held out his hand. The shimmer in his deep red eyes twisted a knot in Roger's gut. Had Anton heard what he'd said about the new year? Had Dmitri given him up? *I can't give in to fear now.* Roger smiled and accepted Anton's invitation. "If the rest of you will excuse me, I'll be back shortly."

"Not too shortly," Anton called over his shoulder as they made their way through the crowd.

The orchestra picked an ominous melody for the next dance. Roger remained as far from Anton as he could, but then Anton put a hand on the small of his back and drew him into a tighter position. Of course, Anton led—Roger wasn't surprised about that—and his pace was swift, constantly shifting and turning them so that Roger strained to keep abreast of where they were in the room.

"You have always been a delight," Anton said, his tone intimate. "Since the night we spotted you, I have admired the way you can simply keep taking everything that has been thrown at you."

"Thank you," Roger said politely.

"And it seems that three decades of sleep did wonders for you."

Roger stiffened. When he tried to catch Anton's eye, Anton continued his now grueling pace. They were chest to chest, and the only way to switch that position would be to fight him. Unwilling to make a scene, Roger was caught in the trap of Anton's arms.

"I spent my time away—"

"In a *coffin*," Anton finished. "Don't bother lying to me further about it. I've known for over a year now."

Yet Seamus had never said a word, never hinted that he knew the truth. Roger frowned, especially as Anton decided that was a perfect moment to make him spin. His balance kept him from slamming up against Anton, though Anton had put effort into making him come back too quickly.

"Does he know?" Roger asked.

"No, no. No, I haven't told him," Anton replied. "I've been caught up in my own affairs, and if I did that, I'd have to admit what I did, and that might be construed as cheating."

"I don't follow."

"You didn't think Quinn came up with that little plot on his own, did you?" Anton chided. He pressed his cheek against Roger's. "He was so terribly distraught about those humans he lost to the Butcher. And I had a flash of inspiration. He could lure that vile hunter to the depths of Nell's sanctuary. Either the hunter would die, or Quinn, or you—or perhaps all three if Nell discovered the ruse and saw a problem!"

"You wanted me killed?" Roger said.

"'Wanted' is such a strong word." Anton put a little distance between Roger's cheek and his, then spun him again. "But once I found you, you couldn't stay in that coma. I needed you out, and if you happened to die, well, then *technically*, it wouldn't have been at my hand, and I would've won."

"So you're not the one that put me in it, then," Roger said.

"Oh, no. Though I could've done it to Dmitri, but that might have been cheating."

Sweating, higher pulse, goose bumps—all of those would have been a mortal's response. Roger was glad that he could smother his fears behind the mental wall of his mind rather than have his body betray him. But when he caught sight of Anton's grin in the corner of his mind, he knew that the ancient vampire could feel every twitch of his inner psyche. *Do what Zack and Takashi would do. Get information.*

"That's the second time you've referenced cheating," Roger said.

"It is. I always knew you were twice as clever as you were pretending to be." Anton beamed at him. "But then you pretended to have all the wit of a worm in a rainstorm."

"You and Seamus scratch your itches with whoever you like, and I doubt that you have love in your heart for anyone else." Roger hoped to spot someone familiar in the crowd, someone who might come to his rescue, but they were moving too quickly. "The only other cheat I can think of is a game."

"Very close!" Anton said patronizingly. "Haven't you ever wondered how you and Dmitri have survived these long centuries? How it is that other vampires died? That some few slipped away from Seamus and I?"

"I only know of one who got away."

Anton rolled his eyes. "Josefina. Formally. But *informally*, vampires have slipped away from time to time. My little rings stop working after fifty miles. You simply haven't heard of them again because they change their name. Two of your own sirelings have vanished that way, Roger. James and Phoenix. I think Phoenix is even still in the city! Have you gone looking for them?"

"No," Roger said shortly.

"No, because you don't want them caught in your hell." Anton pouted his bottom lip and dramatically batted his eyes. "You would have never made it back to the city except for the bet."

Startled, Roger tried to stop the dance, but Anton tugged him onward. "Bet?"

"I'm not supposed to say. Goes against the rules, but then, the gamble has been decisively settled." Anton pulled Roger close so that they were cheek to cheek, and Roger fought the urge to fight Anton in the middle of the dance floor. Continuing in a whisper, Anton said, "We were going through sirelings like tissue paper. One after another. Oh, we had a few loyal ones we liked that had their own ships but no constant companions other than each other. One of us would make someone, then the other would get jealous, and then, oops, we had another dead sireling. We were driving each other insane."

Roger could remember the echoing voices in the dead of night overcoming the creaking of the ship on the waves. The crew, save for what few were needed, would be sleeping. Seamus and Anton would shout at each other in the captain's quarters until a crescendo struck. Most times, there would be another kind of noise after. One that Roger had never stopped to analyze. They could've been having sex. Or they could've been torturing someone. On rare occasion, it had been him, and he had never chalked it up to torture. *But I never truly chose to join them in those years.*

"Dmitri and I," Roger rasped, "we were some gamble between you?"

"Sirelings made on the same night, buried as near to the same grave as possible so that we could see whose would live longest," Anton crooned. "One for him, one for me. We had very few terms. No one was ever supposed to know—that would ruin it entirely. And we weren't allowed to kill the other one's sireling. Anything else could. I grew very cross with you in the 1800s. I can't remember the reason. But you should have died in the house fire that hunter set. Of course, Seamus found out I had an indirect hand in that, and, well, I did have to make up for that little stunt. It's a good thing you survived."

"Our lives have been a *game* to you?" Roger growled.

"The very best," Anton replied with glee. "And look at you! I thought you were neutered and declawed. Instead, you demonstrated a level of skill this evening that I didn't think you had the balls to do, let alone the ability. But after centuries, you are finally using those fine little points to tear holes in the fabric of our coven. You might think you can knit something new from the scraps, but you won't have the chance."

Roger tried to pull away, but Anton had locked his arm around him.

Anton's voice grew colder, a low rumble reverberating through him. "You have finally pissed him off, and with the bet settled, he has nothing more to gain from your continued existence. You have become a nuisance he won't tolerate. Which is a shame. You are so very pretty."

The song came to a close, and Anton released Roger in the center of the floor. All around him, other dancers were finding their next partner or deciding to remain with the one they had. Anton walked backward into the crowd, vanishing between other partygoers in less than the blink of an eye.

A gamble. A *wager*. Roger's immortality had been nothing but a game to the two bastards. Every bit of pain, every trick he'd learned to dazzle and delight them in order to keep them from hurting him further—all of that had been futile because they had made up their minds the night they'd turned him. So long as Dmitri lived, Roger lived. That was it. The two sadistic monsters had merely been trying to prove something to each other. Roger's life had been a lie. His traumas had been their entertainment, not his route to survival.

We can't wait. We need to be armed. We need to kill him tonight. Roger clenched his fist. Someone nearby let out a small shout, and glass shattered. There was some chaos about that, but Roger ignored it and made his way toward Takashi. Without breaking stride, he pivoted toward the direction Zack had hinted he was going.

"We're leaving," Roger told Takashi. "*Now*."

"I'll gather Kit and Carver and meet you at the door."

Roger nodded once and then continued forward.

The vicious waltz that he maintained to please his master was over.

Roger had never felt such freedom. Such anger.

Or so fucking terrified.

CHAPTER 36

The hallway led farther into the Chateau and reconnected with the main floor. The sitting rooms closest to the ballroom still had plenty of people mingling in them, mostly taking the chance to sit down. Zack started down the longer hall, then ran the math on how far Seamus could have gotten, only to reappear a short time later. *Could be doing this for an ungrateful shit.*

But something's not right. Zack stopped near a junction. The second floor would probably have privacy on a night with a massive ball going on, but the staircases were too far. Seamus had the benefit of speed, and he could have dragged Vincent anywhere in the place. Assuming he had done something to him and Vincent hadn't wandered off to the bathroom.

Bathroom. That was a place to check. There were bathrooms not terribly far from the ballroom, and Zack doubled back and stepped into one. Both doors had the same gender-neutral sign. Zack pushed open one door to walk into a face full of hair spray as a woman was reapplying some to her hair. The room had been full of happiness and cheerful conversation as well.

The other bathroom was eerily silent. The quiet made

Zack's hair stand on end, and he crept forward on the balls of his feet. A low moan echoed across the tiles, and for an instant, he worried that he'd stumbled into somewhere he shouldn't. But the sound ended in pain, not pleasure.

"Vincent?" Zack called out hoarsely. He peeked around the corner. Besides a couple of urinals, there were three stalls. Someone dressed in purple was sitting in one of them. "Uh, hey, Vincent?"

A sniff, then a groan, came from the person. Then, a careful voice. "W-who's there?"

"Zack Wright."

"Go away." But a sob was clearly caught in Vincent's throat.

How did I ever think this guy was my nemesis? Zack continued forward. Spatters of blood dotted the otherwise pristine tile. Some had hit the wall. Bracing himself, he pushed on the stall door. It was locked.

"Vincent, let me help."

"There's nothing you can do," Vincent cried.

"You can let me in, or I can crawl in my extremely expensive tuxedo on this ... actually, the floor looks pretty clean." Zack started to lower himself down.

"Fine! Why should I have any fucking dignity?" Vincent screamed.

Zack was about to take back his request when Vincent threw the lock and the door slammed open. Vincent was sitting on the floor, barely out of the swing of the door, and had his legs sprawled out in front of him. He held a wad of toilet paper against his split lip. One eye was red and beginning to puff, and the bridge of his nose had a hint of the same redness. His other cheek was cut, a trickle of blood making its way down to his jaw. Evidence of a handprint around his throat spoke to another bruise in the making.

And all of that was what Zack could easily see. The way

Vincent sat, with his other hand landing on his side, made Zack wonder about other injuries.

"Fuck," Zack said as he sat on his knees. Then he snapped out of his daze and went to the sink. He grabbed a paper towel and dampened it.

"What are you doing?" Vincent demanded, then hissed in pain.

"You need something cold for that eye."

"I tried to ruin your life. Why are you being nice to me?"

"Ruin?" Zack shot him a grin. "That Fang app thing was like *mild* inconvenience at best."

Vincent eyed him warily as Zack handed over the damp paper towel. He placed it against his eye and let out a soft sound of relief that quickly morphed into a flinching groan. "It didn't bother you?"

"Well, it did. But." Zack fussed with his hair, ran into styling gel, and stopped. "I, uh. Did some research."

"What … research?" Vincent asked.

"About Seamus and how long he keeps a head pet. And I realized you were running out of time, and I didn't need to make your life harder."

"Oh." Tears leaked from Vincent's uncovered eye, and then the sob finally broke free from him. "He's going to fucking kill me."

"What if you hid in the Chateau?" Zack asked. "This place is huge. We could get you somewhere upstairs or find a secret compartment or something. Then, when the party's long over, you sneak out."

Vincent shook his head. "Someone tried that last year. Candide turned over the body."

Zack bit his bottom lip. He couldn't just leave Vincent to his fate. If Seamus didn't kill him this night, it could be the next or the one after. The chance that Vincent would live long enough for Roger to kill Seamus and claim the coven was slim.

"You're coming with me." Zack reached forward and started to undo Vincent's collar.

"I can't. Your master—"

"My boyfriend will get on board, or he'll deal with a breakup," Zack muttered. He held the collar out in front of Vincent. "Now, I can leave you here, or you can come with me. Your choice."

Vincent bit his lip for a long moment, then grabbed the collar from Zack and threw it across the bathroom.

Zack nodded. "Great decision. Can you stand?"

"I don't know."

Zack backed up enough to give Vincent room to try, but when Vincent started to tip, he ducked in to support him. From the start, Zack had known Vincent was thin. However, touching him was like holding up a ghost. Zack clenched his jaw and shoved his anger down. How many humans had Seamus done this to? Had he ever hurt Roger like this? *I'm going to burn the bastard's heart out.*

They made it to the hallway. Every foot felt like a triumph. But once they got to the hall, Zack realized he had no idea which direction to go. If he went looking for Roger in the ballroom with an injured, collarless Vincent hanging off him, that would be a slap in the face to Seamus. As much as Zack would love to deliver an actual slap and then some, antagonizing Seamus while they were weaponless was the epitome of poor planning.

Then Roger stepped into the hall from the junction that led toward the ballroom. A lock of hair had slipped from his ponytail and added a moodiness to his striking profile. He glanced down the hall and spotted Zack. Despite the distance of fifteen feet, Zack noticed that his eyes were ruby red. His brows were pinched, and his frown only increased as he neared them.

"What's this?" Roger asked.

"Seamus left him like this," Zack replied. "I couldn't. I know—"

"We're already in deep shit."

Zack drew in a breath to argue that they needed to do the right thing.

Instead of launching into an argument, Roger picked Vincent up and cradled him in his arms. "Give him your bow tie."

Blinking, Zack undid his bow tie and gently draped it around Vincent's neck, though he didn't tie it. "Why am I doing this?"

"This way, he's technically claimed." Roger began to walk down the hall, though he turned away from the ballroom and toward the front door. His steps were long and quick. Zack had to hurry to keep up.

"I can't promise you'll be safe with us, little one," Roger murmured to Vincent. "I may only be giving you minutes."

"I'll take it," Vincent replied and clung to Roger.

That kind of talk made Zack itch for a weapon. They passed what was supposed to be a fancy display of swords in scabbards. Begging a higher power to listen, Zack reached for a hilt and pulled. Steel rang, and he had a saber in hand. It'd be nothing against a vampire as old as Seamus, but it felt useful. Zack swished it twice in the air to get a measure of it. The balance was fine, though he hadn't fenced in ages. *It'll work until I get my dagger. It'll have to.*

"Takashi and the others?" Zack asked.

"Meeting us at the exit," Roger replied.

Meaning Roger had been looking for him to prepare an escape. Zack frowned. "What happened after I left?"

"I'll tell you when we're safe."

What do I feel like safe might take a while? Zack scanned the rooms as they passed. People were starting to take note of them, and the buzz of conversation took on a confidential energy.

The cold gave Seamus away. The creep of his aura drove goose bumps along Zack's skin. He spun and continued to match Roger's pace while moving backward. The shadows were growing deeper behind them. Deep enough to hide a vampire attempting to cloak himself.

Hunters learned a few spells. Without his dagger, Zack lacked the extra focus it could provide, but he honed his anger into the energy he needed. He stretched out his hand and demanded, "Manifestate."

The shadows rippled. They didn't part, but they did reveal the shape of a man striding toward him. Zack lunged and drove the saber point forward.

Seamus twisted to the side, and the blade missed him. Then, he moved with lightning speed.

Thoughts, intuition, *memory* could move faster than a vampire. Zack's higher cognitive functions were registering where the cold had gone to, but he was already in motion, and he slammed his elbow into Seamus's gut hard enough to send the vampire against the wall. Utter surprise filled his features.

Zack let his lips curve into a cruel smile and held the blade to Seamus's throat. "Back. The fuck. Off."

"Thief," Seamus snarled.

"Rapist," Zack replied. "Abuser. Murderer. Should I continue?"

Seamus began to move forward.

Shadow cold as black ice forced Zack against the opposite wall of the hall and shoved Seamus back to where he'd been.

"Boys," Lady Belladonna said as she strode down the hall toward them. Candide was a half step behind her. The archfey had one hand in a gesture that was likely her concentration for the spell, though she showed no signs of any taxing effort to keep the magic going. "This party is a celebration of the might of winter's power. Though we chose a vampire's place, that was a courtesy to the community. This is still a fey party and will remain civil."

"They are stealing my property," Seamus said.

"The Pact of Chicago states that free will remains the most important aspect of any service. That way, we fey do not steal away precious vampires from your coven," Lady Belladonna chided. Her gaze moved to Vincent. "The boy seems to be wearing the crest of Roger, the Wonder."

"Because he snatched off my collar," Seamus snapped.

"He threw it away," Zack replied fiercely. "I saw him do it."

"Roger, have you accepted this new boy into your service?" Lady Belladonna asked.

Standing tall, Roger didn't even look at Seamus. "He is mine so long as he deems me a fit master."

"Boy, do you wish to leave with Roger?"

Vincent managed to nod.

"There we have it. He has chosen a new master, Seamus. Let me find you a drink to commiserate the loss of such a beauty." Lady Belladonna released her gesture.

The icy shadow holding Zack in place released. Everyone in the nearby rooms had pooled at the doorways and even spilled out a little in order to witness the encounter. Acutely aware that every movement would be weighted and judged, Zack turned toward Candide and Lady Belladonna.

Going without a weapon wasn't the hunter way, but he was in the depths of the supernatural and their rules. Lady Belladonna had sided with them for the moment, but she could turn on them. *No one can ignore good manners.*

With a flourish, Zack bowed as he offered the hilt of the saber to Candide. "Mistress, I borrowed this from a wall. Please forgive my use of it."

"It seems in the same condition it was in." Candide took the hilt and lifted the blade to inspect it. Then she handed it off to Dryden and made a shooing motion. "I hope you and your boyfriends will visit the Chateau in the future."

"I would love that, Mistress," Zack replied. He deepened the bow and then gave Lady Belladonna a bow. Afterward, he straightened and spun toward Roger.

Seamus glowered at him.

Zack shot back a triumphant grin and hurried his step to catch up to Roger.

As they reached the exit, Kit, Carver, and Takashi fell in step with them. Kit leaned in close to Zack. "Why is Roger carrying Vincent?"

"Because he sort of claimed him," Zack said.

"You didn't beat the shit out of him, right?" Carver whispered.

"I didn't," Zack replied hotly.

Carver held up his hands. "Just checking."

"Takashi, we need a car without potential eavesdroppers," Roger said.

Blurring ahead on the long walkway, Takashi zipped to where a length of cars were waiting. One of them was probably the limo they'd brought to the party, but Takashi negotiated with the driver of a luxury town car. He took out his phone, and the driver took out theirs. A moment later, the driver walked away and slid their phone back into their pocket.

Takashi opened the door for Roger. "I just dropped thirty grand on this. Please tell me I needed to."

"You did," Roger replied. "And you need to get us to the hotel as fast as you can."

"Are you sure?" Takashi asked.

"We need the blades. *Now*."

"What's going on?" Kit said. "What blades?"

"The enchanted silver blades in the safe." Zack opened the front passenger door and dropped into the seat. He ran his hand through his hair, not giving a crap if he broke it free from the styling gel. "Roger, what changed?"

"The lease on my theater ran out," Roger replied.

The others finished piling in the car. Carver demanded, "Can you translate that from vampire dramatics to common vernacular?"

"Seamus and Anton have been amusing themselves for centuries with a wager on which spawn would last longer, Dmitri or I," Roger said. "Anton said the bet had been settled, and it turns out my little attempts to gain notoriety haven't been as tolerated as I thought."

Meaning, Seamus wants us dead. Zack was grateful Takashi had already taken off down the road. He raked his hand through his hair again, further knocking it out of its ridiculous style. "We get the knives. We get anything, *anything* that could be used as a component to track us, and we get the fuck out of the hotel."

"And go where?" Takashi asked.

"I'll think of somewhere," Roger replied. "After everything, I'm not leaving those bastards in charge."

"Uh, I could use a little more context," Kit said. "Who's in charge of what?"

"Maybe it's time we fill Kit and Carver in," Takashi said. "Considering we might not live through the night."

"Could you drop us off? Maybe we're better off at the party," Carver said.

"You wouldn't be," Vincent whispered. "He's looking for someone to kill."

Without protection, we're fucked. Zack glanced at the speedometer. "You know, I think you could push it another ten over the speed limit. Maybe experiment with fifteen."

"Someone tell me what the hell is going on!" Kit demanded.

Zack glanced to the mirror, but of course, he couldn't see Roger in it. So he half turned in his seat and met his gaze.

They shared one of their briefest staring contests, a battle of wills to decide who would start with the truth.

Zack nodded and then looked to Kit and the others. "Almost five months ago, my family received an email informing us about a vampire that needed to be slain ..."

CHAPTER 37

"What the hell can be used as a spell component?" Carver asked as they entered the hotel suite.

"Technically, anything that's got a connection to you," Zack replied.

"Wait, what about like hair and fingerprints?" Kit said. "We can't possibly get it *all*."

Roger strode into the living room and deposited Vincent on the sofa beside the bar. A few hours ago, the suite had been their hideaway while preparing for an enchanted evening. Now, every second spent in it felt like a casket lid closing on them. Roger motioned to the master bedroom. "Zack."

"Blades." Zack nodded and dashed for the safe.

"I'm grabbing the shotgun from under the bed," Takashi muttered as he followed Zack.

"What good is a shotgun going to do?" Kit demanded. "They're vampires!"

"The child has a point." Anton's voice echoed throughout the suite with no clear point of origin.

One of them had hit the lights as they rushed into the suite. Roger had had his hands full with Vincent and hadn't noticed which of them had done it. But the lights were definitely on.

Only they began to flicker and dim. The darkness from the balcony seeped through the glass and spilled onto the floor. It pooled, condensing and flowing outward, and inch after inch was vanished into the lightlessness.

This could be good. He's expending power. If Roger could find the silver lining, he might find a way to use it to slice through his enemies.

But not everyone shared his hope. Wide-eyed, Carver glanced from the lights to the darkness growing beside the balcony to Roger standing still and shuddered. He spun on his heels. "Fuck this!"

"Wait!" Roger called.

Carver surged forward, grabbed the door handle, and pulled it open.

Seamus stood on the other side. Like them, he still wore the outfit he'd spent the evening in. What little light remained in the hallway flickered as he reached out and snatched Carver by the throat. He strode into the suite with Carver struggling in his grip.

Using every ounce of speed he had, Roger raced toward Carver. Just as his fist was about to connect with Seamus, a tendril of shadow wrapped around his wrist and yanked him away. He hit the wall instead. When he tried to move, another tendril grabbed his other arm. Their strength beat his own, but he fought them. He gained an inch, then two.

It wasn't enough.

Carver's attempt to pry Seamus's hand off his throat was futile. Seamus drew him in and tore into his neck. Fresh blood scented the air, and slickness splattered to the floor underneath him. Seamus latched on and drank.

"No!" Roger tried to find his shadow among the ones around him but couldn't. The darkness was growing too deep.

Cal's silver blade flew toward Seamus. Before it made contact, Seamus released Carver and moved so quickly that he vanished from sight. The knife knocked into the door, then skittered across the floor toward Roger.

But it wasn't close enough to reach.

Carver collapsed to the floor. Blood poured from the wound in his neck.

Kit screamed. Fur erupted across their face, and their ears morphed into long, foxlike ones. A shiver of magic flooded over them. More of their features began to shift, but they remained bipedal.

Roger strained to reach the silver knife.

In all of this commotion, Zack had been following the blade he'd thrown. His own dagger was in his hand, and the runes upon it blazed with white light. It repelled the darkness within a few feet of him but couldn't entirely overcome the power flowing into the suite. Grim determination hardened him to steel. And he didn't slow down. Like he'd done at the Chateau, he pivoted, pirouetting toward a spot at full force, and he sliced with his dagger.

Seamus grunted as he became visible. A sharp red line across his torso was already healing. Somehow, Zack had picked out his movement from the chaos and struck.

And having gotten in one blow, Zack didn't hesitate with the next. Seamus dodged what might have been a killing strike, but he was on the defense for the moment.

Takashi blurred forward with the shotgun in hand. He shouted, "Pull!"

Roger did the best he could. The roar of gunfire told him he'd yanked back far enough. Suddenly, the tendrils holding him released. Cal's weaponry was primed for slaying supernaturals. He'd had silver buckshot, and the blast shredded the shadows.

Roger rolled forward, picking up Cal's bowie knife as he went, and spun to face the deepest of the shadows. Anton was powerful, but he had to be somewhere in the suite. The sort of display he was putting on was too finite in its controls.

The darkness is a fabric. I can tear through fabric. Find the lump where he's hiding. Roger tumbled into that mental space he had discovered while fighting Nell. It had been with him all his nights. He was a *vampire*, and that had meaning. Power of its own. His own.

And there, not where the shadows were darkest but beside them. Roger ran for the spot, shouting, and he drove the blade forward.

Shadow tendrils erupted from the floor. Multiple ones wrapped around each of Roger's appendages and hauled him downward.

As Takashi brought the shotgun up for another blast, Anton stepped out of the darkness. The shadows released him like they'd miss him, and he rushed Takashi. He grabbed the shotgun before Takashi pulled the trigger and yanked it from him. Then, he swung it with the force of a truck. The stock connected with Takashi's skull, and Takashi dropped to the floor.

The blow wouldn't kill a vampire, but Takashi was knocked out of the fight.

"Silver bullets," Anton said as if he were actually impressed. He tossed the shotgun onto the floor beside Takashi. The stock and barrel were mangled. "How very *hunter* of you, Roger. And what's this in your hand?"

In the distance, there was a cry and the shattering of glass. Roger couldn't afford to look away, but his heart fractured into a thousand pieces. Zack. Kit. Vincent. They were in danger, and he was stuck in a mess of shadow.

Roaring, he reached for his own darkness, that piece of the shadows that belonged entirely to him. He found it and brought it like a blade across the tendrils holding his left side. His shadow became a blade in his right hand, and he had

Cal's silver knife in his left. Using them, he cut away at the other shadows.

"My, my, my. You are interesting at last, Roger," Anton said, his voice echoing with a sliver of ethereal power.

Launching himself, Roger aimed for Anton's midsection. He clipped Anton's side, and his move landed him past his prey. He turned, knives cutting through shadows that attempted to claim him, and danced to a safer spot.

"Oh, let's *play*." Anton's eyes flared a brighter red. He stretched out his hands, and his hair flowed backward as if in a wind.

Shadows undulated across the floor and sprang into dozens of tendrils. Roger sliced and cut as many as he could while forever pursuing Anton across the suite. But Anton was always just out of reach. Every roar and strike were drips of Roger's strength until a dam broke within him, and his power waned.

But Carver was dying.

Takashi was lying motionless on the floor.

Vincent was out of sight.

Kit … Kit had to be injured. Roger could smell their blood.

And Zack. The sound of him fighting carried into the room. At some point, he'd been driven out onto the balcony.

We're losing. Roger forced his leg forward, though the tendrils wrapped around him. Another slew of them covered his left leg, and one tugged on his knee and broke it. He screamed as he went down.

From there, his wrists were caught in the gluey shadows, and he was pulled onto his hands and knees. Centuries of pain and fear flood through him.

Anton sank to his knees in front of Roger and pressed his head against Roger's. He slid his hands along Roger's back. "Shh, shh. Seamus insists that our little wager isn't truly done yet. You're not going to die tonight."

A shiver of relief poured through Roger on reflex. "You ... you aren't going to kill us?"

Anton put a finger under Roger's chin and made him meet his gaze. His smile froze what little heat Roger had left. "Darling, I said *you* weren't going to die tonight. I said nothing about anyone else."

Then Anton snapped Roger's neck, and oblivion swallowed his thoughts.

CHAPTER 38

Flying through a glass door *sucked*. Zack rolled as he hit the concrete balcony and let his momentum carry him farther away from the shattered glass. His dagger had slipped from his hand. He'd brought his arms up to protect his face, and it had been a danger. He came to a stop and hurried to his knees.

The dagger was close to the broken glass door. It was his only protection. He had to have it. He scrambled, and a sliver of glass sliced through his palm. *Not my good hand. I'll deal with it later.*

The thunk of flesh on flesh threatened to distract him, but ingrained training kicked in. A defenseless hunter couldn't help anyone. *Arm yourself first. Then save who you can*, Dad had always said.

Will I ever see him again?

Another distraction that Zack pushed away. He grabbed his dagger and rose into a fighting stance. His breath clouded the air in front of his face, and the icy air fought his lungs. But he could do this. He had to do this.

Kit snarled as they struck Seamus with their claws. They

continued pushing him out onto the balcony with every slice. Seamus took them, each with a laugh, and the wounds healed by the time Kit scratched him anew.

However, they were keeping Seamus distracted, and Zack could work with that. He slipped around so that he was behind Seamus. When the timing was right, he plunged his dagger toward the center of Seamus's back.

Only for Seamus to blur with vampiric speed. Seamus locked his hand around Zack's right wrist and forced him onward.

The blade sliced into Kit's stomach.

"No!" Zack tried to wrench free of Seamus's grip, but the vampire was a granite block.

"Now, now, little blade, do what you're meant to do. *Kill*," Seamus snarled into Zack's ear.

With a speed and effort that wasn't his, Zack cut across Kit's abdomen. The wound was deep. Too deep. And made with silver, which meant Kit wasn't healing right away. Kit put their hands over the wound and staggered backward. Their foxlike features began to melt away, but not entirely. The golden eyes remained and the hurt that was in them.

"Kit!"

Seamus laughed.

Cal used to laugh like that.

Right before Zack usually found a way to win a sparring match.

Fear and anger melted into pure determination. Though Seamus had a strong hold on him, physics could still serve Zack. Breaking grips was the first and most repeated lesson among hunters. Because what they had to fight was always stronger. Faster. Had a longer reach. Winning was never about besting their opponent but surviving them in any way possible.

Zack pivoted his wrist, wincing from the pinch, and he yanked his hand free using the one small weak point in

Seamus's grip. He spun away from him, then swung out a wild punch. Seamus grabbed that wrist, but that meant he dragged Zack in closer. Zack drove the blade into Seamus. As he stepped toward him, he shoved upward on it.

Flesh parted on the blade, and Seamus grunted. His eyes fluttered shut for a heartbeat, but then he grinned. He brought his arm down and pushed Zack's elbow down, sliding the dagger back out of its wound.

"Missed the heart," Seamus taunted.

"Don't worry. I'll get it in the end." Zack cracked his head against Seamus's. The vampire lost a step, and Zack shoved him forward. They crashed against the outdoor couch and tumbled together onto the concrete. Zack continued to stab him. Over and over. He wasn't quite reaching the heart. He hadn't angled it upward enough.

Seamus rolled them and slammed Zack against the concrete. One blow to the head made Zack's head spin. The second knock made his grip loose. Seamus stood and delivered a swift kick to Zack's side, but that was an old tactic Cousin Denny had liked to do when he thought he'd won. Zack caught Seamus's leg by the ankle, pulled it upward, and twisted as hard as he could.

Seamus fell onto the concrete with a crack. He growled as he got onto his knees.

Zack was already finding his feet, already had his dagger in hand. He feinted with his blade, then connected a punch across the jaw with his free hand and brought the dagger down into Seamus's shoulder.

Seamus's eyes flared bright, burning red.

The burst of cold against Zack's back was a warning that registered in his mind a fraction of a second too late. He was spinning, aiming, but Seamus knocked him down with a punch. As he struggled to his feet, Seamus kicked Zack's knee.

It doesn't bend that way, Zack's rational voice said as a

scream tore from his throat. *And now I'm disassociating. This is shock.*

Breathing was a task he couldn't ignore anymore. He'd relied on the power of a sprint and not the long haul of a marathon fight. He pushed himself up onto his elbows.

Seamus grabbed his left arm and wrenched it.

The pop should have hurt more. But the pain was fading away.

Definitely shock.

Muffling his pained cries, Zack flipped over onto his back and held his left arm to his chest. His dagger was … was somewhere close. Not in his hand. But it was tied to him, and he could feel its location.

Seamus leaned over him, foot on either side to straddle him though he remained standing. He had the dagger in his hands, and he admired it closely.

Zack tried to wiggle backward. If he could inch back far enough, he might be able to deliver a kick that would send Seamus over the balcony. That probably wouldn't do much. Seamus might even be able to fly. But Zack wouldn't give up. He couldn't.

Seamus tilted his head like he'd heard some distant melody and was trying to catch the tune. With a calm expression, he twirled the dagger in his hand and then drove it downward into Zack's chest. The blade lacerated his right lung, and breathing changed from hard to painfully impossible.

Not impossible. Still breathing. I can still kill him. I have to. Zack gritted his teeth. Seamus left the blade in him and stood.

So Zack wrenched it free with his good hand and forced himself upward.

Seamus was sitting on the other goddamn outdoor couch. He had his arm across the back of it like he was relaxing during a night with friends, and he continued to hold his head as if he heard some song he was remembering. "What do you think, darling?"

Zack was about to tell him to go to hell.

But Anton had come to the broken door. He slid the remaining piece open and leaned against the frame. "Are you certain? Last time, it didn't work out so well."

"It's been six hundred years. I think I'm ready to try again."

"Try—" Zack managed the one word, but blood filled his throat. He coughed, and once he started, he struggled to stop. His vision swam.

Where is Roger? Did Anton kill him? Did he kill Takashi? The others? Zack tightened his grip around his dagger's hilt, but he knew his grasp wasn't as firm as it had been. His strength was melting away, slipping from him like the blood leaving his body.

"That annoying tattoo is in the way, but you can feel it, can't you? The whisper of it." Seamus stood smoothly. "Here, let me show you."

The strike for Zack's jaw came too slow, and even in his weakened state, Zack managed to sway out of the way. But that left him straighter in stance so Seamus's fist connected firmly in his stomach. Zack doubled over. *I'll kill him. I'll fucking kill them both.*

"That mangled and that desire is that strong in him?" Anton said.

"You felt it, then?"

"Like a shadow cast upon the wall, but I know the shape of it." Anton retreated into the suite. "If you're going to do it, be sure about it, though. Wouldn't want you to waste the time."

"I suppose that's fair," Seamus murmured.

Then he struck Zack. And he hit him again.

Bones were cracking. Breaking. Pain was becoming too

much to hold on to, and the world was a spin of color except for Seamus. His fist. His foot. His bright red eyes.

And Zack clung to one hope. That he would live long enough to shove his dagger into Seamus's heart. That he might have one turn of luck that would drive the silver into Seamus in just the right way. He could keep breathing. He could force what little of his body might still respond, and he would fucking *kill*.

He was lying on the cold concrete again, staring up at the stars. The lights of the city dulled out the best of the view, but the silent witnesses continued on their treks across the night sky. His left eye wouldn't open. He couldn't breathe through his nose.

Yet, when Seamus leaned into view, the desire came back. *I'll kill him.*

"You are a special one," Seamus whispered with reverence as he knelt down. He ran his fingers through Zack's hair.

Vincent.

Carver.

Kit.

Takashi.

Roger.

They could all be dead because of the bastard leaning over Zack.

I'll kill him. I'll fucking kill him.

"I wish I could know your mind, little dagger, but I do sense the beat of your heart." Seamus stroked Zack's forehead and then his cheek. "I can guess at the thoughts. Perhaps I shouldn't blame you for that hate in this moment. You've been led here by the weak, but there is something worthy in you."

Zack spat out blood. He drew in a ragged breath.

"I'll give you a choice," Seamus whispered. "You'll know when it comes."

Zack would've frowned, but that required energy, and the pain was all he could handle. Even as many pieces as his mind was in, the pain slid into each one.

With an odd gentleness, Seamus moved and slipped under Zack, bringing him up to a sitting position. Half cradling him, Seamus bit into his neck. His fangs sliced into his skin like a hot knife through a snowbank.

The world was falling away to nothing. Only the sound of swallowing and his heavy breathing broke the stillness.

A crunch of flesh happened. Zack expected that to end his agony, but no new pain registered. Seamus pressed his cheek to Zack's temple. When he spoke, his voice was so close it felt like it was inside Zack's mind. "You'll slip away in a moment. You only have to lie here."

A cry bubbled in Zack's throat and threatened to strangle him. He attempted to buck, but Seamus had an arm latched over his chest.

"Shh, shh. I promised you a choice. You can slip away. Or."

Zack couldn't see much. His left eye was swelling shut.

But he could smell the strangely sweet liquid not far from his nose. He could see a smudge of red against ivory-pale flesh.

"All you have to do is open your mouth, and it's yours," Seamus whispered. "But you have fought so bravely, little one. If you want to slip away, I will stay with you."

He meant die.

Zack was going to die.

Unless he …

That would make him a vampire.

But.

But I won't be truly dead.

And he would be able to survive. If Roger and Takashi were gone, he'd be able to have his revenge, and if they weren't, then he would have them again. They could be together. Forever.

Zack opened his mouth, and Seamus put his bloody wrist against his lips. Honey-sweet blood filled Zack's mouth. A chilling tingle crept over his lips and across his tongue.

He swallowed.

ACKNOWLEDGMENTS

This time around, my thanks start with my incredibly supportive family. One of the hardest feats with writing is finding the time to do the work. My family did their best to give me the space to write and publish this book despite all the challenges we faced this last year.

Another thank you goes out to Sue, my dev editor. Also, if you're *dying* to read the next book, you can thank Sue for the cliffhanger ;) Originally book two and three were only one novel, but Sue nudged me into exploring the vampires' world more. She reminded me that half the fun of projects like these is falling into the fictional world. And she pushed me to go for more bite. I've learned a lot writing this novel, and I'm really proud of how it's turned out.

A big thank you goes out to you, dear readers. I keep going because readers keep showing interest. An extra big thank you to anyone who recognized my Soul Bond characters. (Yes, that was the same Noah and Ben from the book. I'm excited that the two story worlds were compatible and just make so much sense together.)

And an extra extra big thank you goes out to anyone who's taken the time to review or recommend my books. We all thought the machines would rule us Terminator-style, but we know it's the algorithms that can have a huge impact. Each mention grows this world bit by bit.

Hopefully, I'll see lots of readers around for book three. We're only getting started, friends.

ALSO BY JS HARKER

Soul Bond

Keep Me Safe

The Tit For Tat Series

Tit For Tat

His Fairy Prince

A Midsummer Night's Party

The Fang and Dagger Series

Wrong Hunt

Vicious Waltz

To get the latest on new releases

sign up at

www.jsharker.com/newsletter

ABOUT THE AUTHOR

JS Harker loves stories. She was one of those kids who constantly had a book in her hands and spent countless hours adventuring with her siblings. These days she wanders into her imaginary worlds and conjures up tales of magic, passion, and happily-ever-afters. She currently lives in the part of the Midwest that makes Tatooine look interesting by comparison (not that she's ever obsessively thought about becoming a Jedi or anything).

Follow her on Facebook or go to www.jsharker.com and sign up for her newsletter to receive updates!